STRATEGOS

RISE OF THE GOLDEN HEART

by Gordon Doherty

www.gordondoherty.co.uk

GORDON DOHERTY

Published in 2013 by FeedARead.com Publishing – Arts Council funded

Copyright © The author as named on the book cover.

First Edition

Also by Gordon Doherty:

STRATEGOS: BORN IN THE BORDERLANDS
When the falcon has flown, the mountain lion will charge from the east, and all Byzantium will quake. Only one man can save the empire . . . the Haga!

LEGIONARY
Numerius Vitellius Pavo, enslaved as a boy after the death of his legionary father, is thrust into the border legions just before they are sent to recapture the long-lost eastern Kingdom of Bosporus. This sees him thrown into the jaws of a plot, so twisted that the survival of the entire Roman world hangs in the balance...

LEGIONARY: VIPER OF THE NORTH
In the frozen lands north of the Danubius a dark legend, thought long dead, has risen again. The name is on the lips of every warrior in Gutthiuda; the one who will unite the tribes, the one whose armies will march upon the empire, the one who will bathe in Roman blood . . . The Viper!

GORDON DOHERTY

They poured around me eagerly like eagles,
Some striking at arm's length with rapid sword cuts,
Some thrusting mightily at me with lances,
Who was my ally then? My guard and shelter?

'Digenis Akritas, the Two-Blooded Border Lord', the Grottaferrata Version.

GORDON DOHERTY

Sarah, Mum, Alun . . .
Thank you doesn't come close to covering it, but thank you indeed!

The Byzantine Empire circa 1067 AD

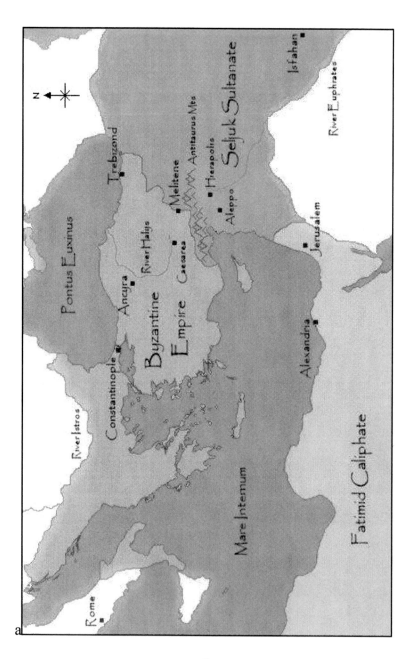

The Byzantine Themata of Anatolia circa 1067 AD

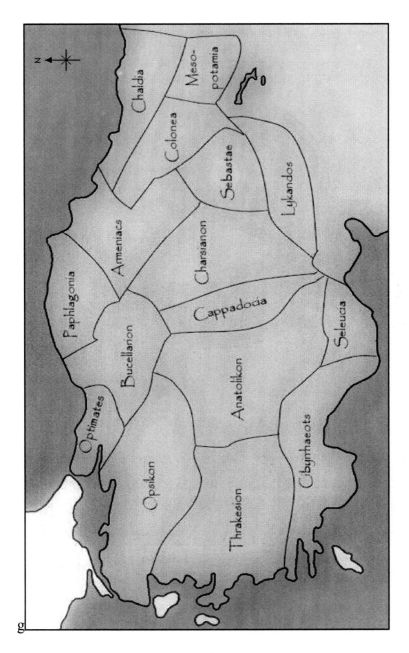

Constantinople circa 1067 AD

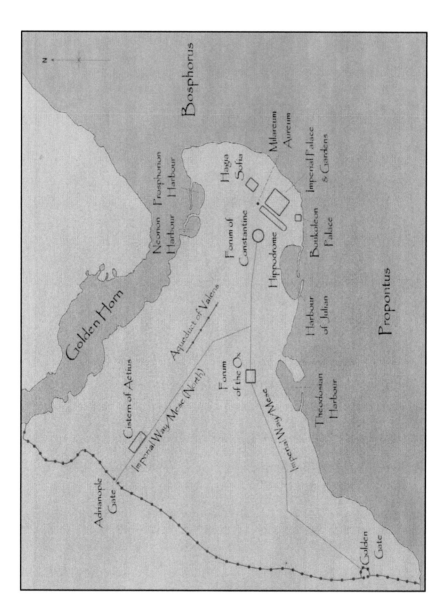

Structure of a Typical Byzantine Thema

See glossary (at the back of the book) for description of terms.

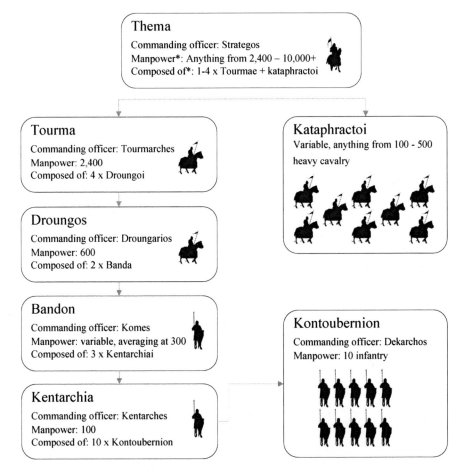

Thema
Commanding officer: Strategos
Manpower*: Anything from 2,400 – 10,000+
Composed of*: 1-4 x Tourmae + kataphractoi

Tourma
Commanding officer: Tourmarches
Manpower: 2,400
Composed of: 4 x Droungoi

Kataphractoi
Variable, anything from 100 - 500 heavy cavalry

Droungos
Commanding officer: Droungarios
Manpower: 600
Composed of: 2 x Banda

Bandon
Commanding officer: Komes
Manpower: variable, averaging at 300
Composed of: 3 x Kentarchiai

Kontoubernion
Commanding officer: Dekarchos
Manpower: 10 infantry

Kentarchia
Commanding officer: Kentarches
Manpower: 100
Composed of: 10 x Kontoubernion

*There was no standard number of soldiers in a Byzantine Thema, though most could theoretically muster between one and four tourmae. However, in the mid 11th century, many themata had suffered grievous neglect, and some could muster barely hundreds, let alone thousands.

GORDON DOHERTY

1. April 1067 AD, Charsianon, Eastern Byzantium

A zephyr lifts me ever higher and the spring sun beats upon my outstretched wings as I soar across the rugged, golden heartlands of Anatolia. The first navigators to set foot on this realm named it the Land of Sunrise. Yet had they only known what torment was to be played out in the ages ahead, they may have chosen a more suitable moniker.

These last years have been more brutal than many past. Driven by the death of his uncle Tugrul, Sultan Alp Arslan and his Seljuk hordes have torn these lands asunder, smashing against the dying embers of Byzantine resistance with the tenacity of a beating black heart. The boots and hooves of his armies and the broad wheels of his war machines have ploughed the earth year upon year, sowing the corpses of Byzantine farmer-soldiers in their wake.

Of the few Byzantine souls who refuse to crumble under this pressure, one troubles me greatly. Once I thought he was the man capable of defying my greatest adversary, Fate. Now I see in him more darkness than light. The boy once known to me as Apion has become an embittered husk of a man, a strategos who leads his beleaguered border army into battle as though he relishes the prospect of death. In victory, he sees only the failures of his past, while his men chant the name that has come to define him.

The Haga!

Twelve long and bloody years have passed since I last spoke with him, but I know that I must visit him once again. For I see a

13

tumult of portents as to what Fate might throw in his path. I see bitter conflict, bloodshed, betrayal, loss and pain . . .

But, most vitally, I see hope.

Yet before I go to Apion, there is another to whom I must speak. One who has lost himself in hatred. He has pursued Apion like a vulture for so long that I fear he has forgotten those lost years when they were once like brothers.

***

Bey Nasir scoured the noon heat haze, his grey eyes framed by the studded rim and noseguard of his helm. The jagged, sun-bleached valleys of Charsianon seemed to be devoid of life. Still, he thought as he eyed the bend in the valley ahead, they were in enemy territory and there was much potential for ambush.

He twisted in the saddle of his chestnut mare to glance over his Seljuk warband. Two thousand men marched with him. Seven hundred were *ghazi* riders. These nimble steppe horsemen were armoured in light quilted vests and armed with composite bows, scimitars, war hammers and lassos. Bolstering the ghazis were one hundred Syrian camel archers, swift and hardy. They rode at a good thirty paces behind the ghazis though, as the ghazi mounts were notoriously skittish around camels. To the rear marched the infantry; over one thousand *akhi* spearmen, wearing iron mail vests or padded jackets, iron conical helms and carrying circular shields painted in turquoise, green and tan. In their midst marched one hundred of the finest engineers from the heart of Persia along with the wagons that carried their siege implements and the warband's supplies.

No, he assured himself, squaring his broad shoulders, his scale vest glinting in the sun, *the Byzantine forces are weak and scattered. No ambush can trouble my forces today.*

But almost as soon as the thought started to calm him, one of the nearest ghazi riders called out, pointing to the western end of the valley. 'Sir!'

Nasir spun to face front once more. His gaze locked onto the dust plume approaching. In the heat haze, he could see only a blotch of darkness at its source.

'Halt!' he barked, raising one hand and tugging on the reins of his mount. Behind him, the warband rippled to a standstill, the drumming of hooves and boots died and was replaced by a rattle of spears being levelled.

Nasir's brow dipped as he watched the approaching shape. A bead of sweat danced down his cinnamon skin. For just a heartbeat, he imagined the two-blooded cur who had plagued his life for so many years now; the black-plumed helm, the crimson cloak, the ivory-hilted scimitar. The whoreson who had led the Byzantine resistance for so long. Too long. His lips curled into a grimace and he raised a hand, readying to wave his riders forward.

Then, from the heat haze emerged a rider in a light linen robe, saddled on a piebald steppe pony. It was merely the scout rider he had sent out earlier. A chorus of relieved muttering rang out from the column and Nasir's heart slowed, his hand dropping and his grimace melting.

The young scout slid from the saddle, his robe drenched with sweat, panting as he crouched on one knee before Nasir. 'Bey Nasir, by noon we will be in sight of the town of Kryapege. From the end of the valley I saw the farmers retreating behind its gates and the defenders bolstering the battlements.'

Nasir's eyes narrowed. 'So the Byzantines will not face us in the field? Instead they choose to cower inside their decrepit walls?'

The rider nodded with zeal. 'It seems they fear even the news of your approach!'

Hubris laced Nasir's blood and he waved the warband forward once more. He would strangle the life from the place, then destroy the dog who had cursed his being. Memories of his childhood flitted through his mind and his knuckles trembled white on his reins. He saw all that he had lost since then. All that he had lost because of that bastard. He saw her face.

Maria.

Then as they rounded a bend in the valley, he slowed, his blood cooling.

'Bey Nasir?' the rider nearest him asked nervously as the men slowed behind him.

Nasir's eyes hung on an ancient Hittite carving etched into the rock, high up on the valley side. A two-headed eagle, its wings vast, clutching a bull in its dagger-like talons.

The *Haga.*

At this, the grimace returned and his heart thundered once more. He grappled his scimitar hilt and slid it clear of his scabbard, holding the blade aloft in a clenched and shaking fist. Then he kicked his mare round to face his warband.

'On the plain ahead we will hew timber for our siege engines and we will sharpen our blades. Then we will strike Kryapege from history!' He boomed, then punched his free hand against his chest. 'Allahu Akbar!'

Two thousand cries filled the valley in reply like raging thunder.

'*Alla-hu Ak-bar!*'

16

***

Within a day, Kryapege was surrounded. Nasir's two thousand had wrapped around the crumbling red brick walls like a noose while a sparse line of Byzantine defenders looked on from the battlements.

For the next week the blockade continued, and the Seljuk siege line was abuzz with activity as they prepared for war. Hammers tap-tapped as the siege engineers went about their work. Horses snorted and whinnied as their riders groomed and fed them. The screeching of iron upon whetstone filled the plain like the gnashing fangs of a predator readying to feast. Today, they were almost ready to crush Kryapege and those within its walls.

Nasir stood in the midday sun by a semi-circle of yurts, a small fire and a stack of fresh kindling. He swirled his cup of freshly brewed *salep* and supped at it again. The heat of the sweet, creamy cinnamon and orchid root drink was just enough to bring a mild sweat from his pores, cooling his skin. He smoothed at his pony tail with one hand and his eyes flitted from the town's eastern gate to the siege plan he had etched into the dust before him. But he could not focus his thoughts. Instead, the words of the oath he had once made with the *Haga*, in a lost age, pushed to the fore.

Until we're both dust.

He frowned and pinched the top of his nose between his fingers.

Then the screeching of an eagle startled him. He looked up to see only an unbroken, azure sky and shook his head. He looked to the nearby chief engineer, who was barking his men into a rhythm as they hauled a trebuchet frame upright. He made to stride over to inspect the goings-on, when he noticed something from the corner of his eye.

17

GORDON DOHERTY

A hobbling form walked towards him, cloaked and hooded in white.

He frowned at the painful gait of this figure. There were no elderly or crippled amongst his army, and the plain was deserted before and behind his siege line. Agitated at this distraction, he filled his lungs to bellow at the figure.

But the figure pre-empted this, and lifted a hand, extending a bony finger. 'Save your breath, Bey Nasir,' an old woman's voice croaked from the hood, 'for we have much to discuss.'

Nasir spluttered at the nerve of this crone. 'You are no Seljuk . . . and how do you know my name?'

She ignored the question and lifted the hood down, revealing puckered features framed by silver, web-like hair. Her eyes were milky-white and sightless; despite this, they seemed to scrape at his soul. At once, he recognised her. It was the hag who had come to him many years ago, when Maria slipped towards death. When the darkness had first gripped his soul.

'You . . . '

'Sit, sit!' she said impatiently, waving him down.

Anger flared in Nasir's chest and then, like the passing eye of a storm, it disappeared and was replaced with a warm sense of ease. Bemused, he found himself sitting. Now he had no inclination to yell for his guards, all of whom seemed oblivious to this intruder.

'So, Nasir,' she said, sitting across from him, resting her back against the kindling pile and pouring herself a cup of salep from the urn over the fire, 'where do we start?'

'Why are you here?' he asked. It seemed like the correct question.

She smiled ruefully. 'Ah, that is one answer I cannot offer you. Like you, I have been drawn here. But I have many questions for you.'

18

Nasir nodded. 'Very well.'

She supped her salep and puckered her lips, then let out a contented sigh. 'You are a brave warrior – that so many men follow you is testament to your greatness. But do you not fear your leader, the Mountain Lion?'

Nasir's heart clenched at the mention of the name. Alp Arslan, the Mountain Lion, the Seljuk Sultan. The sole monarch of all Persia from the river Oxus to the Tigris. The sultan was engaged in war far to the south, and had demanded that the beys he left behind were to resist raiding Byzantium until he could return to join them. He looked to the crone, his lips taut. 'I respect him, but I do not fear him,' he lied.

'Clearly,' the crone chuckled, her eyes widening.

Nasir frowned and shuffled where he sat. 'He is the finest of warriors, a master of the sword . . . '

The crone raised her eyebrows and cut him off. 'That is the least of his talents. His mind is far sharper than any blade.'

'Aye,' Nasir conceded, 'yet his strategy drives a wedge between him and his armies.' He swept a hand around the Seljuk siege works. 'These men are hungry to complete the conquest of Byzantium that was promised to them many years ago when his uncle Tugrul was sultan. That is why they are here. Because while Alp Arslan chooses to war with the Fatimids in the south this year, he denies the warriors he left behind the chance to seize that glory.' He cast his gaze over his warband and thought of the other seven thousand who besieged the nearby city of Caesarea. 'Bey Afsin and I have given them that chance once more.'

The crone nodded wistfully. 'Yet when Tugrul led his armies here, he was beaten back. And Alp Arslan has led his vast armies here many times in retaliation for that defeat and been repelled every time. Many Byzantines have been slain, but still they resist. Now your sultan chooses to wait until he can focus his armies entirely on Byzantium before he strikes again. Do you not think this strategy is shrewd?'

Nasir looked away from her and to the walls of Kryapege.

'Your silence speaks volumes, Nasir,' the crone said, then stabbed a bony finger towards him. 'You are not here for conquest; you do not share Bey Afsin's impetuous motives or those of the men you will lead in this siege. You are here for Apion.'

Nasir felt the mention of the name like a blade to his heart. 'What of it? I have lost much because of that whoreson.'

She raised her eyebrows. 'Loss? I'm not sure that . . . '

'Loss comes in many forms, old woman,' Nasir snapped, cutting her off. He fixed his baleful gaze upon the walls as he thought of Maria.

'Perhaps,' the crone nodded in acquiescence. 'But have you ever considered how much more you have lost in the pursuit of the man who was once your friend?'

With every breath, Nasir thought.

'And what makes you think you can best him?' The crone continued. 'Despite years of trying, both you and Alp Arslan have been unable to defeat the *Haga*.'

Nasir feigned a scoff at this, his mind flitting back to the carving of the two-headed eagle on the valleyside. 'The *Haga*? Do not try to dazzle me with myth, old woman. The Strategos of Chaldia is flesh and blood and nothing more. He rallies the few wretches that remain of the Byzantine border armies, yet he carries a curved Seljuk blade in his hand.' His heartbeat quickened and his breath grew shorter. 'He doesn't even know who he is anymore, fighting for a cause he no longer believes in because he cannot remember how to live beyond the battlefield. He chases answers at the edge of a blade –

answers he will never find,' he said, unable to contain the wavering in his voice.

'Because those who could allay his torment withhold those answers,' the crone cut in, wagging a finger at him in reproach.

Her gaze seemed to pierce into his heart, and he felt a welling of guilt there. At last, he dropped his gaze, swiping a hand through the air as if to break the crone's glare. 'I alone am not to blame for the *Haga's* torment. There are many ghosts in his past, and they have all but destroyed him!'

'The ghosts of his past have all but destroyed him . . . have they? Have they indeed?' The crone stared at him. 'When you next look upon a mirror, think upon those words, Nasir.'

Nasir looked up with a frown. But the crone was gone.

The kindling pile was charred to the core, with silvery wisps of smoke curling into the air. An eagle screeched once more, and Nasir shot his gaze skywards.

The sky was pure, unbroken blue.

2. The Cold Spring

In a baking, whitewashed alley in the heart of Kryapege, a calico cat was perched by an open blue door. It peered into the cool shade inside, transfixed on the cumbersome, red-faced man cutting up a piece of carp. Then, the moment his back was turned, it pounced onto the table and snatched up a scrap of flesh in its fangs. The ruddy man's ears perked up, then he spun round and roared at the creature. The cat scrabbled from the table and sped for the door, tripping and tumbling down the steps before tearing along the alleyway. The cat's eyes darted all around as it looked for an escape route. Then it saw the figure of an amber-haired man in a light tunic sitting on a doorstep. The man was statue-still and staring into a dagger blade. The cat darted in to cower in his shadow.

Apion looked up as the ruddy fishmonger thundered past and on down the alleyway, threatening to do all manner of things to the cat, including removing its tail and inserting his boot in its back end. When the fishmonger was out of sight, he looked down and stroked the cat's ears and the creature purred as it devoured its meal. Then he looked up to see a group of six more cats piling into the fishmonger's doorway in his absence, each helping themselves to the rest of the carp. He welcomed the dry chuckle this sight conjured. For a moment, his thoughts were clear.

Then he returned his gaze to his dagger blade and his thoughts darkened once more. The scarred features staring back at him from its polished surface were wrinkled in a frown. His amber locks were grey-streaked at the temples, and hung tousled and matted with sweat. His beard was equally unkempt. His thick brow shaded deep-set emerald eyes, lined with age and weariness, their gaze fixed along the length of his battered nose. *What am I?* he asked himself bitterly. *A Byzantine boy brought up by a Seljuk guardian. A man who has slain like a demon. A strategos ill-suited to the empire of God.* He looked to the small, wooden war chariot carving in his other hand. The *shatranj* piece was well-worn and stained with the blood of Mansur, his old Seljuk mentor. Then he looked to the white band of skin around his wrist where he had once worn a Christian prayer rope, and then to his forearm and the red-ink *stigma* of the two headed eagle that had supplanted his faith. *What am I?* he asked again.

He looked to both ends of the snaking alleyway. At one end, the remains of the citadel stood – shards of brick jutting from a hillock, now only manned by the goats that grazed on the grass there. At the other end, the red-brick town wall could be seen. Beyond waited a powerful Seljuk warband. But it was not their number that vexed him, it was the man that led them. Nasir would never relent, and he knew this. He lifted the cup of brackish water by his side and sipped carefully, then closed his eyes as a name rang in his thoughts. A name that had fused their paths through life.

Maria.

Nasir had pursued him like a starved wolf since she had died. Perhaps today was the day one of them would find peace.

He sheathed his dagger and took a deep breath, looking to the walls again. There, he caught sight of one of his men up on the battlements. One of just three hundred men of the Chaldian *Thema* waiting for the Seljuk assault to begin. In response to the Seljuk invasion, Apion and his army had been summoned south to the lands of the Charsianon Thema by the obnoxious *Doux* Fulco – a man nominally in charge of the eastern border defences and even more of a mercenary than the rogues he hired using imperial coin. The headstrong doux had then carved up the Chaldian ranks, sending just this few hundred here to guard Kryapege while leading the other nine hundred plus his own rabble of two thousand mercenary Rus and Normans with him inside Caesarea's tall and broad walls. According to reports, Fulco and his men now awaited a similar fate there, besieged by Bey Afsin and the rest of his vast horde. In every direction, the empire was being pressed out of existence.

Years ago, Apion had thought that the empire could resist the Seljuk pressure. The border armies were dogged in their defiance if nothing else. But it was the man at the heart of the empire who had spawned decay and undermined their efforts. Emperor Constantine Doukas was a blinkered and parsimonious ruler, championing a regressive tax system that punished all but the rich. His reign had seen forts fall into disrepair across the land. Equally, the thematic armies had fallen into grievous condition with scant number and little equipment, some even falling out of existence altogether. Now mercenary tagmata led by men like Doux Fulco held sway, caring more for their gold than for the people they were paid to defend. A gentle breeze danced along the alleyway and stirred him from his thoughts. He shook his head and sighed.

Then, as if to remind him of its presence, the calico cat licked at his arm. He looked down, and the cat fell onto its back and writhed in the sunshine, purring.

'To have such carefree days would be a fine thing,' he smiled and stroked its full belly. Then it took to playfully biting at his fingers and grappling with his forearm. 'But I imagine your day will be truly spoiled if you don't have a drink to wash down your meal?'

He reached out to pick up the cup of water by his other side.

But his hand froze and his eyes narrowed on the water's surface.

***

Tourmarches Sha ignored his burning thirst as he climbed the steps to the battlements of the east wall, his charcoal-dark skin glistening with sweat. It was a bitter irony that this arid, crumbling settlement was still known as 'the cold spring' given that the stubborn town well had run dry weeks ago. Even before that, the water it did yield was brackish and polluted. Indeed, there was precious little to say in praise of Kryapege other than its importance as a strategic choke point to the west of Caesarea and the Antitaurus Mountains.

Reaching the top of the eastern gatehouse, he straightened his conical helmet to offer some shade to his silver eyes. Then he rested his palms on the crenellations and ran his gaze along the line of the siege. Two thousand Seljuk warriors had this ruin of a town in their grasp. All along their ranks, fang-like speartips glinted, men grimaced in anticipation and horses and camels snorted in impatience.

Then he turned to look along the crumbling lower town walls. The single and depleted *bandon* of just over two hundred *skutatoi* stretched thinly along the battlements and the scattering of riders and archers inside the town were to face this storm alone.

His eyes fell on the nearest spearman. The man's skin was slick with sweat and he wore only the lightest of tunics. His *spathion* was sheathed in his swordbelt and he gripped his *kontarion* spear firmly. But Sha eyed the soldier's *klibanion*; the iron lamellar vest lay by the man's feet. Beside it rested his *skutum*, the crimson, kite-shaped shield adorned with a gold Chi-Rho emblem. In contrast, Sha wore his armour vest, weapons and helmet and carried his shield at all times

25

despite the heat and despite his fatigue. He looked back to the sentry; a single arrow, let alone a volley, from the Seljuk warband outside and this man would be dead. He considered for a moment whether to bark his disapproval, then he saw a similar sight all along the dilapidated battlements. Weary sentries, baking in the heat, few having eaten or drank in days. Even the *komes*, their superior officer with the knotted white sash around his torso, had set down his armour.

As a tourmarches, answering only to the strategos, it was Sha's place to bark them into order. But in his time as an officer, he had learned that sometimes a deft touch was most effective. He bit back his censure and instead held out his water skin – containing barely a mouthful of liquid – to the man. The soldier looked nervously to his superior. 'Take your ration, soldier. Slake your thirst,' Sha encouraged him. Then he squinted into the sunlight and nodded to the dust-coated embroidery of the Virgin Mary that hung proudly from a timber frame atop the gatehouse. Another precious breeze wafted across the battlements at that moment, lifting the fabric. 'God knows you've earned it.'

'Thank you, sir,' the soldier nodded, poking out his tongue to moisten his cracked lips before gulping hungrily at the skin as if the tepid water was an elixir. 'Sir . . . the strategos . . . he hasn't come to the walls for two days now. But he will come soon, won't he?' he nodded over the wall to the Seljuk lines. 'For when they advance?'

Sha stared at the man then shifted his gaze to the network of alleys leading into the heart of the town. 'He will come when he is ready,' was all he could offer. 'In the meantime, be sure to wear your armour,' he nodded to the klibanion by the man's feet, 'I know how draining it is in this heat, but better to be hot than dead, eh?'

The man saluted and immediately lifted his klibanion vest and buckled it on. Sha nodded in satisfaction as he saw the other men nearby follow suit, then he turned to flit down the steps and into the town.

The fifty Chaldian *toxotai* were clustered together near the makeshift archery range beside the granary. These archers were not burdened with armour, wearing only linen tunics, dagger belts and wide-brimmed hats tilted at a jaunty angle to shade their eyes from the sun. They looked tense as they honed their marksmanship with their composite bows in near-silence. They were scared, Sha realised.

When he passed the stables, near the empty cistern, the fifty Chaldian *kataphractoi* were nervously brushing their mounts or polishing their armour. Even these heavy cavalrymen, precious and near invincible on the battlefield, were nervous.

Then he stalked up through the narrow streets of the lower town. The townsfolk and the rabble of farmers who had rushed inside the walls for protection darted across his path from door to door, panicked and cradling provisions. They needed a salve to ease the fear in their hearts. They needed the strategos to come forward and lead them.

Suddenly, a half-rotten door crashed open before him. Two men tumbled onto the street, brawling. A huge Greek with wild hair and sunken eyes and a shaven-headed man with a trident beard. They scuffled and traded blows, the Greek smashing the bearded man with a left hook and then the bearded man knocking teeth from the Greek's mouth in reply.

'Enough!' Sha barked. But the two men barely offered him a glance as they broke apart and circled one another.

'Those figs are to feed my family. Give them back to me!' the bearded man roared, pointing at a small parcel the Greek had tucked under his belt.

27

'Not a chance – I will not go another night with an empty belly,' the Greek spat, blood washing from his bloodied lips. Then, taunting the trident-bearded man, he thrust a hand into the parcel and scooped out a handful of the shrivelled fruit before cramming it into his mouth.

The bearded man roared at this and then leapt forward, drawing a dagger.

Sha's eyes locked onto the blade. Instinctively, he leapt forward to thrust his shield between the pair. But he fell square in the path of the big Greek's left hook that was aimed at the bearded man.

Sha heard a crunch of bone and saw only blackness and a shower of white sparks as he staggered back and slumped against the wall. Dazed, he heard screaming women and the *swish-swish* of the dagger being swept at the big Greek, along with the bearded man's angered grunts. Then footsteps approached. Heavy footsteps. Sha shook his head clear and blinked his eyes open.

'I haven't had a drop of ale or wine in *weeks!*' Tourmarches Blastares cooed, resting his oak-like limbs on his hips. The giant sported a broken nose and a network of scars under his close-shaven scalp. 'And when I'm without a drink to warm my blood, I become bloody angry. It makes me want to fight. Then I wander along here and it seems that you whoresons are having all the fun! So, who wants a broken face first?'

Sha staggered to his feet as Blastares cracked his knuckles and eyed the pair – both of whom had suddenly lost their pluck. Then, behind Blastares, the prune-faced and white-haired Tourmarches Procopius arrived. He led a party of five skutatoi who fanned out in a line, spears levelled, faces twisted in snarls under their conical helmets.

'Or you can call it a day, hand back what you've taken, and put your blades away,' Procopius added.

The Greek seemed cowed and reached to lift the parcel from his belt. But, in a moment of very poor judgement, he opted to barge past Blastares in an attempt to escape with the fruit. As if swatting a gnat, the big tourmarches stopped him with a crunching jab. The crack of the Greek's jaw breaking rang out as he crumpled to the ground, shuddering then snoring violently.

Procopius clicked his fingers and the five skutatoi lifted the Greek and dragged him into the shade. Then the aged tourmarches picked up the parcel and tossed it to the bearded man.

'Anyone else?' Blastares asked, eyeing the rest of the locals that had gathered to watch. To a man, they slunk away, heads bowed, refusing to meet Blastares' glare.

Sha looked to Blastares and Procopius, touching his split cheek gingerly. 'Well timed.'

But Blastares' nonchalant expression faded as soon as the populace dispersed. The big man wore a troubled frown, as did Procopius.

'Blastares?'

'Have you seen the strategos?'

'I was on my way to find him,' Sha started.

'Then we must hurry,' Procopius cut in. 'Bey Nasir has sent a messenger to the walls – he readies to advance upon the walls and end the siege!'

***

Apion stared at the cup, frowning. Now it was absolutely still. Had it been a trick of the light?

Then footsteps echoed down the narrow alley. He looked up to see his three tourmarchai hurrying towards him. These were his trusted three – the men who had been like brothers in his years in the ranks: Sha the pragmatist, Blastares the infantry lion and Procopius, whose knowledge of siege craft was legendary.

'Sir, we need to act,' Sha spoke first, crouching before him. 'Bey Nasir has addressed the walls. He demands our surrender and insists he will attack at noon tomorrow if we do not comply.'

Apion's gaze narrowed, falling back to the water's surface. 'Then our fears of thirst and starvation matter little!' he chuckled dryly.

Blastares frowned at the other two, then nodded to the cup. 'Hold on, I recognise that cup – you're drinking the piss-brew from the tavern?'

Apion shot him a stern glare. 'It's water, Blastares. If I visited a whorehouse would that mean I was there only for the rutting?'

Blastares and Procopius looked at one another, eyebrows raised and bottom lips curled down, nodding.

Apion scowled at this. 'I came here to think . . . ' he stopped, shook his head, rubbed his face with his palms and then affixed his three with a steely look. 'You said noon tomorrow? You are sure of his intentions?'

Procopius nodded hurriedly. 'They are readying their war engines. I have seen them treating the ropes and the timbers of their stone throwers.' He stopped and cupped his jaw, his eyes narrowing. 'But I have a feeling in the pit of my stomach that they're up to something else . . . '

'Aye, they are,' Apion frowned. 'If Nasir says they will attack at noon tomorrow then I can assure you he will strike our walls tonight. Has word of this message spr . . . ' his words trailed off and his gaze locked onto the water in the cup once more.

'Sir?' Sha asked. Then he, Blastares and Procopius all looked to the water's surface.

The surface was still.

Then it rippled from the faintest of tremors. Apion's eyes widened.

Procopius' jaw dropped and he glanced to the ground beneath their feet. 'Sappers!'

Blastares sprung to his feet. 'If they get under the walls . . . '

Procopius raised a finger, cutting him off, and waited until the liquid rippled again. 'See how the ripple emanates from the side of the cup nearest the walls? I'd say they are already under the walls, but they're not finished tunnelling yet.' The aged tourmarches' eyes darted this way and that.

'Either way we must act, immediately,' Blastares appealed.

'I will deal with the tunnels,' Apion replied. 'Sha, we need to discuss how the men should be deployed.' Then he turned to Blastares and Procopius. 'You two need to deal with the Seljuk artillery.'

Blastares frowned. 'The artillery? You mean the artillery *outside* the walls?' he crouched back down on his haunches with a dry chuckle, folding his arms. Then he jabbed a thumb at Procopius and cracked a wry smile. 'This old bastard knows all there is to know about artillery, but are you proposing that he and I walk out there and eliminate, what, six catapults, and two trebuchets? Then stroll back in here for some of the foetid, briny brew from the tavern?'

'Yes, yes, that might work,' Procopius cut in, stroking his chin with his thumb and forefinger.

'Eh?' Blastares frowned, his face like an angered bull. Then he saw the old tourmarches was deep in thought.

'You know a bit of the Seljuk tongue now, as do I,' Procopius continued as if Blastares had not spoken. He looked to Apion, who had taught them some basics of the language, before continuing; 'A pair of thick cloaks and two serrated daggers, and a bit of stealth . . . aye . . . '

Blastares frowned, his bottom lip trembling in exasperation. 'What are you muttering about?'

'I think I'll leave you to it?' Apion said, cocking an eyebrow as he stood. 'I believe I am needed at the walls.'

3. Cutting the Noose

Nasir buckled on his scimitar, straightened his scale vest then stepped out of his tent and into the light of a waxing moon and a glitter of stars. The blessed cool of night saw the soldiers of his warband both armoured and cloaked. The infantry were poised, mounted archers eager, all eyes on Kryapege's walls. The artillery was primed. They were ready. He was ready. For twelve years he had been ready. He lifted a neatly braided lock of Maria's hair from his purse, inhaled its scent and kissed it gently.

Forgive me, he mouthed.

'Sir, I implore you, wait here,' a voice interrupted his thoughts. 'Let your men lead the tunnelling party . . . '

Nasir snapped his glare round upon the akhi captain, halting and silencing him. Then he placed his conical helm on his head. As the ornate noseguard slid into place and the mail aventail gathered around his shoulders, Nasir turned from the walls and set his sights on the small hillock just behind his readied ranks. To the rear of this rise, hidden from Byzantine view, a timber frame outlined a broad cavity, gouged into the red earth.

Nasir clicked his fingers. At this, some two-hundred akhi spearmen rushed to form up behind him. Only the whites of their eyes, speartips and helms showed above their shields. He waved them forward, their horn and iron lamellar armour like the scales of a giant serpent as they snaked towards the tunnel entrance.

He slowed only when two men – a bulky figure and a smaller one, both wrapped in cloaks – cut across his path. The hooded pair

33

stumbled as they hurried out of the way, the smaller of the two muttering some apology in a broken Seljuk tongue. 'Cursed Mercenaries!' Nasir grumbled as the pair made their way towards the artillery lines and the other Persian engineers.

Shaking the distraction from his thoughts, Nasir snatched a torch from the sapper who stood beside the tunnel's entrance. Then he strode into its depths, the serpent of men diving underground with him. He marched past the collection of Persian workers, still fitting and making good the timber struts that held the tunnel in place. The tunnel descended sharply until the rock was damp and cool and the gloomy corridor rattled with the echo of iron and crunching boots. Then, when they reached one set of struts with a turquoise rag tied around each side, Nasir raised a hand. They were nearly under the walls of Kryapege.

At once they slowed the pace of the march, cupping their weapons gingerly, padding forward in near silence. They continued like this for several hundred feet, noticing the tunnel rise again, towards ground level. Then, up ahead in the torchlight a wall of red earth and rubble appeared, marking the tunnel's end. This section was heavily strutted, given the proximity to the surface. Nasir grinned; from here, his column could spill into the heart of the Byzantine town and seize the walls under cover of darkness.

'How far?' he whispered to the head sapper.

The burly, moustachioed man wiped the sweat from his brow and squinted. 'Seven feet,' he replied, jabbing a finger upwards. 'With my best men I can break through very soon.'

Nasir gave him a cold nod. 'Then you must begin at once.'

Nasir turned to his waiting men, raising a clenched and shaking fist. 'Let every swing of your blades stain the earth with Byzantine blood,' he hissed through gritted teeth. Then he raised one finger. 'But leave the *Haga*. For he is mine to slay!'

***

Apion stood in near-darkness. Expressionless iron masks hovered all around him in the chill, a faint orange underglow betraying their unforgiving, empty-eyed stares. He thought again of the past. He thought of the few he had once loved, and then the countless number he had slain since those precious few were taken from him. A ghost of that past was coming for him now.

Then the darkness and the silence were pierced by a dull, almost apologetic chink of iron upon rock, directly in front of him.

It was time.

At once, his gaze sharpened. He placed his helm on his head, the three black eagle feathers jutting from the crest and the cool, iron scale aventail slithering down his neck like an asp's skin. He squared his shoulders, the iron plates of his klibanion rustling and his crimson cloak slipping back from his shoulders as he did so. He rested his palm on the ivory hilt of old Mansur's scimitar and glared into the darkness. In the void, a vision formed of a dark, arched doorway, the orange glow behind it beckoning him forward, a sibilant voice beyond it taunting him. This image had plagued him even before his first days of war, the voice drawing him into the hell that lay behind the timbers. He knew for certain that he would walk in those flames today.

'Ready?' he hissed to the iron masks around him.

The masks nodded in silence.

Let the past come for me.

***

35

The air was growing stale and thin in the tunnel, and Nasir's breath came and went like fire in the gloom. His teeth grated as he watched the head sapper and his engineers chip carefully at the rock face. They were heartbeats from seizing victory. *A breath from ending the Haga's days,* he enthused, his grimace bending into a rapacious grin. Then he frowned.

The head sapper was stepping back from the tunnel end, confusion pinching his features.

Nasir followed the man's gaze; the centre of the rock face had crumbled away under the sapper's chiselling. But instead of more rock as expected, a hole the size of a coin had appeared. Darkness lay beyond.

'We should still have another six feet to go, should we not?' one hunchbacked sapper asked his leader. 'Did we misjudge our depth?'

The head sapper shook his head, pushed his eye to the hole. Then he twisted round to Nasir, his face pale, his mouth agape and his pupils dilated in panic.

The breath caught in Nasir's lungs as an acrid tang curled into his nostrils from the opening. For just a heartbeat, the tunnel was deathly silent. Then his eyes bulged in realisation. He swept his hands up. 'Back . . . BACK!'

The roar had barely left his lips when an almighty crash shook the tunnel. At once, the tunnel end crumbled like a falling veil. The coin-sized hole became a gaping maw from which a clutch of demons glared out, a dull orange light dancing across their iron faces. Then the dust of the fallen rock swept over the Seljuks. Nasir staggered back, gagging and wiping at his eyes.

As the dust settled, he saw the reality of what stood inside the countermine – men in iron masks, conical helms and klibania. A pair at either side held miniature battering rams, still caked in the dust of the thin partition they had just demolished. The band of them in the centre carried iron canisters under one arm and held leather-bound iron siphons in the other, gentle flames licking from the ends.

Siphonarioi. The dreaded Greek fire throwers.

In their midst stood an amber-bearded warrior with three black eagle feathers on his helmet, his deep-set eyes shaded under a dipped brow.

The *Haga* raised one hand, and it was enough to send the Seljuk warriors scrambling backwards, toppling over one another.

'At them!' Nasir screamed, ripping his blade from its sheath to rally his men.

But his words were drowned out by a thunderous roar as the *Haga* dropped his hand and the siphonarioi unleashed their fury. The tunnel was filled with wrathful orange plumes and an acerbic black smoke. The akhi warriors fled in panic, screaming, many ablaze from head to toe as the fire clung to them like wet clay. In moments, blackened bodies fell to their knees and then toppled to the dust.

Nasir pressed up against the tunnel-side behind one strut. His skin was tormented by the searing heat but he was untouched by the spouting flames. Cutting out the glare of the blaze through narrowed eyes, he saw the *Haga* watching the destruction like a scavenger waiting for the predator to finish its meal. Then at last the siphons fell silent, leaving a carpet of fire and thrashing men. With a roar, Nasir leapt out from the strut and charged over the flames. He pushed past the screaming inferno that was the chief sapper and leapt for the *Haga*, scimitar raised over his left shoulder.

In a flash of iron, the *Haga* spun to him, ripping his own blade from its scabbard. They clashed at the edge of the carpet of fire. The flames licked at their boots. Their swords met in a screech of iron, sparks dancing and adding to the fiery hell all around them. For the briefest of moments, the pair's faces were inches apart, grimacing as they fought for supremacy, each pushing their blade towards the other. Nasir's lips trembled with rage as he saw the *Haga's* features illuminated in the firelight; the callous emerald eyes that had haunted his every thought. At last, Nasir slid his blade from the contest and ducked back. As the *Haga* stumbled forward under his own momentum, Nasir ripped his scimitar up, the tip scoring across his foe's face. The *Haga* staggered back from the blow, but he was unblinking, his face set like stone despite the blood that washed from the bridge of his nose and his cheek. Then Nasir lunged forward, the tip of his blade plunging towards his enemy's heart.

At the last, the *Haga* swept his scimitar up and parried, then he drove forward, deftly and fiercely, swiping his blade in a flurry of silver. Nasir felt the force of each blow and could only parry. In moments, he had been driven back into the carpet of fire and then he tripped over the smoking corpse of the head sapper. He flailed, toppling into the blaze.

The flames enveloped the right side of his face, clinging to his flesh. Unearthly pain gripped him. He scrambled back from the blaze to the strut behind which he had sheltered. There he beat at the flames until at last his skin was free of them. Over his own screaming, he heard a lone voice.

'It doesn't have to end like this, Nasir. Leave, while you still can,' the *Haga* spoke.

Nasir winced at the stinging agony and the pungent stench of melted flesh on his face. He looked up across the carpet of flames, dipped his brow and pinned his nemesis with a gimlet stare. Then he gripped his scimitar, readying to strike again. At this, the *Haga* shook his head in resignation, then turned and nodded to the men carrying the battering rams.

With a crash, they battered at the nearest struts of the Seljuk tunnel. The wooden posts cracked and bent and a shower of earth and rock rained down around Nasir in a grim portent. Through the tumbling rocks, Nasir fixed the *Haga* with his glare, raising his scimitar point like an accusing finger. Then he turned, just as the battering rams shattered the struts completely. This time the tunnel capitulated. Nasir leapt back from the rockfall and fled back through the tunnel, leaping over the charred corpses of his men, hearing the abruptly severed screams of the stricken that were caught under the collapsing earth.

He burst from the end of the tunnel, only paces ahead of the collapse, then toppled to his knees, panting. Rubble and dust shot out of the tunnel behind him and then the entrance collapsed too. All around him were the few of his tunnelling party that had escaped. They lay blackened and groaning like shards of a shattered blade.

Nasir struggled to his feet, batting away the helping hands of his men, some bringing balms and bandages. He lifted his scimitar and looked upon his reflection. The skin was gone from his jaw and cheek, and the sinew and muscle underneath was blistered and angry, while the white of one eye was blood-red and bulging. A voice barged into his thoughts uninvited. *The ghosts of his past have all but destroyed him . . . when you next look upon a mirror, think upon those words.* He shook the crone's musings from his mind with a low growl. The pain and the disfigurement were a fine price to pay if it meant the *Haga* would be slain today.

Then he heard a faint chanting rise from within the walls of Kryapege.

'*Nobiscum Deus!*' mixed with '*Ha-ga! Ha-ga! Ha-ga!*'

He turned his searing gaze upon the town.

***

Apion and two skutatoi bundled the trio of captured Seljuk akhi from the countermine, then on through the lower town and towards the eastern gate. The Chaldian soldiers and the native garrison alike chanted and cheered as he passed, their breath clouding in the dawn chill. Even the townsfolk joined in, roused from doubtless fitful sleeps, hope sparkling in their eyes at last.

Stow your hopes and be ready to fight for your lives, he thought as he marched through them. His body still trembled with shock from the clash with Nasir, and the dark door lay ajar in his thoughts. Today was far from over.

The skutatoi shoved the three captured akhi up the stairs onto the battlements and Apion followed. There, he looked to the east. The first orange of dawn licked at the horizon, framing the plume of dust that stretched from the mouth of the collapsed Seljuk tunnel. He saw that Nasir's men were in disarray. For the briefest of moments, he considered the possibility that these three prisoners could live beyond today. Then the chanting behind him fell to silence, and the dry cackle from behind the dark door rattled through his thoughts as if mocking him for his naiveté.

He felt all eyes upon him: the soldiers of the thema, looking to their strategos; the people of the town, desperate for a show of authority. Apion looked over his shoulder and shared a glance with his tourmarchai. Sha, Blastares and Procopius offered him stony looks, knowing what had to come next. Without ceremony, Apion drew the dagger from his belt and wrapped a forearm around the chest of the middle of the three akhi, while the two skutatoi did likewise with the remaining pair.

Apion composed himself. The Seljuk prisoner had been stripped of his weapons and his skin was black with soot, his eyes wide with terror. He could feel the man's heart thundering through his horn vest. Apion felt pity pawing at his chest for an instant, then shook the emotion clear and steeled himself.

As the sun slowly breached the horizon, he felt its warmth on his face. He leaned in to whisper in the man's ear, speaking in the Seljuk tongue. 'It was a brave act to march into that tunnel, and I commend you for that. But I cannot release you, for my people would strip the flesh from your bones before you even reached the gates. And I cannot send you into slavery, for I know only too well the horrors a man can suffer at the hands of a Byzantine master.' With that, he pressed the dagger against the man's throat. 'Forgive me.'

'Your god will never forgive you,' the Seljuk croaked as the two skutatoi either side despatched their prisoners swiftly.

Apion hesitated for but a moment, his eyes falling to the white band of skin around his wrist. At once, his heart hardened. 'Tell me,' he whispered into the akhi's ear. 'Who is my god?'

With a swift wrench of his wrist, it was over. The Seljuk's hot blood flooded across his arm and he caught the man's weight, lowering his body to the battlements. He crouched there for a moment, shame creeping over his heart. Then he looked out to the enemy lines, already being marshalled into position for a frontal assault on the eastern walls. As the Seljuk war horns wailed out, he sought out the figure of Nasir, standing in their midst.

What choice did you give me?

41

**

All along the Seljuk lines, laments rang out at seeing their comrades executed. Eyes turned this way and that, then, almost universally, they looked to Nasir. They looked at his mutilated features with a mixture of horror and expectation.

The blood pounded in Nasir's ears. He looked along his readied lines as the rising sun bathed his ranks from behind. The gentle heat stung like fire on the melted flesh of his face.

'Ready the artillery, ready the men. This town will be razed into the dust by noon!'

At this, a raucous cheer filled the air.

Nasir raised his left hand.

'Catapults, ready!'

At this, the crew around the six bulky timber frames groaned, taking the strain, bending the stone-throwing arms back.

'Ready!' they cried.

Then Nasir raised his right hand.

'Trebuchets, ready!'

'Ready!' The crews around the two hulking devices responded, fifteen pairs of men straining at the end of the ropes, holding the giant timber throwing arms almost at their full stretch.

Nasir's brow dipped and he threw both hands forward, towards the walls of Kryapege.

'Destroy them!'

A deafening cheer filled the plain as the two sets of crews pulled down on their devices to gain every last morsel of extra power before letting loose their load of rocks.

This was the fatal mistake.

All along the lines of the Seljuk artillery, sharp cracking rang out as the tensed ropes split. The ropes whipped up from the devices and the throwing arms spluttered, dropping their payload or hurling it weakly or wildly askew. One crew was struck with the lashing ropes of their device, the lead crewman's eyes dashed out by the ferocity of the thrashing tether. Another could only gawp in terror as the massive boulder on his catapult hopped up just a few feet before coming down upon him, crushing him like an egg.

Only one crew's device remained intact – having been a fraction slower than their comrades. The lead crewman examined the ropes, then spun to his leader. 'The ropes have been half sawn!'

Nasir's eyes bulged as he looked across his line of siege engines, hanging limply like snapped branches after a storm. Then he yelled back at the men of the last trebuchet; 'Loose your weapon!'

'It will fall short of the battlements,' the man started.

'Do it!' Nasir bellowed.

The man nodded, then barked his crew into loosing at less than full stretch. The timber arm swung round and hurled a jagged limestone block towards the walls. The distant Byzantines on the battlements to the right of the eastern gate watched in silence, only scattering moments before the missile smashed into the base of the walls below them. Dry and in extreme disrepair, this section of wall shuddered and crumbled. The few sentries too slow to disperse toppled with the stone and were crushed, their screams drowned out by the thunderous collapse. As the dust cleared, the lower town of Kryapege was revealed through the gaping fissure – wider than any other on the decrepit walls.

At this, a roar erupted from the watching Seljuk ranks.

Nasir drew his scimitar and raised it overhead. 'Forward!'

The akhi burst into life, their boots drumming on the dust, spears levelled, eyes peering over shield rims. The camel archers followed closely, forming a thin line behind the infantry. Screening the rear, seven hundred strong, were the ghazi riders who heeled their mounts into a gentle canter, their faces etched with anticipation as they picked arrows from their full quivers and nocked them to their bows. Nearly two thousand men washed towards Kryapege's walls.

Nasir leapt onto his mare and raced to the head of the ghazis. 'With me!' he cried to a group of forty of the riders, waving them to the front. 'Put your bows away, today you will use your swords and lances as we drive the Byzantines onto the spears of our akhi.' He twisted to the rest of the riders. 'The rest of you, stay to the rear and let the Byzantines feel the pain of an arrow storm!' he roared, punching the air.

'Allahu Akbar!' the Seljuk ranks cried out in reply, then burst into a chorus of ululating battle cries.

Nasir led his forty riders to the fore. He scanned the battlements and was pleased with what he saw. There were even fewer Byzantine soldiers than he had anticipated. The precious kataphractoi riders were penned inside the town now and could not use their might on the open plain to threaten his army. There were barely fifty men stretched across the walls – all toxotai. Then, for the second time that morning, doubt gripped his gut like an iron fist. The Byzantines were few indeed – too few. One toxotes atop the gatehouse seemed to be watching their advance intently, and he was gripping something – a red rag. Then the man held it in the air and swiftly swiped it from side to side.

At that moment, Nasir noticed something from the corner of his eye. He twisted in his saddle to look back over his left shoulder; behind and to the left of his advancing ranks, the red dust of the ground itself puckered. A circle as large as a grand yurt crumbled away. His eyes locked on this unearthly sight. The Seljuk advance slowed, men looking over their shoulders likewise. Then he heard the men on his right flank burst into a babble of confusion. His head snapped round; the same spectacle lay behind that flank too. The men looked to the two gaping holes in the ground behind them and then to their leader. Nasir realised what was to rise from those pits, but a heartbeat too late.

Like dead warriors rising, a clutch of Byzantine kataphractoi riders poured from each of these tunnels that had been dug from inside the town. There were barely twenty in each party, but every one of them, horse and rider, was clad in iron. The riders were crowned by gleaming conical helmets, plumed with coloured feathers. Their faces were hidden behind triple-layered mail veils, their bodies were wrapped in iron lamellar with vivid cloaks draped on their backs and their arms were encased in splinted greaves and plated gloves. Composite bows and spathion blades were strapped to their backs while curved *paramerion* blades and viciously flanged maces and war hammers hung from their belts. Even the mounts looked demonic, wearing iron scale coats and plate facemasks, breath clouding before them in the last of the dawn freshness. These two wings of kataphractoi lowered in their saddles and levelled their lengthy kontarion spears, decorated with a knotted triangle of crimson cloth near the tip, held on one arm that was protected by a small round shield strapped to the bicep. Then they charged for the ghazi rear like two sharpened talons.

'*Nobiscum Deus!*'

Nasir stood on his stirrups and twisted to bellow at the ghazis. 'Turn!' he cried. Then he realised that this group of riders had never been this far west before, and had never faced kataphractoi.

The ghazis to the rear at first seemed bemused by the hubris of this handful of charging Byzantine riders, whom they outnumbered hugely. They simply raised their shields, expecting the riders to hurl missiles and then peel away at the last moment. But as the kataphractoi thundered to within fifty paces, the ghazis realised the charge was no feint and they jolted into action, some turning nocked bows upon the Byzantine riders. With a chorus of twanging bowstrings, a cloud of arrows hissed through the short distance between the Seljuk rear and the kataphractoi. Cries rang out, shoulders were thrown back where arms were pierced, and a cloud of crimson puffed into the air where one rider was felled – an arrow through the eye. That apart, the kataphractoi had weathered the storm and were now only paces away.

At this, the Seljuk riders fumbled, throwing down their bows, struggling to pull their scimitars from their sheaths and heel their mounts round to face their foe. But they were too slow.

The two kataphractoi wedges plunged into the Seljuk rear, the momentum carving the ghazi riders open like fangs tearing through tender meat. The ghazis were armoured only in quilt vests – no match for the tip of a Byzantine kontarion – and they were felled in swathes. Blood spray filled the air as spears gutted and impaled the ghazi riders, whose panicked sword swipes did little to trouble their ironclad Byzantine attackers. In moments, the Seljuk rear was in turmoil.

Nasir could only watch. His riders were being cut to pieces. He clenched a fist. *Do not let them break and charge again!* As if his thoughts had been heard, the ghazi did not scatter before this onslaught. In moments, they had absorbed the shock of the kataphractoi charge. Now they were clustering around the Byzantine riders and retaliating with venom, hacking speartips off, then driving their scimitars up and under the iron plates of kataphractoi body armour, bringing forth torrents of blood. Now the seemingly invincible

Byzantine riders were locked in a mortal struggle, discarding their spears and ripping their spathions and maces from their baldrics to fight for their lives. Many of Nasir's ghazi would die in tempering their might. *So be it,* he thought.

He turned back to his spear line. They had slowed, casting glances over their shoulders at the cavalry melee. 'To the walls!' He rode round behind them and whacked the flat of his scimitar down on their backs. But still they were hesitant. He saw fear on their faces, and followed the gaze of one – fixed on the breach in the town walls.

The breach was filled with a blur of silver. Another cluster of kataphractoi – this time only ten of them – picked over the rubble and then trotted out before the walls. The crimson-cloaked *Haga* led them forward at a slow trot on a broad and muscular chestnut gelding. His face was now obscured behind a triple-mail veil. Those flanking him were the ones who had been by his side for some years, Nasir thought, seeing the coal-skinned Malian to the *Haga's* right and the brutish rider saddled alongside another aged comrade on the left.

Nasir grimaced at his own hesitancy, then he battered his sword hilt against his shield and kicked his mare into a gallop up and down the front of the akhi line. 'We have nigh on one thousand spears! Do not let his myth blind you,' he cried, pointing his scimitar tip at the *Haga*. 'He is but a man! Like the many of our people that he has slain, he will bleed!' He drummed his sword hilt on his shield once more, in time with his words. 'He will bleed! Onwards!'

At this, the Seljuk spearmen seemed roused once more and resumed their advance. Only a hundred paces separated them and the *Haga's* meagre contingent of riders. His thousand akhi would envelop this tiny pocket of riders and impale man and beast on their spears. *Best to make use of what weapons I possess,* he thought, twisting in his saddle to wave his Syrian camel archers forward. 'Let them feel the wrath of your deadly hail!' Nasir roared. But then he turned back to see that the *Haga* had also raised a hand. At this, the ten kataphractoi flanking the *Haga* had taken up their composite bows, each nocked with flaming arrows – torch wielding skutatoi scurrying away from them and back into the town. Nasir's eyes locked onto the flaming tips. Then, just as the akhi bounded ever closer to the Byzantine riders, the *Haga* dropped his hand.

The ten fiery missiles arced up and over the Seljuk spearmen, over Nasir's head, to hammer down around and into the line of camel archers who were still nocking their own bows. With a chorus of terrified lowing, the camels thrashed and bucked, throwing their riders. Then they scattered, some ablaze, away from the town. The terrified beasts found themselves confronted with the rear of the melee between the ghazi riders and the kataphractoi, and they raced headlong into and around this fray. The horses in that conflict whinnied in terror at the arrival of these blazing creatures. Then they, too, scattered in panic from the scene. Some ghazi riders were thrown to the ground, their skulls dashed against rocks. Others were dragged like wet rags, feet tangled in stirrups, their mounts in blind flight. Even the surviving Byzantine kataphractoi in the centre of the melee broke away, struggling to control their mounts. But the ghazis were scattered, as were the camels.

As the dust of this furious exodus began to settle, Nasir looked all around him. His camel archers were gone, and only a handful of seventy or so ghazi riders had reformed, clustering behind him. Before him, his akhi spearline had halted less than twenty paces from the *Haga*, paralysed by fear after seeing almost their entire mounted reserve dismissed with one volley of flaming arrows. The *Haga* and his riders glared back at them.

Then the crunch-crunch of boots on earth rang out as the Byzantine skutatoi marched from the town gates. There were barely two hundred of them, and they carried with them a dust-coated Chi-Rho crimson banner. The *Haga* raised a hand and they marched out to form a shallow line in front of him. The line was only one man deep, but it matched the width of that formed by the Seljuk akhi. They came to a halt and then they each lifted a *rhiptarion* overhead, the slender javelins trained on the akhi ranks. Then the surviving kataphractoi who had risen from the tunnels – only twenty two left in total – split into two groups once more before clopping round to form up on the flanks of this line like pincers. Finally, atop the gatehouse, a handful of fifty toxotai archers clustered, arrows nocked to bows and trained on the Seljuks stood on this perfect killing ground.

The opposing lines eyed one another.

One of the Seljuk spearmen looked up at the tips of the arrows trained upon him, then at the arc of Byzantines facing him on the ground. Then he looked over his shoulder, to the east. The only direction left open. Then he looked up at Nasir, eyes bulging, before throwing down his spear and turning to run for the rising sun. In one fluid motion, Nasir tore the composite bow from his back, nocked and loosed an arrow that punched into the deserter's spine. In a spray of blood, the man crumpled. At this, the few others whose gaze had been drawn to the east now fixed their eyes forward.

Silence hung over the standoff momentarily before Nasir roared to his ranks. 'Do not fear the few who stand before us. Their deception is a measure of their character, and they have run out of guiles!' he roared. At this, a rumble of defiant jeers rang out from the Seljuk ranks, and they bristled, fixing their eyes on the skutatoi line. 'But now we come to it – only courage and steel will seize victory!'

He levelled his scimitar at the *Haga*. 'Forward, men! Take glory in the name of Allah!'

The akhi ranks exploded in a chorus of roars. 'Allahu Akbar!'

At the same time the *Haga*, in the Byzantine centre, lifted his scimitar and roared; 'Stand your ground! For the empire!'

With a thunder of boots and iron, the Seljuk swarm raced forward.

***

First, the Byzantine rhiptaria hammered down on the akhi front line, the javelins punching through shields and driving through flesh and bone. Ninety or more of the Seljuk spearmen fell under this hail.

Then the akhi charge smashed into the Byzantine line with a clattering of shields and screeching of iron. Blood jetted into the air where spears punched through armour and flesh. Limbs spun from bodies as spathions and scimitars were swept to and fro. Stricken men disappeared underfoot where their corpses were churned into the dust. The few ghazi riders who had regrouped loosed arrow after arrow into the skutatoi ranks, and the toxotai on the walls replied in kind with volley after volley.

But the Seljuk numbers were telling, and they drove the skutatoi line back towards the breached walls. Meanwhile, the kataphractoi held back. Still and silent. Watching.

'Crush them!' Nasir cried over the din of battle, firing his steely glare across the fray at Apion and his waiting riders.

'Steady!' Apion growled to his clutch of ten as the skutatoi line backed towards them. Then he flicked a glance up to ensure the two groups of riders on the flanks were holding back likewise.

The skutatoi were being overwhelmed by the akhi. The centre was bending inwards like a bow. But, hubris coursing through their veins and in their haste for a decisive victory, the Seljuk spearmen did not notice the orderly manner of this bending.

But Apion saw the moment like a hammer hovering above an anvil. The akhi had lost their flat front. They were hungry for blood.

'Break!' he bellowed. The skutatoi line heard his command and broke back at the centre, like a pair of doors swinging open. The two halves rolled up like a coiling rope, forming two small, packed masses of speartips and snarling faces. The Seljuk lines spilled around these two pockets of resistance.

Nasir's cries to them went unheard as he saw the snare.

'Forward!' Apion roared. In harmony, the three pockets of Byzantine kataphractoi charged into the fray. Each of the iron riders lay low in their saddles and extended their spears. Apion raced at the head of the central wedge. The blood thundered in his ears as his body juddered with each stride. Ahead he saw the frenzy of the warring infantry and the mass of disorganised akhi, backs turned.

The nearest akhi spun around. His blood-spattered face flashed with panic for a heartbeat, before he roared to his comrades. A cluster of them turned, instinctively swinging their spears down to meet the oncoming cavalry charge. But they were too late.

Apion's shoulder shuddered as his spear burst through the neck of the nearest Seljuk spearman, almost tearing the man's head off. Shaking his lance free of carrion, he carried on, bracing as he then plunged the spear into the chest of the next man. The shaft of the spear splintered as he tried to wrench it free, and he threw down the useless weapon. Another akhi leapt up and swiped a blade against his forearm, shattering the splinted greaves there and cleaving into his flesh. Apion stifled a roar of pain as blood washed from the wound, then kicked out at his attacker, leaving a nearby skutatos to despatch him.

He twisted in his saddle to see another kataphractos hacking through the melee, only for a scimitar blow to scythe through the rider's already-torn armour, cleaving the man open from shoulder to lung. By his other side, a fellow rider from his ten was barging his way through the fray manfully, only for a Seljuk spear to burst through his chest from behind, sending him toppling from his mount, limbs flailing. His riders were taking heavy losses, but the skutatoi spears were holding good and the akhi were beginning to panic. Many hundreds had fallen and now some were backing away from the fray, their eyes darting to the east once more.

But this glimmer of hope was swept from his thoughts as a clutch of akhi rushed to surround him, swords and spears hefted to lacerate him, and the pocket of remaining ghazi riders had circled around to aid them. In one motion, he reached over his shoulder and lifted his spathion from his baldric, and with the other hand, he pulled the flanged mace from his belt.

The first spearman that leapt for him would have felt nothing. Apion's blade passed through his neck without resistance, blood showering like rain, and the man was dead before his body hit the ground. The next akhi slid to his knees, aiming his sword-strike at the unarmoured legs of Apion's mount. Apion saw this, flicked his sword up and caught it overhand, then threw it down like a spear, the blade punching into the man's gut.

Barely able to snatch a breath, Apion spun just in time to see a ghazi rider swing down at him with a hand axe. He dipped to the left, the axe blow whooshing past his helmet. Then he grappled the rider's shoulder and took purchase to swing his mace up and round with venom, bringing the blade-sharp flanges of the weighty iron head crashing into the ghazi's helmet. The mace smashed through the iron helm as if it was made of parchment, and then shattered the rider's skull like an eggshell. A spray of grey matter and black blood burst from the rider's right eye socket, coating Apion's veil and spilling inside the eyeholes. The familiar stench of death permeated his senses once more. He drew his scimitar and sought out his next opponent.

These were the fleeting moments when he did not hear the voices of the past. When he was beyond the dark door, consumed by its fire. When he could see only his next foe and hear only the shrill song of battle.

At last, he found himself surrounded only by comrades. Now the Seljuk infantry were breaking in droves, throwing down their spears and running to the east. His sword arm was numb and trembling. The dark door faded as his heartbeat slowed and he heard the rasping of his own breath.

Only a handful of ghazis remained. Nasir was in their midst, berating the deserters and cutting down those nearby. His face was twisted in fury. But, at last, he relented. 'Withdraw!' he cried, waving his riders back. As a group they turned and heeled their mounts into a gallop.

As one, the Byzantine ranks broke into a chorus of cheering; 'Nobiscum Deus!' they cried. Then the familiar, rhythmic chant rang out; '*Ha-ga! Ha-ga! Ha-ga!*'

The riders gathered around Apion and looked to him. 'Sir? Give the order!' Sha panted. The Malian was coated in gore, readied to kick his mount and give chase.

Apion looked around to see that nearly half his men had fallen and many were injured, yet those still standing seemed eager to give chase too. 'No, it is over,' he said as he watched the remnant of the Seljuk force flee towards the now fully risen sun.

Then, silhouetted in the distance, Nasir twisted in the saddle, hurling some defiant cry over his shoulder and lifting something from his back.

Apion only saw the arrow at the last. He slid to one side in his saddle, but not soon enough. The arrow smacked into the collar of his klibanion, gouging one of the iron plates from the leather binding and tearing the flesh on his shoulder. The blow sent him toppling from his mount and he thudded to the dust.

At this, the chanting fell into a shocked silence. Sha, Blastares and Procopius rushed to surround him, throwing their veiled helms to the ground and leaping from their mounts. Apion waved them away and pushed himself up to stand, grateful that his agony was concealed behind his veil.

'The siege is over,' he snarled, snapping the arrow and clutching at the wound, 'get back inside the town.'

4. An Echo from the Past

Apion sat alone on the crenellations of the east wall, wearing a faded grey tunic, leather riding boots and his crimson cloak. The late afternoon sun behind him was a gentle salve on his battered body, soothing the wounds under the bloodied bandages hugging his shoulder and forearm. He chewed on a chunk of smoked carp skewered on the end of his dagger. The tangy flesh flaked on his tongue and he savoured the momentary sensation of wellbeing. Once they had broken the siege, Sha had led some of the town garrison to a tributary river and they had returned with barrels of fresh water and this bountiful catch. He washed down each mouthful with a swig of well-watered soured wine – the tart liquid reinvigorating his taste buds.

His belly full for the first time since the siege began, he cleaned his hands on a rag and enjoyed the blanket of drowsiness that settled on his mind. Then the air was pierced by the first rumblings of a kettledrum and a few high-spirited voices. He looked down into the town; in the square near the gate, fires crackled to life and men, women, children and elderly spilled into the square. The drums grew louder and then flutes joined in as the people danced and sang, ruddy-cheeked and boisterous, satiated after many days of starvation and thirst. After the sombre burial procession east of the walls that had dominated the day, this was the outpouring of relief. A sense of calm touched Apion's heart at the sight, so rare in the borderlands. Then he frowned, noticing a shape down one shadowy alleyway, writhing. Making out hairy, naked, gyrating buttocks, and the faint grunting of a rutting couple, he immediately realised that it was Blastares, indulging fully in the celebrations. A wry smile spread across his face; the usual post-battle penance and forgoing of wine and meat would come, but not today. He turned away to give his hulking tourmarches privacy, and looked along the battlements to the east gate.

His smile faded instantly.

Three gawping, grey heads rested on stakes atop the gatehouse, gazing out to the east. Veins and strings of congealed blood hung from their necks. Shame snaked through his thoughts once more.

It was the three Seljuk akhi he had brought to the walls to be slain. He had ended their lives. That, he could justify. He had justified it to the man whose throat he had cut. But what he had done after the battle, when Nasir's arrow wound was still fresh, when he had stood in the fire beyond the dark door . . . that, he could not justify.

He could still remember the sound of his own half-panting, half-growling as he had stormed back into the town, hobbled up to the battlements where the bodies lay, drawn his scimitar and desecrated the corpses.

He turned his gaze from the heads and held up the dagger blade, gazing at the creature that stared back at him.

An eagle cried out from high above the town.

Apion saw the silver-haired crone in the dagger blade. She sat silently by his side. Her milky, sightless eyes were fixed on him, unblinking. 'It has been some time since we last spoke,' he nodded faintly to her.

'You sought revenge, Apion. You drank the bitter foulness from its cup,' she said. 'You thought you could do so and then purge it from your life. Yet you found that once you have bathed in blood, the urge to spill it follows you forever more. It is a cycle I have long since grown weary of watching. It draws the worst from good men.' She extended a bony finger to the three impaled heads. 'Those men should have been buried, their bodies intact.'

'I know this,' Apion said stoically, spinning his dagger on its tip. 'Why do you remind me of my lot?'

Her sightless eyes seemed to search his face. 'I could remind you of much more. It has been twelve years since we last spoke. I have watched over you in that time. I have seen the grim deeds you have carried out or that have been performed by others at your behest. There have been noble exploits at times,' she nodded in concession, 'but always, your anger and hatred have brought shame upon you with your actions.'

'So you come to chide me?' Apion turned to her, frowning.

'No, not to chide you. I thought the darkness had consumed you entirely but I see that a chink of light remains. I come to offer you hope.'

'Hope? Hope is not a word to be used carelessly,' Apion offered her a mirthless half-grin. He swept a hand out across the surrounding countryside. 'With every passing day, hope dies in men's hearts all across these lands. Our borders are guarded by mercenaries who care little for those they protect,' then he cast a half-scowl over his shoulder to the west, 'and our emperor sponsors this. All the people of these lands have left is their God.' He ground his dagger into the mortar between two pieces of stone. 'So tell me, what hope can you offer?'

She paused, her expression falling stony. 'I have seen a future where this land can be free of struggle, for you and for all. But once again, Fate toys with me, showing me only what might be, dangling half-truths and allusions before me.'

'You have offered me wise words in the past, old lady. But you trouble me with riddles today. And today I have enough troubles and my mind is already awash with riddles. Please, if you have been blessed with the knowledge of what is to be, then tell me.'

The crone cackled shrilly, her eyes bulging, her lips rolling back to reveal worn and yellowed teeth. 'Ah, to hear a man speak of foresight as if it is a boon – that is rich indeed. If you were plagued with the knowledge of what might be then, truly, your life would be troubled indeed, and your mind would never be free from torment.' She tapped her temple with a bony finger. 'Believe me, I speak from experience.'

Apion sighed. 'But you have something to tell me, else you would not have come to me?'

She nodded, then turned to the east. 'I see a future where a great conquest has taken place. A battlefield by a vast lake lies soaked in blood. A great leader has fallen. This land is no longer in torment.'

Apion's eyes widened and he searched the crone's face, waiting on some bitter twist. But there was none. 'The conflict can end?'

She nodded in silence.

He mused over her words again and frowned. 'But you do not say who the victor is?'

She gazed through him. 'It is not the victor that matters, Apion, but the outcome. A time of peace across Anatolia. A chance for this land to know summer after winter, free of bloodshed.'

'You speak of a dream I have lived only in my early years,' Apion spoke absently, then his frown returned and he shook his head. 'But you must also see the victor, surely? What use is the knowledge that one runner will win a race, or that a dice will yield a number?'

The crone sighed and nodded in resignation, her features lengthening. Then she fixed Apion with her milky glare. 'I see a battlefield by an azure lake flanked by two mighty pillars. Walking

58

that battlefield is Alp Arslan. The mighty Mountain Lion is . . . dressed in a shroud.'

Apion's eyes widened and darted.

'Be wary of what you take from my words,' she added quickly. 'Many men have met their end by reading good from ill-omens. Many more have thrown their lives away by sensing wickedness from the mildest of portents.'

'That is the lot of any man. I accept this,' Apion said. 'But that you have come to me tells me that you have also seen my part in this future?'

'Aye,' she nodded, 'since the first time we spoke, and all throughout the dark years of war, I knew you would be part of it.'

'Part of what?' Apion leaned closer to her.

She grasped his wrist. 'Stay strong, *Haga*, for the Golden Heart will rise in the west. At dawn, he will wear the guise of a lion hunter. At noon, he will march to the east as if to counter the sun itself . . . '

Apion shuffled, his lips readying to speak.

The crone held up a finger, silencing his coming words. ' . . . at dusk you will stand with him in the final battle, like an island in the storm.'

Apion's eyes became shaded under a frown. 'What does it mean?' he sighed.

'I can offer you no more than this,' she said with candour, 'for this is all that Fate dangles before me.'

'But where should I go to find this . . . Golden Heart?' he asked.

'Go where you feel you must, Apion. If it is meant to be, then you will meet him.' Her face grew sullen. 'It seems that to defy Fate you must also submit to his whims.'

Apion made to protest, then caught the words in his throat and nodded with a sigh. 'I think I am beginning to understand your torment, old lady. Very well,' he prodded his dagger to the east. 'Tomorrow, once my men are rested, we will make haste to Caesarea. Many citizens and men of my ranks are trapped within Bey Afsin's siege lines.' Then he sighed and added through gritted teeth. 'As is Doux Fulco.'

'He is as good as dead, Apion,' she spoke gravely. 'This is no vision. This is a fact. His craven heart has led him inside the city's walls. He would have been as well sealing himself in his own grave. He and the people inside cannot be saved.'

Apion nodded. 'But I must try.'

Her puckered face at last creased into a smile. 'And that is what makes you what you are, under all those layers of bitterness, a flicker of light in the darkness. That is why I know you can be saved. That,' she placed a hand over her heart, 'is why I know you can defy Fate.'

Apion felt warmth in his own heart at this, as if she had placed her hand there. He looked coyly down to his dagger blade once more, surprised to see a smile in his reflection. 'By all accounts my path will be long and arduous. But tell me, old woman, was there ever a future for me where war did not hold sway?' In his heart, he imagined Maria, alive and in his arms. The sweet scent of her skin, the warmth of her touch. Their children playing around them. His eyes moistened.

The crone's lips moved as if to speak, but then she hesitated. 'We will talk again, Apion,' she said at last, 'when the time is right.'

He looked up with a frown, but the crone was gone.

The deep-red sky yielded nothing but the distant screech of an eagle.

***

The Seljuk-held city of Hierapolis dominated the arid plain of northern Syria. Its old, Byzantine walls were lined with an akhi garrison, and the vividly tiled minarets and the dome of the great mosque glistened in the rich sunset. High on the acropolis mount, the mighty limestone citadel stretched for the heavens, topped by the fluttering golden bow banners of the sultanate.

But the city was merely a speck on the western horizon for the Seljuk women of Hierapolis, washing their garments in the shallows of the River Euphrates at this hour when the sun was less fierce. Most gossiped as they worked, laughing or, more commonly, lamenting their absent husbands. One woman worked alone.

She wore a fine, dark-red silk robe. Her slave girl had laid this out for her in the morning. The girl had insisted on washing these garments, but her mistress had said no, insisting the slave should remain in their modest villa to rest, eat and build up the strength she so clearly lacked since they had bought her. So the woman had come here alone, ignoring the glances fired at her from the various cliques of jabbering wives and slaves. *The wife of a bey, deigning to dip her fine hands in the river?*

When she had finished washing each piece, she wrung the river water from it before bashing it against the rock. She reached out and lifted the next robe, humming a tune her father had once taught her – this helped block out the jabbering and whispering around her. The melody conjured up memories of the days when she would sit on Father's knee and the goat kids would skip nearby as they sung it together. A smile spread across her face at this. Then a meadow brown butterfly fluttered down to rest on the tip of a reed in the shallows before her. For a moment, she stopped washing, admiring the creature.

When she caught sight of her reflection in the momentarily still shallows, a tinge of sadness stung behind her nose. She saw the lines to the sides of her eyes and the few strands of silver in her charcoal hair. She was not her father's little girl anymore. Worse was the thought that she could no longer remember what her father had looked like. A coldness set around her heart as she remembered the last time she had seen him. The blood seeping from his awful wounds, the life slipping from him. She blinked away the thoughts before they could materialise and set about scrubbing at the robe vigorously and in silence. The butterfly fled in fright.

Then a distant wail echoed across the plain from the west. She shivered at the noise, then turned to see a party of ghazi riders race out from Hierapolis' gates. They were little more than a blur of hooves, speartips and dust cloud as they thundered across the plain towards the north-west. The Antitaurus Mountains loomed there, silhouetted by the sunset. Beyond them were the borderlands with Byzantium. Out there, somewhere far over the horizon, her husband roamed with his warband, eager to spill Byzantine blood.

Bey Afsin is the true leader of the Seljuk people – where Alp Arslan hesitates, Afsin is ready and willing to strike down our enemies!

She turned back to her washing, shaking her head at the memory of her husband's rant. Such a thinly veiled guise for his true motives. The playful boy she had grown up with, the young man she had once loved, had been consumed by bitterness.

I have brought you wealth and a fine home, have I not? Is that not enough? he would say.

'When we were young and in love, we had nothing,' she muttered, her gaze lost in the waters of the Euphrates.

Love. The words lingered in her thoughts. Once again, the sorrow stung at her eyes and her mind drifted to the past. She saw a face from those lost days. A face she thought of like this every day. The Byzantine boy father had brought to the farm. They had lived together for a few years. First she had loved him like a brother, then they had been lovers. Despite all that had happened since those days, he was never far from her thoughts.

She heard a laboured sighing behind her. Turning, she saw a portly old woman – one of the few less inclined to gossiping about her presence at the river – struggling to carry her washing on the long trek back to the city before darkness fell. She gathered up her things and rushed over, taking some of the old woman's burden. 'Allow me.'

The old woman smiled warmly. 'Thank you, Maria.'

***

That night, the grizzled and hulking Komes Stypiotes was on sentry duty atop the eastern gate, nearby the three staked heads.

Each komes had been assigned one wall and the eastern wall was his. But while his thirty men up and down the battlements stood rigidly to attention, Stypiotes felt tiredness overcome him. The wine he had supped before his shift had been unwatered and he had emptied most of the skin, and his belly was heavy with mutton and fish. He let out a serrated and smoky-tasting belch. He had definitely eaten far too much of the carp, he asserted, not for the first time tonight.

The crackling of the torch nearby grew rhythmic and soothing. Soon, his eyelids drooped and his mind turned to some fleeting whimsy, where a buxom lady was leading him by the hand to her bed. She slipped off her robe and lay down before him, beckoning him forward with a coiling finger wedged between her full breasts. A weak smile spread across his face at this and his head nodded forward as if accepting the invitation. Then, as quickly as the buxom lady had appeared in his dream, she transformed into a gruesome creature, oddly reminiscent of a giant carp, silver-scaled and with fangs like sabres. Before he could gather breath to scream, the creature leapt up from the bed to sink its fangs into his shoulder and a wet, sucking of ripping meat belched out.

With a yelp, Stypiotes jolted awake, his face pale and his eyes wide. 'Oh for . . . ' he muttered as he realised he had been dreaming. 'Bloody carp!' He spat, then cast a sour glare at the nearest of his skutatoi, who was stifling a snigger.

He squared his jaw, facing forward again, taking some comfort from the fact that his embarrassment would keep him awake for some time. Then something caught his attention, from the corner of his eye. Something was missing. He turned to his left.

The three stakes, some twenty paces away, were shorn of the severed Seljuk heads. They had definitely been there moments ago. He had certainly not imagined their gruesome presence. Frowning, he levelled his spear and stalked over to the blood-tipped stakes, looking around. But the battlements were still and empty apart from the few sentries. He looked down the steps and into the town, but all was dark and silent, the celebrations having long since ended. Then he turned to the blackness outside the town, and froze.

A single dot of orange candlelight illuminated the night, near the graves of the fallen. Stypiotes peered at it, then discerned a lone figure, back turned. The figure carried a spade and a hemp sack. His lungs filled to raise the alarm, when he recognised the amber locks and crimson cloak. He watched as the strategos then proceeded to bury three fleshy masses in the grave.

Then, the footsteps of the nearest skutatos rattled up by his side. 'Sir?' The youngster gasped in panic, pointing to the candlelit figure.

'At ease, soldier. There's a man doing what he must do. Nothing more.'

Stypiotes looked on as the burial was finished. Then the figure crouched on one knee, head bowed.

The strategos' shoulders shuddered silently.

5. Death of an Emperor

Eudokia gripped the edge of the balcony. Her ivory skin and fine-boned features were expressionless. Her silver-flecked, blonde locks were tied up in a swirl as she drew her bloodshot gaze over the eastern gardens of the Imperial Palace.

Here, the incessant babble of Constantinople was little more than a dull murmur. The morning sun bathed the vast and verdant space, edged with a marble colonnade and studded with ornate carvings and fountains. A web of paved footpaths picked their way through pockets of exotic blooms that lent their honeyed scents to the air. There were orange trees studded with fruit, palms that stretched high overhead, a family of parakeets flitting between them, and jasmine and wisteria that yawned across the marble walls.

A slave boy and a girl of similar age, thinking themselves unobserved, took a moment to rest in the shade under one orange tree. Eudokia saw them smile as they chatted. Their bodies bore the bruises of their master's wrath, and their lot was meagre. Yet still they found time to sit together and smile, taking turns to offer seed to a mother parakeet, which would peck at the seed then swoop back up to her nest and feed her three screeching hatchlings. Eudokia looked to her hands, creased with age, and remembered the lost days of her childhood when she had last known such companionship. Her gaze was fond momentarily, then it turned stony as she remembered how that had played out.

She turned away from the balcony edge and faced the black silk curtain that separated her from the bedchamber. She steeled herself as she stepped towards it. For while outside was verdant, vibrant and abound with life, inside was rife with the stench of death.

She brushed through the curtain, the silk cool on her skin. Instantly, the baritone chanting of priests met her ears and echoed around the cavernous and ornate bedchamber. The gilt frescoes tried in vain to spice the room with vitality. The fine sculptures in brass, porphyry and veined marble portrayed muscular men in the prime of their youth and health, as if mocking the shrivelled figure on the bed at the centre of the chamber.

This was Emperor Constantine Doukas, the ruler of all Byzantium. God's chosen one. He was bald, and what little hair remained was plastered to the back and sides of his scalp with sweat. His beard was unkempt and he was dressed only in a linen shirt that failed to hide his jutting ribs.

His emaciated form was a pitiful sight, yet she was bereft of pity for him. Indeed, she had never loved him, and it was all she could manage not to fear him. Their marriage had been more of a business arrangement between their families – wine and oil magnates of Paphlagonia and Ephesus – and they had barely met before the wedding ceremony. Regardless, she had hoped they would learn to love one another early in their marriage, but that hope had quickly dissolved when, pressed by his father, Doukas set out to ascend to the imperial throne. He swiftly became a guarded and devious creature, suspicious of all around him, sure they were eager to snatch his power away. She had hoped this was just a carapace he had adopted on his quest for power. But when he had found her writing a letter to her family in Ephesus, she realised his ambition had truly pickled his soul. He had torn the half-written letter from her, his eyes bulging, accusing her of plotting to ruin his bid to become emperor. He had ripped the paper in half, pinned her by the throat to the wall and then pulled out a dagger, pressing it to her breast until a droplet of blood darted from the skin. Never before had she seen such coldness in another's eyes as he glared at her. *You have no family. You are mine and mine alone. You will provide me with heirs. You will obey me.*

When he had taken the imperial throne, Constantine's advisers played upon his fears, whispering suggestions of duplicity in his ear, and these ideas burrowed like the tentacles of a parasite into his mind. Members of the court were tortured and executed on the merest hint of subterfuge or resistance to his designs. She shuddered, remembering the time he had summoned her into the underground torture chambers to watch one mild-mannered senator having his rib cage prised open and his lungs plucked from his chest to be held before his disbelieving eyes.

Equally, the populace hated him as much as they feared him. At first, the bravest of the citizens heckled him at the races in the Hippodrome, their cries vociferous. But then they were bundled away by his loyal garrison, never to be seen again. Soon the cries stopped altogether, and an air of oppression settled across the city. A stifling air that had remained ever since.

Until today, she thought without a hint of emotion.

An audience watched the emperor's last moments in silence. A pair of red-haired and white-armoured *varangoi* stood either side of the bed. These loyal Rus axemen were good-hearted yet bound to serve the emperor, whoever he may be, to the last. A handful of slaves and attendants knelt by the foot of the bed, cradling bowls of hot and cold water, salves and tinctures. Xiphilinos, the Patriarch of Constantinople, stood at the head of the bed, flanked by sceptre-wielding priests, leading them in their incantations.

At the near side of the bed stood her three sons: broad and tall Michael, young Andronikos, barely ten, and little Konstantious, just seven years old. Michael bore the cold scowl he had learned from his father, while Andronikos and Konstantious wore wrinkled looks of fear and sadness.

At the far side of the bed, the emperor's brothers, advisers and sycophants clustered like a colony of vultures, watching the body of the man whose death they waited on like a fresh meal. For once her husband was dead, the dice of power would be cast into the air.

The emperor looked up at this point, pinning her with his bloodshot glare. His breath was shallow and his skin bathed was with sweat as he reached out a hand to her. 'Come to my side, my dear,' he croaked. 'I fear that my time is short. I have something I must tell you.'

Eudokia saw the fear in his eyes, and for the first time in so many years, her heart responded with just a trace of pity. At first she was disgusted with herself. *After all he has done?* She looked to his outstretched hand and thought of the two slaves sitting outside. It was too late for any notion of companionship. But could this be one final act that would set her free? An apology for his deeds? She strode forward, hiding her emotion impeccably as she had learned to do, then sat on the bedside. She took his hand. 'My Emperor?'

'We have had many years together, Eudokia,' He held her gaze, his eyes moistening, 'and in that time I have been a poor husband to you.'

That does little justice to your foul deeds, Eudokia thought, keeping her face expressionless. Then she leaned in to whisper in his ear. 'Do not trouble your mind with what has gone before, just tell me you are sorry. Just once.' She even squeezed his hand just a fraction in reassurance, leaning back.

But the emperor continued as if she had not spoken. 'I expect that you will seek such companionship when I am gone by marrying another.' At this, he tightened his grip on her hand. The grip was fierce and belied his frailty, his bloodshot and bulging eyes searching hers. It was that look again. Colder than a winter's night.

Constantine hauled himself to sitting, his face only inches from hers. 'But you must *not!*' his teeth were rotten and his breath reeked of decay. 'Any stranger in this palace is a threat to the Doukid line, a line that must . . . *will* continue to sit on the imperial throne!' He said, a hint of his old booming tones breaking through his infirmity. But it was fleeting, and he collapsed back in a fit of coughing and wheezing, his eyes glazing over from the effort.

Eudokia's breath grew short and she felt numb inside. Across from her, she sensed the barely disguised grins from the watching vultures. Then an adviser sidled over to her and thrust a sheaf of paper before her. She did not look up.

'Make the oath that your emperor asks of you,' the adviser purred.

Eudokia snatched at the paper and scanned the wording of the agreement; she was to remain a widow. Her son, Michael, was to take the title of emperor. That alone would have been palatable, but the document also stated that Constantine's brother, John, was to be Michael's chief regent. The first inchoate tears blurred her vision as she realised that this was the parting demand of her husband – to have their son as a puppet and his vile brother and his advisers as the masters. Then she bit back on the urge to let her sorrow flow freely. *Stay strong*, she chided herself as she signed the document, pledging her acceptance of this.

She took a deep breath, blinked her eyes clear and then shot to standing. Rage pounded through her veins. But she was statue-still and unflinching as she glared across at those on the opposite side of the bed. John and his colony of advisers replied with barely disguised sneers. *You arrogant fool, when the husk of man who calls himself my husband breathes his last, power will go not to those with sheaves of paper. It will go to the strongest.*

Then, without another glance at the dying emperor, she strode from the room.

6. Into the Lion's Den

Apion led the remainder of his thema through a sun-bleached plain studded with green shrubs. The crunch of boots and the incessant cicada song had grown entrancing. This and the late May afternoon sun had a way of lulling men into a relaxed state.

Some men, Apion thought, looking to Blastares who rode alongside him.

The big tourmarches' scarred face was twisted in a sweat-bathed scowl. He suppressed a sigh as he crammed the last of his ration – a chunk of cheese wrapped in charred flatbread – into his mouth and chewed vigorously before washing it down with a swig of watered wine. Then he shuffled in his saddle and scratched roughly at his crotch.

Apion sensed the question coming before it was asked.

'Remind me exactly why, sir, we are trailing across the dust, throwing ourselves at the back of a massive Seljuk army, just to save that arsehole, Fulco? The men long to return to Chaldia.'

Apion did well to stifle a chuckle at Blastares' obvious agitation. But the big tourmarches' question was fair.

'What good can we do?' Blastares continued, twisting in his saddle, scanning the depleted banda and riders behind them. 'We have just one hundred and forty six men left. The scouts insist that Afsin has some seven thousand warriors in his army, and Bey Nasir and those that we scattered will surely have retreated to swell his ranks as well.'

'We won't be fighting when we get there, Blastares,' Apion replied calmly. 'We'll be looking to save as many of those trapped inside the city as possible.'

'Including Doux Fulco?' Blastares cocked an eyebrow with a hint of mischief.

Apion thought of the recalcitrant Doux. Fulco's brazen and blood-stirring rhetoric on the muster yard was matched only by his vagary for self-preservation on the battlefield.

'I don't value Doux Fulco's life any more highly than I do those of the smiths, tanners, beggars and whores within those walls,' Apion replied.

At this, Blastares relented. 'Aye, well we agree on that.'

They rode on in silence until they came to a rise in the plain where a stream cut across the land. A baked-red ridge lay ahead. Apion raised a hand and the column slowed to a halt. 'Rest your legs and slake your thirst, men,' he said. Then he slid from his mount and beckoned his trusted three with him. Sha, Procopius and Blastares followed him on foot as he stalked up to the rocky ridge.

They crouched as they reached the lip, and were silent for some time as they took in the sight before them. Below them, the land opened out in a vast, shallow bowl, baked terracotta and gold, shimmering in the heat haze, framed to the south by the magnificent Mount Argaeus, its tip teasingly capped with cool, crisp snow. In the centre of the bowl lay Caesarea. The city walls were, tall, solid and broad, constructed of huge blocks of dark, sombre stone. The battlements were speckled with the glinting iron helmets and speartips of Fulco's garrison and the vibrant fabrics of the Virgin Mary and the saints were erected above the towers. The domes, columns and aqueduct within the city seemed to huddle together behind those walls. For outside the walls, a horde of Seljuks lay wrapped around the city.

It was like a grotesque magnification of the scene around Kryapege only weeks ago.

There was an almost permanent dust cloud above the Seljuk lines that enshrouded the city as ghazi riders galloped to and fro, relaying commands to each of the large tents pitched at regular intervals around the blockade. Some of them cursed at the inhabitants as they rode, others loosed arrows upon the walls like a cat toying with its catch. Then a faint breeze brought with it shouting and the clashing of iron upon iron as the Seljuk infantry were drilled by their commanders. All the while the tap-tapping of hammers rang out from the Seljuk siege works as trebuchets, catapults and great towers were constructed.

'So the reports were wrong,' Blastares gawped, breaking the silence at last, 'seven thousand strong they said – but there are nearly nine thousand, I'd say.'

Apion scoured the siege lines. 'nine thousand or one hundred thousand – it doesn't matter; we're not taking them on, Blastares. We just need to find a way in.'

Sha whistled as he looked along the unbroken siege line. 'We'll need stealth or deception.'

Apion cut into an apple with his dagger, lifting a slice and chewing on it. 'Both,' he said.

Procopius nodded. 'Aye, but we need to plan this carefully. This won't be like sliding into a whore's bed.'

Apion was momentarily thrown by the turn of phrase. Then his gaze snagged on the wagons that rumbled into the bowl-shaped landscape. There was a thin train of them, skirting round the base of Mount Argaeus and then along the track towards the siege lines. He watched the nearest one; it seemed destined for a compound that formed part of the siege line. The enclosure was basic, presenting

74

palisade stakes to the city and a strapped timber gate to the south, and it was manned by only a handful of akhi. The wagon entered the compound via the timber gate. Inside, forage, game, fodder and barrels of water were unloaded before the driver whipped his horses and set off to the south once more. Interestingly, this wagon and the others approaching had no armed escort.

He looked to see that his trusted three were shrewdly watching the wagons too. Then they looked to one another, their eyes sparkling.

'We wait until dark then we make our move,' he said calmly.

***

Apion shivered and pulled his woollen cloak a little tighter as he crouched in the undergrowth, his face and hair blackened with soot and earth. The waning moon betrayed little of the track that lay a few metres before them. This kept the narrow rut they had dug in the path obscured. This was a blessing, the bitter night chill and agonising wait were not.

'Come on, come on,' Sha whispered in the darkness beside him. The Malian was rubbing his calves to prevent his muscles from seizing up. Like the rest of them, the tourmarches wore only a tunic, cloak and swordbelt.

Then, at last, a crunching of wheels on scree betrayed an approaching vehicle and snapped Apion from his thoughts. All of them fell silent and utterly still. He gestured to them to remain that way and peered into the blackness. A single wagon. This was perfect – they would spring from the brush and the driver would surely spur his mounts on, taking a wheel over the rut at speed, stalling the vehicle for a few precious moments. 'On my command,' Apion hissed, raising one finger as the wagon neared.

But then the clopping of more hooves halted him just as the words tumbled towards his lips.

Ghazis.

The two riders trotted along behind the flanks of the wagon, arrows nocked to their bows, eyes keen and alert. A night escort. So Bey Afsin was shrewder than he had anticipated.

His mind spun. Should they withdraw and come back with more men the following night? By then it could be too late – Caesarea might have fallen. His eyes darted this way and that, until the groan of a straining cartwheel rang out. A front wheel of the vehicle had sunk into the rut and the driver called out in alarm. The two ghazis instantly pulled back, ignoring the driver's protests, first scouring the tracksides for bandits. Then the gaze of one of them pinned Apion where he crouched. The whites of the man's eyes bulged. His bow loosed and Apion froze. The arrow smacked into the dirt, an inch from his boot.

As the rider fumbled to nock another bow, Apion realised the decision was made. He leapt up, drew his scimitar and roared his men forward.

***

Mezut rested his elbows on the edge of the squat timber watchtower at the southern edge of the supply enclosure. From his vantage point he could smell the cooking meat and baked bread waft in from all around the yurts and fires forming the blockade. Yet he was stuck here with sack upon sack of grain, raw, bloodied animal corpses and cursed horse fodder. It summarised his feelings about this whole endeavour.

Bey Afsin had promised much to him and the many men he had led away from the east against Alp Arslan's wishes. They had ridden from the Seljuk lands, hearts full of hubris and in awe of

Afsin's dream to finally conquer Byzantium. Allah seemed to be truly with them at first. But after many months far from home, the men had become disillusioned with their leader, who now seemed to be hungrier for the spoils of victory than the glory of conquest. Indeed, rumours had spread that his tent was piled high with gold and silver stripped from the Byzantine settlements they had raided so far. Worse, whispers were spreading that Alp Arslan had broken from his Fatimid campaign, assembled a vast army and now marched this way, intent on crushing his renegade Bey.

Mezut shook his head at this. 'Afsin is a fool,' he realised with a weary heart, 'and I am a fool also for following him.' He sighed, then stood a little straighter. Soon, his shift would be over. It would not do to be anything other than diligent whilst looking after the stores. Afsin was notorious for his brutality. Indiscipline amongst his ranks in these last months had been swiftly and ruthlessly ended at the end of a blade or a barbed whip.

At that moment, the crunching of cartwheels on scree and the clopping of hooves rang out. Mezut lifted a torch and peered into the darkness to see the next supply wagon approach with the two night escort riders.

The wagon driver wore a blue felt cap and a woollen robe and was hunched over his reins, no doubt tired of his work. 'Open the gates,' the driver called again in an odd Seljuk twang.

He called to the two akhi down below. The pair hauled the palisade gate open, the strapped timber groaning. Mezut descended the ladder as the wagon rolled in and wheeled round to a halt, then the riders followed it. Mezut stepped from the compound and gazed south.

'There are no more?' He asked, scanning the darkness outside. Two thuds sounded behind him and a cold wave of fear washed across his heart. He turned just in time to see the driver lurching for him. He

77

saw the dirt-streaked face and the piercing, emerald eyes. Then, with a flash of iron, the flat of a scimitar blade smacked against his temple.

Bright lights filled Mezut's vision and he toppled to the ground. He watched, helpless, as a group of five figures, blackened and crouched, stole over the southern palisade then flitted across to the walls of Caesarea.

***

Inside the map room atop the thick-walled citadel at the heart of Caesarea, Doux Fulco felt the wine swash in his belly and knew the precious moments of gladness were over. He rubbed his pale, polished bald pate as a dry throbbing began in the centre of his head. This was accompanied by a dull, bloating nausea in his gut. He pulled his chair closer to the cracked oak table, rested his weight on his elbows and sighed, gazing across the plethora of maps and city plans that were spread before him. The diagrams and texts were but a blur now. He lifted the wine jug and, when only the last few droplets trickled into his mouth, he snarled and hurled the terracotta piece to the hearth.

The jug shattered across the dying fire and the crash echoed through the chamber. He looked up to his mercenary captains, his pointed features and stark black brow wrinkling as he eyed them. Only the fire crackling in the hearth broke the silence and a cloying scent of woodsmoke crept from the dying flames.

'There's definitely no word of a relief column?' Fulco rasped.

The biggest of them, a Rus warrior, looked on with a blank expression. 'We *were* the relief column,' he replied in a jagged accent.

'Watch your tongue, Rus!' Fulco growled, then dropped his head into his hands once more. Fifteen hundred men made up his tagma. Barely enough to man the southern and eastern walls, where the Seljuk blockade was thickest. There were the nine hundred he had commandeered from the Chaldian ranks – yet all he heard from them was mutterings of discontent at being separated from their strategos. Fulco's top lip curled at this. Apart from that, the garrison in the city was paltry; three hundred skutatoi and fifty toxotai. At the outset of the siege and despite the truth of his Rus captain's words, he had sent riders to the north, calling for a relief force from the Colonea Thema. The following dawn, the riders' heads had thudded onto the flagstoned streets, fired from Seljuk trebuchets. Since the blockade had been put in place, there was little hope of getting word out. They were alone against Afsin's horde.

He stood up from the table and strode to the open shutters, hands behind his back as he looked across the night skyline, illuminated by torchlight. The broad and sturdy imperial mint towered high, rivalled only by the stilts of the aqueduct and the Monastery of St Basil. Mighty Caesarea, the jewel at the heart of Byzantine Anatolia, would fall. That was almost a certainty. His brief had been to defend the city and prevent its fall, thus he would be seen as a failure. But the cold terror at the prospect of a violent death troubled him far more than the fate of this place or his reputation. His top lip curled as he scanned the ant-like populace scurrying to and fro in the streets below. *When it comes to it, the dogs that dwell here can keep the Seljuk blades busy whilst I escape.*

Then one figure stepped forward, clearing his throat. 'If I may interject, sir?'

Fulco's neck snapped round to glare at the figure. It was Dederic the Norman rider, distinguished from the Rus and his own comrades by his diminutive stature – only shoulder-high to the rest. He was younger than most of them too – only in his twenty-third year. His head was shaved to the scalp at the back and sides with a dark mop of

79

hair on top. As if to compensate for his size, his jaw was broad as was his nose, and his eyes were a piercing gold. Like the rest of the Normans, he wore a mail hauberk, the hood lowered and gathered around his shoulders. 'Speak,' Fulco grunted.

'There is still time to call upon the Strategos of Chaldia, sir. Under cover of night, we at least have a chance of getting a rider or even a runner through the blockade.'

Fulco's blood heated at the mention of the man. Despite his imperially bestowed authority over the north-eastern themata, the men of the local militias there still spoke only of one name. *The Haga.* He shook his head, his teeth gritting.

'There is a weak spot to the north of the city,' Dederic continued. 'If the strategos attacked from his side and we sally at the same point, then perhaps we could break through there – at least see the citizens clear of the walls and into the northern hills? The banks of the Halys are thick with fishing vessels that could transport . . . '

'Enough!' Fulco bawled. *Put my life at risk to save these wretches?* He wracked his mind for stirring words to mask his true motive. 'Not a soul will leave this city. This is a city of God, and God's people will not flee like rats under the Seljuk glare. Honour is at stake, soldier. *Honour!*' Fulco lifted the purse from his belt and shook it. 'A concept you may not be familiar with. For you are here only to accrue gold, are you not?'

Dederic's nose wrinkled at this. Fulco willed him to speak, his fingers curling into a fist inside his iron-plated glove.

But it was another voice that spoke.

'If we stay here then we will die. There is no honour in dying needlessly, though I doubt that is your true motive in any case.'

Fulco spun on the spot, to the arched doorway. A silhouetted figure strode into the room. His blood iced. He clapped his hands together and two Rus leapt forward, pulling their axes from their belts.

But, in a flash of iron, another figure leapt through the doorway and ripped a spathion from his belt, countering the Rus. A flicker of firelight betrayed this second stranger's coal-dark skin.

'At ease,' the first figure spoke, gently pushing the axes and blades down and walking into the light. His battered features and amber hair were soot and earth-blackened. But the murmur of recognition rang around the room instantly.

'*Haga!*'

Fulco frowned. 'Strategos? The blockade is breached?' A flutter of blessed relief touched his heart – was his life to be spared?

'No,' Apion spoke in a stolid tone. Then he strode forward and rested his palms on the table to cast his gaze across the litter of papers. 'Sha,' he beckoned his companion, 'what do you make of the city plan? Are the streets broad enough for a clean evacuation?'

The brief notion of reprieve snatched away, Fulco's blood bubbled with fury at the man's ease – flicking through the maps as if his superior was not present. 'Then you will give me a full report, Strategos. How did you enter the city and what forces do you bring?'

Apion turned to him with a slight frown at the interruption. 'There are five of us. Your guards opened the gate hatch to let us in.'

Fulco slammed a fist on the table. 'And the blockade?'

'It is as tight as ever, Doux, we were lucky to slip through.' Apion offered him a weary look. 'It will not be broken by force.'

Fulco rubbed at his temples, wishing he had resisted that last jug of wine whilst eyeing the next. 'Then what do you bring to us – five extra men to defend the walls?'

'No, I bring a slim chance for some of the people of this city to slip through the blockade and escape the fate that awaits them.'

Fulco knew he could not air his thoughts on their deserved fate. Instead he decided to call the *Haga's* bluff. 'The Seljuk blockade – the same blockade that *cannot* be broken?'

'I said it could not be broken by force, but it can be broken.' Apion stood back from the table and turned to Dederic. The little Norman straightened up under the *Haga's* gaze. 'And if it is to break, then your captain has already identified the area to the north of the blockade as the most suitable point for the citizens to flee.'

At this, Dederic offered a faint nod of gratitude.

This riled Fulco even more. 'Your riddles will save nobody, Strategos,' he scoffed, 'we need clear plans.'

Apion addressed Fulco and the rest of the room. 'Think about it, we cannot fight our way through Afsin's lines, but what if his men are compelled to abandon those lines, albeit temporarily?' The watching mercenary captains frowned at this.

'What would bring them to this action?' Dederic asked.

Apion tapped a finger to his temple. 'The thing that Afsin and his ranks out there fear more than anything else.'

The Norman's gaze fell to the flagstoned floor and darted this way and that. 'Alp Arslan . . . '

Apion nodded. 'It has been rumoured since this invasion began that the sultan would come to tame his renegade bey. Afsin's ranks quake at the very thought of the Mountain Lion's wrath.'

Fulco's eyes widened as a babble of murmuring broke out among the captains. His chest tightened as he felt his authority diminish like the dying fire in the hearth.

Apion addressed the captains. 'Afsin will pay dearly for acting against the sultan's orders, and his men already look over their shoulders in fear.' Then he turned to Fulco. 'So if we play on that fear, then maybe, just maybe, the chance to escape this walled grave will present itself.'

The image of the city as a tomb chilled Fulco to his core. He held the strategos' gaze with a firm and cold glare. 'Your plan will see the ranks to safety also?' he asked meekly, gulping, his eyes darting to those watching.

Apion's face remained stony. 'Every soldier will have a role to play in seeing the citizens to safety. But I will not lie to you – your blades will taste blood tonight and many of you will not see tomorrow.'

Fulco felt his gut curdle at this. Suddenly the strategos' plan seemed significantly less agreeable. 'Bey Afsin will surely not fall for any such ruse,' he said, trying to disguise the tremor in his voice.

Apion nodded at this. 'But if we do not try, then every one of us will die.'

'Aye,' Fulco's face streamed with a cold sweat, his gaze growing distant.

'Give the word, sir,' Apion said. Then he lowered his voice to a whisper; 'Seize this chance and you might live to fight another day.'

Fulco looked into his eyes in silence, then nodded faintly.

The tourmarches, Sha, saw this and left the room, his footsteps pattering up to the roof of the citadel.

'Where do we start?' Fulco asked.

Apion pointed through the shutters.

Fulco turned to see a single, fiery arrow arc into the sky from the citadel rooftop and then drop silently. His skin crawled. To the south, far beyond the Seljuk blockade, the lower slopes of Mount Argaeus gradually illuminated with the glow of first a handful, then hundreds of torches.

He spun back to Apion, sensing control spiralling from his grasp. 'What have you done?'

***

Blastares dropped his torch as the flame died then stood back, panting. The lower slopes of the great mountain were speckled with some five hundred resin-soaked stakes, his men scurrying to light the remaining few. 'That's it,' he barked, 'get 'em all ablaze!'

Then Procopius hobbled past, marshalling his men likewise, his craggy features black with soot. 'Watch you don't set yourself alight, you old bastard!' he cackled.

For once, Procopius didn't have time for a riposte.

'It's working – look!' the sharp-featured Komes Peleus cried out.

Blastares spun to peer at the band of orange torchlight wrapped around the city, then saw that it was peeling away like a layer of skin. The faint moan of Seljuk war horns carried on the night breeze as Afsin's men hurried to form a line, facing south.

'Ha! Let's hear it for Blastares' army!' he barked, patting one stake as if in congratulation. Then he nodded to the lip of the vast bowl that encircled Caesarea. 'Now form up – we have a quick march ahead of us, to the north to help with the evacuation.'

The men scurried into formation. All but Komes Stypiotes, whose face had paled, his mouth agape, gazing south.

'Komes?' Blastares frowned, then turned away from the city to follow Stypiotes' gaze. There, where there had previously been pure, unbroken darkness. Another orange glow emerged around the southern base of Mount Argaeus.

More torches. Hundreds of them, spilling into view. Then thousands, like some mocking reflection of the illusion they had set up right here. But these torches bobbed and flickered as they grew closer, and they came with the rumble of hooves and boots. Then a Seljuk war horn moaned.

Blastares' skin prickled as he discerned the first of the banners in this approaching army. The golden bow emblem was unmistakable.

Alp Arslan had arrived to tame his bey.

***

Apion feared he had made a terrible mistake. He was hoarse from barking and marshalling the citizens towards the northern gate. Every time he looked down a street or alley there were more and more citizens pouring from the tenements, clutching their possessions, stumbling and falling before others. But they were not moving fast enough, many clustering around the skutatoi, begging for information, demanding to know why they had been flushed from their homes in the dead of night. Added to this, many of Fulco's Norman riders were breaking from their positions to ride clear of the city with the citizens, then he saw some of the Rus axemen doing likewise, saving their own necks. One even swung his axe at a Chaldian skutatos who tried to stop him. Only a handful of Fulco's riders remained where Apion had placed them – a group of thirty or so Norman riders led by Dederic, who had hopped from his saddle to help usher a family from the alleys and towards safety. By his reckoning they had a few short hours at best before Afsin would uncover the ruse, wrap his forces around the walls once more and surely ensnare and slay any Byzantines caught in the open ground.

85

'Make haste – you will be safe to the north,' he said as he helped one woman from her knees and bundled her towards the gate. Peering through the gateway, he was heartened to see the first streams of evacuees reaching the northern hills. From there it would be a short journey to the banks of the River Halys. If his riders had carried out their job, then the local fishing fleets and trade vessels would be clustered there.

But then panicked cries rang out from the south of the city.

'The Seljuks have breached the walls!'

He looked down the broad street to see fighting on the southern battlements. Skutatoi were tumbling into the streets below, impaled on akhi spears and peppered with arrows. *Surely Bey Afsin has not uncovered our ruse already?* Then he heard a thunderous cry spill around the walls from outside the city;

Alp Ars-lan! Allahu Akbar!

No! He stumbled back, eyes wide, as ladders clattered into place all along the battlements. In every direction he looked akhi spilled onto the walls and then swamped and cut down the skutatoi there.

The Mountain Lion had come after all.

From the southern, eastern and western walls, the first parties of akhi descended the stairs then spilled into the streets, slicing through the terrified citizens in their path. Within moments, the granary and a sweeping row of tenements were ablaze and the streets sparkled with spilled blood. Panicked horses bolted from the nearby stables, adding to the chaos. Then he spun to the sound of crashing stone from the east of the city. A great cry rang out of the Monastery of St Basil, and akhi spilled from its doors, carrying shattered chunks of marble from the saint's tomb like trophies. At the same time, the southern gates crashed open, shattered by an iron-tipped ram. A sea of ghazis spilled into the streets and headed straight for the citadel. The stronghold was barely manned and it fell in a heartbeat.

The walls were gone and Caesarea was on the brink.

Apion shepherded an elderly man carrying two babies to the north gate, denying the sense of futility in his heart. Then looked up to the north walls – the last high ground still in Byzantine hands. There he saw Doux Fulco, framed by the waning moon. He was fleeing from the advancing akhi, making his way towards the nearest stairs, barging the few hundred Chaldian skutatoi who still fought out of the way. Then the doux stumbled in his haste, pitching headlong from the battlements. His cry was as shrill as a vulture's, and Apion saw the man's eyes bulging, his arms flailing. Finally, the cry was cut short; his skull shattered against the flagstones, a soup of blood and grey matter bursting across the street, his body crumpling on top of it. At the last, it was Fulco's craven nature and not a Seljuk blade that killed him.

But Apion spared only a heartbeat of thought for the man's fate. For he realised he had sent the citizens out onto the open plain where thousands of Seljuk blades would now be converging on them. The mocking voice from behind the dark door rasped in a dry laughter as he looked to the open northern gate. Outside, the flood of women, elderly, children and babies screamed as, from either side, a horde of ghazi riders closed in on them, arrows nocked to bows. The cowering citizens halted their flight and the riders waited on the order to fire.

'Sir!' Sha emerged from the chaos and backed up to him, his eyes bulging. The pair lifted their blades and turned; every direction offered only blazing fires, pockets of bloodied and cowering citizens and retreating skutatoi. Closing in on them was a wall of Seljuk spearmen. They were spilling through the gates, filling the streets, swarming over the walls. 'Is this the end?' the Malian panted.

Apion could offer him no answer.

Then a Seljuk war horn sounded three times. Gradually, the war cries of the akhi tumbled into silence. They slowed their advance and then halted, forming a spearwall in an arc around the last clutches of Byzantine defenders before disarming them. The skutatoi atop the northern gatehouse finally laid down their weapons as they saw that defeat was inevitable. A line of Seljuk archers hurried to kick the discarded weapons away, before nocking arrows to their bows and herding the Byzantine soldiers from the walls.

Apion looked all around, seeing only bloodstained Seljuk warriors grimacing back at him. Then, three riders trotted in through the northern gate and the noise seemed to fall away.

A pair of ironclad ghulam riders carried banners bearing a golden bow emblem. They flanked the broad-shouldered central rider, saddled upon a sturdy dappled steppe pony. He wore a gilded conical helmet with an ornate nose-guard and an iron plated vest that hung to his knees. He carried a scimitar and a finely crafted composite bow. His skin was sallow, his expression stony and gaunt and his nose long and narrow. His dark brown eyes were sharp like a hawk's. He sported a thick and long moustache, the ends looping round the back of his neck where they were tied together. A pair of akhi hurried to surround Apion and Sha, pushing spearpoints into the flesh of their necks as this rider approached to within a few feet.

Apion threw down his scimitar and Sha followed suit.

'Have I finally captured the legend of the Byzantine borderlands?' Alp Arslan spoke stonily. 'I know it is you,' the sultan eyed him, examining his blackened, unarmoured form then gazing into his eyes. 'We have clashed many times, *Haga*. All I have seen of you behind the iron veil you wear on the battlefield is those eyes and . . . ' he dismounted and strode forward, lifting the sleeve of Apion's woollen robe, revealing the red ink *stigma*. 'Aye, *Haga*, it is you,' he nodded.

Apion stared at the sultan, expressionless. 'Do your bidding, spill our blood. But do not seek glory in the slaughter, for there is none to be found.'

'Years ago, Haga, I longed to take your head,' Alp Arslan raised a clenched fist, his eyes sparkling, 'dreamt of a moment like this.' He lowered his fist and shook his head. 'But now that the moment is upon me, I feel no wish to spill Byzantine blood. It *will* happen – but not today. I have seen enough Fatimid blood in these last months to sicken myself of all things crimson.' He nodded to the bloody soup staining the battlements and the bodies of slain citizens strewn through the streets. 'But, fifteen thousand souls march with me. Food and fodder are paramount, and so your fine city had to be taken. You know as well as I that at times some bloodshed cannot be avoided. But it is over now.' At this, he barked to the ghazis outside the gate. Mercifully, they lowered their bows. Gradually, and in disbelief at first, the cowering citizens there stood once more, then they wasted no time in fleeing northwards. The sultan then clapped his hands and issued orders to the swell of akhi, despatching them to the cisterns with orders to put out the flames that threatened to consume parts of the city.

He looked back to Apion. 'I came here to settle a dispute.' He clicked his fingers. A clutch of akhi led forward a bedraggled form who wore only a torn robe, his grey hair loose and matted in gore like his beard. Bey Afsin's rebellion was over. Beside him was Nasir, shackled, one side of his face lined with the fresh and angry welt of melted flesh.

'That it spilled into Byzantine lands was a regrettable occurrence,' the sultan continued, snapping Apion's gaze away from his old foe, 'and one I could not allow to burgeon any further.' He turned to Bey Afsin. 'Why did you turn from me, my once most loyal Bey?' Afsin could not meet the sultan's gaze.

Then Alp Arslan turned to Nasir. Nasir looked his leader in the eye. 'And you, noble Nasir. I fear you are an even greater loss to my ranks. My plan was to have you elevated to my side. At the helm of the finest riders of my army, controlling a *ghulam* wing. Yet you throw your loyalty behind Bey Afsin's hot-headed scheme and charge to the west like a blinded bull?' His eyes hung on the melted flesh dominating one side of Nasir's face. 'The scars you bear will surely serve to remind you of your folly. But for how long?'

At this, a pair of akhi stepped forward and drew their scimitars, resting the curved blades on Afsin and Nasir's necks, looking to their sultan.

Apion and Nasir shared a lasting, stony gaze.

'In my time I have had men put to excruciating torture,' Alp Arslan continued, twisting to address the watching thousands. 'There was one ambitious soul who thought the sultanate would be better steered by his hand and so he set his mind to plotting my assassination. He had plenty of time to rethink his ambitions when I had him staked onto the hot sand, his eyes dashed from his skull and ants set loose upon the bleeding sockets. It took him a day to die and by then, the ants had burrowed through and infested every space inside his head.'

At this, the hordes looking on cheered in bloodlust and anticipation. Afsin squirmed in the grip of the akhi. Nasir did not flinch.

Then Alp Arslan turned to the pair. 'Your acts were criminal,' he paused and all around murmured in expectation, 'but they were not treasonous, and your motivation is noble. Patience is all that separates us,' he looked to both of them in turn, then boomed so all could hear;

90

'We all seek glory for Allah. We all seek the conquest of Byzantium and the peace that will come after that.' The sultan lifted his arms up, palms outwards. 'So let it be known here and now that you will not be put to torture or death. Instead you will be placed back in my ranks and given the opportunity to demonstrate your loyalty. For we are stronger together. That this mighty Byzantine city has capitulated is but a precursor of what could be. First, you will ride south with me and put an end to the ambitions of the proud, misguided Fatimids. Then, when the time is right, we will return to this land, and deliver glory to Allah *together!*'

The thick swathes of Alp Arslan's horde packing the battlements and the city streets erupted in a colossal roar. Nasir did not blink as the blade was taken away from his neck. His gaze remained on Apion.

Then the sultan too looked to Apion. 'Does this not serve to demonstrate the futility of Byzantium's resistance? While your forces grow weaker every day, my armies simply grow.'

Apion stared back in silence.

'In these past years I have heard much of the *Haga's* wit – sharper even than his blade, apparently. Yet I find you reluctant to utter but a word?'

Apion seared a glare at Alp Arslan. 'I find that conversation held at spearpoint tends to be rather one-sided.'

Alp Arslan frowned. Then the sultan threw his head back and let loose a lungful of laughter that rang into the night. With that, he raised a hand to the spearmen behind Apion, who lowered their weapons.

'Come then, *Haga*. Let us talk as simple men. Weaponless and alone.'

***

Dawn was approaching and the newly kindled fire cast the map room in an orange glow. Apion gazed into the flames. He wore a fresh, soft woollen robe. He had washed the worst of the grime from his face and beard, and wore his damp hair knotted atop his head. It was as if the events of the evening had been some kind of nightmare.

But then he looked up; where Doux Fulco had been sitting only hours ago, Sultan Alp Arslan now sat, supping the remains of the jug of wine left behind by the previous incumbent. On the table between them, a chequered shatranj board had been set up. The pieces had not yet been moved.

The sultan had shed his armour and now wore only a *yalma,* a green silk close-fitting robe trimmed with gold embroidery. His dark locks hung down his back, and his flowing moustache was tied back there too. Apart from the finery of his garment, the sultan looked very much like the many Seljuk traders and farmers Apion had encountered in his time. He did not look particularly like Mansur, yet, looking at the sultan across the shatranj board, Apion could not help but think of his old guardian; the man whose sword he carried to this day; a man whose memory he loved and loathed.

The sultan was flanked by two standing figures. One was a towering rock of a man named Kilic, the sultan's bodyguard. Kilic wore a permanent scowl on his flat-boned face, and was dressed only in a sleeveless linen tunic that displayed his bulging, scarred arms. The other was Nizam, a small, stout, grey-bearded vizier wearing a blue silk cap. He had seen this pair watching in the distance when his and Alp Arslan's armies had clashed in the past, and Apion guessed that they were to the sultan what Sha, Blastares and Procopius were to him. Just then, a slave hurried in to place a platter of bread and a pot of honey upon the table along with a fresh jug of wine. At this, Alp Arslan nodded to the two behind him.

'Leave us, please.'

Nizam bowed and Kilic grunted, his eyes never leaving Apion as they departed.

'Eat and drink, Strategos. There is no victory, moral or otherwise, in starving yourself after a battle.' The sultan went at the bread and honey before him like a man who had not seen food in days. Then he washed it down with a mouthful of wine before reaching out to tap the board. 'When I was a boy, I used to play this game with my Uncle Tugrul. You remember the *Falcon?*' he asked, pushing a central pawn forward, looking up with a stony gaze.

Apion let the question hang in the air. He had never spoken with the previous sultan, but they had clashed in battle, over twelve years ago. He had led his men in a ferocious counter-charge that had broken Tugrul's great horde and shattered the Falcon's reputation terminally. Alp Arslan knew all of this and knew it well. Indeed, it had been the driving force for his subsequent battering of the Byzantine borderlands in the first few years afterwards. Back then, rumour had been rife that Alp Arslan lived only to crush the Byzantine armies and to see Apion's head on a spike. Mercy had seldom marched with the Mountain Lion. He eyed the sultan's blade, resting by the hearth, and wondered what had changed in the intervening years; he tore a piece of bread, dipped it in the honey and then chewed. Instantly it invigorated him and soothed his knotted stomach. He reached over to move one of his own pawns forward, opening a path to develop his war elephant. 'I remember the Falcon. At least, I knew of the warrior whose hordes I faced in battle, but I did not know the man behind the armour.'

The sultan's stony gaze faltered a little, growing distant. 'They were one and the same, Strategos. Some men can never truly shed their armour. I realised this when I was very young. I used to be known as Muhammud back then,' he said. 'I was a happy boy. Yet I always longed to emulate the *Falcon's* greatness. I coveted a battle name as if it would make me a man.' The sultan mused over his next move, then plucked a knight and moved it ahead of the pawn line. 'Tugrul once told me that many years ago, when my people dwelt upon the open steppe, they would go to the foot of Mount Otuken. The drums would rumble like thunder and the tribesmen would watch on as the *khagan* approached, adorned with yak tails and bright pennants and his skin laced with paint. Then he would bestow the *er ati* upon the bravest of warriors. That was how Tugrul gained his battle name. That was how the *Falcon* first spread his wings. From the moment Tugrul told me this, he put an elusive goal before me. For I could never earn my battle name in such a fashion. Our people left the steppe long ago and now Mount Otuken lies windswept and deserted, its glory reserved for the ghosts of the past alone.' The sultan's lips tightened. 'He knew the fire this would stoke within me.'

Apion eyed the sultan. He had dealt with many Seljuk *emirs* and beys in his time. Some wise, some haughty, some devious, some blunt. This man, the sultan who ruled above them all, was not what he had expected. 'In these last years, your reputation has far outshone the *Falcon's*,' he said tersely, moving another pawn out to limit the knight's movement, 'and the name *Alp Arslan* is known across my empire and yours.'

The sultan nodded, moving a pawn forward to bring his vizier into play. 'I first heard that name when I was saddled on my mount, soaked with blood. We had just subdued the last of the rebel *Daylamid* spearmen, high in the rugged mountains of Persia. A thousand men around me lauded the slaughter I had led, a thousand more lifeless faces gazed up at me from the blood-sodden earth. *Alp Arslan!* they

94

chanted all around me. As a boy, I had expected to feel pride at that moment, but when it came, I felt only emptiness.' The fire dimmed a little more as the sultan swirled his wine cup, his hawk-like eyes peering into the past. 'The glory of Mount Otuken will forever evade me, but the cursed fire Tugrul stoked within me will never die. Sometimes I find myself pining for those days when I used to be known simply as Muhammud.'

The sultan's words were like an echo of Apion's thoughts. 'Any moniker earned by the spilling of a man's blood is a curse rather than a boon. Indeed, every time they chant *Haga* after a battle, I find myself awakening as if from some awful dream, surrounded by death. Yet I find myself drawn back to that numb netherworld, time and again.' He lifted his war elephant out to counter the threat of the sultan's vizier piece. 'I detest my battle name,' he leaned back in his chair with a dry, mirthless laugh, one finger absently tracing the white band of skin on his wrist, 'yet when I think back to the days when I was known simply as Apion, I have no wish to return there.'

The sultan lifted his war elephant and sent it across almost to the edge of the board, lining up to strike Apion's pawn line. 'A riotous mixture of my ambitions and my uncle's ambitions for me spawned the creature I have become. I have watched my family tear at each other, murdering and plotting against one another in their lust for power. Now I find myself as sultan, does that make me at once the best and the worst of them? Regardless, it is what I am. The boy Muhammud is gone, and my destiny is set in stone. There will be many more bloody battlefields.' Alp Arslan looked into the crackling flames for a moment. Then he leaned forward, his expression earnest. 'I have faced curs, cowards, mindless butchers and men who would slaughter their children for a purse of gold. But I have faced few like you, *Haga*; your tenacity is unparalleled. After twelve years, still you resist my armies. What happened to you to make you this way?'

Apion's gaze drifted as the question hung in the air. Then he reached down to lift Mansur's bloodied shatranj piece from his purse, his eyes examining its worn surface. Then he took up an empty cup, filled it with wine and took a deep gulp. A long silence passed, broken only by the spitting of the fire. Then he looked the sultan in the eye and, without thinking, he slipped into the Seljuk tongue; 'Everyone I have ever loved has been slain.' His words echoed around the map room as he lifted a pawn out to block the sultan's chariot and present a lure to the nearby knight.

Alp Arslan's eyes narrowed and he replied in his native tongue; 'Then this is the source of your hatred of my people?'

Apion shook his head almost imperceptibly. 'Of those lost to me, there were my Byzantine birth parents, slain by Seljuk scimitars. Then there were my Seljuk guardians, butchered by Byzantine spathions. So, no, I do not hate your people, Sultan. I judge men on their merits and not their origins. Quite simply, I hate what this land has become.'

'There will always be a borderland, Strategos,' the sultan said as lifted his vizier forward. 'Were people not suffering here, then they certainly would be, elsewhere.'

'Perhaps. But now you have your answer. I can never relent until I am cut down, or until conflict is driven from this land.'

Alp Arslan supped his wine as if considering his next words carefully. 'Your empire is putrefying at its heart. Your emperor is blinkered and your armies are in decay. Your empire fights the same battle as mine. But we fight the winning battle, Strategos. You will lose this struggle. You must know this.'

Apion felt the steel wrap around his heart once more. 'I know little of assured futures, Sultan.' He thought over the crone's words. *I see a battlefield by an azure lake flanked by two mighty pillars. Walking that battlefield is Alp Arslan. The mighty Mountain Lion is dressed in a shroud.* 'Indeed, I have been told that destiny is for the strongest to define.'

Alp Arslan held his gaze. A log snapped in the hearth. 'Men fight on either side of this conflict, and that is all we are. Men. Beating hearts, red blood and sharpened steel. I ask you this as a man, and I will not repeat the offer.' The sultan's eyes sparkled. 'You seek an end to the war, Strategos. Perhaps you could find a swifter end to it . . . by my side.'

Apion's breath stilled. He held the sultan's gaze. He thought of the many valourous and the many more bloody deeds committed by those who fought under the imperial banner. The Seljuk armies had shown him a similar mix of virtue and vice in his time. It seemed that an age had passed before he replied. 'There is more to it than that, Sultan. Some men are little more than blood, bone and blade. But others have something that sets them apart. A touch of charm in their blood, coursing through their hearts. A light that will never dim. I have little doubt that you are one such,' he prodded a finger into the table top gently, 'but there are a precious few more who fight for the empire's cause. Now that all else has been taken from me, my purpose is to fight for those few. And if I die for them and the cause is lost, then I know at least I have stayed true to my heart.'

Alp Arslan smiled wearily at this, leaning back from Apion and then standing as the first rays of dawn spilled through the map room. 'So be it, *Haga*. Tonight, no more blood will be spilled. Tomorrow, you, your men and the rest of your people are free to leave this city under amnesty. You will travel safely to your farms and barracks. My

97

men and I will remain here until the next moon. Then we will return to Seljuk territory.' Then his expression darkened. 'But know this; the next time we meet, there will be no amnesty. The actions of Bey Afsin illustrate the will of my people.' He clasped a hand over his heart. 'The conquest of Byzantium is coming, and I will not relent.'

'Likewise, you must know I will never yield.' Apion tapped the shatranj board. 'I hope that one day we will finish this game. But if not, then we will make our final moves on the battlefield.'

Alp Arslan nodded wistfully, then turned to leave.

Apion was alone. The fire crackled and spat as it died to nothing.

7. Return to Chaldia

The journey home for the weary men of the Chaldian Thema was long and troublesome, and it had taken some months to finally set eyes on their homeland.

They had stalled at first on the banks of the River Halys. In the stifling summer heat, Apion found himself charged with the care of tens of thousands of displaced citizens and farmers. While Caesarea lay in Seljuk hands, there would be no return home for these people. Alp Arslan's show of magnanimity had been shrewd, for allowing the populace safe passage from their homes had effectively tied up the remaining forces of the mustered themata in organising and policing the homeless rabble. Gaunt and filthy, they lived for weeks in makeshift tents and timber lean-tos under the welcome shade of the beech groves lining the banks of the Halys. It was fortunate that the river was abundant with fish and the surrounding lands rich with game. For without such bounty, thousands would have perished.

Still, the days were long and troublesome. Theft, rape and brawling were rife and the atmosphere suffocating. So, Apion took to waking each morning just before dawn, then setting out to run along the banks of the river, barefoot and dressed only in a light linen tunic. He found the chill air and the babble of the river cleansing to the mind, and he would only stop when the sun was fully past the eastern horizon. After stopping he would stretch his muscles and wash in the shallows. Then he would eat his usual breakfast of bread and honey, washing it down with river water. His mind fresh, he would then return to face the latest troubles of the refugees.

As the weeks passed, imperial trade cogs and the occasional galley docked by the camp and transported some of the refugees to the more westerly themata and gradually the camp shrank. By the ides of August, the camp held only a few thousand souls. It was then that Apion saw fit to delegate his command of the site to the newly appointed strategos of the Charsianon Thema – a young man who had previously been a tourmarches, one of the few who had survived the initial incursions of Bey Afsin.

After that, Apion and the men of Chaldia had set off on the journey home, crossing the Halys and then heading north-east. It was a steady and quiet march as they dotted between rivers and wells, eating from their rations and trapping game. Now, some six months after they had left their farms and towns, they were finally within sight of their homeland once more.

Apion squinted into the morning sun and eyed the plain ahead; russet and gold stretches of dust dappled with beech thickets and studded with shrubs. He could not help but focus on the crunch of boots and hooves on the dirt track behind him. Far fewer than there should have been. Of the twelve hundred Chaldians summoned to Charsianon by Doux Fulco, less than four hundred men would be returning home to Chaldia. Two households in every three would know only grief in the months ahead.

'Many widows we make of waiting wives, with so little thought we squander men's lives,' a baritone voice spoke as if reading his thoughts.

Apion turned to Sha. The tourmarches had drawn level on his grey stallion.

'It's a saying from back home, in the sands of Mali. It is not just this land that suffers the pox of bloodshed. But I doubt that offers you any comfort?'

Apion looked off into the distance. 'Not a crumb, Sha, not a crumb. That more young men of these lands will step up to take their fathers' places is a joy for a strategos and a tragedy for those families he leaves behind.' He twisted in his saddle once more. His gaze fell upon the short rider behind him.

Dederic the Norman rode in his mail hauberk. His skin was the colour of cooked salmon under the sun's glare, and he looked almost as agitated as big Blastares. The Norman was one of the few of Fulco's tagma who had stayed to defend the city when many others had fled. He had also been eager to accept Apion's offer to enlist with the thema. Apion was equally eager for his acceptance, as only twenty seven of the precious kataphractoi had survived the Charsianon campaign, and Dederic and his knights would help to cover those losses.

Sha followed his strategos' gaze. 'He's a good rider, sir. Some of his comrades are a touch feisty. But at least now they act under *your* command.'

Apion smiled dryly. 'For a time, perhaps. But it will not be long before the emperor sees fit to appoint another puppet doux in Fulco's place. Only then can he have a tentacle in every thema of his empire. Was such greed for power rife in your homeland too?'

'In Mali?' Sha mused, then shook his head. 'When I was a boy, our king would be sure to ride to the borders of his realm at least once every season. To see what threats lay outwith and, more importantly, within. He rode without luxury and slept little, and some say he was permanently callused from the exercise. My people loved him for this.' Sha looked to Apion and extended a finger. 'Emperor Doukas would only have to ride out here once to see what lies in store for Byzantium should he continue his policy of neglect and greed.' He wagged his finger. 'Only once.'

Apion grinned wryly at this. 'Perhaps the emperor feels it would be beneath him. After all, rumour has it he considers himself divine.'

Sha cocked an eyebrow. 'Sir?'

Apion shrugged. 'I heard it from the last mule-post from the west. It may be true or it may be hearsay. A few years ago, the Oghuz tribes raided in the west – nearly half a million of them spilled across the River Istros and into the empire.' He frowned. 'I do not know those lands, but I know what half a million armed men must look like. At one point they had Doukas and his retinue of just a few hundred riders trapped near the Haemus Mountains. He was a dead man, and the Oghuz are well-known for putting their enemies to miserable deaths – slicing off arms and legs then hanging the moaning torso from a tree for the wolves and bears to tear at. One night, while camped in some miserable hilltop bog in the middle of a rainstorm, Doukas did not pray to God, instead he cursed God for having put him in so miserable a predicament. Then he went on to curse the Oghuz who would surely put him to an excruciating end in the next few days. Then, almost overnight, as if his word had been deific, the Oghuz raiders were stricken by a terrible plague. They fell in their hundreds of thousands. Those who survived were leaderless and panicked. Many fled back to the wastelands across the Istros, but many more surrendered to Doukas. At once the raid was over and tens of thousands of these Oghuz pleaded to serve Doukas as mercenaries. An immense victory – won by his words alone, or so he believed.'

Sha held out his palms. 'Perhaps that is why he chooses to neglect his borders and the themata armies so?'

Apion thought of Alp Arslan's threat without airing it, 'well he may well find that one day soon that those borders are pushed back until they encroach upon Constantinople's walls. I fear that his words will offer little providence then. Hope is hard to conjure when such a prospect looms.' He sighed and squinted into the sun. 'What keeps you here, Sha, when the empire you serve shrivels in upon itself? Do you never pine for a return to Mali?'

'Hope comes when we least expect it, sir. I remember that always, ever since I was a slave in the Seljuk heartlands. One day I hobbled back to the slave quarters, my back was more blood than flesh. I wept, knowing I could not sleep due to the pain. That night, I took a piece of root from under my pillow. I had been given it by an old slave months before as he lay dying. He said it would turn my blood to fire and I would suffer for only moments, and then I would be free.' Sha's eyes grew glassy and he paused for a moment. 'I held the root in my hand for what seemed like an eternity, preparing to die. It was at the last moment that I realised that I had not heard the usual scuffle and chatter of the guards outside, nor the door to my filthy quarters being locked. When I opened the door and saw that the guards were indeed absent, I had my freedom.' Sha frowned as he spoke. 'On the cusp of death, hope presented itself.'

Sha sat up straight on his saddle, blinking the glassiness from his eyes and forcing a smile. 'And as for returning to Mali?' he shook his head. 'I don't think so – that king was an arsehole,' he said and then roared with baritone laughter.

Apion chuckled too as Sha fell back to marshal the column.

They rode on across the plain and through the valleys. At dusk on the third day they reached the south banks of the River Lykos and made camp there, each *kontoubernion* of ten men setting to work on erecting their tent and lighting a campfire. The following morning the sun rose and grew fierce once more. The men of the thema were settled in the lacy shade offered by the beech trees, bantering as they waited on a passing vessel to transport them across the water. They

103

kindled fires, boiled river water in their pots and then added balls of dried yoghurt, almonds and sesame oil, which blended with the water to form a thick and nutritious porridge. Their banter dropped to a lull as they filled their bellies with this, supplemented it with hard tack biscuit and smoked fish then washed it all down with well-watered wine.

To one side of the camp, Apion sat alone, his limbs still supple from his morning run and his hair still damp from bathing. He ate a meal of bread, cheese and dried berries, washing it down with cool river water. Then he settled down to cook a small pot of salep over his fire, the orchid root and cinnamon blending with the milk and releasing a delightfully sweet fragrance. The smell triggered many memories.

As did the sight a few hundred paces along the riverbank.

There, the charred foundations of a hut were embedded by the ruins of a simple ferry dock – little more than a few posts of timber driven into the silt of the shallows. On the opposite riverbank another post stood, with a frayed tether hanging from its tip where once a horn had hung. Once, years ago, the old ferryman Petzeas and his boys had run this crossing. In those days before Apion had enlisted with the thema, he had spent many hours chatting with the old goat as he crossed the river on his travels between the market towns dotted across the land. But then, five years ago, war had devoured the old man's simple life. Apion had been too slow to meet the Seljuk incursion that ravaged these southern tracts of Chaldia. The ghazi warbands had razed, plundered and murdered everything in their path. Peaceable Seljuk settlers and Byzantine citizens alike were slaughtered like animals. Old Petzeas had been trampled to death and his home set to the torch. His sons, Isaac and Maro, had joined the thema ranks, embittered and thinking only of revenge. Apion had felt compelled to talk them out of this, but had found he could offer no rationale, no reasoning that would seem fair or fitting. He himself had joined the ranks intent on revenge, and knew that some fires in the soul could not be doused. So Isaac and Maro had fought like lions in Blastares' tourma, only to be cut down in a Seljuk ambush in Southern Armenia. An entire family gone, consumed by the treacherous borderlands.

He was stirred from his thoughts as, at last, a small, well-weathered *pamphylos* drifted downriver. The bowl-shaped transport vessel had sun-bleached sails, desiccated timbers and an equally well-weathered crew. Sha hailed it, summoning its captain to the vessel side. The captain reluctantly agreed to ferry the men of the thema across to the north banks, forty men at a time. Apion waited until the end to cross, and his eyes rarely left the sad, blackened stumps of old Petzeas' home.

They reformed on the opposite bank and then continued northwards. Apion sensed his men's weariness and fell back to offer them words of encouragement, slipping from his saddle to lead his Thessalian on foot for a while. It was then that the Norman, Dederic dropped back also.

'It's not often you see a strategos or a doux deigning to forego the relative comfort of the saddle and tread the land,' he said.

Apion shot a glare up at him and saw the little rider's nervous grin fade. It was then he realised he was scowling. He sighed and chuckled. 'At ease, Dederic. I sometimes forget that my troubles are etched on my face.' Then he looked down at the dusty track. 'And now that you mention it, by now my feet are probably just as callused as my arse.' He slipped one foot into a stirrup and hauled himself up and into the saddle, relieved to hear Dederic laughing. He winced at the rawness of the little rider's sunburnt skin once more and frowned. 'So, tell me, where in the west do you hail from?'

'Rouen,' Dederic broke into a broad grin, his gaze growing distant, 'a dear and green land. The soil is rich, the air is crisp in the winter and hot in the summer,' his grin dropped for a moment, 'but not this hot.'

Apion frowned. 'Then what brings you east?' Apion knew the usual motives of mercenaries were plunder, titles and lust for bloody adventure. But he could not pin one of these on Dederic with any certainty.

Dederic's features darkened just a fraction. 'I had little choice but to leave my home, Strategos. I came this way two years ago, and I can still taste the tears that stained my face on the day I left my family behind. We have a small landholding on the outskirts of Rouen. A patch of farmland by a fresh brook, ringed by oaks that look like they have grown there for a thousand years or more. It is where I grew up – where my father and his father lived out their lives in relative peace. I took on the working of that land to feed my wife, Emelin, my three girls and my boy. But had I remained there, they would have ended up in poverty, homeless and starving,' he frowned, 'or worse.'

Apion recognised the little Norman's expression only too well.

'My father died heavily indebted to the lord of the land – a fat and uncompromising whoreson who insisted we had inherited the debt. Then the harvests were scant for four years, and we could not hope to pay our dues let alone put gruel on the table for the children. I promised the fat lord the arrears we owed, if only he would wait on my return from these lands. So I set off in the service of a neighbouring lord, seeking out the coin that would spare my family a grim future.'

Apion frowned, seeing that Dederic's hands were typical of a landworker; the skin mottled with scars and his fingers were short and stumpy. 'You worked the soil, yet you are a rider?' he gestured to Dederic's fine iron garb and well-kept fawn stallion, usually only

106

owned by the rich lords and knights of the west – those who reigned over the serfs.

Dederic nodded, then shot a furtive glance behind. 'All of my men and I were serfs before we came east, sir. We served as squires, pikemen and light infantry, the first to be thrown into the fray while the lancers waited for us to break the enemy or be broken before they would enter battle on their fine steeds.'

'So how . . . ' Apion begun.

'Slain, sir. Every last one of them. The Seljuks surrounded them near Ikonium and butchered them. Cut off their heads before the city walls. Their riches did little to protect them at the last,' Dederic laughed mirthlessly and shook his head. 'The bitter irony is that while the Seljuks slaughtered the lancers, they ignored the fleeing serfs, seeing us as little threat. Later that night, we crept from our hiding places in the rocks, we reined in the panicked horses, we gathered the armour . . . we buried the corpses. Then we fought on in place of the dead lords.' He stared straight ahead, his gaze flinty. 'We fought on, because we had to.' He patted his purse. 'I need many more coins, but one day I will be able to return home. My family will be freed from the bonds of the fat lord.'

Apion felt a glow in his breast at the little rider's conviction. 'You fight for your family. I have heard only a few noble motives from the mercenaries that pour into our lands, Dederic. Today I have heard one more.'

Dederic nodded, his gaze sullen and his lips pursed.

There was much more Apion wanted to say to the little rider, but the steel around his heart would not allow him to do so. Perhaps there would come a day when he could share his past with this man. He offered an earnest nod, then rode ahead to the front of the column.

By late afternoon they entered the valleys of the River Piksidis and the foothills of the Parhar Mountains. Here the pale gold landscape gave way to a lighter terracotta earth, with thicker patches of green shrub that dotting the ground and the gentle hillsides. The cicada song echoed through these valleys and the heat was only just beginning to ease as the sun dropped to the western horizon.

Apion was all too aware of the babbling Piksidis, only a short ride away. Nestled on its banks was a place he had not visited for twelve years. The ruins of old Mansur's farm. After witnessing the grim remains of Petzeas' home, he knew he could not afford to set his eyes upon the place. He had tried to come here once before, alone, and found that he could not face it. Now, with his men in tow, he could not trust himself to retain his iron veneer. It was not far from here, and its presence pulled at his heart. They passed by the far side of the cluster of gentle hills that marked Apion's old stamping ground, and he kept his head bowed as they did so. From the corner of his eye, he could not help but see the outline of the beech thicket atop one hill, and the rock in its midst. A reminiscence of his precious few moments alone with Maria up there danced through his mind. Her scent, her soft skin, her sweet voice.

'Sir!'

Apion snapped from his thoughts and twisted in his saddle. Procopius sat bolt upright on his mount, one hand shielding his eyes from the sun, the other pointing to the north. Up ahead, a lone rider galloped towards them, a red dust plume billowing in his wake.

It was a *kursoris*, a thematic scout rider wearing an off-white linen tunic, riding boots and a dark-blue felt cap, armed only with a spathion and a bow. He was dipped in the saddle and his dappled grey rode at full gallop. At this haste, Apion's heart steeled and his shoulders tensed.

The rider reined in his mount, paces from Apion.

'Strategos!' the man saluted.

Apion nodded. 'Rider?'

The man pulled off his cap and mopped the sweat from his brow. 'I thought we might never find you,' he panted. 'You must make haste, to Trebizond.'

'The capital is in danger?' At this, Sha, Blastares and Procopius gathered round, Dederic joining them with his clutch of Normans.

The rider shook his head. 'No, Strategos. The capital is safe. But Cydones requests your presence with the utmost urgency.'

Apion's gaze shot to the northern horizon, behind the rider. His eyes narrowed. Cydones, his old mentor in the ranks, would never create a commotion without good cause.

He raised a hand and circled it overhead. 'Infantry, proceed to Trebizond at quick march.' Then he pinned his gaze on two figures near the head of the first two banda of infantry. 'Komes Stypiotes, Komes Peleus, you have the lead.'

'Aye, sir!' the pair saluted in reply.

Then Apion beckoned to the kataphractoi and the Norman knights.

'Riders, with me – we leave for the capital at full gallop!'

***

They rode through the night. While the riders grew cold as the chill rushed over them, their mounts glistened with sweat, a lather of saliva gathering at their iron bits.

Then, as dawn broke, they neared the northern coastline of Chaldia. Overnight it seemed that the land had transformed around them. The arid rock and patchy shrubs were gone and in their place were verdant grasses and forests that hugged the cliffs and hillsides. Striped birds chirruped and squawked, flitting from tree to tree in celebration of their victory over the ubiquitous cicada song. The air had changed too, growing fresher and spiced with the tang of sea salt.

Then, when the sun had fully risen, the snaking track broadened, becoming a speckling of ancient flagstones and then a full stone road. Up ahead, the sun-bleached and well-walled city of Trebizond rose into view, capped by the citadel perched on the city's acropolis and framed by the azure sky and the sparkling waters of the *Pontus Euxinus*.

The riders slowed as they entered the stream of trade wagons, camels, oxen and mules ambling to and from the city gates. At the rumble of hooves, some turned and moved aside, others seemed less than enamoured by the inconvenience. Until they heard the cry from Sha, who rode out ahead.

'Move aside for the strategos!'

At this, all heads turned, then wagons and animals drew in to the roadside.

The skutatoi above the gatehouse cried out as they approached and the gates groaned open.

Inside, the broad main street stretched out before them. Islands of palms in the centre of the street hung motionless in the windless air, while a sea of citizens swarmed to and fro. It was market day, and the populace of the city was out in force, joined by the swathes of thematic farmers, here to trade their crops and wares and buy tools and fodder. This throng was hemmed on one side by the towering red-tiled dome of the Church of St Andreas and on the other by the tall-walled granary. Overlooking all of this from the far end of the street was the citadel, perched on the green hillside by the coast.

Apion slowed as he and his riders entered the bustle of bodies. The air was thick with the chatter of friends, the yelling of traders, the crying of babies and the cackling of drunks. The stench of horse dung was ripe, only combated by the succulent tang of sizzling goat meat, garlic and strong wine. They trotted into the heart of the city, past the market square and the gushing fountain at its centre, then peeled from the main street and rounded the squat stone walls of the city barracks at the foot of the citadel hill. Here, the streets were narrow, cool, shaded and blessedly quiet.

To the rear of the barracks was the imperial stable compound; a run of timber sheds with a small patch of enclosed, hay-strewn ground for the mounts to be exercised. Piles of fodder and a water trough lay at one end, where stablehands groomed the precious few spare mounts. The tink-tink of iron upon iron rang out from the larger shed at the end of the compound where the stable smith worked on new stirrups and snaffle bits for the beasts.

Apion slid from the saddle as they entered the stable area, his legs numb from the ride. He offered his reins to the nearest hand then removed his helmet, running his fingers through his sweat-matted locks. 'Where is Cydones?'

The hand opened his mouth to speak and then stopped.

'I know the *clop-clop* of a Thessalian from a mile away!' a voice croaked.

Apion spun to see old Cydones hobbling through the narrow arched entrance that led from the main barrack compound. He was dressed in a white woollen robe and sandals, resting his weight on a cane as he moved. The man who had been strategos of Chaldia before him was now in his sixty-seventh year. The onset of age had been swift since he had laid down his sword for the last time. He was now a frail and withered form, bald-headed, with snow-white hair around the

111

back and sides and a rather unkempt white beard. This sparked a tinge of sadness in Apion's heart. He remembered the tall and broad figure that had mentored him through his early years as an officer. Back then, Cydones sported a dark and pristinely forked beard, and would seldom be seen without his iron klibanion hugging his torso and his swordbelt strapped to his waist. Now, without family to care for him in his retirement, he resided here at the barracks, advising Apion and the men.

Cydones hobbled over to the dismounting riders. Then he reached out a knotted hand, grasping at Apion's wrist.

'I knew you'd be back soon,' Cydones spoke warmly, his sightless eyes darting all around and his hand moving to touch Apion's jaw. 'I have momentous news for you, Ferro . . . sorry . . . Apion.'

Apion winced at the old man's forgetfulness. Age had taken its toll on Cydones' mind as much as it had on his body. Ferro had been Cydones' chief tourmarches, but had died over ten years ago – impaled by a raiding ghazi warband before the walls of Argyroupolis.

'We rushed back to see this old bastard?' a foreign voice chuckled in a muted tone. 'He doesn't even know the strategos' name!'

Apion spun to the voice. It was one of Dederic's men. A tall and red-haired Norman rider with a bent nose. His smirk dropped immediately as Apion's glare fell upon him. Then Apion strode forward, his face twisting into a grimace, his fingers curling into fists. Under Apion's glare, the big Norman wilted, his gaze dropping to his boots.

'Sir!' Dederic cut in, moving to stand before the big Norman. 'Let me discipline him, if you will allow it?'

Apion looked down to Dederic. His first urge was to shove the little rider out of the way and smash the teeth from the big man's mouth. Then Cydones spoke in a mirthful tone;

'Ah, but he is right, Apion. An old bastard I am,' then he moved towards the big red-haired Norman, tapping his cane before him to find his way, ' . . . but a *wily* old bastard. So he'd better watch his tongue around me.' With that, Cydones swished his cane up and whipped it down, striking the calves of the big Norman. The Norman howled and sunk to his knees.

At this, a chorus of laughter erupted from all watching on.

Apion looked on, eyebrows raised for a heartbeat. Then he looked back to Dederic and issued a sigh that morphed into a dry chuckle.

'No need. I think he has learned his lesson.'

'Sir!' Dederic backed away, relief etched on his features.

Apion offered him a faint nod, then raised his voice to address his men. 'Now, tend to your armour and weapons, then fall out. You will return to your farms soon, but first we have much work ahead of us to reform and replenish the ranks. Visit the taverns if you must, but be ready for morning muster.'

With a guttural cheering, the men dispersed, leaving Apion and Cydones alone. They walked together into the barracks and strolled around the near-deserted muster yard.

'The workers have discovered a fresh seam in the silver mines,' Cydones enthused, 'so the next mustering should see the new men we gather clad in good fighting garb.'

Apion nodded. The silver caves had been mined for these last twelve years unbeknownst to the imperial tax collectors. Those seams had been the difference between the Chaldian army standing firm along the borders and falling out of existence like some neighbouring themata. This was indeed good news, but not momentous – surely not the reason he had been called back to Trebizond in a rush. 'So tell me, sir, what trouble is brewing?' he asked the old man.

Cydones snorted. 'You insist on calling me sir, even years into your stewardship of this land. I remember when I was first promoted, I would never dream of calling the stubborn bastard I replaced sir. In fact I . . .'

'Cydones?' Apion cut in, barely masking his frustration.

'Oh, right . . . I,' Cydones started, then a frown wrinkled his brow as he searched through his thoughts. Then his face lit up in realisation and was momentarily free of wrinkles. 'Ah, yes!' he wagged his index finger in the air. 'There is no trouble, Apion.'

Apion frowned.

'No, instead there is news that may change the ills of these lands.'

'Sir?'

Cydones' face fell stony. 'Emperor Doukas is dead, Apion.'

The breath stilled in Apion's lungs. Many emperors had risen and fallen in his lifetime; some had abdicated, a lucky few had died a peaceful death, but many had been slain in their sleep and some even mutilated by the fervent masses of Constantinople. 'How did it happen?'

'He died of a lung infection, on the ides of May. Word travelled slowly and we only found out last month. I've had scouts looking for you since then.'

Apion frowned. 'That a man has passed gives me no pleasure. But Emperor Doukas has a lot to answer for, and now he never will. Sir, I fail to see anything to be joyous of in this news? If there has been no coup, no shift in power, then surely one of Doukas' sons will take the throne and continue his policies of neglect?'

Cydones stopped, rested his weight on his cane and wagged one finger from side to side. 'No, it is not to be – and that is where the hope lies. Doukas' wife, Eudokia, has contested the succession of her own son, Michael.'

Apion spluttered at this, turning to Cydones. 'In that snakepit? How have we even come to hear of this? Usually such an act all but guarantees a stealthy dagger blade between the ribs, does it not?'

'Eudokia is a brave spirit, Apion. She went against her late husband's demands that she should never remarry. She signed an oath to that effect. But after Doukas' passing, she appealed to the patriarch, Xiphilinos. I can only imagine what discussions took place or what dealings were made, but now she is to remarry. Her new husband will become emperor. The Doukid dynasty is over, Apion.'

Apion's eyes widened. Doukas had overseen eight years of military neglect. He had quickly filled the senate with his supporters and tuned taxation to punish the poor and keep the rich magnates happy and supportive of his reign. He was hated throughout the capital and the themata. But the end of his dynasty could easily be the start of another, more loathsome one. 'That alone is not cause to rejoice, sir. It is entirely possible that Eudokia will wed another haughty figure who is equally damaging, or more so.'

Cydones reached out to grasp Apion by the shoulders. 'No, Apion. For she is to wed a man of the army. Romanus Diogenes; a legend from the battlefields of the west. He understands the plight of the empire's borders. The cause has been reignited. There is once more hope that this land *can* be saved!'

One word echoed in Apion's ears.

Hope.

His eyes darted across Cydones' face, then he glanced to the barrack gates. 'I must tell my men. They have gone so long with only harsh news.'

'Aye, tell your men, Apion. Then select the best of them to accompany you and wish the rest farewell.'

Apion frowned at this. 'Farewell?'

Cydones face lit up. 'Eudokia has summoned every strategos and doux to the capital to set out her plans and to hail the new emperor. A berth awaits you in the harbour.' He stretched out an arm, pointing westwards. 'You are to set sail for Constantinople.'

A shiver danced over Apion's skin.

The Golden Heart will rise in the west.

8. The Snakepit

The imperial *dromon* cut through the choppy waters of the *Pontus Euxinus*, headed west. Its twin triangular linen sails were sun-bleached and patched with leather, and they billowed in the morning winds, carrying the craft along at a fine pace. Every wave that crashed against the bow dissolved into a cool salt spray that soaked the decks of the vessel. Free from the oars, the *kopelatoi* roamed the deck, tying down cargo and shinning up the rigging to tighten and twist the sails. The *kentarches* also strode the decks, roaring encouragement to his crewmen.

'Cleanses the body and the mind, does it not?' Cydones spoke, inhaling deeply at the lip of the boat, his chin thrust out defiantly. His robe was sodden with brine.

Apion, sitting nearby, chuckled at this. 'Get any closer to the edge and it'll cleanse you a little more thoroughly than you might wish!' But he could not deny the freshness of the sea air. He was dressed in a faded red tunic and leather boots. His amber locks whipped back with the breeze as he cut at an apple with his dagger, lifting slices to his lips. The sea stretched out unbroken to the northern horizon where the waters met with the hazy blue sky. Then he glanced to the other side of the ship; about three miles to the south, the northern coastline of Anatolia rolled past. The mountains and thick forests of the Bucellarion Thema were occasionally punctuated by sun-baked city walls or timber port-towns and imperial watchtowers. Finally, he stood to join Cydones, looking west. A faint outline of the coastline far ahead betrayed a break in the hinterland. This was the

Bosphorus strait, the narrow channel that would take them right into the heart of the empire.

To Constantinople.

Cydones sighed, clenching a fist. 'We are on the cusp, Apion. When Romanus Diogenes takes the throne, he will revitalise our armies.'

Apion felt a swirl of emotion in his blood. Hope had indeed sparked in his heart at the prospect of a military man rising to the purple. But the days since the news had given him time enough to realise that such hope was sure to be fraught with danger. 'Perhaps. But until then, we must deal with those he left behind, those who oversee the empire in the interregnum.' For a moment, he recalled the dark spectre of the *Agentes*. The shadowy organisation that murdered and plotted on the emperor's whims had collapsed some years ago. But darkness never truly disappeared, he mused, it only ever seemed to change its form. He turned his mind to those they were to meet; Doukas' widow, Eudokia, and the rest of his bloodline and advisers. 'I have seen what a droplet of power can do, even to a good soul. Do you not wonder endlessly of their motives in summoning us to the capital?'

The old man frowned and turned to Apion, his sightless eyes narrowed. 'I'd be sick with worry if I was to allow myself to dwell upon it, Apion.' For an instant, he wore a sharp expression, the fog of age falling away. 'I have not set foot inside the city since I was a young man. Back then I had no dealings with the imperial court or the military, but that matters little; emperors and beggars find little providence in that place . . . you said it yourself, Constantinople is a snakepit, and you have never even been there. Yes, the coming of a new emperor brings with it a promise of rejuvenation. But the Doukids will be livid at Eudokia's actions, and they are but one faction that covets the imperial throne.' Then Cydones shook his head and grinned wryly. 'In fact, if I had any sight at all I would certainly sleep with one eye open for the duration of our stay.'

Apion roared with laughter at this, and the effect was cathartic. The tension that had started to cluster around his heart dissipated like the salt spray. He swigged fresh water from the skin on his belt and mused instead on the positive. 'But if it is true. If we are to have an emperor who will invest in the themata armies once more . . . '

Cydones nodded. 'We could dispense with the mercenaries who protect our lands when it suits them. Yes, I can see in my mind a time when the themata return to their past greatness. Every warrior with good boots and a fine iron vest. A helm that is crafted to fit him well. A spathion honed to perfection and a shield painted freshly. Every household would have a bow and forty arrows so a man could protect his family whether he was a man of the ranks or not. Every imperial stable replete with tall and muscular mounts. The forts and watchtowers across the land in good repair and with full garrison, watching the tracks, passes and highways across the land. That is the dream I once strived for.'

'And I,' Apion added.

Cydones smiled. 'Then that's one thing we agree on. Still, your choice of *best* men to accompany you on this journey still befuddles me. Dragging along a blind, dithering old fellow like me when you could have brought any of your fine tourmarchai?'

Apion smiled at this. 'You don't know your own strengths, sir. You see far more than many a sharp-eyed youth,' he grinned, 'and you are a fine shatranj opponent. Besides, Sha, Blastares and Procopius are best placed to stay in Chaldia. They will keep the people safe in my absence.'

He turned to rest his back against the lip of the dromon then gazed to the aft, his hair whipping up across his face. While the crew scuttled across the deck and shinned up and down the mast and rigging, one figure was bent double over the edge of the vessel, near the stern. Dederic's shoulders lurched as he retched violently into the white churn that stretched out behind the dromon. Apion had brought him because he had proved a worthy addition to the thema, helping his Norman riders integrate well with the kataphractoi. Dederic had a dry sense of humour and a shrewd mind as well. Added to that, the Norman had spent some months in Constantinople within the last few years, and his knowledge of the place could be useful.

'You think Dederic has it in him to lead a tourma for you?' Cydones said as if reading his mind.

'Aye, he's already a leader, even if he doesn't realise it yet,' Apion said, thinking of how the Norman had led thirty lost and frightened serfs and moulded them into a disciplined band of lancers. Then he recalled Dederic's steadfast commitment to saving the citizens of Caesarea. 'And he has a good heart.'

'A good heart? There is no such thing,' Cydones replied wistfully. 'All men can do is struggle to stave off the darkness in there. Light cannot exist without darkness. To be a man is to be both.'

Apion saw the old man's brow furrow and wondered at what grim memory he was replaying right now.

Then the shrieking of gulls pierced the air. They turned to the coast to see a series of broad stone watchtowers dotted along the shores as they approached the Bosphorus strait. Atop each, purple banners fluttered bearing the Chi-Rho and the Cross.

They were coming to the city of God.

***

The sails were brought down and the oars extended as the dromon entered the warm, turquoise and placid waters of the Bosphorus strait. The surface ahead was dotted with fishing vessels and trade cogs. Ferries cut to and fro, from one rocky and verdant coastline to the other. Thick shoals of silvery fish darted this way and that before the dromon, and then a school of dolphins broke the surface and tumbled through the waters alongside the vessel.

Apion stood at the prow with Cydones and Dederic – the Norman having at last lost the green tinge to his skin.

The three were silent in anticipation, until Cydones cupped a hand to his ear at the gentle splashing of oars from the ferries up ahead. 'Ah, Europe to Asia and back in a single morning – that brings back memories!'

Then the old man clasped a hand on Apion's shoulder as they approached a jutting outcrop of headland. 'We're nearly there,' he said, his nostrils flaring and his sightless eyes closed, 'I can smell it . . . the fruits of the palace orchards, the sweat of the mounts in the Hippodrome, the dust of the emperor's stonemasons, the spices of the traders . . . and the bullshit of the senate!'

Apion and Dederic roared at this. Then they rounded the headland and all three fell silent.

Constantinople was revealed, dominating the western skyline, conquering the peninsula that spliced the waters.

Apion wondered at the sight. Never in all his years in the borderlands had he seen a city to rival this. The ancient walls were broad and all-encompassing with pristine purple banners fluttering in the faint breeze atop every fortress-like tower. Silvery flashes along the battlements affirmed that it was well garrisoned at every section. Behind the walls, the city rose up on its seven hills. The gentle, lush green slopes of the first hill curved around the tip of the peninsula in the shape of a hawk's beak. The mountainous domed church of the Hagia Sofia was perched there, then, a stone's throw away was the Imperial Palace. This magnificent gilded marble complex was ringed by collonaded walkways and topped with a wide, red-domed portico.

'This is our destination?' Dederic said with a touch of disbelief in his voice as he eyed the palace. 'The last time I was in this city I slept in a pile of hay next to a cesspit that was shared by a brothel and a tanner's yard.'

Behind the first hill, the dark-brick walls of the Hippodrome seemed to mark an end to the fertile area around the palace. After this was a sea of marble. The aqueduct of Valens rose up and picked its way through the other slopes of the city, each seeming to jostle for supremacy. Domes studded every hilltop and arches, obelisks and columns stretched for the sky, bearing brass and gold statues of heroes and emperors. Around this finery, a sea of red-tiled tenements and villas, stairs, streets and alleys filled every available inch.

The dromon slowed and the oarsmen guided it around the tip of the peninsula and under the gaze of a thick cloud of circling gulls. They came to a section of the sea walls that jutted out into the waters – a spacious, fortified harbour complex, with a sturdy timber bar blocking entry.

'We must be nearing the Port of Julian?' Cydones asked, feeling the direction of the sun on his face and cocking an ear to the gentle lapping of water on the harbour walls.

'Aye, it would seem so,' Apion answered, casting his gaze up to the nearest of the two towers overlooking the harbour mouth. An iron fire siphon lay still and silent up there, and he wondered when they would next be put to use.

Then a finely-garbed skutatos appeared atop the tower and yelled down to the ship. 'State your business.'

'I bring wine and oil . . . ' the ship's kentarches yelled back from the decks.

The skutatos looked irritated at this, waving one hand to the north. 'Merchant vessels are to dock at the Neorion harbour. You can trade for honey, wax, hides and slaves in the northern city mar . . . '

' . . . and I bring the Strategos of Chaldia!' the kentarches cut him off.

At this, the skutatos fell silent, then waved down into the harbour. The timber bar groaned as it was hoisted clear.

The capital had so far presented an image of polished invincibility, but as the dromon manoeuvred inside the harbour, there was no pristine imperial fleet. Instead, Apion frowned as the ship drew into an empty berth alongside a row of nearly forty dilapidated war galleys. The best of these ships were dried out with damaged rigging and hulls. The rest were semi-submerged, water lapping over parts of the deck.

'The crafts of the imperial fleet used to sit proudly with their hulls well above the water and their masts stretching for the sky,' Cydones said, hearing the creaking of damp timber all around him. 'But not any more? The *vasilikoploimon* is not what it once was?'

'It appears not,' Apion agreed.

'Then it has been this way for some time,' Dederic offered. 'At least, it was in this condition when I first came east. There are only ten galleys maintained, and they exist merely to sail this strait and escort the imperial flagship – a vessel less suited to war than to entertaining those of the palace court,' he snorted in derision. 'The riders I served had to purchase a berth on a trade ferry to cross the water on our way to meet with Doux Fulco. We sailed to war with cattle!'

The kentarches laid the gangplank onto the flagstoned harbour side then saluted to Apion. The gulls shrieked all around, swooping and darting in the sunshine, convinced a meal was to be had.

'Well the fleet may be neglected,' Apion nodded to the skutatoi all around the harbour walls as they disembarked, 'but the imperial tagmata are certainly not.' These were the armies traditionally stationed in and around Constantinople. Unlike the wretched mercenary border tagmata, these soldiers were the cream of the empire's fighting force.

'Describe them to me,' Cydones asked as, all around the three, the crew began unloading crates and hemp sacks onto the wharfside.

Apion looked to the two skutatoi who stood either side of the iron-studded gateway that separated the harbour from the city. Like the others, these two were tall and broad-shouldered, their jaws set in determined grimaces – a far cry from the often ragged and rake-thin themata skutatoi. But it was their garb that set them apart. 'Finely armoured – each of them wears an iron klibanion over a pure-white tunic. On their heads they wear a helm and a scale aventail. Their shields are painted purple with a white Cross in the centre.'

Cydones nodded. 'So the *Numeroi* still run the city walls? Aye, you will seldom find a meagrely armed soldier in this city, Apion. While the emperors have let their outlying armies and their fleet rot, they would never let the blades that protect them succumb to rust.'

At that moment, the iron gates groaned open. From the shadows, a block of eight broad and tall warriors marched purposefully towards Apion. They were markedly different from the numeroi. They wore pristine white breastplates and white cloaks trimmed with gold thread. Even their boots were white, and emblazoned with a black motif of a long-legged spider on the shin. Their hair was red or blonde, hanging in richly oiled-curls and braids

124

and they wore kohl under their eyes – Rus who had fallen for the charms of Byzantium, Apion reckoned. Decorative shields hung like turtle-shells on their backs and they carried thick-shafted axes, the finely honed edges glinting in the sun. Their leader was a granite-faced individual. His features were creased with age and a scar ran vertically over one eye. His grey locks were braided into two tails, his moustache was thick and full and his eyes were shaded by the kohl and a heavy brow. He threw up an arm promptly.

'Igor, Komes of the Varangoi, sworn protectors of the imperial blood.'

Apion returned the salute. 'Apion, Strategos of Chaldia,' he replied.

'My men and I will escort you to the palace, sir,' Igor barked. 'Many of the other doukes and strategoi are already here,' he faltered momentarily and his voice grew hushed, ' . . . but there have been some unfortunate events since their arrival.'

Apion's brow dipped. 'Komes?'

'Walk with us,' Igor replied, 'and do not stray.'

Apion shot Dederic a troubled look, then he took Cydones' elbow and the three followed the varangoi. He noticed Igor glancing furtively at the watching numeroi on the harbour walls. In reply, the numeroi burned equally baleful glares at the Rus.

'The populace are . . . excitable,' Igor continued in a muted tone. 'The races are on today and have been every day for the last week – funded by those who see the contested throne as an opportunity.'

The iron gates before them groaned once more, opening up to reveal a blur of citizens darting to and fro. As they passed under the gateway and out into the broad street, the rabble broke around them like a river. Many faces washed past, some lost in thought, some inebriated, many more bearing malignant scowls. The jabbering of a thousand voices was incessant, until it was suddenly drowned out by the deafening wall of noise that tumbled from the Hippodrome; a raucous cheer that shook Apion to his bones, the likes of which he had only ever heard on the battlefield. A shiver danced up his spine, despite the stifling heat, as he craned his neck to look up at the vast arena's towering collonaded walls and the purple banners fluttering above.

Then he turned back to the Varangoi komes.

'Tell me, Igor,' he said, 'tell me what you could not under the gaze of the numeroi?'

Igor leaned in close, still darting glances to see who was within earshot. 'There are some within the palace who seek to ruin Lady Eudokia's plan to bring Romanus Diogenes to the throne. They see the gathering of your ilk as an opportunity to leverage support for their cause. And those who spurn their advances . . . ' Igor's face fell grave and he shook his head. 'The Strategos of Paphlagonia was found in his palace bedchamber the night before last, dead in only his twenty third year. Then the Doux of Lykandos was killed by thieves in the Forum of the Ox while he browsed for spices – they sliced his head from his body.' He looked up, above the Hippodrome, where the rooftop portico of the Imperial Palace pierced the skyline. 'Out here and in there, it would be wise to stay on your guard, Strategos.'

Apion followed the Rus' solemn gaze. 'So this is the heart of the empire I have fought for all these years? I will heed your words well, Komes.'

***

Zenobius rested his palms on the crenellations of the inner harbour walls and swept his gaze along the packed streets of Constantinople. He was a young man still, but his lank hair was pure white, like his skin, and his eyes were ghostly silver. Behind those eyes lay bitterness and a primal instinct to survive. When he was a tot, his mother had assured him that his striking appearance had marked him out as one destined for greatness. Yet when she had died, Father had shunned him as much as Mother had coddled him. Father had taken to drinking neat wine at every hour of the day when their crop failed, and had then taken to blaming Zenobius, insisting he was a curse from God. Then, one day, Father had even joined in when the villagers had battered Zenobius until blood ran from his eyes and ears. Zenobius had quickly learned to disguise all emotion and to show little reaction to the taunts of his aggressors. He did not wince. He did not cry. Neither did he smile – but this came easy. This veneer caused the beatings to be no less painful, but it did deny his attackers much of their enjoyment. After years of this, he realised he could not remember what it was to be human.

It was shortly after this that he had come here, to the heart of the empire, to seek out the destiny his mother had promised him. Indeed, he had found it in his new employ. *Yes*, he thought, examining the pale skin of his fingers, *now they cannot hurt me. For I am the master of pain.* Then his gaze swept back to the party of three that stood below, like a rock in the river of pedestrians. A broad-shouldered warrior with battered, bearded features and amber locks stood with a short, dark-haired Norman and a feeble and sightless old man.

'Is it him?' a voice grunted.

Zenobius turned to the bald, burly torturer by his side. 'Aye, it is the Strategos of Chaldia,' he said, then nodded to the clutch of

127

varangoi who milled around the three newcomers. 'Look, proud Igor is with them.'

The burly torturer uttered a hushed, baritone laugh, emitting a waft of vile breath as he did so. 'Then I look forward to welcoming them.'

9. The Cold Heart

Apion waded into the cool, scented water, tracing his fingers across the surface. He glanced at the marbled opulence surrounding him – all was still apart from the delicate corner fountains, carved from blood-red porphyry, babbling as they spilled fresh water into the pool. The palace baths were empty and he was alone. So he lay back and sunk under the surface, washing the dust and salt from his skin. For an instant he could hear only the gentle thumping of his heart and the water coursing in his ears. It was a blissful moment of calm. Then he opened his eyes and through the waters he saw the ceiling frescoes ripple. Dancing reflections from the water's surface lent a vivid lustre to the colourful figures there. Emperors past, reaching up to the sky as if to talk with God. Warriors of the arena streaked in crimson, standing over slain opponents and saluting fervent crowds. Chariots racing, riders crying out, mounts' eyes wide and bulging. Around the edges were images of wild beasts; lions, elephants, wolves and scorpions. Then his gaze fell on one creature; an olive-scaled serpent, glaring down on him, its eyes a portent of the venom in its fangs.

Igor's words of warning from earlier that day rang in his ears. Suddenly feeling less than calm, he rose to standing, sweeping his locks back from his face. As the water drained from his ears, he heard a noise.

A sandal scraping on the tiles behind him.

He spun to the doorway, muscles tensed. The two slave girls there yelped in fright, then ran from the room, giggling. With a sigh and brisk shake of the head, he waded from the pool to the chair where his tunic hung.

He wiped the excess water from his body and lifted the filthy and faded garment. But he hesitated, noticing the blue silk robe the slave girls had left for him. He touched it, then reticently lifted it and dropped it over his body. It was cool and soft on his skin. Then he sat by the platter of fruit, bread and honey the girls had also left. Blueberries, apricots, figs, freshly baked bread and rose-scented water. He took a mouthful of blueberries, the skin bursting to release their tart and fresh juices.

Still not a patch on Chaldian crop, he mused with a pensive half-smile, thinking back to those lost days on Mansur's farm.

He tore at the still-warm bread, dipping it in the honey before chewing. As he washed it down with a swig of rosewater, a warming shaft of afternoon sunlight crept across his legs. He followed the light over to the collonaded outer wall of the bath chamber. Most of the arches were covered by timber lattice screens to provide bathers with privacy, but the sunlight was pouring in through the one archway with no screen. Outside, a vibrant garden square shimmered. There were orange trees, palms and exotic blooms jostling for space while parakeets flitted to and fro between the branches. This was in pleasant contrast to the packed city streets pulsating against the other side of the palace. Such beauty should have soothed his thoughts. Instead, he found his foot tapping incessantly. For now he could only imagine big Blastares' waggish reaction to seeing his strategos in such luxury, wearing a silken robe. He grumbled then hurriedly stood to change back into his grubby tunic, lifting the robe off and dropping it to the floor. But as he picked up his tunic, something caught his eye.

There, on the central balcony above the colonnade on the far side of the gardens, a figure looked down upon him. She was tall and slender and wore her golden, silver-flecked hair tied up on her head. Apion frowned, wondering why she stared at him with such a foul look on her fine features. He stepped forward, towards the sunlit ground under the open archway. From there he could see that her expression was more one of shock than disdain. It was then that a sudden breeze reminded him he was stark naked.

To save further embarrassment, he fumbled to wrap his tunic around his waist and started to mouth an apology. But she turned from the balcony and was gone in a heartbeat.

Cursing under his breath, he pulled his tunic on and strode from the room through the inner doorway, glowering at the silk robe as if it was to blame. He was intent on dressing fully and then seeking out the woman to apologise to her but found his pace somewhat cowed by the vastness of the palace interior. The cavernous ceilings shone with a gilt lustre and the forest of veined marble columns and sparkling porphyry served to remind him how far from home he was. His every footstep echoed and the eyes of the white-garbed varangoi followed him as he flitted up the marble staircase. At last he reached the upper floor then made his way along a corridor lined with tall, arched windows through which the afternoon sun bathed the mosaics on the walls and floors. He came to the three rooms assigned to Dederic, Cydones and himself. A serrated snoring echoed from old Cydones' room. This took the edge off of his annoyance, and his lips played with a smile. 'Aye, the noise from the streets will not be an issue with you nearby, Cydones,' he thought aloud.

Then he stepped inside his own chamber, a high-ceilinged, cool, light and spacious room with a wide oak bed, a chest and a table. He stretched his calves and his shoulders and then sat by the chest, reaching for his boots and his cloak. But he stopped, his blood chilling as he felt a breeze from the arched windows.

They had been closed when he left the room earlier.

His eyes locked upon the pure-white, silken veil that hung over the central window and the faint shadow behind it. Then the veil billowed as the breeze picked up once more, revealing a short and aged man, back turned, hands clasped. The man looked through the open window and down the slopes of the first hill, where the grounds of the imperial palace deigned to merge with the city streets. He wore a gold-trimmed, purple cloak and a purple felt cap atop his tightly curled, grey crop of hair.

Apion stood, frowning, cursing the absence of his swordbelt. Indeed, Igor had seemed reluctant to relieve him of his weapons when they entered the palace, but could not risk letting anyone bar the Varangoi bear arms within the building. Apion considered his next move.

Just then, a roar erupted from the Hippodrome. At this, the man tilted his head back, extending his hands to his sides as if refreshed by the incoming breeze.

'Can you hear it?' the man said. 'The people are exultant. It is a golden melody.'

'I hear only the bleating of a stranger in my quarters,' Apion replied flatly.

'The people are so easily swayed,' the figure continued as if Apion had not spoken. 'A dash of entertainment, a shipment of Paphlagonian wine,' he snapped his fingers, adorned with thick gold rings, 'and they are acquired. A prudent expense, it would seem.'

'I will ask you once; who are you?' Apion said, his voice echoing around the room.

The man turned to him at last, fixing him with the kind of gaze a gull would cast upon a discarded fish head. He was narrow-eyed with a shrivelled, pinched face. 'Psellos, chief adviser to the imperial throne.' He bowed slightly, his eyes never leaving Apion. 'And you are the Strategos of Chaldia, I believe?'

Apion nodded.

'Many of your ilk have arrived here in recent weeks,' Psellos started.

'So I have heard,' Apion spoke over him. 'and some of those have had their visits . . . cut short. So forgive my abruptness, but when I find a stranger in my quarters, I have little time for decorum.'

Psellos smiled, extending his arms wide. 'Ah, set your mind at ease, Strategos. I come here only to welcome you.'

Apion noticed that Psellos' smile never reached his eyes.

'And to offer you a morsel of advice,' Psellos continued. 'In my years as adviser, I have seen how vital you and your kind are in making or breaking an emperor, or even a whole dynasty. That is why you have been called here; to make choices that will determine the fate of the empire.'

'Weighty choices plague my every day back in the east, but not here,' Apion replied prosaically. 'I have come here simply to hail the arrival of the new emperor. Then the rebuilding of the borderlands can begin as soon as Romanus Diogenes takes the throne.'

The little man's features creased with a tight and bitter smile. He raised a hand, one finger extended and wagging. 'Ah, now there is the first of the problems. An assumption that has little basis in legality . . . contrary to current thinking, the throne does not lie unoccupied. The young Michael Doukas sits upon it. His father's dynasty is unbroken.'

'I understand that it is merely a formality that he and his regents will step aside when Romanus Diogenes comes to be crowned?'

Psellos was unblinking. 'That remains to be seen, Strategos. As I said; the coming months will reveal many truths. In that time, I urge you to remain open to those who choose to confer with you.'

'Why would I be anything but?'

Psellos chuckled mirthlessly at this, stroking his chin as he strolled to the door. 'Why indeed?' he said as he left the room.

Apion's mind darkened as his thoughts tangled. He had been lured here by the promise of hope. Yet he had been received with only dark insinuations. *But they can wait,* he thought, shaking his head clear of this muddle as he slid on his boots, focusing only on the fine-featured woman on the balcony, *for I have an apology to make.*

He stood and swept his crimson cloak across his shoulders. Then he hurried downstairs and past the two varangoi bookending the archway that led outside into the gardens. The afternoon sunlight was warm and a welcome contrast to the cool, shady interior of the palace. Indeed, the trilling cicada song reminded him of home. He glanced up at the balcony above the far side of the gardens where he had seen the woman. She was not there so he picked his way along the narrow paths that wound between the fruit trees and colourful blooms. The tang of oranges spiced the air first, and then the lazy scent of jasmine and narcissus. Fountains babbled near the heart of the gardens, and he found it an effort not to forget his troubles.

Until he heard footsteps, rushing towards him. At once, he was alert.

He looked this way and that, then spun to his right. The dark-green leaves of a rhododendron bush wriggled and rustled. He grasped at his absent scimitar hilt and cursed aloud, bracing himself for this unseen attacker.

Then the tension washed from him as a boy tumbled from the bush, giggling, twigs in his blonde hair. The broad grin on his cherubic face fell as he skidded to a halt before Apion. The lad was no more than seven. Apion's eyes fell to the sword belt the boy carried. It contained a spathion.

'A weighty weapon for a young lad, is it not?' he cocked an eyebrow.

The boy squared his shoulders and lifted his chin at this insult, and Apion had to work to resist chuckling at this.

'I'm going to be emperor one day, so I must be ready!' the boy replied. Then he jabbed a finger at a nesting parakeet and its hatchlings, high up on one orange tree, an impish grin creeping onto his face. 'My feathered army are loyal to me!'

Just then, a weightier set of footsteps sounded nearby, accompanied by a low growl. 'Konstantious! I have no time for your foolish games!'

The boy's haughty look faltered at this and he spun round, lifting the sword from the belt, two-handed. His limbs shook under the weight of the blade.

A small but broad-shouldered young man stomped into view. He was sixteen, perhaps. He wore a purple tunic hemmed with gold thread. His jaw was broad and well-defined, his hair light brown and short and his eyes shaded under a scowl. Apion saw the resemblance between the two as the young man marched up to little Konstantious and tore the sword from his grip, threw the blade to the ground, then moved towards the young lad, fists balled.

Apion stepped between the two, frowning at the young man. 'Perhaps in ten years or so you two could have a fair fight. Until then, you should keep your sword belt somewhere safe.'

The young man's face burned with anger. 'How dare you address your emperor in such a tone?'

Apion's breath froze in his lungs. So this was Michael. Constantine Doukas' eldest son and acting emperor. The boy whose grasp of the purple would be torn from him when Eudokia remarried.

Michael Doukas continued to glare up at him. 'Drop your gaze and fall to one knee or I'll have you flogged until the bones in your back are shattered.'

Apion simply gazed back at the boy. Then Konstantious, hiding behind Apion, peeked round to yell; 'Nobody has to do what you say, puppet emperor!'

At this, Michael's face turned crimson, and he readied to leap for little Konstantious.

'Easy, easy!' Apion held up his hands, then bowed on one knee. They were at eye level now. 'You are emperor and so I will kneel before you. But know that in the past I've been flogged until the barbs on the whip wrenched at my ribs. So I do not wilt under such threats, Michael. Men who do may fear you, but they will never respect you.'

Michael's gratified grin faded a fraction at this and he looked every inch the lost young man that he was.

Then a woman's voice pierced the air and the young man's face fell completely; 'You'll control that foul temper of yours, Michael.'

Apion glanced up. The tall, slender lady from the balcony walked towards them. She was draped in red silken robes and he could now see her face clearly; beauty sullied only slightly with age, her golden locks flecked with silver. Most interestingly, she was flanked by two varangoi, each bearing their heavy axes as if ready to strike.

Konstantious ran to her, throwing his arms around her waist. 'Mother!' he sobbed.

Apion's ears perked up at this. So this was Lady Eudokia.

She wrapped an arm around Konstantious then stabbed a finger at her elder son. 'You will adhere to my rules, Michael. Until the new emperor arrives, you will obey my every word.'

'What if Uncle John contradicts your word, Mother?' Michael spat back. He glared at Eudokia, Konstantious and then Apion in turn, then stormed off into the main wing of the palace. Apion watched him go, frowning. He felt only sympathy for the young man. Snared in some power-struggle like a butterfly in a web, anger seemed to be Michael's only way of venting his frustration.

'And you,' Eudokia spoke in an accusatory tone.

Apion spun back round and looked up at her, wide-eyed.

'I can only congratulate you on your success in putting on clothes this time!' She barked.

Apion felt the beginnings of an embarrassed smile creep onto his face, only for it to fall away as Eudokia's face twisted further in scorn.

'And stand up, you fool. There is no true emperor in this palace.'

He stood and her gaze narrowed on him for a heartbeat as he rose above her.

Then she nodded to her guards, turned and swept back towards the palace, taking Konstantious by the hand. As she disappeared under the shadows of the brightly-painted colonnade, she raised a hand and snapped her fingers.

At this, the two varangoi grinned, then one of them motioned with his axe, beckoning Apion.

'Come with us – Lady Eudokia requests your presence.'

***

Apion stood in the magnificent rooftop portico, the pinnacle of the imperial palace. A circle of narrow, finely sculpted marble columns supported the red-tiled dome overhead. This offered him a pleasant shade from which to enjoy the almost unbroken vista of the magnificent city. Young Konstantious played with wooden blocks and carved soldiers on the polished floor. A pair of the omnipresent varangoi stood guard by the top of the marble stairs that led back down into the depths of the palace. But it was Eudokia who held his attention.

She had not spoken a word since they had come up here, preferring instead to prepare herself a drink of iced water and crushed petals. Then she had moved to the edge of the portico, sipping from a silver cup, her eyes darting across the western city skyline, lost in thought as she traced a fingertip along the sun-warmed balcony edge. Her fine-boned face was bathed in the hue of sunset, and this washed away the lines of age and gave her hair a fiery-golden sheen.

Apion glimpsed the nape of her neck. His unease faded a little as the delicate skin there conjured up a lost memory of Maria. Of kissing her there, his arms around her waist, her scent dancing in his nostrils.

'It is for the simplest of reasons that you are here,' she spoke at last, shrilly and suddenly. 'Absurdly simple.'

Apion snapped to attention. '*Basileia?*'

'I am no empress,' she replied flatly, 'do not address me as such.'

Apion felt her rebuke sting like the lash. 'Very well . . . my lady.'

She turned to him, her face expressionless. 'The reason I had you brought up here,' she reached out to clasp the fabric of his tunic, 'is because of this.'

Apion frowned.

'Earlier, when you were bathing, I had the silk robe sent to you. I wanted to see how quickly you would accept such finery. But instead you chose to keep your filthy, worn tunic. That tells me something about you. You may yet turn out to be an untrustworthy snake, but I can afford you a sliver of doubt. And,' she looked away, sipping her drink again, 'I was not watching you for any other reason, and certainly did not expect your vulgar display of nudity.'

Apion's skin burned in embarrassment again. 'I can only apologise, my lady. I have spent so long with my armies that sometimes I forget myself.' A memory barged into his thoughts uninvited: Blastares strutting through the barracks in the nude, cupping his testicles, breaking wind every few paces and grunting the words to a song about two whores smearing each other with honey. His eyes widened and he quickly shook the thought from his head.

'Well, I suppose much about this place must be unfamiliar to you,' she conceded. 'The border themata . . . I hear those distant lands are rife with warfare. Life there is brutal and short, is it not?'

'For many,' Apion agreed.

Then she frowned at the red-ink stigma on his arm. 'What of this – is it some symbol of your army?'

Apion shook his head. 'This is the *Haga*. An ancient Hittite myth. My men laud me with this moniker as if it represents only glory. But for me it is a constant reminder of all that I have lost.'

Eudokia's eyes darted across his face. Apion braced for another abrupt and awkward question. 'What is your name, Strategos?'

Apion felt the tension ease from him at this. She was the first person to ask this since he had arrived at the capital. Indeed, she was the first to ask this for many months. To all others he was simply the Strategos of Chaldia. 'Apion,' he replied.

'So tell me, Apion, this loss, does it bring you sadness?' she asked, gazing into the horizon once more.

Apion's expression turned grave as dark memories surfaced. 'Sometimes, my lady. Sometimes it brings only anger.' He saw her flex her fingers on her cup, her tongue darting out to moisten her lips, her fine neck swelling a little as she gulped. The sunset betrayed a hint of glassiness in her eyes. He felt a question tingle on his lips.

'You have something to say, Apion?' she said, sensing his hesitation.

Apion braced himself. 'Do you miss your husband, my lady?'

She raised her eyebrows at this, as if taken aback. 'I hated him with all my being.'

Apion nodded, dropping his gaze. 'You can still yearn for someone, even if you did not like them.'

Her lips trembled as if to reply, but she simply looked away, falling silent once more. She paced around the edge of the portico, one hand tracing the marble balcony.

'Perhaps. But I did not bring you here to talk of loss, or of the past,' she said at last, her gaze falling on the waters to the south, bathed in shimmering crimson as the sun slipped behind the western hills of the city. 'I wanted to speak of the dark intrigue that hangs over this city like a thundercloud.'

Apion felt a wave of relief at her frankness. 'I would welcome such talk. For I came here in search of hope, hope that might see my homelands free of the strife that plagues its peoples. Yet since I stepped onto the harbour this morning, I have heard nothing but insinuation, uncertainty and barely veiled swipes at those who occupy this palace in the interregnum. Tell me, my lady, what is afoot? Who can I trust? Who must I be wary of?'

She pointed to the south.

Apion looked to the grand vessel anchored just outside the Theodosian Harbour. The hull was painted brilliant white and the lip of the vessel was gilt and sculpted. It had three banks of oars and its crew scurried up and down the network of rigging on its broad masts, unfurling two vast, white linen sails, each adorned with a purple Chi-Rho emblem. On the deck, there were silk awnings shading an area ringed with cushions and padded seats. Slaves dashed around this area, carrying platters of food and amphorae of wine. Anchored around this vessel were ten dromons, utilitarian in contrast. These smaller war galleys were utterly free of finery, each deck studded with a glimmering square of fifty numeroi.

'Now I understand why the imperial fleet lies in such ruin – if such funds have been poured into the decoration of this one vessel and its escort,' Apion said. Then he turned to her. 'I mean no offence . . . '

'The offence comes not from you, Apion. The opulence lavished on the imperial flagship is but one of the follies of my dead husband.' Then she stabbed a finger at a small white rowing boat cutting through the still waters towards the flagship. 'The greatest of his follies, however, was his failure to shed the malignant leech that clung to him throughout his reign.'

The tiny boat drew alongside the huge vessel, docking with a timber staircase that led to the decks. The figures on the rowing boat boarded the larger vessel. Apion made out a clutch of six numeroi and a pair of slaves amongst their number. But one central figure was the focus of attention, slaves dashing from below deck to hold silken canopies above his head and to offer silver platters laden with jugs and fine foods. It was Psellos, the shrivelled adviser.

'I have met with this one already,' Apion said.

At this, Eudokia balked, glancing to the varangoi. The nearest of the Rus axemen shook his head. 'They spoke only for moments, my lady.'

Apion pinned her with his gaze. 'My lady, what is this?'

Eudokia composed herself. 'I have to be sure of you, Apion.'

'I can offer you only my word.'

She searched his eyes, and he wondered what she found in there.

Finally, she nodded. 'Psellos is a parasite. He rose to prominence after establishing the University of Constantinople. He used that leverage to worm his way into the political sphere. From there, he attached himself to the emperor's court, and that was over twenty years ago. The man has sponsored the rise of the last three emperors, feeding from them during their reign and lurking at each of their deathbeds. It is he who conjures the thundercloud over this city. The continuation of the Doukid dynasty is his only hope of retaining control. He has my late husband's brother John on his side, and already he poisons the mind of my eldest boy against my designs to break the Doukid line.'

Apion watched as the purple robed Psellos reclined on the cushions and took bread from the slaves. Then another figure emerged from below deck. Tall and dark-bearded. He greeted Psellos heartily, then took to gulping at a cup of wine.

'John has always aspired to the throne,' Eudokia said, 'yet he is a wrathful and short-sighted man – even more so than his brother was. It took little for Psellos to tether him. Indeed, Psellos calls him master without a hint of irony.'

Apion's gaze hardened as he watched. John Doukas pushed away a young slave who offered to water his wine, then took to punching the cowering, screaming boy. He stopped when the slave collapsed to the deck. Then he took up a baton and proceeded to thrash at the slave's head.

Cold memories of Apion's days as a slave surfaced. 'Then you have chosen well in contesting their push for power. Equally, from what I hear, you have chosen well in summoning Romanus Diogenes to be the new emperor.'

Eudokia looked to him with an expression of mild shock. 'You believe my choice to be wise and well thought out? Are you aware that I had Romanus Diogenes exiled, only days after my husband died?'

'My lady?' Apion frowned.

'He could have been executed on my word. There were strong rumours that he planned to seize the throne in a violent coup. Had he done so, my sons would have been blinded,' her voice hushed a little and she darted a glance at young Konstantious, 'or killed.' Then she turned her gaze back upon the flagship, and her face wrinkled in fury. 'Now, in those intervening months I have found out that those rumours were fuelled by those they served best.'

Apion nodded. 'Regardless of what journey brought us here, my lady, we are here now.'

Eudokia nodded. 'Yet Romanus Diogenes is still engaged in campaigning on the Istrian frontier and will not arrive in the capital until December. Much can happen in that time. Can I count on your support until then, Strategos?'

Apion nodded. 'The promise of a new emperor spirited my men and I here all the way from Chaldia, my lady. I do not intend for that to be a wasted journey.'

'That pleases me,' she replied.

The pair gazed bitterly at the scene on the flagship. Now the slave lay still and lifeless, a crimson pool forming around his head as

John Doukas poured another cup of neat wine. All the while, Psellos looked on, reclined and sipping from a goblet.

Eudokia's shoulders tensed, and then she clicked her fingers. At once, the two varangoi rushed to flank Apion. 'That will be all, Strategos,' she said, her gaze fixed on the boat.

Apion bowed, then turned with the varangoi and walked to the staircase.

'Apion,' she called out, just as he was about to descend the stairs.

Apion turned. She wore a wrinkle of concern on her face, the iciness in her eyes gone momentarily. 'My lady?'

'My guards will protect you as they would me,' Eudokia replied. 'But sleep lightly. Trust no one.'

'Yes, my lady.'

10. Affinity

Summer seemed reluctant to give way to autumn, and the Ides of October saw a muggy heat settle over Constantinople. While the city streets, harbours and forums swarmed with crowds on this particular day, the Hippodrome was deserted. Until Apion and Dederic emerged onto the racetrack from the shade of the western tunnel. They were both barefoot and wore only light linen tunics.

Apion squinted into the mid-morning sun, shading his eyes with one hand as he swept his gaze along the vast, empty banks of seating that hugged the arena. The gilt copper statue of the four horsemen mounted at the north end gazed back at him lifelessly. In the narrow strip of raised land marking the centre of the arena, an eclectic line of obelisks, columns and monuments jutted skywards. Some of these were crowned with statues of great chariot riders of the past and of immortal heroes and the old gods, Heracles and Apollo being the finest.

But it was not to admire such finery that they had come here, he thought, running his eyes around the lengthy sides of the track and the tight u-shaped bends at either end. The surface was even, though the tracks of the last chariots to have raced here were still marked in the dust, along with splinters of wood, shards of bronze and dark patches where blood had been spilled. But after a week of confinement within the palace, this was a meagre hardship to endure in return for the freedom of an open piece of ground and the chance to run.

He glanced around once more as he swept his hair up in his hands and knotted it atop his head. They were definitely alone. Igor

145

had been reluctant to let them come here, and so they had slipped out here when the big Rus left them to attend to the Doux of Mesopotamia's arrival.

Beside him, Dederic dropped his water skin and a hemp sack by the trackside, then contemplated the length of the racetrack. 'How many laps of this did you say we should run?'

'Three laps is roughly a mile. So I'll be running thirty of them. You just do as many as you wish.'

Dederic wiped at his brow and nodded to the Imperial Palace, the tip of which peeked over the eastern terrace. 'I wonder that old Cydones had the right idea?'

'Sleeping through the midday heat?' Apion gasped sarcastically. 'Nonsense – where's the fun in that?' Then he shrugged. 'Aye, we'll do this at dawn in future, but let us not wait for tomorrow. It is as I said, when you engage your body,' he tapped a finger to his temple, 'it frees your mind of troubling thoughts.'

Dederic's gaze grew distant and he fell silent. Then, at last, he nodded. 'Aye . . . aye, I'll go with that.'

They walked to the northern bend in the track and then stopped in a patch of shade. 'We'll start from here,' Apion said as he stretched his calves and hamstrings. Dederic followed his routine. 'This'll keep you limber and stop you from aching quite as much later on.'

They set off at a light jog, side-by-side. Apion noticed Dederic's breathing growing laboured before they had even reached the southern bend.

'Feels like my heart is going to burst from my chest,' the Norman gasped between breaths.

'That will pass quickly, it is just your body over-reacting to the stress. It is akin to battle, is it not?'

146

'Aye,' Dederic panted, 'but this feels somewhat . . . more deadly!'

Apion roared with laughter at this. 'Take a breath over two strides, then exhale on your next. Find a rhythm and your heart will settle into it. Also, keep your shoulders back – this will increase your intake of breath.'

They came round to the northern bend and past their starting line and then Apion picked up the pace into a run. Dederic kept up, breathing faster to do so.

'The physical battle is easily won,' Apion spoke between strides as they came round to start their third lap. 'After that comes the battle of endurance – a test of the mind.'

'Aye,' Dederic panted, 'All I can . . . think of . . . is one word. Stop!'

'You will stop,' Apion replied, 'but only when you choose to. The negative thoughts won't have their way.'

They fell silent after this, both men utterly focused. Apion felt his heart pounding in his chest and the blood throbbing in his ears. By the sixth lap his skin was slick with sweat and, blessedly, he realised he was thinking of nothing other than the track ahead and of his stride. Past and present troubles had been shed somewhere in those first few circuits. He glanced to Dederic and hoped the Norman had found similar peace.

The sun was rising towards its zenith when they started their fifteenth lap and the heat was fierce. At this point, Dederic fell back and then stopped, slumping down in the shade of the western tunnel, gulping hungrily at his water skin between heaving breaths.

Apion continued until he came to the northern bend for the thirtieth time. His thighs were on fire, but now it seemed more of an effort to stop and break the rhythm than to keep going. But he did slow gradually as he rounded the southern bend. Then his breathing calmed as he came to a halt by Dederic. After stretching his muscles once more, he sat and wiped the worst of the sweat from his brow, then took up Dederic's offer of the water skin. He could manage only sips, but it instantly cooled his chest. After a short while, the Norman rummaged in his hemp sack and brought out two eggs and a small loaf of bread. They ate swiftly and washed the meal down with the last of the cool water.

Apion pushed up, readying to stand, when Dederic's words stopped him.

'Sir, does it last longer if you run more?' he said.

Apion looked to him. The Norman's brow was furrowed as he studied the dust before him. 'Longer? The silence in your mind, you mean?'

'Aye,' Dederic looked up. 'It is as you said it would be; I thought nothing of the fat lord while I ran nor while we ate. Emelin and the children were a warm glow in my heart and their troubles seemed distant, conquerable.' He scratched a line in the dust with his finger. 'But now those troubles clamour to return to my mind.'

'Running only staves off my troubles for a short while, Dederic,' Apion settled back down cross-legged once more. 'I understand the torment.'

The pair shared a lasting silence, each man gazing into their own past.

'I've heard things, sir,' Dederic said at last, tentatively, 'the men in the Chaldian ranks spoke of what happened to you. To those you loved.'

Apion tensed.

'I'm sorry,' Dederic waved a hand, 'I didn't mean to bring your attention to that which you seek to forget. I can only pray that the same fate does not befall my family.'

Apion nodded. Then he leaned forward and clasped a hand to the Norman's shoulder. 'Then don't let it happen, Dederic.'

Dederic frowned.

'Back then,' Apion said, gulping back the gall of sorrow and bitterness, 'I should have saved those I lost. But I failed. Not a breath passes without the question gnawing on my thoughts like a pox; what could I have done differently? The answers come thick and fast, mocking me. But there is only one answer that I know to be true,' he held Dederic's earnest gaze. 'If I was back in that time now, I would do whatever it took to save them. Whatever it took.'

Apion felt a stinging behind his eyes and he saw the same glassiness in Dederic's gaze.

'Whatever it takes,' the Norman nodded. Then, at last, his familiar smile reappeared. 'In the meantime I think I will run until my heart bursts!'

Apion chuckled at this. Then he looked to the Norman earnestly. 'Something else may well help to set your mind at rest, Dederic.'

'Sir?'

'The Chaldian ranks are bereft of leaders. Without Sha, Blastares and Procopius I would be lost. Indeed, I need more of their ilk. I could use a man like you to lead a tourma for me, when we return to Chaldia. It pays better than a mercenary purse – some two hundred nomismata for a year's service. Within a few years you would perhaps have enough to pay off the fat lord of Rouen? What do you say?'

Dederic gawped for a moment, then his face split with an earnest smile. 'I look forward to serving Chaldia, sir.' He stood and held out a hand. Apion clasped the Norman's forearm and rose.

The pair grinned, then walked into the western tunnel. But there they halted, the breath freezing in their lungs.

They were not alone.

A pair of numeroi approached, emerging from the shadows of the tunnel. The spearmen were fully armoured in their iron klibania, and they wore baleful grimaces under the rims of their helms. One had a broad, stubbled jaw and the other a drawn, sickly pallor. They flexed their grips on their spears as they approached.

Apion's heart shuddered once more, this time with the anticipation of battle. The dark door surfaced in his mind as he saw the pair level their spear tips.

He swept a hand across Dederic's chest, pushing him back. The pair stepped back from the tunnel and into the sunshine-bathed racetrack once more. A glance around the sweeping banks of the Hippodrome revealed no further aggressors. But the pair of numeroi were light on their feet and they split as they came from the shadows to flank he and Dederic.

Instinctively, Dederic and Apion pushed together, back-to-back, twisting round as the spearmen circled them silently. Apion pinned the one nearest him with his gaze.

'Why do you hesitate?' he said flatly, 'two unarmed men should not pose any difficulty to you.'

At this, the stubble-jawed numeros chuckled gruffly, then lunged forward, punching his spear towards Apion's chest. The tip tore Apion's tunic and scored his chest as he leapt clear, pulling Dederic with him. Then he lurched forward and clasped his hands together to bring them down upon the numeros' neck. The stubble-jawed spearman roared at this, his helmet falling to the dust as he staggered back, clutching at his neck, his face boiling red. But the spearmen were quick to come for them once more. Apion and Dederic edged away until they backed against the stone wall that ringed the racetrack.

'I was going to make it quick,' the angered numeros growled, drawing a line across his throat with one finger, 'now I think I'll just spill your guts and let you bleed out while I watch.' His sour glare bent into a shark-like grin. He fired a nod to his colleague and the pair lunged forward like wolves.

Then a crunch of iron upon bone was accompanied by a splatter of hot fluid and a foul stench.

Apion blinked through this mess and stared at the sight before him. The stubble-jawed numeros stood, spear extended, frozen like a statue. A battle axe rested in his forehead, cleaving his brain, and a bloody soup of grey matter pumped from the wound. The man's eyes rolled up in his head and then the body crumpled.

Apion spun to see Dederic gawping at the other numeros. The man flapped his lips wordlessly as he contemplated the axe embedded in his chest, before he, too toppled to the ground.

'I told you not to come here alone, Strategos,' a voice boomed from above. 'The Numeroi watch your every step.'

Apion twisted and looked up. Igor of the Varangoi stood some twelve rows up on the western terrace, flanked by a pair of his men. Each of them wore their pure-white armour and robes.

The big Rus hobbled down the steps and thudded onto the track. He placed a foot on the chest of the dead numeros and wrenched his axe free. Then he gazed at the bloodied iron and sighed, stroking the blade as if it was a pet. 'And I only sharpened you this morning.'

11. Under Darkening Skies

Cydones sniffed at the peach and a smile spread across his face. He squeezed the fruit gently. 'Ripe as a young lady's . . . '

'We'll take three,' Apion cut in, tossing three folles to the stallholder.

The pair stepped out from under the stall's awning and back into the grey autumn morning that hung over the Forum of the Ox. The scent of roasting meat, honey and spices hung in the air as they took in their surroundings again.

Sitting in a valley, the forum was overlooked by the city's third and seventh hills. The square itself was hemmed in by vine-clad porticoes which were packed with stalls, workshops and traders selling their wares. At the western end of the forum was a towering arched gallery, housing a grand statue of Constantine the Great and his Mother Helena clutching at a gilded Cross.

Apion led Cydones towards the centre of the forum, manoeuvring through the throng of shoppers and traders. They were followed closely by the four varangoi Igor had assigned to protect them. The pair stopped by a clutch of Judas trees clustered around a babbling fountain, the golden-brown leaves piling around the roots where they had fallen and some floating on the fountain's waters.

They sat and munched into their fruit.

'When I used to live here as a lad,' Cydones pointed vaguely to the centre of the forum, 'they said there used to be a hollow bronze statue of an ox, right about there. Do you know why it was hollow?'

Apion shrugged absently.

Cydones leaned a little closer, lowering his voice. 'Because the people used to gather to watch as Christians were bundled inside the belly. Kindling and brush would be lit underneath, and then they would be incinerated alive, their screams echoing across the city.' The old man shook his head.

'We are a knotted rope of contradiction,' Apion mused, brushing at the stigma on his forearm and the white band of skin where his prayer rope had once been tied. His fruit seemed less ripe all of a sudden. Then he noticed another furtive glance from the nearest of the four varangoi; they were afraid. Now the peach tasted almost sour and he stopped chewing.

Another doux had been killed the previous day, mutilated under the hooves and wheels of a trade wagon as he strolled the city streets. The wagon driver was discovered later that night, emasculated, eviscerated and left in a dank alley for the rats to feed upon. He cast his gaze around the forum; the spearmen of the numeroi posted at each street corner and atop the higher buildings wore stern grimaces. But he was sure he caught more than one of them glancing at the four varangoi.

'Eat,' Cydones sighed, wiping peach juice from his lips. 'If someone wishes to cut off our balls and gut us then they will. But they'll have to get through those axemen first!'

Apion cocked an eyebrow at the old man's turn of phrase. 'I do not fear being slain, sir. You know me better than that. I merely worry that Eudokia's fears will come to pass.' He thought of the evening a few days past when he, Cydones and Dederic had dined with Eudokia, Igor and a select few of the doukes and strategoi whom Eudokia seemed to trust. She had laid out her concerns and intimated to each of them that tough weeks and months lay ahead. 'She has the loyalty of the patriarch, but he is just one man and his followers are few. The

153

people claim piety but seem to favour Psellos and the games and races he funds. The Varangoi are loyal to her also, but there are only a few hundred posted around the city and less than fifty in the palace. Meanwhile, Psellos can call upon the thousands of spears of the Numeroi at any time he wishes.

'So why does he not force home his massive numerical advantage?' Cydones summarised Apion's question.

'Exactly. The palace could be taken within a morning.'

'This is true,' Cydones nodded, licking his fingers and tossing the peach stone to the ground for the birds. 'But it would be a short-lived victory. Yes, the Numeroi could easily force home the wills of Psellos and see John and Michael seize the throne permanently. But that would incite many more thousands of spears to converge on this city. The themata armies of Lykandos and Paphlagonia would come to avenge any such act, for their strategoi have been slain. Nilos, the Strategos of Opsikon, is loyal to his core – he too would rouse his armies to march against Psellos. Then there are the imperial tagmata, stationed across the Bosphorus. Many thousands of the finest soldiers the empire has to offer – their loyalty is unknown and it would undoubtedly be tested should such a coup occur. The balance is too fine to risk a coup as things stand.'

Apion nodded, smiling. At times, old Cydones' mind was still as sharp as a blade. 'Aye, I know this. But ambition clouds the minds of men. I fear that ambition might drive Psellos to take that risk.'

Cydones frowned. 'I have met that snake only briefly in my time here, and yes, I could smell the ambition seeping from his pores. You are right to be wary of him, not the members of the Doukas family he controls or the thousands of blades he can call upon. For it is the head of the snake that bears the fangs. But Psellos is a cool and shrewd individual. He will not take that risk until the time is right. I am sure of it.'

Apion chewed on the last piece of flesh from his peach, tossed the stone to the ground and washed it down with a swig from his skin of well-watered wine. 'Then it is all we can do to maintain the balance. We must ensure Psellos cannot either slay the remaining strategoi and doukes loyal to Eudokia or buy those whose hearts are venal before Romanus Diogenes arrives.'

Cydones turned to him, his sightless eyes bright as a smile stretched across his lined features. 'Aye, and you have it in your power to do that, Apion. Stay alive, stay true, and Psellos will be thwarted!'

Just then, a sweet aroma of roasted lamb and garlic wafted over them. They looked up. Dederic was wandering over to them, carrying with him a clay pot. He scraped the remaining stew from it, licking at his spoon. There was something about Dederic's swagger that Apion appreciated – as if he cared little for the threat that hung on these streets. The Norman reminded him greatly of Sha, Blastares and Procopius, and it warmed him to know that he had found another with a good heart. Dederic had seemed buoyed by his daily dawn runs at the Hippodrome and Apion hoped that by introducing him to the routine, he had helped the man find some peace of mind.

Just then, a fussing varangos tried to usher Dederic back to where Apion and Cydones sat, but Dederic ignored this, glancing to a brass sundial, then frowning and looking to the sky. The grey clouds were darkening in a portent of rain.

'It must be close to noon, sir. Should we not be heading back, for the gathering?'

Apion tossed the remaining peach to the Norman. 'Aye, we should. And I must say, I do wonder if I've been anticipating anything with less joy.'

Dederic grinned at this, catching the fruit.

Cydones groaned as he stood, then a wry grin spread across his face. 'Indeed! I'd rather face a hundred thousand Seljuks with a wooden sword – splinters on the handle, no less.'

The three chuckled at this, then strode back through the crowd towards the palace, flanked by the varangoi. The first splodges of rain stained the streets before them as they walked.

As the rain grew heavier, Apion snatched glances to the top of the portico from under a furrowed brow.

The numeroi were watching his every footstep.

***

The rain thundered on the palace roof and echoed throughout the main hall. But Eudokia's words boomed over this din;

'On the first day of the new year of our lord, the souls of God's empire will gather to watch as noble Romanus Diogenes joins me in marriage. The empire will have a new leader, a new man who will act under God's will to see our people prosper and our borders secure.'

There were ninety men in her audience. They had set down their klibania, helms and weapons at the gates of the palace and wore only boots, tunics and cloaks. These were the doukes of the provincial tagmata and the strategoi of the themata together with their closest aides. Men who commanded armies of thousands, to victory or death. They listened intently.

Apion stood with Cydones and Dederic. He watched Eudokia as she spoke frankly, her gaze icy. He wondered how many people had ever seen that gaze melt. Few, he reckoned. He had seen it for those precious few moments on the rooftop portico. He had seen it again when they had dined as a group and she had offered him a ghost of a warm smile. No wonder she was so guarded, he thought, given that she had lived in the presence of Psellos and his ilk for so long. Apion furtively eyed the squat, hawk-faced old man who was standing beside Eudokia, his hands clasped and a peaceable expression on his features. Ostensibly, the pair represented imperial unity. But his eyes – his eyes were scouring the room like a predator's, as if seeking out those who had not yet pledged their allegiance to him.

Beside Apion stood Nilos, the strategos of the Opsikon Thema. The big, bearded Greek had embraced him warmly when they had first been introduced over a week past. *Ah, the Haga - the legend of the borderlands!* But when Apion changed the subject to Psellos' background, he became guarded, his eyes darting as he spoke.

A leech! The strategos had hissed under his breath. *The man is a damned leech who seeks puppets for the imperial throne! If you seek reasons for the decline of your borderlands, Haga, then the foremost of them is Psellos.*

Apion realised he was staring at Psellos, and that Psellos was staring back with added intensity. He turned to Eudokia and focused on her words.

'There should be no doubt in your minds,' Eudokia continued, 'that imperial taxes will no longer be squandered on embellishment of the capital or bloating of imperial court bureaucracy.' A rumble of approval broke the silence of the crowd.

Apion could not help but notice Psellos' eyes narrowing at this, darting to a handful of faces in the crowd. Apion glanced sideways to those targeted. One, a young doux, seemed cowed by Psellos' glare and offered a faint nod. Another doux, a wiry, older man with an eyepatch, seemed to hold Psellos' pinched glare momentarily. Apion felt a glow of hope at this, but then the wiry man's forehead broke out in a sweat, then he gulped and dropped his gaze to the floor, offering another faint nod. Psellos then turned his gaze on Nilos, who returned the glare, squaring his jaw. Nilos did not yield, and Apion's heart lifted at this. But Nilos was only one man.

Apion leant to one side, where Cydones and Dederic stood. 'It is as we thought,' he whispered. 'Psellos seeks to tip the balance.'

Cydones' sightless eyes gazed far into the distance. 'Aye, treachery is in the air,' he agreed, his nose wrinkling. 'I can smell it.'

'The armies of the themata will no longer be neglected and the outlying tagmata will be bolstered,' Eudokia continued, 'recruiting Byzantine souls and lessening the dependency on mercenary soldiers.' Eudokia continued. This time, a cheer broke out from the crowd. But nearly half of them remained mute and wary of any show of support.

Psellos' lips tightened at this, as if resisting a satisfied sneer.

Then, Eudokia brought her speech to a close, making sure to catch the eye of every man in the crowd; 'I asked you here to welcome Romanus Diogenes to the city. Now,' she hesitated for just a heartbeat, and Apion saw her lip tremble just a little, 'I ask that you remain here to see us wed.'

Apion's eyebrows shot up at this. He looked to Dederic, who looked equally stunned.

An unfortunately timed clap of thunder rippled through the air outside and reverberated through the hall.

'Tell me I'm going deaf, Apion?' Cydones croaked by his side. 'Did she just say that we are to remain here until the year is out?'

'Aye, unfortunately,' Apion said in a muted tone, his gaze returning to Psellos. 'I feel it will be a long, cold winter.'

***

The rainstorm had raged for days, and the streets of the city were slick and shiny. A clap of thunder tumbled across the night sky and brought with it another sheet-like barrage. Many guttering torches hissed, spat and died at this.

Wrapped in a brown hemp hooded cloak, Psellos splashed through the streets, past the *Milareum Aureum*, the gilded bronze pillar casting him momentarily in its ghostly golden light. When a pair of sunken-cheeked wretches emerged from an alley nearby, Psellos halted and raised one hand just a fraction. Then, as if spawned by the rainstorm, three gleaming numeroi spearmen stole from the shadows behind him and half drew their spathions. The screech of iron was enough to send the wretches scurrying back from whence they came.

Psellos looked at his hand, marvelling at the power it wielded. The city was his. The empire would soon follow.

Then he set off once more towards his destination – the Numera, the barracks of the Numeroi Tagma.

But they're so much more than a simple barracks, he grinned to himself.

Two more numeroi stood in the gloom either side of the entrance, their helms and cloaks fending off the worst of the rain. When he approached they threw up a hand in salute.

Then a komes, denoted by the white sash knotted at his right shoulder, emerged from the door to greet him. 'I will take you to him, sir,' he said.

Psellos nodded in silence as he stepped out of the rainstorm and entered the barracks.

The komes led him through a musty-smelling and dark corridor, until they emerged into the Numera muster ground. It was deserted apart from the sentries who looked down on them from the soaked, grey barrack walls and watchtowers. They skirted round the

159

collonaded edge of the muster ground to stay clear of the rain. Then they came to an iron-lattice gate on the far side, behind which was a corridor lit by a flickering and faint orange torchlight. The komes nodded to the soldier posted here, who fumbled with keys then opened the gate. This revealed a worn stone staircase that descended steeply underground, slick with damp. The komes plucked a torch from the wall and they began their descent.

'He struggled, sir. He killed one of my men. But a club to the back of his head put paid to his resistance. Now he is yours to dispose of as you see fit.'

'Your continued distinction has been noted,' Psellos enthused.

They descended until they reached the prison complex, a series of pitch-black, stinking spaces gouged into the bedrock and fronted by rusting iron bars. Gaunt, sickly faces gawped as the torchlight bobbed past them, some scurrying to the backs of their cells in terror like rats, others lying like broken men, simply rolling their eyes to watch the passing pair.

Then they came to a tall, timber chest that rested against the bedrock. The komes braced his shoulder against one end of the chest and then grunted, putting his full weight into shoving it to one side. The grating of timber on rock echoed around the prison.

Psellos gazed into the opening and down the roughly-hewn stone staircase that was revealed. He could smell the rankness of burnt and rotting flesh, wafting up at them like a wolf's breath. He could even taste the metallic tang of blood. As they descended the staircase, a muffled roar of agony escaped from the depths. Psellos' face split into a grin at this.

Then they finally reached the torture chamber of the *Portatioi*. The most devious of the Numeroi, some would say. *The most efficacious,* Psellos thought.

160

The air was thin and hot in this small and enclosed chamber, probably composed of the dying breaths of the many hundreds he had consigned here.

The only light came from the brazier in one corner, loaded with iron rods and tongs that glowed like hell itself. One torturer was dressed only in a loincloth, his muscular frame dripping with sweat in the stifling heat and the veins pulsing through his shaved scalp as he sharpened a sickle. Meanwhile, from the darker corner of the room, a ghostly figure lurked, his lank hair as white as his skin. This was Zenobius, his chief torturer and a man without a soul. He stoked at a cage in the shadows with a hot poker. This elicited animal grunting and screeching and illuminated fleeting glimpses of some inhuman form, wrinkled and glistening.

Psellos frowned as he scanned the room, then he grinned as he turned round to the wall nearest the door. There his prize lay, like a goose awaiting the butcher. The huge and muscular figure of Nilos the strategos was chained to a table, on his back and spread-eagled, naked. His torso glistened with sweat and blood, and his muscles strained at the shackles. His face was a swollen mess.

Psellos walked over to join him. 'Ah, Nilos, you have inconvenienced yourself so,' he bent over so his nose was inches from Nilos' battered features. 'How much less trouble I would have had with you if you had been as weak-willed as the others.'

Nilos uttered an inhuman roar at this, straining at the irons that held him in place, and aiming a headbutt at Psellos. But the strike fell short as the irons clanked tight. Yet Nilos hovered there, the bulging masses of flesh that were his eyes cracking open just enough for him to glare at Psellos. 'You'll never buy my loyalty, you *whoreson!*' he spat, his words slurred and rasping through his shattered teeth, blood and saliva spraying onto Psellos' face.

161

Psellos stood back, his nose wrinkling as took a silk cloth from his purse and dabbed at the mess. 'Some I can buy. Some I cannot. I need only one thing from those in the latter group . . . I need you to *die,*' he rubbed his hands together, his eyes glinting in the brazier-light, 'and to die in an appalling manner. Then your corpse will serve to persuade the next of my targets.'

At this, Nilos seemed to be fired with a fresh wave of fury. He wrenched up from the table, bawling from the bottom of his lungs.

Psellos erupted in laughter at this.

But then the shackle holding Nilos' right wrist shattered.

Shards of iron sprayed across the room, and the strategos' fist swung round in a powerful hook.

Psellos leapt back, the blow flashing only inches from his face. His bowels turned over and icy fear stabbed at his heart. A shrill cry leapt from his lips as Nilos then wrenched at the shackle on his left wrist.

Then Zenobius stepped forward deftly, snatched the sickle from the big torturer and slashed at Nilos' forearm, cleaving the limb clean off. Nilos crumpled back onto the table, writhing, mouth agape in silent agony, blood pumping from the wound.

Zenobius stepped back, cleaning his sickle in silence, his blood-spattered face expressionless. At this, the bald torturer's hoarse cackle rang out once more, the foetid stench of his breath cutting through the vile smell in the chamber.

Psellos righted himself, then barked at Zenobius. 'Staunch the wound, I want him to die as planned!'

The albino wrenched at the haemorrhaging limb and wrapped a length of filthy cloth around it, tying it as if strangling a victim. Then he barked to his colleague.

162

The bald torturer used the tongs to pluck an iron mask from the coals. It was glowing white, sparks spiralling and dancing from it.

Nilos' pained cries fell silent at this sight. Then Psellos grasped his jaw and glared at him. 'The death mask is but the finishing touch, Strategos,' he purred.

Taking his cue, Zenobius lifted the bolts from the cage in the corner, and the pair of starved hogs were released from their prison. They immediately took to licking and gnawing at Nilos' arm stump. Then Zenobius punched the sickle into Nilos' gut and ripped it across the length of the strategos' belly. As Nilos' guts tumbled from the wound, the hogs leapt upon him, tearing at the steaming entrails.

At that moment, footsteps sounded from the stairs, and another figure entered the chamber. John Doukas' eyes glinted with bloodlust at the sight before him. That and disappointment at having missed some of the proceedings.

'You have joined us just in time, master,' Psellos enthused to John, before turning back to Nilos, writhing under the frenzied hogs. 'Another stubborn strategos is about to breathe his last.'

Nilos could not even utter a croak as the beasts feasted upon his innards. His only solace was that the darkness was closing in. All he could see before him was the trio of faces: Psellos, the man who would be the death of the empire; John Doukas, who looked on like a hungry wolf; and a pale and emotionless creature whose glare cut through him like a blade. This was surely the realm of the Godless.

Then he heard the albino speak calmly to the bald, burly torturer; 'Finish him.'

Nilos' mind swirled with confusion until the tongs and the golden mask filled his field of vision, and descended upon his face. With an untold agony and a stench of searing flesh, the blackness took

163

him. The hoarse cackling of the big torturer was the last thing he heard.

As Nilos' body fell limp, the grin faded from John's face. 'Now we must turn the screw upon our more stubborn visitors.'

Psellos nodded. 'Ah, yes. The Strategos of Chaldia, yet to see sense.'

John shook his head. 'He is even more tenacious than this whoreson ever was.'

'Give me one more chance to speak with him, master.' Psellos' face opened up into a wicked grin. 'He will turn, or he will die.'

**

It was the first morning of December and the rainstorms had abated at last. The air was crisp and a heavy frost had settled across the palace gardens. Near the centre, the parakeets squawked as Apion and young Konstantious played. Apion roared like a lion and stomped forward, arms outstretched, scooping the boy up and swinging him from side to side. Konstantious squealed in mock terror, then wriggled free of Apion's grasp and stumbled towards the orange trees, giggling.

'It is a blessing that I had a thick and restful sleep last night,' Apion panted, doubling over and resting his palms on his knees. Indeed, his body was already tired after his extended morning run with Dederic. Still, this horseplay was refreshing, lightening his mind of troubles.

'I thought you said you were a *brave* lion?' Konstantious jibed. 'You don't seem very brave to me. My parakeets are bigger and stronger than you, and they eat only the seed I feed them.' At this, one fledgling bird fluttered clumsily down to rest upon his shoulder.

164

'Now the worst thing you can do,' Apion wagged a finger, stalking around the orange trees with accentuated footsteps, 'is to goad a wild creature.' His footsteps slowed and he fell silent, then he sprung forward with another roar. Konstantious squealed and then sped away with only inches to spare, darting into the rhododendron bush. The parakeet fled back to its nest.

Apion stood tall, then stalked around the bush. He could see Konstantious hiding in there, waiting, but he pretended not to notice. Then, when he 'carelessly' turned his back on the bush, the youngster burst from the undergrowth, hoisting a thick twig in one hand and leaping into the air.

'Ya!' Konstantious yelled and thrust the 'spear' into Apion's leg.

Apion fell to the ground in an exaggerated fit of choking and thrashing, before falling limp, eyes closed. He held his breath and lay motionless.

Then, when Konstantious stepped closer to inspect his kill, Apion burst back into life, grappling the boy and roaring, lifting him from the ground and swinging him round in circles once more. The pair collapsed into a giggling heap before Konstantious got up and darted to the far side of the garden, his laughter filling the place.

Apion stood, still chuckling. Then, as he stretched his shoulders, his gaze snagged on something. High on the balcony overlooking the gardens.

Eudokia looked back at him, the frosty veneer she wore like a klibanion was absent. She was smiling, and it illuminated her beauty.

Apion found it infectious, and let out a hearty chuckle, resting his hands on his hips.

But the moment was fleeting. A varangos' hand on Eudokia's shoulder and a whispered word in her ear saw her expression fall icy once more. She turned and left the balcony without a word. Apion felt his own smile wane at this.

Then it dissolved completely as he heard a familiar voice behind him.

'These gardens are truly compelling. Once a man knows such finery, he can only think with horror of leaving it behind.'

Apion turned to Psellos. The shrivelled adviser wore a fur-lined purple cloak trimmed with gold thread, hands clasped behind his back.

Apion pinned him with a flinty gaze. 'There may be some comforts I will miss, but I will gladly return to the dirt-tracks and scree-strewn hillsides of Chaldia.'

Psellos smiled coldly at this, then reached up and held out a hand to the orange tree. He clicked his tongue and the striped mother parakeet fluttered down from the tree to rest on his wrist, its three nestlings screeching from above. He stroked the bird's ruby and buttercup yellow feathers and it pecked around his fingers in curiosity.

'A magnificent creature, is it not?' Psellos purred, stroking the bird's neck with one finger. 'A beast of majesty, safe in its opulent home . . . yet cupped in my palm. Watch how its ignorance brings about its fate.'

The bird, angry at the lack of seed in Psellos' hand, pecked a little too hard, pinching the old man's skin and drawing a spot of blood. Psellos did not wince at this. He simply wrapped his free hand around the bird's neck. The creature flapped its wings and squawked in terror and then Psellos wrenched at its body with the other hand. With a snap of bone, it was still. He looked up at Apion once more. 'Emperors, regents and those who sit, ostensibly, in positions of power should be wary of those who lifted them there, Strategos. Remember that.'

'Say your piece, adviser, then leave me.' Apion shot furtive glances around the overlooking balconies and roofs of the palace. The few varangoi who were normally stationed there were absent, doubtless drawn away by the same issue that had troubled Eudokia.

'The axemen are occupied for the moment, Strategos. It is just you and I, and you are one of a . . . *dying* breed,' Psellos said. 'One of the few who choose not to support the continuation of the Doukid line. A wise choice?'

Apion nodded. 'A man's choices define him, so he should always stand by them. There are others who stand with me.'

'Hmm . . . hmmm,' Psellos nodded. 'To the last, it would seem.'

Apion felt a chill on his skin as they gazed at one another in silence. Then a distant, chilling scream pierced the air, from the streets at the far side of the palace. Psellos did not flinch at this. Indeed, his smile only broadened. Then a buccina blared out and the babble of troubled citizens filled the air.

'What have you done?' Apion snarled.

At that moment, Konstantious rushed from the trees, ready to resume play. But he skidded to a halt before Apion and Psellos. His impish grin fell away when he saw the dead parakeet in the adviser's hands. 'What happened?' He gulped, his eyes welling with tears.

'The bird must have fallen from its nest whilst sleeping,' Psellos lied. Then he glanced to Apion with a glint in his eye. 'It would have died instantly, ignorant of its fate.'

Konstantious reached out, taking the parakeet's body from Psellos. 'Then I shall bury her,' he sobbed, 'and make sure she rests well now.' Then he looked up to the mass of twigs in the tree and the screeching nestlings peering over the edge. 'But they will starve without her to nurture them and they will never grow strong enough to leave the nest.'

Apion's thoughts swirled with imaginings of what had happened on the streets. The urge to rush through the palace to see for himself was overwhelming, but that was exactly what Psellos wanted.

He glowered at the adviser, then crouched beside Konstantious, placing a hand on the boy's shoulder. 'Then we can lower the nest and you can feed them yourself. The nestlings will live on and be strong.'

***

Constantinople was cloaked in frost, the wind was bitter and the sky was brushed with wispy, white clouds. The imperial flagship bobbed in the morning swell of the Golden Horn, the oars propelling her gently along the waters of the inlet that hemmed the northern edge of the city. For once, the customary escort of dromons was absent.

On the centre of the flagship, a purple silk tent had been erected. Twenty varangoi stood around this, their faces set in grimaces, their axes held as if they were readying for battle. A small rowing boat approached the vessel. A crimson-cloaked figure stood at the prow, his amber locks billowing in the breeze.

Inside the tent, Eudokia sat at the centre of the plush, quilted floor. But she ignored the comfort of her surroundings and the bountiful platters and amphorae that lined the tent. Neither could she concentrate on the sheaf of paper in her hand. Instead, she could think of nothing but the horrific discovery of the mutilated strategos, Nilos.

The big man's carcass had been found, tied to the foot of the Milareum Aureum, gulls and carrion birds stripping what flesh was left from his bones. Above the corpse on the gilded column's surface, a message had been daubed in blood.

God's wrath will fall upon Diogenes.

The populace had gathered around the sight, babbling in panic, eyes wide and hands covering mouths in disgust. Hyperbole broke out almost immediately, and spread around the streets like wildfire. Some cried out that the impending succession of Romanus Diogenes was folly, that God had chosen another. Others jabbered of a monster that stalked the streets at night. A demon. The antichrist incarnate.

Eudokia looked up from the papers, her lips taut. Indeed, there was a demon in the city, and his scheming had never before been so dark. Such was her mistrust of those who lurked in and around the palace, she had retreated to this yacht with an escort of varangoi in an attempt to understand how she could counter Psellos' push for power.

Like her enemy, she understood that to retaliate directly would only incite the possibility of civil war, dragging the tagmata and the themata into battle against one another around the capital. At a time when the Seljuk forces were rumoured to be readying for a decisive push into Anatolia, this could not be allowed to happen. She tried to piece together the plan in her head once more when a hand swept the tent flap open, sending the winter chill around her bare ankles.

'My lady,' the varangos bowed on one knee to her.

Behind him stood a figure, features silhouetted by the morning sun, eagle feathers rippling in the wind atop his helm.

'Come, sit,' she beckoned him.

Apion handed his swordbelt to the varangos and then entered. It was the first time she had seen him dressed in his full soldier's garb – and he was a fearsome sight. The iron klibanion hugged his torso like the skin of a reptile and the conical helm and scale aventail hid all but his battered face. His emerald gaze was shaded under his brow, his expression dark as he sat before her.

'Nilos' murder still troubles you too?' she asked.

'I cannot change that he was slain, so no, his death does not trouble me.' Apion replied prosaically. He removed his helm and his amber locks tumbled around his face. 'But I worry for the others, those whom Psellos has not yet turned his sights upon.'

'As do I,' she replied.

'Then why summon only me?' Apion replied, his gaze unblinking.

'Because,' Eudokia hesitated at this. 'Because of all the military leaders who have gathered in the palace. You are the only one I still trust.' There was another reason, but that was foolish, she chided herself. Foolish and weak.

'That is praise indeed,' Apion raised his eyebrow at this, smoothing his beard. 'But you know little of me.'

'I know enough, and time is scarce.' She looked over his scarred features and again her gaze locked onto his. For a moment she saw herself on a dusty track that stretched across an open plain. Behind her, the grey, rotting corpse of Constantine Doukas marched for her, arms outstretched as if trying to claw at her. Ahead, she saw Romanus Diogenes, the man she was to marry, the man she had exiled, the man who would gladly take the imperial throne but would never love her. Under Apion's gaze, she felt something she feared she might never feel again. Her heartbeat surged for just a moment, then she buried the thoughts that crept into her mind. 'So, we must turn our attention to the days ahead.'

Apion nodded at this, his expression sincere.

She pushed the sheaf of paper towards him. It was etched with diagrams depicting the walls, towers, barracks and docks of Constantinople. 'Psellos knows that once Romanus Diogenes enters the city, his grasp on power will be as good as over.'

Apion looked up at her, his expression lightening, the edges of his lips lifting.

'Something amuses you?' she frowned.

'Do not take it as a slight. I have spent time with many strategoi, many doukes. Some encounters were pleasurable, others were endured and no more. Few of those men were as succinct and practical as you, my lady.'

She shook her head at this digression and then tapped a finger on the Numeroi barracks and the various strongholds and watchtowers around the city that Psellos' men controlled. 'Psellos' allies within the city will be powerless to flex their muscle without a guarantee of support from the themata and the other tagmata. Thus, I fear that in the coming weeks, he will accelerate his campaign of aggression. He will do whatever it takes to turn the bulk of the empire's armies to his cause. Thus, we cannot allow him the time he needs to achieve this.' She picked out a map of the Balkan region, depicting the empire from the tip of Mystras in southern Greece to the River Istros in the North. She tapped the plains that lay between the city of Adrianople and the great river. 'Diogenes is ending his campaign on the plains, here.' Then she tapped a spot further up, near the river. 'Then he means to establish a winter camp on the banks of the Istros and see that his officers are well bedded in before he travels south in the last week of December, more than three weeks from now. But by then it may be too late.' She looked up to him, her expression earnest. 'You are to ride out to him, Strategos. You are to escort him into the city before then. The fate of the empire rests upon your shoulders.'

Apion took a deep breath at this. 'This is not the first time I have had such weighty expectation placed upon me, my lady.' Then he nodded, his eyes darting across the diagram. 'But I came here in search

of hope, hope that the empire could be saved. So I will do as you ask.'
Then he made to stand. 'And I should waste no time?'

'No,' she shook her head, 'Psellos must not see you leave the
city. So you will leave under cover of night.'

'Then today will be a long day, knowing what lies ahead,'
Apion mused wryly, sitting once more.

She nodded, then gestured to the platters around them; bread,
cheeses, cured meats, fish, fruit, honey, nuts, yoghurt and wine. 'Have
your fill, you will need strength and focus for the journey.'

She realised he was looking at her lips when she said this, and
she turned away in embarrassment.

He seemed not to notice, or at least he pretended he had not. He
lifted the platter nearest, laden with apricots, blueberries, bread and a
fresh honeycomb. 'When I return to Chaldia,' he chuckled, 'I will
remember this fare fondly. Sesame porridge does lose its appeal after
the hundredth day on campaign.' He grinned at her, tearing the bread
in half and holding one piece out to her.

She reached out to take it, then dipped it into the honeycomb,
breaking the wax, the golden syrup spilling free onto the platter. Then,
when she ate, the sweetness of the honey warmed her heart. It had
been days since she had eaten properly, and it felt good. She realised
that, despite herself, she was smiling. Then she noticed that Apion's
gaze hung on her features, his lips playing with a redolent smile. Then
his face fell. In the next heartbeat, he averted his eyes. 'Apion? What
is it?'

He shook his head. 'I just,' he started, his words trailing off.
'You remind me of someone.'

'A woman?' she asked, averting his gaze. 'I did not think to
ask of your family, your wife. I hope you do not think me rude . . . '

'I have no family,' Apion cut in. 'War is my only mistress, and a ferocious one she is at that.' He nodded, his stare growing distant. 'No, you reminded me of someone I once broke bread with many years ago. A woman as brash and strident as you, my lady.' Then he looked up, pinning her once more with his gaze. 'And, if I may say, as beautiful.'

'Did you love her?' she asked, shuffling where she sat.

A long silence passed.

'I did,' Apion replied at last. 'There have been other women, but she is the only one I have ever truly loved.' He shrugged. 'But, like so many others, she was lost to me. Now I often wonder if love and loss are inseparable; if one cannot exist without the other.'

A silence passed between them until something twinged in her heart. This brought forth words she had long ago resolved to never speak to another soul. 'When I was a girl, I lived near Ephesus. I gave my word to a boy, the son of a smith, that I would one day marry him. We walked together every day, we rode in the fields, and we made love in the rain, caring little for anything other than each other's embrace. I have never felt such a bond with any other. I have often wondered if it was love I experienced.' She looked to Apion. 'That love came with loss. A brutal loss that I will never forget.'

'He was killed?'

She hesitated at this, unsure if she could let the next words pass her lips. 'God forgive me, yes.' She clasped a hand to her chest and steadied her thudding heart. 'When the boy raped my sister, he took from her, me and my family more than he could ever give. He took her dignity. The wounds he had inflicted upon her were grave, and she bled until she breathed no more.' She barely disguised the choking of a sob.

Apion reached out, tentatively at first, to place a hand upon her shoulder. 'Loss leaves a bitterness in the veins that never fades.'

She nodded. 'Yes . . . yes it does.' She locked her gaze onto Apion's. 'I found him slumped in an inebriate doze later that night, in the straw behind a tavern. I threw water upon his face until he stirred. I wanted to look into his eyes when I did it . . . I took up a dagger and I . . . I . . . ' she fell silent, searching his eyes for revulsion.

Apion held her gaze, his expression unflinching. 'Then we are more alike than I first realised.'

They hovered there, only inches from one another. She blinked at this, confused at the forgotten sensation of true feeling in her blood.

Then he pressed his lips against hers.

She raised her arms as if to strike him. After years of abhorrence of the asp-like men who stalked the palace corridors, this was her instinct. But she realised she was kissing him back, and her arms wrapped around him, pulling at his cloak until it fell free.

He pushed back at this, grasping her by the shoulders, panting, his eyes shaded under a troubled frown. 'Forgive me, my lady.'

She shook her head, unclasping her robe, which slipped silently from her shoulders to reveal her breasts, her nipples erect and tender. 'Don't speak, Apion. For I sense that a long, dark road lies ahead. Let us have one moment of light.' With that, she drew him closer.

Apion unbuckled his klibanion in silence and then it fell to the floor. Then they came together in a passionate embrace.

***

As the small rowing boat parted from the imperial flagship, Psellos watched from the dromon anchored outside the Neorion Harbour, his eyes fixed on the crimson-cloaked figure. He nodded, his hands clasped behind his back.

'Is it as we suspected? He is to ride to Romanus Diogenes?' John Doukas gasped, leaning over the lip of the vessel as if the truth would be revealed to him under scrutiny.

Psellos grinned at the naiveté, the bluntness. This man was a parody of his hot-headed brother. He would make a fine puppet emperor. 'We have forced Eudokia into a corner, master. We have limited her options to the one we know will serve us best. The *Haga* will make a break for the north in the coming days. That, you can be sure of.'

'Then he must die at the gates,' John hissed, punching a fist down onto the rim of the ship.

'That would be folly, master.'

John turned to scowl at him. 'What? Then you suggest we let him live?'

Psellos nodded, a grin bending under his hooked nose. 'Yes, master. But only for a matter of days. When he meets with Diogenes, then we can slay this troublesome strategos *and* the whoreson who shapes to steal your throne . . . '

12. The Golden Heart

The lush green plains of northern Thracia sparkled with morning frost. Overhead, the sky was an unbroken blue, and the winter sun tried in vain to warm the land. To the south, a band of Macedonian Pine forest stretched across the plain, still and silent.

Then a distant rumbling grew in intensity until the treeline rustled and the ground shook. A flock of bullfinches scattered, chirping a fluted song, before a wedge of thirteen horsemen burst from the forest, lowered in their saddles.

Apion rode at the fore, his crimson cloak and plumage billowing in his slipstream, his arms clad in splinted greaves and his torso hugged by his iron klibanion. Immediately behind him on his right rode Dederic in his hooded mail hauberk, with a conical helm and noseguard and a woollen cloak for warmth. Behind him on his left was Igor, the gruff Komes of the Varangoi, whose braided grey locks whipped up behind him. He, like his ten charges, wore their distinctive snow-white armour, tunics, trousers and gold-edged cloaks. The Rus were notoriously awkward horsemen, but they had kept the pace well.

On this, the third morning of their ride from the capital, they had made good ground northwards and were now in sight of the towering Haemus Mountains. Here, the land became a little more ragged and they soon reached a series of grassy foothills, sparkling with the remaining frost and lined by trickling meltwater streams descending from the rocky heights some miles away. Nearing mid-morning, Apion noticed froth on his Thessalian's iron snaffle bit, and the beast's skin was slick with sweat despite the winter chill. He sat up in his saddle and tugged on the reins. The wedge slowed and then stopped with him.

Dismounting, he smoothed the gelding's mane and whispered soothing words in its ear. As he did so, the men of the wedge gathered around him, awaiting orders. 'We can fill our skins while our mounts recover,' he nodded to the nearest stream, 'and cook some hot porridge to warm our blood.'

The varangoi looked to one another in mild disgust. Apion and Dederic shared a spontaneous grin at this.

Despite their hardy origins in the frozen northlands, the Varangoi had been reared on the finest spiced meats, exotic fruits and poached seafood in their years of service in the palace. Thus, the perfunctory food of the armies had not gone down at all well. Indeed, one of them had spent the previous evening groaning after persevering with the gruel, his skin almost as white as his armour before he retched his meal into the fire. This had served to trigger a similar response from another two of his comrades.

'It's only for another few days – then you can reacquaint yourselves with oak-smoked octopus and the like!' Dederic chirped, sliding from his saddle and juggling two compact balls of dried yoghurt, almonds and sesame oil in his hands as he strolled off to the stream.

Apion turned to Igor and pointed to the nearest two foothills. 'I want one man on each of those hills.'

Igor nodded two of his men forward.

'Keep your thoughts focussed and your bows nocked,' Apion called after them as they jogged to their posts. Then he glanced to the spare ration pack he had brought with him from the palace kitchens. 'I'll have toasted bread and cheese sent up to you as soon as it's ready.' A spring was added to their step at this promise.

Apion watched as Igor and the rest of the varangoi set about kindling a fire, bantering in their native tongue. He prised his helmet from his head, then removed one glove and ran his fingers through his matted locks.

He took up his water skin and sipped absently upon it as he looked around this green, well-watered country. So far removed from the baked, terracotta and gold lands of home. Then his thoughts drifted to Sha, Blastares and Procopius, out in the east. *Damn but I miss them,* he thought.

Equally, he had only been parted from old Cydones for a few days, yet he missed the old man's banter already. They had played shatranj on the afternoon before Apion and the riders had slipped from the city. The loss of his sight had done little to dampen Cydones' enthusiasm – and deft skill – for the game. *So you will leave me behind while you ride?* Cydones had mused as they picked their moves. *Quite right; my body is as worn as my mind, and my bones would surely crumble at the mere thought of the gallop!* Then, in his next move, he had pinned Apion's King to the edge of the board. *Checkmate!* The retired strategos had croaked gently, a grin spreading across his features as he set the pieces up to begin another game immediately, not satisfied with this victory alone. Apion could not contain an equal grin at the infectious memory, and he cast a glance back to the south, wondering how the old man would fare in the palace without familiar company. Well, there was Eudokia, he realised, then chided himself for thinking of her.

Since leaving the imperial yacht, he had resolved to lock away any memory of their warm and lasting bout of lovemaking. Her scent, her beauty and her softness had permeated his every thought and laced his dreams every night since. But through it all, he had thought only of Maria, of what could have been with her in another life. He smiled

178

wryly, shaking the thoughts away; just as Eudokia had used the coming together as a harbour of respite, so had he.

Then his distant gaze faded and settled on the forest from which they had come, now far to the south. His eyes narrowed. Something wasn't right. The flight from the city had felt too smooth and that thought had nagged him all the way here. The numeroi were thin on the walls that night – conspicuously so. He searched the sky, littered with circling wagtails. *Where are you when I need you, old lady?*

Then a hand slapped on his shoulder and his heart lurched in his chest.

'Sir!'

Apion spun to Igor. The varangos' eyes were wide with alarm. Behind him, the pair of varangoi atop the foothills were crouched and waving.

'They've spotted something, coming this way,' Igor said, interpreting the signal.

Apion's vision narrowed on the cleft between the two hills. From the rift beyond, he heard a baritone, inhuman roar. A waft of sweet woodsmoke drifted under Apion's nostrils and he shot a glare at the newly kindled fire. 'Douse it!' he hissed. Silently, he beckoned the men with him, fanning his fingers out to have them separate and line the hillsides.

'Have them guard these hills as if they were the palace gates,' he whispered to Igor. Then he picked up a free spear from beside the doused fire, placed his helmet back on and turned to Dederic. 'With me!'

Apion stalked forward, around the rightmost hillock and then ahead of the varangoi. Then he moved along and up the slope of the uneven ridge that ran northwards from the twin hillocks. As they came to the tip of the ridge, another roar pierced the air. This time it was only paces away, from the other side of the ridge. More, the stench of rotting meat wafted in the chill, northerly breeze.

'Sir?' Dederic's eyes were wide.

'Stay your fears, Dederic,' Apion whispered. 'Has ever a roar and foul breath hurt a man?'

Then he stretched his neck up and over the ridge to look down into the narrow corridor on the other side. What he saw, only a few strides away, turned his blood to ice.

'No, but that thing surely has,' Dederic whispered, gawping beside him.

The beast was as magnificent as it was ferocious. Tawny gold fur and a golden mane, its paws as large as a man's head, the tips of dagger-like claws visible under the fur. The lion's jaw hung slightly open, revealing yellowed fangs and a lolling, pink tongue. These mighty creatures were long thought gone from this part of the world. Indeed, even way out east, in the Armenian mountains, they were becoming a rare sight.

Then Apion frowned, noticing the lion's belly as it padded towards the twin hillocks – its skin was taut and its ribs jutted like blades. The beast was starving.

'It is weak?' Dederic suggested, nodding to the beast's belly as it approached.

'Maybe,' Apion said, 'but never is a predator more dangerous than when it is starved.'

'Then we must slay it?' Dederic's eyes bulged in fear as he shot glances at the distance between them and the rest of the varangoi.

'No, we let it pass,' Apion asserted as the lion padded on towards the south. 'It will find prey on the plain.'

'That's not likely to happen, sir,' Dederic nodded to the cleft between the hillocks that stood between the lion and the plain.

Apion turned to see that the varangoi had spilled to the lower ground and levelled their axes towards the lion, barricading the beast's exit from the corridor. The lion stopped at this, then its growl filled the small valley. Apion closed his eyes and muttered a curse. 'Then we must drive it north, back up the rift in the land.'

The little Norman raised his eyebrows. 'We?'

'Think of this beast as the fat lord back in Rouen!' Apion cocked an eyebrow, issuing a mischievous smirk at the same time. 'Now come!' He hissed, then launched up and over the lip and slid down the steep valley embankment, stumbling to a halt before the lion with the aid of his spear shaft. The beast started, took a few tentative steps backwards, then stood tall and emitted a roar that shook Apion's bones. Having displayed its fangs and the wet of the back of its throat, the beast lowered its head, its eyes trained on Apion, its back legs wriggling and then steadying.

Apion's heart thundered.

But, just as the beast was about to launch forward, Dederic tumbled down the banking less than graciously, his mail hauberk jingling like a whore's purse. Then he righted himself, straightened his helmet and quickly levelled his spear at the lion, following Apion's lead. At the same time, the varangoi rushed up to form a line behind the pair.

At this, the lion aborted its attack and paced backwards, snatching glances at them all. Then it risked a glance over its shoulder. Once, twice, and then once more. But it seemed hesitant to flee to the north.

'It doesn't want to go that way, sir?' Dederic surmised.

181

'No,' Apion's eyes narrowed, looking past the beast to the north. The rift wound on for a hundred paces or so and then it adopted a jagged path, concealing the trail ahead. 'Because it is being hunted. Listen!'

To a man, the party fell silent. Then they heard it; the drumming of hooves, echoing through the rift.

'Coming this way?' Dederic deduced.

'With haste,' Apion nodded. His mind spun with thoughts of the Magyar and Pecheneg warbands it could easily be, for this land was just as volatile and permeable as the eastern borderlands. 'Back to the hillocks,' he waved the men back. 'Let the beast through and . . .' his words were cut off as a clutch of riders burst into view from the north, rounding the jagged edge of the rift.

Startled by this threat to its rear, the lion roared out and, in a flash, leapt for Apion at the heart of the line of varangoi, intent on breaking through to the south.

Apion felt the beast's paws thud against his chest like a rock from a trebuchet. The wind was knocked from his lungs and he crashed back onto the earth. His mind flashed with white light and he was lost momentarily. He heard the grating of the lion's claws against his klibanion, iron segments coming free of the armour. Then his vision cleared, and he saw the beast's face, only inches from his. Its pupils were dilated in terror. Its lips curled back and its jaws extended to crush his neck.

Then there was a crunching of bone and flesh and Apion was showered in hot blood. But there was no pain. The beast's eyes dimmed at this, the fear replaced by resignation as blood washed from its mouth.

Apion wheezed as the creature toppled from his chest, a spear lodged between its shoulder blades. He rolled back from its corpse and looked around him to see that Dederic and the varangoi still held their spears and axes, halted mid-stride in coming to his aid.

'No! This was not to be!' A voice called out from the pack of approaching riders.

Apion stood, gasping for breath and grappling for his sword hilt. But the tension eased from him when he saw that the clutch of horsemen – sixty of them, he estimated – were clearly Byzantine. They were adorned in the fine iron garb of the kataphractoi. Their boots, tunics and armour bore scrapes and stains that told of recent conflict.

From the armies of the north? Apion wondered as they slowed to a trot.

The lead rider trotted forward – a man a few years Apion's senior. His armour was particularly finely crafted, and he wore a fine, white silk cloak on his sturdy shoulders. His broad and handsome face was wrinkled in a scowl, his teeth bared. His flaxen locks were swept back from his forehead and his cobalt glare pinned the lion's corpse.

The rider did not look to any of Apion and his party. Instead, he flicked his glare from the lion to the rider by his side who had thrown the spear. 'You fool,' he grappled the man by the collar and shook him. 'If I wanted another cadaver I could have had my pick from the battlefields!'

'Sir, I was not aiming to strike the beast. I wanted to halt its flight . . . '

While the man who had killed the beast mumbled an apology, Apion eyed the leader, and his gaze fell on something – a tiny trinket that hung around the man's neck. A chain with a small heart pendant dangling over his breastbone. It was pure gold. The hairs on Apion's neck lifted.

The Golden Heart will rise in the west. At dawn, he will wear the guise of a lion hunter. Apion saw the crone's features in his mind's

183

eye. He had forgotten her words in the turmoil of these last months, now they were as crisp and clear as winter meltwater. *At noon, he will march to the east as if to counter the sun itself. At dusk you will stand with him in the final battle, like an island in the storm . . .*

Yet his first words to the man were instinctive. 'Something of an uneven contest, was it not?' He nodded to the lion's corpse then swept a hand around the man and his sixty riders.

The man twisted to Apion, releasing his grip on the spearless rider as he did so. Then, as if waking from a dream, the scowl fell from the man's face. He blinked, almost as if just realising that Apion and the varangoi were present.

'I had no intention of killing such a fine beast,' the man shook his head. 'The Magyar Prince who bestowed him upon me thought I would delight in having such a creature to parade.' His gaze darkened under a frown. 'But the animal was terrified, from the moment the Pecheneg traders dragged him from Armenia and shipped him across the Pontus Euxinus, then for every moment of his wretched life in the war zone along the Istros in these last months.' The man sighed. 'No, I came to recapture the beast after it escaped my camp,' he shot a saturnine look at the rider by his side. 'I did not come to kill it, I wished only to see it returned to its homeland. However, perhaps this outcome is a bittersweet providence – for it is at peace now and will suffer no more torturous journeys.'

'Aye,' Apion nodded at this, 'perhaps.'

'But the spectacle of a lion in these parts is almost rivalled by the sight of imperial Varangoi,' the man mused, stroking his chin. 'Who are you and where are you headed?'

Apion hesitated, searching the man's eyes. Instinct told him that he could trust this one. 'We are in search of the commander of the armies of the north.'

The man's face fell expressionless. 'Romanus Diogenes?'

Apion took a breath to answer and then hesitated. He juggled with the possibility of revealing his mission, remembering his sense of unease, earlier. Then he glanced to the golden heart pendant once more and his doubts faded. He held out a roll of paper, the seal unbroken. 'Lady Eudokia has sent for him.'

The man took the paper and traced a finger across the seal, then he held it to his nose and inhaled the sweet scent Eudokia had laced it with and broke into a broad grin.

'Then you have found him.'

Apion's eyes widened. All around him, the varangoi stooped to one knee, hands across their hearts, heads bowed.

***

Romanus' camp was vast. Apion had seen such a sight only few times in the east; the riders of the Hikanatoi Tagma, together with the infantry of the Paradunavum Thema, stationed together on the plain with innumerable bands of mercenary Oghuz, Pechenegs, Magyars, Normans and Rus. The sea of tents stretched from the banks of the River Istros to the hills in the west and the horizon in the east, all wrapped in a ditch and palisade wall. Banners fluttered in the breeze under a murky sky that threatened snow. The soldiers wandered between the campfires and tents, pulling their cloaks tighter, muttering in muted tones and chewing on their rations.

'This land reeks of conflict,' Dederic spoke.

Apion turned to him. The Norman was standing by a fire with Igor and the other varangoi, just inside the main gate of the camp. The Rus bantered amongst themselves, toasting bread in the flames and supping on their soured wine, some grooming their mounts.

'Aye,' Apion replied, 'So very different from the borderlands I know, yet so very similar.' He looked into the sea of tents. They had ridden north at haste for three more days to finalise Romanus' departure from his armies. Now they waited on the emperor-to-be to return from the depths of the camp and begin the swift journey back to Constantinople. He looked to the south, through the camp gates. 'And that's what worries me – we must stay sharp on our return journey.'

'Why so grim?' A voice called out. 'Bitter at the prospect of leaving such luxury behind after only a short visit?'

Apion turned to face front again; Romanus trotted from the heart of the camp on his white stallion. He led twelve kataphractoi with him, and another twelve scout riders carried supplies on their backs. The soldiers at every point in the camp had risen to their feet, saluting and cheering their leader.

Apion smiled at this. 'Aye, back to bleakness of marble halls, platters of goose meat and jugs of rich wine.'

Romanus returned his wry grin. His riders formed up with Apion's and they readied to leave the camp. Then, at the last, Romanus lifted his sword from his scabbard, pumping it in the air. The men of the camp erupted in a unified roar this time.

'Basileus!'

***

They headed south across the plains at a steady gallop. On the third day they rose early and set off without eating, stopping only at midday to cook a meal of cheese on toasted bread then nuts and honey washed down with soured wine. Then they rode once more. Just as the light began to fade, they reached the conifer forest, thick with the scent of pine. They slowed here, picking through the soft bracken trail.

Romanus had pinpointed a small dell with a stream nearby about three miles into the woods where they could make camp for the night, and this would leave them only two days distant from Constantinople.

A pair of varangoi rode ahead as a vanguard, then Apion and Romanus followed behind, the rest of the riders forming a double breasted column in their wake.

Their chat had been awkward at first, with Apion unable to shake off the memory of the lustful encounter he and Eudokia had shared, and the guilt that came with it whenever he looked her betrothed in the eye. But Romanus seemed as tentative as Eudokia had been with regard to the romantic side of their coming marriage. *A beauty with a heart of pure ice,* he had scoffed bitterly. *Did she tell you she had me exiled and even threatened to have me executed?*

This had set him at ease somewhat. Still, he was glad when the conversation moved on to Romanus' thoughts on how the empire's ills should be addressed.

'The empire has been contracting for too long. Loss has become acceptable,' Romanus continued, his breath clouding in the chill. 'From the loss of Syria and the lucrative trade routes that disappeared with it, to the loss of Tunisia and the precious cereal crop and olive groves.' He shook his head. 'There are many ills to be tackled, Strategos. From the tax system to the armies. From the heart of the empire, stretching out to the borderlands that you and I know only too well.'

Apion nodded. 'In the past, the empire would fund the armies of the outlying themata, allowing them to defend their homes. Now it takes from us, preferring to entrust the empire's welfare to mercenary tagmata loyal only to imperial gold. We are in a sorry state, sir.'

Romanus shrugged, squaring his shoulders and rolling his head. 'It will be corrected. That may not sit well with the magnates of

187

Anatolia. But damn them if they think I'm going to be another lapdog for the rich.'

Apion thought of Psellos and the Doukids. 'There are some who might be cowed, sir. Yet there are others who are rooted in the imperial court. In these last months I have seen terrible deeds carried out by these types.'

Romanus shot him a narrow-eyed look, nodding. 'I know the lie of the imperial court, Strategos. It has festered for too long. It needs washing clean from top to bottom.'

Apion smiled at this. 'Only Lady Eudokia has spoken with such frankness since I came west.'

Romanus grinned. 'That is why we will make a tenacious pairing. I want the capital to become what it once was; a beating heart, a beacon of inspiration. God's true city, as it once was.'

Apion did not reply to this, glancing at the white band of skin on his wrist.

But Romanus continued; 'A city garrisoned with non-partizan tagmata. *Armamenta* stocked high with weapons and armour. Did you know that the capital once held enough ore in its workshops to forge four thousand blades?'

Apion thought over the military treatise he had read through in the library at Trebizond. 'Aye, enough to equip an entire imperial tagma. The city armamenta is to be restored to its past greatness, sir?'

'Indeed,' Romanus leaned in closer, a wry grin spreading across his face. 'And so will those of the outlying themata. The workhouses will provide arms and armour for all our armies.'

Apion thought of Alp Arslan's words, dismissing the empire's demise as a certainty. Suddenly they sounded distant and weak. A warmth grew in his heart, and one word resonated in his thoughts. 'The greatest thing you can bestow upon the empire is hope, sir.'

Romanus nodded. 'That will follow when the people see change around them. But there is much to do. It was once the case that we were strong enough to mount a challenge against our aggressors on the western and the eastern borders simultaneously. It has not been this way for some time. I have watched as, after years of campaigning to bring the Bulgar rebels and Magyar armies to their knees, the armies of the west have been drawn away from the cusp of victory – sent east to push back the armies of the Seljuk Sultanate.'

Apion nodded. 'The converse is equally true. Four summers ago, I led the remainder of the Chaldian and Colonean Themata into Armenia. We pinned Alp Arslan and his army – some twenty thousand riders, twice our strength – in the rocky passes. In such terrain, the advantage of their mounts was lost, and they were hemmed in by a wall of my spears. We were weeks from forcing them into submission, weeks!' Apion clenched a fist as if grasping out for that elusive victory. 'Then a doux led his tagma to our camp. Not to reinforce us, not to elicit surrender or to hammer home victory and seal lasting peace in the east. He handed me a scroll bearing an imperial seal, then led more than half of my men away to the coast, where they were shipped to the west. We were forced to fight a long and bloody retreat from those mountains.'

Romanus patted his stallion's mane, nodded and chuckled mirthlessly. 'Then we have a common history, Strategos. Did you know that I spent my youth in Cappadocia? I rode in the east when I was a boy. And now I must turn my sights to the rising sun once more. I have yet to clash swords with Alp Arslan, but it is only a matter of time. I have heard much rumour of the sultan's guile and ferocity.'

'The rumours are well-founded,' Apion replied earnestly.

'And that is why I need men like you by my side in the years ahead,' Romanus concluded with an earnest gaze.

189

They rode on in silence, and Apion noticed that the light had faded almost completely and that Dederic had struck up a torch. This cast a ghostly orange glow on their immediate surroundings, every shadow dancing like a demon. Only the muted shuffle of hooves, the snort of horses and the crackling of dry bracken pierced the stillness. When an owl hooted from the depths of the woods ahead, Apion started, then chided himself with a ghost of a grin.

Then the piercing shriek of an eagle split the air, high above. The other men of the column glanced up in weary half-interest. But Apion's spine chilled. He frowned, peering into the darkness ahead.

There, a wisp of wintry mist swirled and took shape. He recognised her immediately; the silvery hair, the puckered features. But her sightless eyes were bulging in horror. She pressed one finger to her lips. Then she was gone, and darkness prevailed once more.

Apion slowed his mount to a halt and placed a hand across the chest of Romanus. 'Be still, be silent.'

'Strategos?' Romanus asked, his face creased in confusion. The rest of the column slowed up behind them and the pair of varangoi in the vanguard twisted in their saddles, frowning in puzzlement.

Apion did not answer. His brow dipped as he scanned the forest around them.

Then he heard it, the continued snapping of bracken in the darkness. His eyes widened.

At that instant, hissing filled the air like a hundred asps.

'Shields!' he roared.

The column rustled into life, but not before the arrow hail hit home. The hissing died with a series of wet punches of iron bursting into flesh. Sparks flew as arrowheads hammered into armour, helms and shields. Gurgling cries rang out as the stricken slid from their mounts. Horses whinnied and reared up and at once the column was in disarray.

Finally the arrow hail slowed and stopped. A dozen riders lay slain and still on the forest floor. Apion heeled his mount round, his eyes scanning the blackness over the rim of his shield.

'Brigands?' Romanus gasped as he circled on his mount likewise.

Apion pulled a shaft from his shield – it was squat, thick and the iron heads were heavy; these were no arrows, they were darts launched from a *solenarion*, far more powerful than a normal bow at such close range. A weapon used in these parts only, and sparingly, by the empire. 'No, assassins!'

Romanus' eyes widened as he heard bowstrings stretching once more in the darkness, all around them. 'Dismount and form *foulkon!*' he cried to his men.

The remaining riders slid from their saddles and bundled together with Romanus and Apion, raising their shields around them and overhead to form a miniature protective shell. The bowstrings twanged and another round of hissing filled the air. The huddled group braced and then shuddered as the darts hammered home. A series of gurgling cries rang out and the group shrank further.

'They're coming closer!' Apion realised as he noticed that some of the darts had punched right through the shields this time. He turned to Dederic. 'Give me light!'

Dederic looked at him, wide-eyed, then nodded as realisation dawned. The Norman scrambled out from the foulkon to grasp at the torch, lying on the forest floor where he had dropped it. Then he scurried back into the shield canopy, darts smacking into the dirt in his wake.

Apion tore a strip from his tunic, then handed it to Igor. The varangos hurriedly tied it around the head of an arrow shaft and held it to Dederic's torch. 'Ready? Break!' Apion cried. As one, the foulkon parted, Igor stood and fired the flaming arrow into the depths of the forest. Then, just as quickly, the foulkon reformed. From the gaps in their shields, they watched as the arrow punched down. Sparks ignited the dried leaves all around it. In the glow, the silhouettes of their attackers flitted between the trees. They wore conical Byzantine helmets and padded vests. Apion counted more than fifteen of them before the flames died.

Another hissing volley of solenarion bolts hammered down on the foulkon. Three more varangoi crumpled.

'I can't see them properly. I need more light!' Apion barked, ripping another strip from his tunic. The rest of the men followed suit.

Then one of Romanus' riders nudged Apion, offering him a round, wax sealed clay jar. 'Try this.'

Apion held the wax seal to his nose and caught scent of the acrid stench from inside. His eyes glinted, then he shot up and hurled the jar at the last of the embers from the fire arrow. At once, the jar exploded into an orange vision of hell. Apion watched as the Greek fire engulfed the forest before him like the dark door incarnate. A pair of assassins tumbled around, their skin and clothes ablaze, their cries falling mute as the flames drew the breath from their lungs. Another eighteen silhouettes remained only paces away, hurriedly nocking bolts to their bows.

'Stand!' Apion roared. 'Their strength was the darkness. Now we can fight them. They have assumed that victory is theirs – look how close they have come.' At this, the varangoi stood and formed a line, ready to charge. Then Romanus waved his dismounted riders to their feet likewise, and raised his spathion overhead.

'Advance!' he roared.

Like a mirror shattering, the line exploded forward, each man lurching out, hefting their axes and spathions.

Apion's heart hammered on his ribs as he rushed for the assassin before him. The assassin threw down the solenarion and fumbled to draw his sword. Apion kicked the blade from the assassin's grip and then swiped his own blade down, gouging a crimson trough through the man's chest. Hot blood sprayed on Apion's skin as the man toppled. Then he spun just in time to parry a swipe at his neck, before jabbing his sword hilt into this next attacker's face, feeling bones crunch under the blow. The assassin fell away, his cheekbone caved in.

Apion stalked through the melee to locate his next opponent. He dodged under swinging spathions and swiping Rus axes. Then he saw that three of the assassins had isolated Romanus, and were driving at him with their swords. Romanus fought like a lion, parrying two strikes but taking a cut to his neck from a third, blood spidering over his moulded breastplate. Apion rushed to his aid, slashing the hamstrings of the nearest assassin and then sending a right hook into the jaw of the next, who spun away with a grunt, then twisted back round only to receive Apion's boot on the bridge of his nose followed by the edge of the scimitar across his throat. Romanus despatched the third, punching his spathion through the man's chest and kicking the corpse away.

The pair staked their blades in the ground, panting, hearing the rest of their riders cry out in victory before breaking out in solemn prayer, some dropping to their knees, others clutching hands to their hearts.

'Who were they?' Romanus puffed, nodding to the corpses before them as one of his men tended to his neck wound.

193

Apion pressed his boot on the body of the assassin he had punched, then rolled him over. The man was dressed as a skutatos, there was no doubt of that.

Igor answered, his eyes wide. 'I recognise this cur from the Numera barracks.'

'He is a soldier of the Numeroi?' Romanus' face was creased in a frown, then he looked at Apion. 'Loyal to Psellos and the Doukids?'

'Like a vile stench,' Apion nodded.

Igor looked to Apion and Romanus. 'I doubt he is a mere infantryman,' he said, plucking a solenarion bolt from the man's quiver, then looking around in the darkness. 'This work reeks of the portatioi – the dark-hearted bastards at the core of their ranks that live to spill blood. Torturers and cut-throats.'

'They've followed us all the way here,' Apion realised.

'Strategos?' Romanus exclaimed.

Apion's reply caught in his throat as he heard the stretching of one more bowstring.

He leapt forward, punching Romanus back with the heels of his hands. A bolt sliced through the air and smacked into the tree where Romanus had been a heartbeat before.

Apion and Romanus gawped at each other.

The thudding of a lone set of hooves echoed somewhere in the darkness, heading south and growing fainter.

Apion mounted his gelding, holding Romanus' gaze. 'Out here we are in grave danger. Rest will have to wait. We must ride and reach Constantinople at haste.'

***

A thick fog had settled over the north of Constantinople, filling the valleys and even creeping over the peak of the sixth hill. The shadows of the few who were brave enough to tread these streets at night swirled and faded in the moonlight.

The broad northern imperial way was somewhat imbalanced, lined on one side with a dilapidated tavern and a selection of brothels, and on the other with the marble walls of the Cistern of Aetius. The way ended at the city walls and the Adrianople gate. The gatehouse towered high above, the crenellations and the tiny figures of the sentries silhouetted in the ghostly moonlight.

Hidden in the doorway of a derelict tenement a few doors down from the tavern, two gaunt and filthy men lurked. They watched as a drunken trader staggered from the door of the tavern, casting an ethereal orange glow on the greyness momentarily. He hobbled – partly from inebriation and partly from the festering wound on his leg. A purse dangled from his belt, chinking with coins with his every faltering step. The pair looked at one another and then nodded, before scuttling unnoticed through the fog to flank the drunk, each of them slipping daggers from their belts. Like wolves, they leapt upon the man, muffling his cries with a hand over his mouth. Then one of them hammered a dagger hilt into the man's temple. The man crumpled, and the pair fumbled to free his purse. The first thief batted the hands of the other away, then the other pushed his accomplice back. In an instant, they were growling at one another, like scavengers over a carcass, hands bloodied, daggers levelled. Just then, approaching footsteps echoed down the street. Footsteps and the clanking of iron. They both snapped their glares round on the swirling mist down the street.

'Numeroi!' The first hissed, then scurried back into the silvery veil of fog.

The second grunted at this, flicking his gaze between the purse – still tied to the dead man's belt – and the approaching footsteps. His eyes widened as shapes formed in the mist. Two ironclad numeroi of the city garrison bookended a pair of hooded figures, one hunched and small, the other tall, with ghostly silver eyes peering out from under the hood. Then, at last, the purse came free. He spun and scrambled towards the walls and away from the figures, slipping and sliding on the flagstones. He had run only a handful of steps when a pair of arrows punched into his back. The thief crumpled to his hands and knees, crawling, spluttering black blood from his lips. Then, when the tall, silver-eyed man clicked his fingers, one of the numeroi jogged forward and dragged his spathion blade across the thief's throat and he fell still.

At this, the trader stirred, groaning, clutching his head. In a haze, he looked up at the four who had saved him. 'God bless you!' he clasped his hands together and bowed as he struggled to his feet.

'Nobody must witness my presence here,' the squat, hooded figure hissed, '*nobody!*'

The silver-eyed one by his side nodded at this, then slipped a sickle from his cloak and nicked the trader's neck. The trader's eyes bulged and he mouthed silent words of confusion as black blood haemorrhaged from the arterial tear. Then his skin drained of colour and he slumped to the ground.

Psellos stepped over the corpses and picked his way through the pooling blood. The deaths of these nameless individuals were an irrelevance to him at best. He looked up to the end of the street and the Adrianople Gate. The vast, arched timber gates were as tall as four men, hugged by bands of rusting iron, and barred by a length of timber hewn from a single, tall beech. When they reached the entrance to the gatehouse, another pair of loyal numeroi waited there.

'Where is he?' Psellos spoke abruptly.

'On the walls, sir,' the numeros replied, nodding up to the battlements.

The four ascended the stairway until they emerged onto the battlements. This, the inner wall, stood tall and clear of the carpet of fog. The limestone walkway was bathed in clear moonlight, the towers that studded it were as large as forts. Looking back into the city, only the Hagia Sofia, the Imperial Palace, the Aqueduct of Valens and a militia of fine columns rose above the fog. Looking west, out of the city, the outer wall and the moat were swamped by the fog, and the countryside and crop fields of Thracia were likewise cloaked.

Psellos saw the lone figure standing in the shadows of a crenellation. The rider's face was bathed in sweat, his hair matted to his forehead as he clutched his helmet underarm. He strode to the man. 'It is done?'

The man's eyes gave it away before he spoke.

'No, sir. Romanus lives, though many of his retinue were felled. I have ridden for days without food, rest or shelter. To be sure that news would reach you while you still have time . . . '

'And the *Haga*? I trust that at least this troublesome thorn has been pruned?'

The man's lips trembled. 'He fought like a demon, sir. The men – Romanus' men – they fought on his word.'

'You and your men failed.' Psellos cut the man off, his chest tightening. 'Yet you purport to be one of my finest?' He had promoted this fool into his portatioi on a day when he had been suffering from a crushing headache. The folly of his hasty actions would be costly. He looked to Zenobius. 'Zenobius is an example I had hoped you would follow. He sets aside his soul, his fears, his wants, and he never fails me. Never.'

The rider's lips flapped uselessly and he nodded hurriedly.

'Zenobius, afford this man a lesson in efficacy.'

The albino turned his expressionless gaze upon the shivering rider and grappled him by the throat, crushing the cry of fear from the man's larynx. Then he reached down with his free hand to grasp the rider by the belt. Finally, he lifted the man up and over the dipped section of the crenellations. The rider thrashed like a sturgeon, then the albino released him. His body fell into the fog like a stone, his roar hoarse and muted. Then, a wet crunch of bone echoed between the inner and outer walls.

Psellos inhaled the chill night air through his nostrils and looked to the north-west. 'It is nearing dawn. Romanus must be only a short ride from the walls.'

'You should have sent me,' the albino spoke flatly.

'Aye,' Psellos mused. 'Your time will come, Zenobius.'

'I could have a dagger in Romanus' back even before he reaches the Forum of the Ox?'

Psellos chuckled dryly at the albino's stolid tenacity. 'Once Romanus is inside the city, it will become too dangerous to attempt an assassination. The balance of power will remain, we must bide our time.'

'Hmm,' Zenobius replied flatly. 'And what of the Strategos of Chaldia – I could have his throat opened before noon?'

Psellos sighed, his nose wrinkling as he thought of the aftermath of Nilos' murder. The man's death had put the fear of God into the people, but it had also swayed the Optimates Tagma to favour Romanus Diogenes' rise to the throne. 'He will die, but we do not need another martyr. No, we have to pick our time to slay the *Haga*.'

Then he wagged a finger, a smile creeping across his face. 'But in the meantime, we can wound him.'

Zenobius' silver eyes betrayed absolutely nothing. 'Torture?'

'No. I have found out much about his past in these last months,' Psellos mused. 'To hurt the *Haga*, you must hurt the few that he loves.'

***

Cydones stepped out onto the balcony of his sleeping chamber, then pulled his woollen cloak tight around his shoulders as the bitter fog rolled around him.

'A lungful of night air and a bellyful of salep before I sleep,' he chuckled wryly, wrapping his fingers around his cup, enjoying its warmth.

At this hour, the streets were near silent and he wondered what the great city that was spread out below him might look like. He thumbed at his Chi-Rho necklace, but it did little to fend off the air of melancholy that descended upon him. His memories of the place were all from his boyhood, and they were anything but happy. He wondered, given the tension in the palace since they had arrived – was anyone truly happy in this, God's city? Indeed, the mutilation of the noble and affable strategos, Nilos, had cast a dark shadow on his faith. Cydones felt the chill reach his heart as he remembered Apion reluctantly describing the body they found.

Uttering a weary sigh, he slipped back into his bedchamber, the tap-tapping of his cane echoing as he closed the shutters behind him. Despite being indoors, he kept his cloak on. Even the underfloor heating inside the palace struggled to fend off the winter chill. He decided he would sleep wearing his thick woollen tunic and trousers tonight. So he shuffled across his room, tapping with his cane, then hung his cloak on a nearby chair before sitting on the edge of his bed. He reached out to feel for the bedside table. There sat the shatranj board and the pieces of the unfinished game he and Apion had started. He inhaled the sweet scent of his salep and took a sip, the creamy orchid root and cinnamon flavouring coating his throat. At this, his mood lifted once more.

Apion had first convinced him to try the Seljuk drink many years ago, and now it had become ingrained in his pre-bed ritual. In the darkness behind his sightless eyes he saw the young Apion as he was back then. A boy with a crutch, fresh-faced and sharp-eyed. Now *that* was a memory that stirred happiness from his heart. The crutch was gone now, and when Cydones last had the power of sight, Apion's face was scarred, weathered and battered. But the emerald eyes remained sharp as ever. Then a shadow of guilt passed over his heart as he recalled encouraging Apion to join the ranks of the thema. He wondered what Apion could have been had he not been drawn into the war.

'That boy was destined to hold a sword regardless,' he muttered, breaking into a dry chuckle. 'In any case, an old fool like me can do little to change things now.'

He supped down the last of his salep and then patted around on the bed to find the lip of the blankets.

But as he did so, the icy fingers of a draught danced on the skin of his neck.

He frowned. *I'm sure I closed the shutters?*

Then he realised he was not alone.

'What do you want?' he spoke without fear.

Silence. Only a foetid stench, like rotting meat wedged between foul teeth. Then a hoarse cackle echoed through the room. But there was another presence too, cold and silent.

'There are two of you, aren't there? You think you have an easy job on your hands, don't you?' Cydones felt a burst of the old battle-rage surge through his weary limbs. He grimaced and hefted his cane, his arms trembling with fury. 'Well, come on then . . . you *whoresons!*'

The old man leapt towards the source of the cackling, his bones cracking in protest. He swept the cane back, and his mind flashed with memories of his halcyon years as a mighty strategos. The glory and the bloodshed tore at his emotions as always. Then something cold and hard punched into his chest and he was stilled, mid-leap. His arms fell limply to his sides and his head lolled forward. Was this the fatal wound that he had avoided for all these years? He felt no pain, only numbness.

Then he slid from the lance and crumpled to the floor.

As he lay there, his thoughts dimming, he heard the footsteps of his assassins disappear through the shutters.

He shivered as the life slipped from his body. His last thoughts were of Apion and those he would leave behind.

Yes, it was going to be a long, cold winter.

13. Numb

It was the day of the Nativity of Christ. A faint orange glow tinged the night sky to the east and the land of southern Thracia was quiet and still, the fog clearing at last. The vast tracts of farmland either side of the dilapidated *Via Egnatia* were devoid of workers. The fields sown with garlic, chard, onions, dill, lettuce, cabbages and mint in the warmer months now lay brown and fallow. Then a clutch of riders burst over one hillside from the north, and raced onto the highway, haring to the east.

Apion rode alongside Romanus near the head of the column, their eyes trained on the eastern horizon. The chill winter wind had long since numbed his face and the land seemed to stretch on forever.

Then at last the mighty double walls of Constantinople rose into view, the moat before them sparkling in the dawn light.

Igor cried out at this; 'Nobiscum Deus!'

'Nobiscum Deus!' The rest cried out in reply, raising their swords overhead.

God's city, Apion thought, *and barely a darker place in this world have I ever known.*

'Can you feel it, Strategos?' Romanus gasped over the rush of the air.

Apion fired a glance at him. 'Sir?'

'It's within our grasp now,' he motioned with a clenched fist. 'Everything we have talked of in these last days.'

'We're not inside the city yet, sir.' Apion countered. The irony was that Romanus was probably at his safest near Psellos, for inside the city walls any assassination attempt could not so easily be disguised as brigandage or misfortune. Apion's eyes swept along the tops of the walls as they approached the city.

The purple imperial banners and the embroideries of the Virgin Mary and the saints fluttered defiantly on every tower, and glinting helms and speartips ran the length of the battlements.

Numeroi? Apion wondered. Then he focused on the gate they would enter the city by – if any last-ditch treachery was to happen, it would be here.

The Golden Gate was the ceremonial entrance to the city. The smaller outer wall presented an ornate but squat arched gateway, adorned with sculptures of emperors past on prancing stallions and topped with a ceremonial gilded Cross. The tower-studded inner wall yawned with the vast, marble arch of the main gateway. The two flanking towers were more like citadels, broad and sturdy, and they formed only two corners of the colossal fort that extended inside the city, protecting this entrance.

All seemed sedate. As usual, the gates were open and the first throngs of daily trade traffic rode back and forth – wagons, mule trains and farmers hauling their wares on their shoulders.

Then Apion noticed something. A silhouette emerging from the Golden Gate. A clutch of over one hundred riders. They rode not with the lethargy of tired traders, but at an urgent gallop, haring for Apion and Romanus. The pair looked to one another. The wedge slowed.

'Sir, be on your guard,' Apion pleaded. 'This may be a ploy.'

Romanus nodded with a brisk sigh. 'Aye, be readied, men.' He spoke over his shoulders to the rest of the wedge, while three varangoi moved to shield him.

But as the riders approached, Apion noticed that they too were varangoi, and he instantly recognised the one they surrounded. The slender shoulders and delicate features. The ice-cold gaze, the silver-streaked blonde locks tied tightly atop her head. The tension melted from his heart. 'At ease,' he said, 'it is Lady Eudokia.'

'At ease?' Romanus cocked an eyebrow in an attempt to disguise his relief. 'Then you must know a side to her that I don't,' he said with a dry chuckle.

Apion smiled at this, hiding the trace of guilt in his heart.

The varangoi escorting Eudokia slid from their mounts and formed a rigid line, axes glinting in the rising sun, offering curt nods to Igor and their comrades. Eudokia's eyes narrowed as she looked to Romanus, and a chill breeze lifted a loose lock of her hair.

Apion kept his eyes fixed on the reins of his mount, wary of meeting Eudokia's gaze. Their moment was gone, and now she was to wed the man who would lead the empire from the flames. Yet a more frosty welcome would have been difficult to conjure.

Romanus slipped from his saddle and bowed as he approached her, then lifted her hand and kissed it adroitly. 'My lady, I have ridden at great haste, as you compelled me to. All is well?' Romanus asked her.

'I would not phrase it as such. But you are here now.' Eudokia frowned, seeing the crusted blood on the armour of the emperor-to-be and his men. 'You met with trouble?'

'Trouble tends to follow a man when he is headed for the imperial throne,' Romanus replied with a deadpan expression.

'Indeed,' she sneaked a glance back at the city walls. 'Now let us not linger. The city streets writhe with enemies. But the gate has been garrisoned with men loyal to me, and the Imperial Way is lined with them too.' She extended a hand to the varangoi who had accompanied her. Her gaze was hard. 'My men will escort you. Once we are in the palace grounds, you can bathe, eat and have your bruises and scrapes tended to. Then we can talk.'

Romanus clicked his fingers to his weary kataphractoi riders. 'Indeed, there is much to talk of,' he nodded, remounting and heeling his stallion into a trot. His gaze hung on Eudokia until he broke into a canter and moved ahead with his escort towards the gate.

Eudokia watched him go and then turned to behold Apion, Igor, Dederic and the handful of weary varangoi who had survived the sortie. Then she moved her mount over to Apion.

He felt awkwardness pull at his thoughts as he searched for some form of greeting.

'They nearly slew us, my lady. Psellos had riders track us all the way. They waited until we had rendezvoused with Romanus and then they struck in the forests to the north. I fear that before he ascends the throne, they will . . . '

'Apion,' Eudokia stopped him. Her voice firm, but her eyes were heavy with sadness.

'My lady?' Apion frowned.

Eudokia took a deep breath. 'The subterfuge was widespread. While you were gone . . . ' her voice trailed off. She held something out to him.

Apion stared at Cydones' neatly folded white robe and cane.

***

The winter morning was crisp and clear. Apion sat on the edge of a fountain in the frost-speckled palace gardens, the skeletal trees standing watch around him. He was dressed in his woollen tunic, trousers and crimson cloak. He wore his hair knotted back from his face, his eyes red but dry. His mind was numb after days of grieving and his chest seemed to be hollow and devoid of feeling. The chill December air stung at his nostrils as he searched for his reflection in the fountain's waters, but found only the uninvited image of old Cydones' shattered body. A good-hearted man who had fought for the empire until he could no longer wield a sword. Slain by his own kind in the heart of that empire while he readied to sleep.

He thought of the solemn boat journey past the southern sea walls that morning. Cydones' sarcophagus had sat near the prow of the ship for his final journey. *You always did prefer sea travel, old friend*, Apion reminisced. A half smile touched his lips before sorrow stole it away. The ship had docked near the Golden Gate, and then the sarcophagus had been taken to the Monastery of St Nikolaos where he was buried with ceremony befitting his gallant life. Xiphilinos, the Patriarch of Constantinople, led the prayer, as he had done for the handful of others who had lost their lives in these last months.

The image of Psellos burned in Apion's thoughts.

He did not notice the screeching of an eagle from high above the gardens. Then a silvery-haired figure appeared beside him. She traced her fingers in the fountain's waters.

'I chided you before for the blackness in your heart,' she said, 'but I now realise I was wrong to do so.'

Apion did not turn to her.

'It was something your old friend once said that made me realise this. No man can exist with an entirely pure heart. Darkness has no meaning without light, and light must know darkness to have any purpose. Darkness and light are entwined. To be a man is to be both.'

Apion's eyes welled with tears once more as she said this. 'Then you must know that darkness will cast its shadow on my heart today.'

206

She nodded. 'I know this. I will not chide you for what happens today. But promise me something, Apion,' she clasped his arm. 'After today, let the hope that lies before you flourish. The Golden Heart is rising. All we have spoken of before lies in your grasp.'

Apion saw Psellos' image again. Now it flickered and he saw the dark door, the voice behind it whispering. 'Aye, but that is for tomorrow. Today, darkness will reign.'

A set of footsteps snapped him from his thoughts. 'Who are you talking to, sir?'

He looked up to see Dederic approaching, a fur wrapped around his shoulders. He glanced to his side. On the edge of the fountain where the crone had sat, a creeping winter vine was coiled, its tendrils stretching out over the water's surface. An eagle cried overhead.

'Sir?' Dederic asked again.

'Are they ready?' Apion asked, his breath clouding in the chill.

The Norman nodded, firing glances around the gardens. 'The north hall is empty. The varangoi are waiting on us.'

Apion swept his cloak around his shoulders and followed Dederic inside the palace. This man was noble and he would make a fine tourmarches right enough – just as Cydones had suggested. The thought of the old man's features sent another pang of grief through his chest. Then Apion steeled himself; those who had hurt him in the past had paid dearly for their crimes. Now others would suffer his wrath. Slaying Psellos would pose risk of civil war and so he could not slake that thirst . . . yet. But he could show the adviser just how close a scimitar blade could plunge into his realm of duplicity. His heart thudded under his ribs and the blood pounded in his ears. He focused on the image of the dark door. He longed to feel the flames behind lick at his skin.

Inside the palace, two varangoi waited on them, one carrying a crackling torch. They offered curt nods and then led Apion and Dederic to the north hall, a large room studded with sculptures and busts. The varangoi moved to one statue and pushed it to the side, the grumble of marble upon marble echoing throughout the room. Behind the statue lay a small but thick timber door. Apion and Dederic looked to one another as one varangos unlocked it. From there they were led along a dark and musty corridor, lined with cobwebs as it descended.

'This passage is known to none other than the varangoi,' the nearest of the two guards whispered back over his shoulder. 'Even the emperors have never known of its existence.'

'But it takes us there?' Apion spoke abruptly.

'Right into the heart,' the varangos nodded solemnly. They walked on until the varangoi stopped. 'Look, we are here.' He pointed to a trap door on the floor of the corridor. 'Are you ready?'

Apion took the swordbelt holding his scimitar from the varangos and Dederic took his longsword likewise. They wore no armour, but they would not need it. 'We're ready,' Apion nodded.

The varangoi hauled at a ring of iron and the trap door creaked open, revealing only darkness below, along with the whimpering of broken men.

Apion buckled his swordbelt and then nodded to Dederic. Then he dropped into the space below.

With a muted thud he landed, crouching, enshrouded in his crimson cloak. He perched there, waiting for his eyes to adjust to the darkness. Then, as Dederic thudded down next to him, he saw the iron bars and the gaunt faces of the prisoners. Some were riddled with torture wounds, some without eyes.

'If these men are here on Psellos' orders, then perhaps they are innocent. Should we free them?'

Apion leant in to his ear. 'I have no doubt that their crimes are fabricated to suit the whims of that creature. But less than forty feet above us,' he stabbed a finger up, 'the Numeroi no doubt muster for their morning drill, clad in iron and armed to the hilt. Thousands of them.' His face fell grave. 'No, we came here for one reason, and we must not be distracted.' Then he turned to scan the prison walls. His gaze caught on the hulking timber chest at one end. It was just as the varangoi had described. 'Come, help me,' he beckoned Dederic towards it.

Together, they shifted the chest to one side, and both recoiled at the vile stench that rose from the opening and the descending staircase it revealed. A sweltering heat came from down there, along with the animal moans of a man in agony and the hoarse cackling of another.

As they entered the opening and descended the steps, Apion thought of all he had been through with Cydones, all the man had done for him first as his leader and then as his adviser. His teeth ground like a mill and he felt his vision tremble. He rested his hand on his scimitar's ivory hilt as they emerged into the filthy cavern. It was lined with bloodied torture weapons and a naked man lay strapped to the table, his body twitching its last as his lifeblood leaked from the gaping gash across his throat. At the far side of the chamber, three men stood, backs turned: one was bald and muscular and wore only a loincloth; one was slight with a crooked shoulder, and the third was tall and flat-faced. They bantered as they tended to glowing irons and sharpened serrated blades.

Apion stepped forward into the centre of the room, his eyes cast in shadow and his snarl illuminated by the glow from the brazier. Dederic sidled up to stand beside him. The tall, bald torturer lifted the blade he was polishing, then looked in the reflection and saw the pair. He cried out.

Then the three spun. The flat-faced man took up a glowing poker from the brazier while the slight one grappled the shaft of an axe. The bald one in the middle hefted a blade in each hand.

Then the big torturer's gaze dropped to the red-ink stigma on Apion's arm. 'You are him? You are the *Haga!* You have made a big mistake,' he rasped, his face twisting into a motley-toothed grin and his breath poisoning the air. 'You make my job too easy. Now you will die like the old fool did!' The big man's hoarse cackling filled the cavern.

Apion simply glared until the torturer's confidence faltered. The dark door barged to the forefront of his mind like a pulsing black heart. Then his eyes bulged and he bared his teeth, roaring as he leapt for them, ripping his scimitar from its sheath.

From the prison cells above, the hoarse cackling that had haunted the dreams of those in the cells tapered off nervously. Then there was a rhythmic scything of iron into flesh and the wet splatter of gore, followed by the searing of burning flesh and cries of pain like they had never heard before. On and on this noise continued, until at last it fell silent.

Then, at the sound of ascending footsteps, Zenobius shuffled back into the shadows of the cell in which he had hidden. The two figures that emerged from the stairs were coated in blood. The leader of the pair wore the look of a predator that had just fed, his emerald eyes staring through a mask of crimson.

His time would come, Zenobius vowed.

14. Raising the Shield

The morning of the first day of January, 1068 was the bitterest of the winter so far. Many farmers woke to find their flocks had perished from the cold overnight, and this was the morning that broke even the hardier winter crops of rye and barley. On the northern borders, the Pechenegs were pressing and penetrating into Byzantine lands. In the east, reports of Seljuk raids were widespread and rumours were rife that Alp Arslan was almost free of the Fatimid rebellions and was now readying to turn his armies upon the empire's borders once more.

Despite such woes, the city at the very heart of the empire was more vibrant and joyful than it had been in many years. Romanus and Eudokia stirred the people's hearts with rousing promises of a return to greatness for the people of Byzantium. Today it would culminate with their wedding and then the new emperor's rise to the throne.

The Imperial Way was abuzz with anticipation of the procession that was to come. This broad, flagstoned street, running from the Golden Gate in the west to the Milareum Aureum by the northern end of the Hippodrome, was bathed in crisp winter sunshine. The way was lined with cheering crowds, hemmed in on either side by the Varangoi and the loyal Optimates Tagma, summoned to the city to oversee the ceremony. Every edifice along the way, marble or brick, was topped with finely-robed archers and draped with vibrant fabrics depicting gilt Crosses and images of the saints. Even nature had given the ceremony its blessing, festooning the hardy cypress trees dotted along the processional avenue with a glittering layer of frost.

Near the end of the Imperial Way, the street passed through the collonaded and circular Forum of Constantine. Statues of dolphins, elephants and the old gods competed with the towering effigy of Constantine in the centre of the forum. Sanguine and inebriated citizens clung to these statues and crowded behind the wall of varangoi axemen, vying to get a good view of the procession. The scent of spilled wine, roasting meat and garlic hung in the air. Flutes whistled, kettledrums thundered and the strings of a lyre danced to this melody.

On the western edge of the forum, Apion sat with Dederic atop the steps at the foot of an ancient, blue-speckled marble statue of Minerva, like two men stranded on a tiny island.

'Aaah!' Dederic sucked on his wineskin and marvelled at the festivities all around them. He smacked his lips together. 'Running certainly clears the mind. But this, sir,' he patted his wineskin, 'washes the troubles away in half the time, doesn't it? I haven't thought about that fat bastard of a lord back in Rouen once this morning!' He took another swig. 'Warms the blood!'

'Aye, it should,' Apion shot back with a cocked eyebrow. 'But by any man's measure, your blood should be ablaze by now!'

Dederic cackled at this, then swigged some more. 'Are you sure I can't tempt you?' The Norman said, offering the skin.

Apion shook his head and tore a piece from a round of still-warm bread. As he chewed on it, he glanced around the crowd. In the days since he had dealt the most ruthless of deaths to Psellos' torturers, he had let nothing but pure water pass his lips. But this was pragmatism as opposed to penance. Since they had returned to the city, Romanus had not drawn breath without a ring of varangoi close enough to hear it. Apion had slept little in these last nights, his eyes darting at every noise in the towering palace corridors. But there had been no more incidents. The doukes and the strategoi had remained

212

unharmed, and it seemed as if they would, as agreed, return to their armies at the end of the week. But for Apion, Psellos' seeming withdrawal of hostilities was ominous.

'It's only a morning away, sir.' Dederic spoke as if reading his thoughts. 'By noon today, Romanus will be wed and then he will be emperor. Then we will be free to set out for Chaldia once more.'

Apion stopped chewing and eyed his comrade. 'Ah, I meant to break this to you earlier . . . '

'Sir?' Dederic frowned.

'We are to stay on. Romanus wants counsel in planning his first campaign, to the east, to strike back at Alp Arslan. But there is much to do to consolidate his reign and revitalise the armies before we can set out. So we will remain here for some months.' He grinned as he saw Dederic's initial expression of disappointment faltering. 'I knew you would not be wholly disheartened by this news. You do not have to pretend that you miss the bleakness of the borderlands.'

Dederic held up his wine skin and shrugged as he eyed it. 'Aye, this place has its merits. But for all the wine and fine food I've grown accustomed to in these last months, it is like living in a boiling cauldron.' Then he sighed. 'And the longer I am here, the longer it will take me to earn the coins I need to free my family of the fat lord's attentions.'

'Set your mind at ease,' Apion replied. 'When we do return to Chaldia, I'll see to it that you're paid a tourmarches' wage in arrears.'

'A fine gesture, sir,' Dederic's face widened with a broad smile. Then it faltered.

'Something still plays on your mind?' Apion frowned, thinking of the lost days when he had divulged his dark quandaries to old Mansur. 'A trouble left brewing in your thoughts can be worse than a pox.'

Dederic looked up, his eyes shaded under a perplexed frown. 'It will still take me some years to earn the wealth I need.' Then he shook his head. 'But it is graceless of me to mutter and complain when you have shown such generosity.'

'The wine does that to the best of men,' Apion grinned.

Just then, the crowds erupted in a cheer that grew louder and louder. The pair looked up. The procession approached along the Imperial Way. Patriarch Xiphilinos was dressed in a purple robe that reached to the ground and he carried a tall, gilded and jewel-studded Cross. He walked with silent sobriety – in stark contrast to those who cried out in fervent prayer and inebriate well-wishing. Behind him, a thick wall of white-armoured varangoi marched. Behind them, Romanus rode on a gilded chariot, his flaxen hair whipping in the breeze as he saluted his people.

At this, Apion stood, washing his hands in a fountain at the foot of the statue of Minerva. Then he clasped a hand on Dederic's shoulder. 'I'd best make my way to the Boukoleon Palace for the ceremony. We'll talk later. In the meantime, let your troubles wander and lose themselves in the alleys. I'll leave you to tolerate the celebrations?'

Dederic's frown remained. Then he relaxed into a smile, lifted his wineskin and sucked on it once more. 'Aye, sir.'

***

Apion stood on a balcony, looking down on the smoky grey marble of the Boukoleon Palace floor. This, the ceremonial palace just south of the Imperial Palace and the Hippodrome, was as sedate and ordered as the streets outside were chaotic. Sweet scented oils spiced the air and candles flickered silently all around the cavernous interior, spliced with red-veined marble columns, yawning archways and latticed screens. Senators, priests, military leaders and provincial magnates were packed on the ground floor, leaving only a narrow corridor from the doors to the gilded altar. The corridor was lined with varangoi, and ten more stood vigil either side of the altar. Igor stood there, shuffling in discomfort at being under the gaze of so many, his hair groomed out of its usual braids – doubtless against his will.

Xiphilinos stood before the altar. Eudokia and Romanus stood facing the patriarch. Eudokia wore a rich red silken robe that wound around her slender figure, and was studded with gemstones, just like the headdress that framed her delicate features. Romanus wore fine and embellished armour – a glistening klibanion formed of polished, alternating gold and bronze plates – with white, silk trousers and supple leather boots.

Xiphilinos' joining of the pair had been stilted at best. They had followed the age-old ritual, with the patriarch placing the ceremonial wedding crown on each of their heads, then leading them behind a painted screen to offer them the Eucharist – a sliver of leavened bread and a goblet of wine from which they both sipped. Eudokia had then placed the golden heart chain around Romanus' neck, and Romanus had in turn pinned a gilded brooch to her breast. The exchange of these items was to symbolise their acceptance of one another. As much as Apion saw hope in their joining, he also pitied the loveless relationship that seemed certain to follow.

The imperial coronation that followed at least seemed outright in its intentions. First, Romanus donned the purple cloak, clasping it over his ornate klibanion. Then Xiphilinos brought forth the imperial diadem – a gilded crown, studded with emeralds and rubies, a golden Cross rising from the forehead. Romanus accepted the diadem, placing it upon his head. Twin chains of pearl dangled on each side of his jaw, golden Crosses swinging from the end. Then the patriarch delivered another Eucharist to the new emperor. After this, the palace fell utterly silent. Romanus then turned to the audience, and raised his arms up, looking to the heavens before bowing. Then Xiphilinos called out to the onlookers.

'Bow your heads to the Lord!'

At this, all watching did as commanded. All except Apion. Instead, he thought of all those he had lost, and wondered at their unquestioning faith.

'To you, O Lord!' Romanus and the crowd called out in unison.

Next, Romanus stepped forward, onto a brightly painted circular shield laid on the marbled floor.

Then four varangoi strode forward and hoisted the shield and the man up to their shoulders. With this final gesture, Romanus Diogenes was Emperor of all Byzantium.

A slave boy scampered across the back of the hall and slipped from the grand doorway and cried out; 'All hail Emperor Romanus Diogenes!' Then, from outside a huge roar erupted, shaking the very foundations of the palace.

'Ba-si-le-us! Ba-si-le-us! Ba-si-le-us!'

Apion wondered how many men had been subject to this ceremony in the thousand years of imperial history, and how many of those had been foul-blooded. Not this one, he affirmed, dismissing the distraction of all other finery to focus on one thing. The golden heart pendant.

He had come here in search of hope and he had found it.

***

Psellos' eyes never left Romanus as he was carried from the palace. Every cheer felt like neat acid on his skin, and the man's jutting jaw and bold gaze seemed designed to taunt him. This, after the discovery that three of his finest torturers had been reduced to little more than piles of mutilated skin and bone.

'You said this would *never* happen!' John Doukas hissed by his side.

'I said Romanus would not end the Doukid dynasty, Master. That is very different.' Psellos spoke while barely moving his lips, wary of the magnates, military leaders and priests packed around them either side of the hall.

'But it is too late now. Have you lost your sight?' John shot a hand up at Romanus as he was carried past.

Psellos grabbed his arm before anyone noticed. 'Bide your time, Master, and you will have the throne. Via your nephew, or even for yourself.'

John's face was glowing red now. 'How? He now benefits from Eudokia's guard, and the loyal tagmata surround him also. We cannot get to him.'

Psellos leaned in closer to him. 'Perhaps that is for the best. Look at him, the oaf puffs out his chest upon that shield, and the people will love him for such a cheap show of bravado. If we were to sink a blade in his ribs now, in the city, they would mourn his loss, Master. Equally, they would resent any usurper.'

Psellos and John found themselves left behind as the audience poured from the Boukoleon Palace in Romanus' wake to join the populace for the celebrations that were sure to last for many days.

John's lips were taut. 'Very well, so what do you propose?'

'We have him fail his people, Master. He comes into power on the back of bold designs to reclaim the eastern borderlands for the

217

empire. In the coming months, he will have to vindicate such claims. A campaign will be announced and he will leave for the east. If he was to fail out there, then the people could have no complaint over your succession.'

John's eyes darted as he contemplated the possibilities. 'And if he was to die on the end of a blade . . . ' his whispered words cast a sibilant echo around the now empty palace.

Psellos' brow dipped. 'Oh, I think that in the heat of battle such a thing is commonplace, especially if the sultan's armies were to be one step ahead of the emperor's movements.' Then Psellos placed a hand on John's shoulder and pointed up to the gallery where the *Haga* had stood moments ago. It was deserted apart from one figure, cloaked and hooded, pure white skin and silver eyes bathed in shadow. 'Yes, my finest man will keep abreast of the emperor's plans and weaken his initiatives from within.'

But John's eyes narrowed. 'Yet one man alone may not be enough. Perhaps we should also look to seed Romanus' ranks with another? A man in his very retinue, one who will ride by his side in this coming campaign. A man who answers to us?'

Psellos' nose bent over a shark-like grin. He had led his puppet to yet another conclusion. 'A fine idea, master. But those who can get close to the emperor are loyal to him.'

John plucked a thick, pure-gold nomisma from his purse, then stroked it as if it was a pet. 'Even the fiercest loyalty has its price,' he grinned.

***

Dederic sipped at his wine as the wedding feast and celebrations carried on all around him. The Forum of Constantine was cloaked in the blackness of the winter night, but the festivities seemed determined to stave off the bitter chill. The collonades glowed orange in the torchlight. The streets were packed with cheering inebriates and playing children. The air was alive with the beating of kettledrums and lilting melodies from flutes.

Dederic had met Apion after the ceremony then lost him again a while after dusk. *Probably wanted to be alone . . . as usual!* He chuckled to himself. Before him was a ruddy-faced group of old men, jabbering at each other, barely containing their laughter as they bantered. All around him were sanguine faces and joyous tones.

But Dederic had never felt so alone. His gaze grew distant, and he saw only his wife, Emelin, his three daughters and his son. Then he saw the rubber-chinned countenance of the fat lord who had plagued their life. He recalled the time the sweating lord had turned up at their home, flanked by two huge axe-bearing bodyguards, then proceeded to slide Emelin's robe from her shoulders and fondle her breasts while the children looked on, crying. When Dederic had taken up his longsword and lunged for the cur, the bodyguards simply drew their axes around the throats of his youngest two, eager for the excuse to murder them. So Dederic could only set his sword down and sit, head in hands, as the fat lord raped Emelin before him. The lord controlled him. Anger snaked through his wine-warmed mind. Were there no innocents to protect, he would have ripped the spine from the corpulent fool's back before now. His hand trembled as he gripped his wine cup with a clenched fist, and he heard his teeth grind like millstones in his head.

Suddenly, two of the old men before him bashed their cups together with a loud *clack!*

Wine showered Dederic and he was torn from his thoughts. He waved away their apologies with a forced grin. *Enough wine for one*

219

day; time to rest, he affirmed, setting down his near-full cup. Then he turned to leave the forum. But his gaze halted on something like a tunic catching on a barbed hook.

Psellos and John Doukas moved through the edge of the crowd like eels in the shallows of a murky river. These two were as vile as the bastard who stained his life back in the west. Anger flared in his heart.

Then he noticed that they were not, for once, flanked by their usual escort of numeroi guards. A thought stirred in Dederic's tired mind, mixing with the wine that washed around in there.

He stared long and hard at the pair as they cut into a dark alleyway that led to the Hippodrome and the Numera. The blood he and Apion had spilled in the cellars of that place had clearly done little to ease the strategos' pain. *Perhaps,* he thought, his fists balling and his lips trembling, *the slaying of this pair will.*

The wine coursed through his blood and his heart thundered. He lifted his cup once more and drained it in one gulp, then stalked through the crowd after the pair.

The babble fell away as he broke from the crowd and into the backstreets. The chill air stung at his nostrils as he stalked down the darkness of the alley, his brow dipped in determination. It was only when he stumbled and flailed to right himself that he realised how drunk he was. At that moment, Emelin's voice echoed through his mind and he saw her, hands on hips, berating him after he had dropped and smashed a clay pot in the hearth room of their home.

Sometimes, you are as clumsy as a one-eyed ox!

A ghost of a smile passed across his lips for a moment as he remembered how he had calmed her by wrapping his arms around her waist and nuzzling into her neck.

He thought of turning back at that moment, then he saw Psellos' and Doukas' silhouettes slipping down another alley, and imagined what misery the fat lord was subjecting Emelin to right now. *After them!* He gritted his teeth and hurried round the corner.

Then he skidded to a halt as he saw that Psellos and Doukas had stopped up ahead and now others had joined them. He ducked down behind a pile of half-rotten timber crates, then stretched his neck to peer out at this clandestine encounter. Psellos was talking to a clutch of hooded figures, flanked by a pair of ironclad numeroi. Dederic's vision was blurring and he shook his head. He could make out a pale face and lank, white hair under one hood.

What intrigue is this? Dederic mused, his eyes narrowing.

Psellos' features were shrivelled and grey like a corpse as he spoke in muted tones, then held out a bulging purse. The pale, hooded figure took the purse and folded the edges down. At once, the faces of Psellos, John Doukas, the hooded figures and the numeroi were illuminated with the lustre of gold. Thick and pure nomismata. Hundreds of them.

Dederic stared at the sight, more coin than he had ever seen in his life. For a few heartbeats he forgot where he was, the lustre of the gold hypnotic.

Then, the scuffing of a boot on the flagstones snapped him back to reality. Three more numeroi had entered the alley at the far end.

'Keep watch at either end of the alley,' John Doukas barked at them. Then two of the three spearmen jogged towards the timber crates.

Panic shot through Dederic's blood. He stumbled back through the shadows, his mind awash with wine and confusion.

15. To Conquer the Sun

Apion finished his morning run and then ascended the stairs of the Hippodrome. He nodded to the pair of varangoi seated in the otherwise deserted arena as he passed them. 'I won't be long,' he panted.

He carried on up the stairs until he reached the southern lip. Up here, a gentle salt-tanged breeze from the Propontus offered some respite from the fiery July heat, cooling his sweat-slicked skin. He inhaled deeply and looked far to the west, where the hazy and distant Mount Olympus pierced the azure skyline, still capped with snow at its summit. Then he drew his gaze in along the southern edge of the bustling city.

The waters of the Propontus were coral blue and peaceful. Storks and herons picked through the shallows while dolphin schools tumbled and played further out amidst the fishing vessels dotted on the placid surface. Inside the sun-baked sea walls, the marbled finery of the southern wards were cloaked in a verdant blanket of vines, rooftop gardens and orchards. Bullfinches, skylarks and parakeets chirruped in competition with the cicada song, and the populace babbled throughout the streets. Crowds clustered around the fish market by the Harbour of Theodosius, where oysters and tuna seemed to be in high demand.

But the busiest part of all was around the fortified Harbour of Julian. Here, the infantry of the finely armoured Optimates Tagma and the riders of the Scholae Tagma filtered towards the harbour. Following them was the *touldon,* the precious supply train of mules and wagons that would pull rations, tents, artillery, spare weapons and armour along with an assortment of tools such as mallets, axes, sickles and shovels. This gathering of an army had been inevitable since the ceremonial gilded shield had been hung from the gates of the Imperial Palace.

For today, the first great campaign for many years was to set off to the east.

He turned to look across the Bosphorus strait. Beyond the woods on the far shore, the mountains of Anatolia lined the eastern horizon. A shiver danced up his spine. Beyond those mountains lay Chaldia and the borderlands. But they were headed beyond the borderlands – right into the Seljuk dominion. He cast his mind back to Romanus' brash address in this very arena in the early summer.

The armies of God's empire will march to the east. Rejuvenated, with pride in our hearts, we will recoup the vital lands that have been long lost to us. We will walk over fire to see the Seljuk threat quelled. To the east and into the flames! To Syria!

His heart beat just a fraction faster at the memory. The words became intermingled with those of the crone.

In the afternoon, he will march to the east as if to conquer the sun itself.

At last, it all seemed possible. Psellos and the Doukids had been tempered, apparently. They still clung to the imperial court, but the murders and plotting had ceased since Romanus had taken the throne. Romanus had wanted to have Psellos exiled. But Eudokia had insisted that to do so would incite bitter retribution and that he could still garner enough support to spark a civil war. *Let the snake slither in our midst. Is it not better that he is within our sights than plotting unseen?*

Apion frowned, weighing this logic, not for the first time in recent months.

223

Then the rippling of heavy linen snapped him from his thoughts. He looked down into the interior of the fortified harbour. There, the newly crafted fleet was readying to sail. Each of the thirty dromons had fresh white sails adorned with purple Chi-Rho emblems. Their timbers were supple and fresh, their hulls high in the water and their sides studded with fire siphons. It was in stark contrast to the crippled, rotting hulks they had witnessed upon their arrival in the city.

This was just one of Romanus' immediate reforms. The rotting fleet had been scuttled. The senate had protested vigorously about this, but to Apion it had seemed like the merciful thrust of a blade into a wounded stallion's chest. *What use is a fleet that cannot sail even from its own harbour?* Romanus had insisted. *The empire needs a fresh and compact fleet to allow us to cross the Bosphorus without need of private ferrymen.* The church had backed his stance. Then they had recoiled in horror as the emperor had set the Varangoi loose to strip the gilded artifices of the city's churches to pay for the initiative. But Romanus was undeterred. Apion had led the Rus in their endeavours, the pleas of the clergy like distant echoes as he set about chiselling obscene quantities of precious metal from the holy buildings all across the city. Only the Hagia Sofia was spared this harvesting.

Then he heard the tink-tink of hammer upon metal from the *armamenta* workshop. The long-neglected furnaces had been fired into life once more, devouring the vast quantities of iron ore purchased with the church gold. Over these last months, great stockpiles of spathion swords, kite shields, kontarion lances, iron and leather klibania, well-crafted leather boots and iron helms were formed. Now each and every man in the ranks of the Scholae and Optimates tagmata had been furnished with full armour and weapons. Indeed, as they gathered inside the harbour, they formed up in neat squares and wedges of shimmering iron.

The Optimates Tagma were two thousand strong, comprising fifteen hundred skutatoi in full iron garb, carrying spears, spathions and shields, and five hundred toxotai in wide brimmed felt hats with bows and full quivers.

The Scholae Tagma was fifteen hundred strong and all cavalry, man and mount encased in iron. They would form the hammer to the anvil of the infantry. They were led by Doux Philaretos, a scowling man with receding cropped hair who Apion placed as shrewd and easily angered. But Romanus trusted him implicitly, it seemed. *The most loyal of my men,* he had spoken of the doux with a sparkle in his eye. Apion was less enamoured with the man, and could not decide whether his judgement was coloured by his experiences with the late Doux Fulco and his like. Regardless, the Scholae riders under Philaretos' command seemed like good men.

These two tagmata were to form the core of the campaign army. But the spears of the Optimates Tagma alone were too few. More infantry were needed. Far more. As such, Romanus planned to muster the themata. They were to cross the Bosphorus and disembark in Anatolia, then march to the centre of the Bucellarion Thema where the armies would muster. Apion had worked hard to convince Romanus that the themata needed a vast investment if they were to be ready – significantly more than the funds used to bring the tagmata up to scratch. So, Romanus had despatched wagons of gold to each of the themata they were to call upon for this campaign. That moment had been like water to a parched throat for Apion, as he thought of the many thousands of lives that would be saved under the protection of finely garbed soldiers.

You would have been proud, Apion whispered, seeing Cydones' features in his mind. A refreshing breeze lifted his grey-flecked amber locks as he saw the old man standing alongside Mother, Father, Mansur . . . Maria. The memories ached like an open wound.

Then footsteps scraped behind him, echoing around the arena and jolting him from his thoughts.

'Sir!' A voice spoke, echoing like the announcer at the races.

Apion turned to scan the arena. The two varangoi had not spoken. Finally, his gaze snagged on Dederic, standing near the centre of the track, dwarfed by the central array of columns and obelisks.

'Sir?' Dederic repeated.

Apion flitted down the steps and padded out across the racecourse, the varangoi following a handful of paces behind. As he approached the Norman, he noticed once again how much the little man had changed. His skin was burnished from the summer sun. He had even taken to wearing kohl under his eyes like some of the varangoi, and had let the severely shaved back and sides of his hair grow into long, dark curls.

'It is time?' Apion asked.

'Aye, our dromon will set sail before noon.'

The pair shared a taciturn gaze for a few moments.

'Then let us not keep fate waiting,' Apion said at last, clasping a hand to Dederic's shoulder and smiling. 'We will meet my army on the voyage ahead, and I know you will lead your tourma well. This campaign will be arduous, but it can be won.'

'Whatever it takes, sir,' Dederic replied with an earnest gaze.

They walked into the western tunnel. There, Dederic stopped. 'Sir?' he said, his voice echoing in the cool space. 'I've fought in central Anatolia, but that's as far as I've been. What awaits us beyond the borderlands?'

Apion looked through the Norman as his mind replayed the years of bitter bloodshed.

'You believe in God and heaven don't you, Dederic?'

The Norman frowned, then nodded. 'Of course I do, sir.'

'Then you will soon know hell also . . . '

***

A hot, dry August breeze swept across the mustering point near the banks of the River Halys in the heart of Anatolia. Outside the vast marching camp, weed and dust whipped up and over the gathered men of the Thrakesion Thema, who shuffled in discomfort under the afternoon sun.

Emperor Romanus Diogenes stood in full armour; a white and silver moulded bronze breastplate over a white linen tunic and trousers, iron greaves and fine doeskin boots. He carried his silver, purple-plumed helm underarm. Once more he swept his steely glare across the few hundred who stood before him – their appearance in stark contrast to his. They were gaunt, with soot-blackened faces, motley teeth and tousled hair. They wore ripped and darned tunics, faded and stained. Only a handful of them wore quilted and felt armour jackets, and even less had iron helms – the majority wearing only felt caps. Precious few carried the shield, spathion and spear of a skutatos or the composite bow of a toxotes. Most were armed only with farming tools and rudimentary weapons; hoes, scythes, clubs and woodcutting axes. But the banners were most telling of all. Each of these was supposed to represent an infantry bandon of between two hundred and three hundred men. He had bargained on each thema bringing anything up to thirty of these banners, yet here before him were only six, frayed, faded and smoke-stained. Barely fifty men clustered under each.

Anger bubbled in Romanus' veins. Where were the thousands that he had been told to expect? What had become of the gold he had released to these themata from the imperial treasury to equip them? He cast a dry look to Igor and Apion, by his side, then turned his gaze on the man who had presented this ragged bunch to him.

Gregoras, the Strategos of Thrakesion, was a ruddy-faced individual with shifty eyes. He was mounted with his retinue of ninety kataphractoi. Few of his riders wore armour while he wore a fine, moulded breastplate. In the previous year, Gregoras had held firm and stayed loyal to Romanus' rise to the throne while others sided with Psellos. But in the months leading up to this campaign, Romanus had received little communication from the man, and what word he did receive was brief and terse.

Under Romanus' glare, Gregoras' gaze faltered, his eyes darting to the left. Romanus noticed how his chin bulged over the collar of his klibanion. A man who had enjoyed plenty in recent times, unlike his men.

'I assume that others will be coming?' Romanus asked through taut lips.

Gregoras' tongue darted out to dampen his lips before he spoke. 'These have been hard times, *Basileus*. The availability of fighting men has dwindled. Many have paid their exemption tax for this year in order to tend to their farms.'

And I have a damned good idea as to where a wedge of that tax has ended up, Romanus seethed, eyeing the pure-gold chain Gregoras wore around his neck. 'What became of the gold that was issued earlier this year? It was supposed to see each man armed and armoured as they should be.'

Gregoras' gaze once again faltered. 'There were . . . complications. The armamenta struggled to acquire the resources needed to produce the goods on time.'

'So they produced nothing? In six months?' Romanus hissed, striding over to reach up and grapple Gregoras' klibanion. '*Nothing?*'

'*Basileus!*' Igor spoke in a low but demanding tone.

Romanus glowered at the plump strategos. Then, with a sigh, he released his grip and gestured over his shoulder. 'Take your rabble into the camp and have them set up their tents. I had space reserved for many thousands,' he said, barely containing a sneer, 'so you will have ample room to sleep in comfort.'

'As you command, *Basileus*,' Gregoras gushed, backing away before barking orders to his weary infantry.

Romanus turned to the marching camp as Gregoras, his riders and his ragged collection of men flooded past them and inside. The camp was vast, ringed by an outer ditch and then palisade stakes punctuated by timber watchtowers. The tips of pavilion tents and vivid banners were visible above these defence works. But so were the yawning stretches where there should have been more. The strategoi of two other themata they had summoned – the Bucellarion and Anatolikon – had turned up with a similar following and suspicious tale of woe to that of the Strategos of Thrakesion. Only the Strategos of Opsikon – a young man who had succeeded the murdered Nilos – had mustered a decent number of spearmen and archers to complement his two hundred kataphractoi. The campaign army now numbered barely seven thousand men, when Romanus had planned to have at least twice that number, and over half of them resembled little more than a peasant militia.

'We only have your men and the border tagmata to add to this rabble,' Romanus muttered to Apion absently.

229

'I cannot speak for the border tagmata, *Basileus*,' Apion said, a shadow crossing his thoughts as he recalled the odious Doux Fulco and his ilk, 'but the men of Chaldia will not disappoint you.' The shadow lifted as he thought of Sha, Blastares and Procopius and the well-drilled if depleted tourmae they led.

'I don't doubt you, Strategos,' Romanus sighed. 'But even if the army of Chaldia offered a full complement, we still could not set out for Syria in this condition. Despite our efforts in these last months, there is still much work to be done.' The emperor scoured the camp again and again, as if in search of an answer. 'It seems that intrigue clings to this campaign like a plague carried from Constantinople – that three of the four themata have been unable to utilise the grants we provided is interesting indeed.' He sighed through taut lips. 'At this, the most desperate days for the empire, must I fight a war in my own camp?'

Both men looked at one another. One name remained tacit between them.

Psellos.

'*Basileus*,' Apion spoke firmly, his emerald eyes fixed on Romanus. 'Indeed, there is much to be done. But we must start somewhere,' Apion said.

'Aye. Suggestions?' Romanus asked wearily.

Apion raised a finger to point at the trudging smatter of infantry as they filed inside the camp. 'Those filthy banners, they epitomise the poverty of the ranks. The men feel as worthless as those rags look. Have the craftsmen set up their looms – fresh banners can be woven within the week.'

Romanus cracked a grin. 'Aye, that seems a fine place to start. Then tomorrow, we ride to visit these armamenta who, in over half a year, could not stitch together a single felt vest.'

Then Igor joined in, a manic grin sweeping across his face as he drummed his fingers on his axe shaft. 'Yes, tomorrow we will crack some heads!'

The group split up and Apion wandered through the camp picking through the sea of fluttering banners and brightly coloured tents to reach the one he shared with Dederic and some of the varangoi. Inside was empty and stifling hot, so he pegged the tent flap back to allow fresh air to circulate. The ten sets of quilted bedding were laid out around the centre pole and the spears and armour of each man were balanced at the head. He ate a light meal of cheese and hard tack biscuit, washing it down with a swig of rather tepid water. Then he took the opportunity to rest, slipping off his cloak and boots then reclining on his blanket. As he closed his eyes, a merciful breeze danced over his tired limbs, lulling him to sleep.

As his thoughts slipped away, he saw her again, and her name echoed in his dreams.

Maria.

***

Maria sat, cross-legged by the poolside in a pale-green linen robe. The coral-blue water was absolutely still, reflecting the vibrant tiles of the villa courtyard and the unblemished August sky that hung over Hierapolis. Honey-gold finches chirruped from their nest in the palm tree in the corner. Dragonflies hovered in the shade and around the verdant vines that scaled the walls. She closed her eyes and tried to let the serenity cleanse the fear from her heart.

Then the creaking of a thick wooden door shook her back to reality. Her chest tightened at once, her heartbeat galloping. She

231

looked into the shaded hearth room to see the silhouetted figure entering the villa. A thousand doubts raced through her mind. She had been told what to expect; that her husband would return to her today after more than two summers since he had ridden west with his warband, and that he had been horribly disfigured.

When Nasir stepped out into the sunlight, she shuddered. Not at the sagging, blistered welt of skin and patchy hair that clung like a mask to one side of his face. But at the look in his eyes. He had found no vent for his anger in his latest foray.

She clapped her hands. The slave girl came running. 'Bring bandages, balms and salves,' she called out, sending her off back inside the villa.

'It is too late to heal the wounds,' Nasir spoke, his voice dry from the dust of the ride.

'But you will still be weary and saddle sore from your ride, will you not?' she approached him gingerly, extending her arms as if to embrace him. Deep in his grey eyes, she saw an echo of the young man she had once loved, before he had descended into bitterness. Then his gaze steeled and his nose wrinkled.

'Is it too much even to embrace me?' she spoke weakly.

Nasir shook his head, waving one hand at her as if swatting a fly away, then headed back inside the villa.

She stared at the spot where he had stood. Sometimes, when he was gone with his riders, she imagined that the iciness between them was just a trick of her memory. Yet when he returned, she always felt such a fool for deluding herself.

She entered the villa. It was cool and gloomy inside. Nasir sat on a wooden bench, unstrapping his scale vest, facing away from her.

'How did it happen,' she asked, 'your wounds?'

He halted, trembling with rage.

At that moment she knew the answer. 'Apion did this? I'm sorry, I . . . '

'You're not sorry. You never were,' he spat at the mention of the name. 'Your father's blood is on his hands. Don't you remember what they did to him? All because that Byzantine whoreson was not there to protect him!'

Maria choked back a sob. It was this distorted truth that had convinced her to perpetuate Nasir's cruel deception. To let Apion live all these years believing that she too had been slain with her father on that day.

'Aye, he has burned the flesh from my face,' Nasir snapped his head round at that moment, showing the ruined side of his face; gritted teeth, the melted folds of skin and one bulging eye. 'But the pain of these wounds is nothing compared to knowing that . . . '

'Father!' a voice called out. Footsteps pattered through the villa and then a broad and tall boy raced into the room like a blur, rushing straight for Nasir. He slid to his knees and threw his arms around Nasir, back turned to Maria. Nasir returned the embrace, kissing the top of the boy's head and smoothing his charcoal locks. His voice had softened now, but he cast baleful looks up at Maria.

'Aye, Taylan, I have returned, but not for long. The sultan has already tasked me with another mission.'

Taylan looked up, then recoiled in shock. 'Your face,' he said, lifting a fawn hand to Nasir's wounds. 'The Byzantines did this to you?'

'It is but an old scar now. Many of them fell to my blade in penance.'

'And many more must fall when you ride out again!' Taylan growled, trying in vain to disguise his sobs.

Maria clasped her hands to her breast at this. This was the one thing she feared more than anything. That Taylan would inherit Nasir's anger. He was only thirteen, but was already familiar with the scimitar, and Nasir had sent him to ride with the sultan and watch battles from afar.

'Aye, many will fall, Taylan,' he said, his chill glare never leaving Maria, 'but there is one whose blood must be spilled above all others.'

Maria's heart turned to ice.

Bey Nasir had been away on campaign for more than two summers, but the Nasir she had once loved had been absent far longer.

***

A baritone chanting rang out from the dusty, sun-baked streets of Ancyra as the bishop led the populace in morning prayer. The few skutatoi posted on the walls were the only ones to notice the tiny dust plume approaching from the south, winding through the russet and gold hills. One squinted at the banner that emerged from the plume, then looked to the other, frowning.

'I drank a lot of wine last night, and I mean a *lot*. Unwatered too. Tell me my mind is still addled with merriness?'

'Eh?' the other skutatos frowned, then squinted at the banner himself. His jaw dropped. 'Is that . . . '

Neither noticed the cloaked and hooded figure watching from an adjacent rooftop. The figure saw the approaching horsemen. Then three rapid glints of reflected sunlight flashed from their midst. The figure noticed this then scurried back from the roof's edge.

Leo the smith was a simple man, a man who could only enjoy reward after a hard day's work. That was why the events of the last few months had been so confusing for him, he mused, weighing the full wineskin in his grasp. He wiped a rag over his wrinkled scalp and spat a gobbet of phlegm onto the streetside, then looked both ways before lifting the keys to the armamenta from his pocket.

'What is there to be scared of?' he chided himself as he unlocked the door. 'They're all in on it. Every whoreson in the city.'

The half-rotten timber door opened with a clunk and he stepped inside the cavernous red-brick workhouse. Where normally there would be a riot of hammers on iron, sawing, shouting and sweltering furnaces blazing, there was only stillness and silence. The furnaces lay black and cold, the lathes and anvils still and silent and the long workbenches were empty, all apart from one bearing a brass bell upon it. He stalked across the floor of the main workroom, the place echoing with his every footstep, then slumped down on the chair and lifted his feet onto the battered old table before him. He sighed and looked to the wineskin, made to pull the cork from its top, then hesitated as he felt a touch of guilt.

He looked around. Wool, flax, ore and timber were piled high but untouched and the furnaces, looms and lathes lay inactive. Likewise, Leo thought, the tannery at the edge of the city was empty and blessedly free of the noxious stench. This, despite the surplus of hides that lay untreated by its doorway.

Yes, it felt wrong. He lifted the wineskin to his lips and sucked upon it, the tart liquid washing into his gut and further lifting his mood. But it felt so, so good. Being paid twice his usual wage to do nothing? That was quite something. Besides, he thought, every other worker was taking the money without questioning their morals. Yes, he grew bored easily without daily labour. But then, he grinned, he could simply spend his wage on whores and drink to whittle away the time.

He shrugged wearily as he thought of his wife's tears that morning. He had thought this relative wealth would have at least brought a smile to her face. Instead she seemed determined to focus on the scent of the whore he had spent the previous night with.

'Cah!' he swept a hand through the air as if batting his troubles away. 'She'll learn that it's better this way.' He tipped the skin up once more. Today, like the last few days when it had been his job simply to keep an eye on the building, he planned to get so drunk that he would sleep through his shift. Already he felt a fuzziness right behind his eyes. A smile crept across his face as he lifted the skin a third time.

'Be on your guard,' an urgent voice filled the room.

Leo sat bolt upright. His heart thundered and he looked this way and that.

He felt fright drain from his body, convinced he had just fallen asleep for a moment. Then he saw a hooded figure stride towards him across the workroom.

He leapt up, yelping, spilling his winesack on the flagstones, backing up against the wall, his chair tumbling to its side.

The figure halted suddenly, only a pace from him.

Within the shade of the hood, Leo saw the ghostly pallor of the man and recognised him at once. It was Zenobius, the curious stranger who had ridden into the city some months ago. The albino had also been in the armamenta that day when the Strategos of Bucellarion had ordered the workers to stand down. Bizarrely, he seemed to be overseeing the strategos' actions that day. He had the look of a soulless bird of prey that day and now he looked like a hungry one.

'Gather the workers,' Zenobius said, flatly.

'What?' Leo stammered.

Zenobius grappled his collar and hefted him from his feet and against the wall. The albino's glare was empty. 'This is all you were asked to do for your coin. Now do it, or I will cut you to pieces,' he said, then pointed a finger at the brass bell on the workbench.

'The workers, yes!' Leo nodded hurriedly, rushing over to lift the bell. This was left in place to be rung whenever the works needed to be resumed. 'But who is coming?'

Zenobius simply moved a hand to his belt, where the edge of a sickle blade glinted.

At this, panic washed through Leo's veins and he stumbled through the double doors into the workyard up the timber stairs onto the roof, clanging the bell with all his strength.

***

Apion clutched at the handle of the armamenta door. It rattled but would not open. He looked to Dederic and shook his head, then he twisted round. Romanus and a party of forty varangoi in their pure-white armour were mounted in the middle of the street. Philaretos and Gregoras were mounted alongside them.

Romanus' lips grew taut. Then he waved Igor and a clutch of the varangoi forward.

'Stand back!' Igor grunted.

Apion twisted just in time to see the scarred Rus begin his charge, head down, growling. He leapt back as Igor threw his sturdy frame at the door. With a sharp crack, the lock gave way and the door burst in, falling from its hinges in the process. Igor dusted his hands together then cricked his head towards either shoulder until a popping noise sounded from his collarbone. Then the party filed inside, halting on the main workroom floor as a pair of young men cut across their path carrying timber to the furnace.

Apion frowned as he swept his gaze around. The furnaces were lit, women were sitting at the looms and a small, bald smith seemed engrossed by a sheaf of paper with diagrams inked upon it. Through the double doors, in the yard, he saw two men buzzing around what looked like a fletcher's workshop. Then he looked back to the smith – and caught the man's furtive glance for a heartbeat before it was dropped back to the paper. Apion dipped his brow and strode over to the furnace area.

'You oversee this workhouse, smith?'

The man nodded, as if irritated by the interruption.

'And how are the works going?' Apion asked.

The smith took a moment to stroke his chin before looking up.

'Slowly, we have had some difficulty with the materials. The ore has many impurities, and the wool is coarse and . . . '

As the smith listed his complaints, Apion looked to the pile of ore in the adjacent storeroom. He noticed two things at that moment. The thick coating of dust upon the iron ore and the bead of sweat on the smith's forehead, despite the relative cool of the workhouse.

' . . . we really are struggling to meet the emperor's demands,' the smith gestured to the furnaces, 'but we've been working night and day to . . . '

Apion barged past the smith, then placed a hand against the furnace door, tentatively at first, then without fear. It was cold and only beginning to heat from the flames inside. He looked up at the others in the room. One of the lads carrying timber had a wet, red stain down the front of his linen tunic. Wine. The other lad's clothes were pristine white, despite the soot around the works. Then he saw that another few faces had appeared in the yard outside. They looked anxious until the fletcher whispered to them and they hurriedly took up tools.

'There have been no works here for some time,' Apion stated.

'I . . . how dare you suggest,' the smith started, his eyes bulging. All around the workshop had slowed, eyes fixed on the scene.

'You reek of wine!' Apion spat back. 'And your drudges have obviously come here in haste from the inn,' he gestured to the lad with the stained tunic. Then he nodded to the white-robed lad, 'or from prayer.'

'This is an outrageous claim!'

Igor barged forward, lifting his axe from his back, hefting it up to strike at the man with the shaft. The smith staggered back and fell in anticipation of the blow, shielding himself with his arms.

Dederic stepped forward and caught Igor's arm just in time. The gasps of the onlooking workers filled the cavernous workhouse.

Igor grunted and glared at Dederic, wide-eyed.

'This is not how it is supposed to be,' the Norman muttered, frowning.

'Strategos?' Igor bawled, looking to Apion.

Apion twisted round. 'Dederic is right. If we knock this man unconscious, who will see our weapons forged?'

With a grunt, Igor stepped back.

Apion crouched by the smith and stared at him. 'The emperor waits in the street outside,' at this, the smith gawped to the shattered door and then to Apion, 'and he is minded to execute those who have jeopardised his campaign.'

'I . . . I . . . ' the smith stammered.

'You will not be hurt or punished, smith, unless you fail to do as I ask.'

The smith nodded hurriedly.

'The emperor's army is set to march into Seljuk lands to protect the empire, to protect you, to protect your family. Yet near half of them, over three thousand men, have only tunics and the grace of their god to protect them from Seljuk steel,' he gripped the smith's tunic, lifting him to his feet and pulling him close. 'We need klibania, do you understand?'

The smith nodded hurriedly.

'Iron is best but leather will do,' Apion continued. 'They need boots also – we have already visited the sot dozing at the tannery, so he knows his responsibilities. Helms, blades, spears and shields are in short supply also, as are arrows. You have a busy few weeks ahead of you, smith, but I'm sure your appetite for hard work has grown in the time you have taken coin to do nothing.'

The smith gulped, a steely resolve growing and replacing the terror in his eyes. 'Aye, it has. Idleness has made me do some bad things.'

Apion pinned him with a gimlet stare and lowered his voice. 'A man rarely finds opportunity to redeem himself for past evils. Seize your opportunity.' At last. the man nodded vigorously and Apion released his grip on him. Then Apion strode back to the shattered door. Igor's barked orders echoed around him as he left.

Outside, Romanus waited on horseback. The varangoi clustered around him. Philaretos and Gregoras looked on with narrowed eyes.

Apion squinted as he looked up to the emperor. 'It is as we thought, *Basileus*. Some treachery has seen the armamenta lie idle for months. But it is rectified now. Igor is posting his men here to oversee that the works are completed with haste.'

'Good,' Romanus nodded, the tension easing from his expression just a fraction. 'Now we must ride around the farmlands and muster what other men we can.'

***

Zenobius lay flat on his belly, inching forward until he could curl his fingers around the lip of the armamenta roof and peer down into the flagstoned street below. While he had taught himself to disguise his emotions, it meant they were all the fiercer in his heart. The signal from his man in the emperor's retinue had been too late. Psellos would think him some kind of fool. Childhood memories swirled in his agitated mind. His mother's promise of greatness seemed ever more distant and he heard the drunken jeers of Father and his cronies as they beat him. *Father was right. I am a curse!* At this, his expressionless face twitched and the beginnings of a frown wrinkled his brow. But he clenched his fists until his nails broke the skin and his palms bled. *No,* he insisted, his face settling once more, *this is merely a setback.*

He looked to the nearby stables where a dappled grey was loosely tethered. It was time to move on to the next step of the plan.

***

Apion walked with Romanus, Igor, Dederic and Philaretos in the watery morning sunshine by the banks of the Halys, north of the camp. It had been a hectic few weeks of kicking the armamenta into life and rounding up what few recruits they could find in the nearby farmlands, villages and towns.

Just outside the camp on a patch of flat ground clear of rhododendrons and rocks, the skutatoi of the Opsikon Thema were being put through their paces by their *kampidoktores*. The gruff man orchestrated the drill of running and leaping with a chorus of barks and a gleeful and sadistic grin. Adjacent to this, the thock-thock of arrows

241

punching into wood rang out as the toxotai of the Bucellarion Thema fired into rings of tree trunk, each emptying one quiver before taking up another.

Then, further north, the imperial tagmata trained. One glance could distinguish these more ancient regiments from the mercenary rabbles on the borders led by the likes of Doux Fulco. The skutatoi of the Optimates Tagma – the only infantry unit that could present with every man armed and armoured – formed up in a silvery line, those with the longest spears to the fore, their green banners splicing the line at regular intervals of each bandon of three hundred men. One barking command saw their flanks fold swiftly to form a defensive square. Then, *buccinators* by the side of the river raised their horns to their lips. The wail of the instruments rang out and the earth shook; from the banks upriver, the kataphractoi of the Scholae Tagma mock-charged this square. They were a fine sight; fifteen hundred mounted men encased in iron, thundering forwards together in a thick wedge. At the last moment, they split into two and broke around the square. Then the men of the Optimates cheered as they fended off this 'charge'.

Apion noticed a contented smile touch the corners of Romanus' lips as he watched. Then the emperor turned to those with him, recounting the next steps for the campaign once more. 'A trade flotilla is due to come downriver within the week. They will bring the last shipment of arms and armour from Ancyra and they will ferry us upriver.'

'Another week of training should surely see the vermin of the themata hardy enough for the march,' Doux Philaretos said with a sneer as they peeled away from the riverbank.

Apion bit his tongue at this.

Then they came to the men of the Thrakesion Thema. They had been bolstered with the extra few hundred that had been mustered in the last weeks.

Apion eyed the man who barked them into formation. It was Gregoras, the ruddy-faced strategos. The new recruits of his thema were easy to spot, their shoulders bowed under the weight of all they carried. Apion thought of Philaretos' jibe and sighed. Then he strode from the emperor's group and past Gregoras. All the men in the Thrakesion ranks broke into a muted murmur at the disturbance.

'What do you think you're . . . ' Gregoras barked at Apion.

Apion turned to him. 'Permit me this one thing, sir.'

Gregoras' eyes narrowed and his lips grew pursed. 'Be swift, strategos.'

Apion carried on before stopping in front of the recruit at the end of the line. He was gaunt and unshaven, with nervous eyes and foul teeth.

'At ease,' Apion said.

He lifted the pack from the recruit's shoulders. 'A column is only as strong as its weakest point,' he barked to the line, lifting from the hemp bag three pots, a hand-held grain mill, a small sack of barley, another sack of wheat. Then he shook his head and crouched, lifting the sack by its corners and tipping out a pile of tools and blankets.

'A marching soldier must carry only what he needs. The temptation is always there to be prepared with everything you might need, but think only of the essentials.' He kicked the sack of barley to one side, then all but one blanket, then the majority of the tools. 'You carry your weapons and your armour, a cloak or a blanket – not both, two skins of water, one sack of grain, one pot, a cup, and a mill,' he said, scooping each of these things back into the pack. 'I have spent months in the arid east with only these things.'

He noticed one squat recruit nearby stifling a smug grin, firing glances at the man whose possessions were on display. 'Don't look at this man,' Apion patted the gaunt recruit on the shoulder, handing him back his pack, then scowled at the short recruit's pack before sweeping his gaze across the rest of the line, 'for he isn't the worst offender.' At this, the squat man's face froze in alarm, fearful that he would be made an example of next. 'Sell what you do not need to the touldon or at the next market we cross. When you are clashing swords with a seven foot Seljuk, you will not be glad of an extra cooking pot. Though he may find use for it after he has cut off your balls and fancies a meal.'

A flurry of nervous laughter was followed by the thudding of knees hitting the dust and the clatter of packs being unloaded.

As he left the line, he nodded to the seething Gregoras then made to catch up with the emperor and his party. He noticed that one deathly pale recruit was kneeling but not unloading his pack nor chatting with his comrades. He seemed to be more interested in Romanus and his party, still walking some distance away.

'Zenobius!' a komes cried at the soldier. 'Get on with it - empty your pack!'

***

The Halys babbled incessantly in the darkness and the sky was studded with stars and a waning moon. At the heart of the camp, crackling torches illuminated the night and cast an ethereal glow up onto the gilded campaign Cross erected by the emperor's tent.

Gregoras, the Strategos of Thrakesion, was seated at the campfire, eating a strip of greasy goat meat, staring silently into the flames. Paces away, Apion, Romanus, Philaretos and Dederic sat around a small table just outside the tent. On the table was a shatranj board, a plate of fruit and a jug of wine.

Philaretos' eyelids drooped, then he jolted awake. Hearing Igor and the pair of nearby varangoi sentries chuckling at him, he rubbed at his eyes and scowled them into silence. Then he drummed his fingers on his knee and tapped his foot. Then he shuffled and scoffed, drained his wine cup and stood, casting an accusing finger at the shatranj board. 'Torture, this is. Watching even more so than playing. Give me a sword and a thousand men any day.' With a further sigh, he stood and stalked over to sit next to Gregoras at the nearby campfire, where he took to honing his spathion on a whetstone.

Apion and Romanus looked at one another, chuckling.

At the same time, Dederic stood. 'The doux has a point; there is a certain level of patience required for this,' he said, nodding to the board. 'A level of patience that turns the mind to otherwise loathsome tasks.' He strolled over to his fawn stallion, tethered only paces away, then took to brushing at the beast's mane and coat.

Romanus chewed on a piece of dried fish then supped at his watered wine. 'Just us then, Strategos?'

'Aye,' Apion nodded, lifting a pawn forward from his front rank.

The emperor lifted a pawn of his own, moving it out over two squares to allow development of his chariot piece. His face was stern, his mind clearly not on the game. 'There is one thing the men must learn. Something long forgotten by all but our border armies. Not just how to fight, but how to fight the Seljuk war machine.'

Apion nodded, shuffling to sit forward. 'The Seljuks employ more than one style of warfare, *Basileus*. When they muster the armies of Persia, they present spearmen, archers and cavalry – a mix not unlike our forces. But the core of the Seljuk armies is and always has been their mounted archers. The steppe cavalry that swept across and seized all of the lands that they now possess are still the beating heart of their forces. They ride their sturdy steppe ponies like centaurs, and they only ride mares – always mares. They can fire an arrow for every heartbeat, so while one is being nocked, another is in flight and another is punching into its target.' His gaze grew distant. 'Like flies that can be beaten off but not driven away. They call themselves ghazis now, but they are the jewel in Alp Arslan's hordes. He knows this and that is why he is a master of the feigned retreat, employing the ghazis as the lure and the Persian might as the snare. It is vital to disarm to lure first.' He leaned forward and plucked a war elephant piece and had it shoot across the board, taking the emperor's vizier.

Romanus rubbed at his temples, ignoring the loss. 'Tell me though, Strategos; I am walking into hell in the east, yet I fear more for what is going on in my absence, in Constantinople. Why is that?'

Apion's mind flashed with images of Psellos, John Doukas and the Numeroi, then of Eudokia and her boys. A trace of guilt spidered through Apion's veins as the image of Eudokia stayed a little longer than the others.

'You fear for Lady Eudokia?'

Romanus burst out with laughter. It was mirthless. 'I fear more for any who would try to harm her – Eudokia is very capable of defending herself.' His face fell sombre. 'I do not wish her to come to any harm, Apion, but there is no love there. Yes, we rut. It is often fraught and frantic. But it is never with the passion of lovers. It serves its purpose, as does our marriage.' Romanus leant forward, his eyes bloodshot and weary in the torchlight. 'It is the presence of Psellos writhing like an asp in my palace that troubles me. He has been quiet for some months, yes, but I see him as a wounded wolf. I know he will never accept my reign.' He shook his head, punching a fist into his palm. 'That is why this campaign must succeed, Apion, at all costs. Failure will see him prise me from the throne and the Doukids will reign once more.'

Apion nodded. 'Then let us fix our minds on the east, *Basileus*. Let us take victory in Syria. The people of the empire will never accept a coup against a victorious leader.'

Romanus' sour look dissolved into a grin. 'Leave the rousing homilies to me, Strategos.'

Apion found the grin infectious. 'Gladly,' he said, sitting back, crunching into an apple.

Romanus chuckled, then stifled a yawn and tapped the shatranj board. 'My body is telling me that it is late, and that I should retire. But we will finish this game one evening soon.' He swigged the last of his wine and readied to stand. 'But the east is indeed where we must focus. Firstly we must look at the march that will take us there. Lykandos lies in our path. Our touldon is light and so we must march through the heart of that torn land and the supply points I have organised. I hear that the valleys there are notorious?'

Apion nodded. Lykandos was one area of the borderlands that he particularly loathed visiting. Ostensibly it was a Byzantine Thema, but, pressed against Seljuk-held territory, it was even more permeable a border than Chaldia. 'The valleys are stifling, even in this month. We must take the widest of those valleys, but even that is long and winding. The sunlight blinds you as you ride, and you hear only the echo of your mount's hooves. It can feel like you are the only man alive after a while, and that is when it is at its most dangerous.'

Romanus stood, then clasped a hand to Apion's shoulder. 'Then that will be when I need my finest men by my side. Until tomorrow, Strategos.' With that, he turned and spoke with the varangoi, before entering his tent.

247

Then Apion stood and stretched. He stepped over to feed his apple core to Dederic's stallion. 'Feed him well, for the march to come will be arduous.'

'Aye, sir,' Dederic nodded, busying himself brushing the stallion's coat.

'And don't wake me when you come back to the tent,' he grinned.

Dederic flashed a smile in reply.

Then Apion turned to the campfire. Philaretos and Gregoras were in a whispered discussion there. He offered his half-full wine cup to the pair. 'Any more of this and I'll be in a foul mood come the morning.'

They fell silent instantly. Gregoras shot a prickly glare up at him. Philaretos looked up too; the sleepiness in his eyes from moments ago was gone. Apion noticed the whetstone in his other hand had barely been used. Then, in a heartbeat, the Doux's features melted into a smile and took the cup. 'Aye, it would be a shame for Paphlagonian red go to waste.'

Apion nodded to the pair. 'Savour it . . . and let it wash the tension from your mind,' he said, trying to disguise a frown.

Then he wandered over to where Igor and the varangoi stood. 'Until morning,' he said.

Igor offered him a warm grin. 'Sleep well, Strategos. Tomorrow is the start of a long journey.'

'As is every day, Komes,' Apion smiled. 'As is every day.'

As he walked through the torchlit camp, he glanced back to the campfire and wondered at the mood of some of the men. The tension of the campaign was building, it seemed.

***

Zenobius knelt in his kontoubernion tent, hands on his thighs, his eyes closed. In the darkness, he was truly alone. Just like those days he had hidden under the floor of his father's house. Four winter days without food or water, insects crawling in his hair, rats biting at his flesh. Meanwhile the villagers searched for him outside, baying for his blood, sure that he had been responsible for the death of a newborn baby. That the baby's corpse bore the scratches of a wildcat meant nothing to them. They wanted his blood. Father seemed happy to let them have it and even helped the mob in their quest. That was when he had first killed, emerging from beneath the floor late on the fourth night, then clubbing to death the sot who had spawned him. The power had first flowed through him in those moments as the blood spilled.

His memories were wrenched away when he heard footsteps approaching. He glanced around the circle of nine unoccupied sets of bedding in the tent. Was it one of the nine fools of his kontoubernion he had been forced to endure? Then the tent flap was pulled back gingerly. His glower melted into a cold smile as he recognised the shadowy figure stood there. It was his accomplice, the one in the emperor's party who had signalled him on their approach to Ancyra.

'Ah, you have something new for me at last? You had better or I will see to it that you never receive the gold my master promised you.'

'I heard everything. The emperor is to march the column through Lykandos,' the figure said, flatly. 'Through the central valleys.'

'Good, good,' Zenobius mused. 'Then they will come to the Scorpion Pass on their journey.'

'What is to happen there?' The shadowy figure asked.

Zenobius stared at him. 'Do not plead ignorance to the consequences of your actions. You know well what will happen.' Then the albino leaned forward, just far enough for the moonlight to dance in his ghostly silver eyes. 'They will come to the Scorpion Pass . . . and they will die there. All of them.'

16. The Scorpion Pass

It was a baking-hot morning when the imperial campaign crossed into the golden, steep-sided valleys of the Lykandos Thema.

Apion rode alongside Igor, Dederic, Romanus and Gregoras. He found plentiful excuse to cast a look over his shoulder and take pride in the spectacle of the column. Over seven thousand men, snaking out for miles behind them like a silvery asp. In the few weeks they had been stationed by the Halys, the army had been transformed.

At the tail, Doux Philaretos had been entrusted with the rearguard. He along with five hundred kataphractoi – a mixture of riders from the themata and the Scholae Tagma – and a large detachment of toxotai were on the lookout for ambushers and deserters. Fortunately, since the bolstering of the column's fortunes, there had been few of the latter.

In front of this rearguard, and forming the bulk of the column, the much-improved infantry banda of the themata marched, sixteen abreast. Those who had previously been filthy and unarmed now possessed a shield, spear and sword. The majority were clad in quilted vests and leather klibania, and the select few who would fight on the front ranks had been afforded iron klibania. The medley of bright, clean banners identifying each of the banda bobbed on a sea of vertical speartips as they strode, bulging around the centre to protect the supply touldon. Equally rejuvenated, the toxotai marching with them each had a bow, a full quiver and a wide-brimmed felt hat to keep the sun from their eyes, affording them a truer aim.

Leading the thematic infantry were the all-iron-garbed skutatoi of the Optimates Tagma. Then, heading up the column were the rest of the Scholae Tagma; twelve hundred riders on muscular mounts. The priests marched before these riders, carrying the bejewelled campaign Cross. The *signophoroi* flanked them, carrying their purple Chi-Rho campaign banners with pride. Then, at the head, the emperor rode, surrounded by his white-armoured varangoi.

Since leaving his Chaldian army behind almost a year ago, Apion had felt short of a limb. This sight, however, was a fine comfort. Having equipped the men well, their self-belief and attitude had lifted also – just as old Cydones had always preached.

'A well-tempered anvil, indeed,' Romanus spoke in a hushed tone, 'probably the finest I have led in some years.'

Apion turned to see that the emperor was grinning at him.

'Not quite; wait until we rendezvous with the men of Chaldia . . .' Apion grinned in reply.

Romanus frowned momentarily, then threw his head back and boomed with laughter.

***

The mood of the march had been buoyant for the next few days. The priests had led prayers and chanting as the column wound its way deeper into the valleys of Lykandos. Apion had dropped back from time to time, offering words of encouragement to the marching men. He had noticed to his amusement that, when the priests were well out of earshot, some of the men struck up more ribald songs. Indeed, the further away the priests were the more bawdy the men became.

At the end of each day they would set up a vast, palisade-ringed marching camp, with each thema and tagma forming smaller

252

camps within for their own ranks. After evening prayer, the men laughed as they ground their grain, cooked their porridge and sipped their soured wine by the campfires. The nights passed without incident and the soldiers awoke refreshed in the mornings, ready for another days' march.

Vitally, each man had set out from the eastern banks of the Halys with two full skins of water, knowing that the heart of Lykandos was notoriously dry. Those skins had served them well for those first few days. Indeed, they should have been enough to see them to the first well and the supply dump the emperor had arranged.

But then, on the fourth day, things changed.

They came to the wide valley with the well at its centre, the column had slowed to a standstill and looked on in silence, the ribald tunes and prayer falling away.

There were no wagons, no sacks of grain, fodder or water skins. Likewise, the group of skutatoi they had expected to find guarding the well was nowhere to be seen. The valley floor was deserted. Romanus had sent a clutch of kursores scout riders on to the end of the valley to check for signs of the men or even for ambush. But the land was deserted in every direction. Then they approached the well, but it yielded only sand. The mood had understandably darkened at this. But out in these parched valleys, they could do little other than carry on to the next well with only the emergency water rations on the touldon wagons to fall back on.

Two days later, they had approached the second well in weariness, the men bearing dark lines under their eyes. Again there were no supplies and no guards. They were apprehensive as they moved to the well, then spirits soared as the bucket splashed into the darkness at the bottom. The cheering and expectation plummeted though, when the bucket became wedged. Apion had tossed a flaming torch into its depths, and then recoiled at the rotting body of the skutatos that lay down there – his neck and back snapped at absurd angles and the water slick with his putrefying flesh. Again, they had little option but to move on.

Now, another three days on from that second well, they trekked in silence, all water long gone. As if to mock them, the noon sky was pure azure and the heat in the valley was relentless, the air stale and dry. The bulk of the kataphractoi had taken to riding only in their tunics, boots and swordbelts, their weighty armour stowed in the touldon. Many of the skutatoi had done likewise, now marching only with their packs, spears and shields. Even the usually hardy mules of the supply train brayed in exhaustion.

Apion too rode in his light linen tunic and boots, with a felt cap on his head to shield his scalp from the worst of the sun. His hair hung loose around his face and neck. His mind was foggy, having slept fitfully the past few evenings, waking unrefreshed. His throat was as dry as his tunic was damp with sweat – he had drained the last of his water the previous day.

Damn, but this land is dryer than the wit of a Cretan.

He felt guilt at his own discomfort, wondering how the infantry behind him, largely from the more temperate north-western themata and unaccustomed to this parched land, would be faring right now. Then he looked ahead to the vanguard of three hundred kataphractoi, riding a half-mile in front of the main column. Their role required them to remain in full armour, and they were but a shimmering dot of iron on the horizon. *Poor bastards*, he sympathised, *no doubt cooked through by now.*

Gregoras, the Strategos of Thrakesion, rode nearby in silence, his ruddy skin dripping with sweat. Apion noticed how his eyes seemed to be alive though, combing the valleysides, taking everything in. He felt both reassured and unnerved by this.

In contrast, Dederic rode with his head down, his eyes on the dust before him. The Norman was shorn of his weighty mail hauberk. His neck was burnt red.

'I'd cut off my cock for a skinful of water,' Igor croaked beside him. The Rus' face was the shade of cooked salmon, giving him a demonic appearance.

'It is enough to drive a man to madness,' Romanus observed, frowning slightly at Igor's choice of words. 'The echo of boots and hooves grows spellbinding, and all my thoughts are fixed only on when we will next enjoy a modicum of shade.'

'Aye,' Apion straightened up on his saddle, 'yet thirst and heatstroke are but a few of the dangers out here.' He took to scouring the valley sides as he said this. In their discomfort the vigilance had ebbed, he realised. 'We must keep the men focused, *Basileus*.'

At that moment, a clopping of galloping hooves rang out. Doux Philaretos slowed alongside them, having rode from the rearguard. 'Fresh water would focus the mind like nothing else right now,' he suggested, then cast his narrowed eyes around the emperor's retinue. 'Perhaps we should stop here and find a source?'

Romanus punched a fist into his palm, then swivelled his gaze along the valley sides. 'But if we stay on our route, the River Pyramos is, what, just over a day's march from here?'

At this, Gregoras' eyes shot to the emperor. 'A day's march for well-watered men, perhaps. I would agree with the doux, *Basileus*. Let us stop here and find a closer source.'

'It seems that the River Saros is but a short distance from here – just over two miles,' Philaretos continued, squinting at a dog-eared map. 'Look, there,' the doux said, tapping his map then pointing at a narrow crevasse a few hundred paces ahead in the southern valleyside. A finger of rock jutted into the sky from one side of the opening, curving round like a half coiled finger, the tip weathered to a fine point. 'That's it, the only passable terrain to the banks of the Saros, by the looks of it. It's called . . . the Scorpion Pass.'

'Sounds lovely,' Igor muttered.

Apion looked to the jagged opening, struggling to hear anything other than the trickling of water in his mind. He rubbed at his eyes and examined the fissure again. It was narrow, and even from here he could see that the ground was uneven and littered with rockfall. The men would have to march two abreast at best, and the horses in single file. 'That valley is narrow and treacherous underfoot – we could only send a few men through it to bring water to the column and it would take many trips to slake the thirst of our ranks. It would mean halting here for some time. I feel we should press on to the east, *Basileus*.'

Romanus mulled over a response. 'Yes, we should not be distracted from our course . . . '

Before he had finished his sentence a groan came from behind them, followed by a thudding. They twisted in their saddles to see that a pair of skutatoi at the head of the Thrakesion Thema had crumpled, one to his knees, the other flat-out, face down. The one on his knees panted, his eyes like slits, his limbs trembling, his face pale. *Ghostly white,* Apion thought, seeing a lock of pure white hair hanging from the felt cap the man wore. It was the albino recruit he had noticed before.

'Clearly, we must stop here,' Gregoras raised his eyebrows at this as if to underline the point. The other banda of the thema looked on, their faces a sea of weariness.

'*Basileus*, morale is low,' Doux Philaretos agreed. 'At the rear of the column, we have had to ride down deserters – it started this morning.'

Romanus swithered. Then he looked to Apion. 'I can't let morale fall away, Strategos. Worse, I can't afford to have them perish. They need water.' His gaze darted from his weary men to the silent, shimmering valley sides.

Philaretos and Gregoras shared a shrewd glance then looked to the emperor with narrowed eyes.

At last, the emperor nodded, heeling his mount round to face the head of the column. 'Down your burdens and rest,' he boomed. 'We will remain here until the midday heat relents.' He motioned to the blanket of shade that had formed on the northern side of the valley as the afternoon begun. 'Keep your weapons close and maintain a stringent watch. But know that your water rations will be replenished before long.'

As the news filtered back along the column, a chorus of relieved sighs broke out and then escalated into a raucous cheering. Like a silver asp, the body of men moved from the centre of the valley into the shade at the northern edge. Then a clatter of helmets and shields hitting the dust filled the air. The vanguard trotted back to join their comrades.

'Kursores!' Romanus barked.

A pack of thirty scout riders trotted over on their lithe mounts. Their leader was Himerius, an aged man. His crisp bald pate was an angry shade of red from the sun. His face was fixed in a sour and puckered grimace, as if he had been sucking on a ripe lemon. '*Basileus!*' the rider barked.

'Load your saddles with water skins, as much as you can carry when full. Make your way to the Saros then ferry the skins back to the column. It will take many trips, but know this;' Romanus' cobalt eyes sparkled, 'today, you can be our saviour.'

***

Zenobius stepped away from the collapsed skutatos and moved into the shade. Here, he offered a furtive nod to his accomplice, mounted by the emperor's side. Then he abandoned his pretence of feebleness and watched as the skribones tried in vain to revive the fallen man he had been marching alongside. Perhaps if the man merely had heatstroke then they would be able to bring him round, Zenobius thought. Then he reached into his purse and thumbed at the small pewter vial in there, half of its contents gone. No, there would be no reviving of this one, he grinned. Then his eyes drifted to the Scorpion Pass.

Perhaps I have offered him a small mercy, given what is to come . . .

***

Atop a sun-baked plateau in the north of Lykandos, Sha chewed on a strip of goat meat as he eyed his weary men. There were nearly four thousand of them. They were gathered round small cooking fires, munching on their rations of hardtack, slurping at their stew of honey, almonds and yoghurt, stopping only to slake their thirst with their plentiful water supply. They needed every last drop, for up here they were exposed to the mid-afternoon sun that baked them as they ate. Their necks were angry red and their faces slick with sweat. He considered giving the order to move out, then hesitated. *Give them a little longer,* he affirmed, *after all, it has been a long and tiring march.*

258

It had been three weeks since the eighteen hundred men of the Chaldian Thema – four banda of skutatoi, one of toxotai and nearly two hundred kataphractoi – had set off from the verdant coastal area near Trebizond. They had headed south-west, mustering the men of the eastern themata as the letter from Apion had instructed.

Their first stop had been the city of Nicopolis to levy a tourma from the narrow-shouldered Strategos of Colonea. Sha smiled as he recalled the man's initial belligerence and refusal. The man's stance had quickly melted when Sha mentioned that the order came from the emperor and that the *Haga* would be coming to enforce the order. On paper, they should have complemented his column with another two thousand four hundred men; six banda of skutatoi and two of toxotai. In reality, there were less than four hundred men, and he could barely tell the spearmen and the archers apart – each wearing only a tunic, a few with boots, and a handful with shields and weapons. He had hidden his dismay though. At least these thematic troops had mixed well with their Chaldian brothers – some of them exchanging food and others playing dice, their banter rising and falling.

Next they had marched south-west from Colonea to cross into the rocky highlands of the Sebastae Thema. Some years ago, the thema soldiers there had retired to their farms permanently, stowing their swords and putting their lives in the hands of Doux Ausinalios and his mercenary tagma that had been sent to replace them. Now Ausinalios was to join Sha's column. The doux brought with him two hundred Norman riders, five hundred Pecheneg horse archers, five hundred Oghuz steppe cavalry and over a thousand Rus axemen. Ausinalios' army was welcome in terms of the numbers, but there had been an uncomfortable rift between them and the native Byzantine troops. Fights and goading had been commonplace on the march and in camp. One man had even been blinded in a dagger fight.

259

The sooner we meet with Apion and the emperor, he thought, glancing south, *the sooner I will be relieved of this lot.* Decision made, he filled his lungs. 'Rest is over. Douse the fires and ready yourselves to move out!'

'Aye, we're not far from the rendezvous point now,' Procopius sighed.

'By tomorrow we'll be there,' Sha replied.

Then a tinkling of water and an angry hiss split the air. Sha and Procopius spun to see Blastares, staring skywards, a look of bliss on his face. A plume of grey smoke billowed around his ankles as he emptied his bladder onto a campfire and the skutatoi nearby yelped as they scrambled clear of the spray.

The big tourmarches grunted and shuffled a few times to get every last drop out, then blinked, realising Sha and Procopius were gawping at him in disbelief. His blissful expression morphed swiftly into a scowl. 'What're you looking at?' he growled.

Procopius screwed up his eyes in exaggerated fashion; 'Not sure – hard to tell from here.'

'Aye, well at least I can do more than piss through this, you old bastard,' Blastares fired back, and then cackled, shaking his head in disbelief at his own comeback as he tucked himself away again.

Sha stifled a chuckle then turned to the edge of the plateau, looking out over the wrinkled network of valleys below. He raised a hand, readying to wave the men into a march towards the snaking path that led down there. But as he did so, something caught his eye and his breath. Many miles away, a dust plume approached from the west, rising from the broad valley that spliced Lykandos.

'Ours?' Procopius whispered, crouching by his side, an elbow resting on Sha's shoulder. Then Blastares moved to his other side.

'Got to be,' Blastares affirmed.

'They may well be,' Sha agreed. 'But if they are, then who or what is *that?*'

Blastares and Procopius followed Sha's stabbed finger. There along the hilly ground south of the dust plume, a faint glinting pierced the heat haze. It was there and then not there at the same time . . . and it was moving, like an arrowhead shooting for the flank of an unsuspecting warrior.

***

Hooves echoed through the narrow, shaded pass. Himerius, the komes of the scout riders muttered under his breath. He had lost his felt cap that morning and now his bald pate was lobster-pink and crisp. The dust all around him was thick and clung to the throat. He winced as his mare stumbled and whinnied. No part of this pass was even close to level, with slivers of broken bedrock and scree under every step. So far, they had been forced to dismount to round piles of rockfall and to lead their horses through the narrowest parts. Then, when they ducked low in their saddles to ride under yet another jagged overhang, the serrated rock scraped his angry scalp.

'The only damned grace is that we are in the shade,' he croaked, shaking a fist at the offending rock as he sat tall once more.

Niketas, the young rider behind him, laughed stoically at this. 'Just think of ducking into the shallows of the river, sir.'

'I'm thinking of the state of my mount after six or seven sessions of stumbling through this crack in the ground.' He patted his grey on the neck. 'They won't be replaced or tended to if they are injured – we're not tagma riders, lad.' The spite in his tone silenced his fellow rider. He closed his eyes, sighed and then twisted in his saddle to the youngster. 'I'm sorry, Niketas. A grumpy old bastard like me and heat like this do not mix well.'

But Niketas' gaunt features were illuminated with a smile. He was pointing ahead.

Himerius spun forward again to see that the pass was opening out above them, the blue sky yawning overhead. The rushing of the rapids met his ears before the tumbling waters came into sight. A smile cracked across his aged features. He closed his eyes, clutched the Chi-Rho on his neck chain and mouthed a prayer to God.

Then he blinked at the clatter of a small rock tumbling down the side of the crevasse. He squinted up into the sunlight. Confusion wrinkled his features at what he saw up above.

A single man, crouching. He wore a jet-black pony tail and grey eyes that seared under a v-shaped brow. One side of his face was an angry smear of scars and drooping flesh. He wore a scale vest and a fine Seljuk conical helm. Then the man stood tall and barked. At once, both sides of the pass writhed as warriors rose. There were hundreds of them, and hundreds more behind. Himerius dropped the Chi-Rho, his entire being suddenly awash with icy cold dread.

'Get back to the column!' he roared. 'Warn the emp . . . '

His words were ended in a gurgling roar as a spear punched through his throat and a pair of arrows hammered into his chest.

***

Nasir crouched above the craggy pass, biting his lip in vexation. All along the high flat ground beside him, his three thousand men were stilled likewise, breath bated, crouched or lying flat. His eyes never left the thirty scrawny imperial scout riders below. They could not be allowed to foil his plan.

When the sultan had given him the opportunity to redeem himself, sending him west to seek out and counter Romanus' expected campaign, it had been a fine gift indeed. Then, when a lone rider had come to him just days ago advising him of the Byzantine route, it had been like a gift from Allah. This was his chance to seize glory. This was his chance to slay the *Haga*. But now, only a mile from the edge of the broad valley where the ambush was to take place, these scout riders could ruin it all. One glance upwards. One careless noise from his warband.

Then the clack-clack of a tumbling pebble rang out. He shot a deathly glare at the akhi whose shuffling had dislodged the stone. Then his breath stilled as the echo of the falling stone died.

The lead rider gawped at it and then up at the edges of the pass.

The Byzantine locked eyes with Nasir.

There was no turning back now. Nasir stood to his full height, filled his lungs and ripped his scimitar from its sheath. 'At them! Kill them all!'

As one, his warband rose to hurls spears and loose arrows upon the Byzantine scout riders. The old rider crumpled mid-cry, convulsing, his body punctured. The cluster of riders behind him descended into chaos. The quickest to react kicked their mounts into a turn, only to crash into those behind them. Backs exposed, these riders were swiftly pierced with missiles and slid from their mounts, corpses tangling under hooves.

Nasir slid down the scree-strewn pass side then leapt forward to hack at the panicked mass of riders. A clutch of akhi joined him, jabbing their spears forward at man and mount alike. He wrenched one fleeing rider from the saddle and smashed his mace into the back of the man's skull, crushing his head. Then he tossed the corpse aside and looked for his next foe.

Only a few Byzantines fought on. One, a gaunt-faced young rider who had fallen from his horse, hobbled towards a riderless stallion further back in the pass.

'That one!' Nasir stabbed his mace towards the fleeing young rider, sinew, skin and bone dangling from the tip. 'Stop him!'

Nasir leapt over the pile of the dead and hurled his mace as the young rider reached out to mount the stallion. The weighty metal bludgeon spun towards the man's head and Nasir grinned in bloodlust. But the young rider stumbled and the mace only scraped across his crown, tearing the felt cap and a section of scalp clear. Heedless of this gruesome injury, the rider mounted and heeled the stallion into a frantic gallop.

Seljuk arrows hissed and smacked against the sides of the pass, some punching into the man's back. But the rider did not fall and in moments he was gone. The drum of hooves died and for a heartbeat, the pass was silent bar the panting of the Seljuk warriors.

'Sir, we should consider turning back. If the Byzantines know we are coming . . . ' an akhi panted.

Nasir spun to him. It was the man who had dislodged the stone. In one motion, he pulled his scimitar from its sheath, then drove it hard into the man's gut. The akhi's eyes bulged and blood pumped from his lips, then Nasir ripped his blade clear. As the corpse toppled, he cast his gaze around his men in the narrow passage and the swathes of them lining the tops of the pass.

'There is no turning back. Riders, mount! Spearmen, be ready for a quick march. To the north!'

***

Apion's belly groaned. It was loud enough to draw startled looks from Igor and his axemen. He stared at the hardtack he had been holding for some time now, touching his parched tongue to his cracked lips. Hunger and thirst seemed to be playing dice with him and every other man sat in the shade at the northern edge of the valley.

'You'd be as well eating rocks,' Igor croaked, mopping the sweat from his brow.

'Washed down with a cup of dust,' Philaretos, sitting nearby, rasped with a throaty chuckle, his eyes shaded under a scowl.

The ruddy-faced and sweating Gregoras smirked at this, his beady eyes fixed on Apion.

Apion shrugged in resignation and placed the biscuit back in his ration pack. Himerius and the riders were not due back for a while yet. Even then the water would rightly go to the infantry first, so it would be near sunset by the time they received their share. He looked to Romanus, striding along the lines of his column, offering words of encouragement to his men. The emperor had insisted on being the last to receive water.

'We're being led by a good man,' Dederic muttered absently, by his side.

Apion looked to him. The little Norman's face was bathed in sweat. He had taken to carving at a wooden stake, hewing it vigorously into a point.

'Preparing that for the fat lord?' Apion nudged him with an elbow.

Dederic nodded. 'Something like that.' Then he looked up, squinting at the sun. 'Tell me, sir . . . in your time leading the ranks, you must have had to make tough choices?'

'Indeed,' Apion replied instantly, 'Almost every day. I have had men and their families retreat from their defences and their homes,

265

ceding hard-won ground to the Seljuks but saving them from unavoidable slaughter. I have allowed captured ghazi warbands to return to their lands unharmed – thinking that perhaps the next time we meet on the battlefield they will remember that. I would say these were good choices.' Then he thought of the bloody massacres he had led, the wailing of children spattered in their parents' blood, the stench of burning flesh. His thoughts spiralled back to those last days on Mansur's farm – the time that spawned that darkness. He flicked a finger at the Chi-Rho banner hanging limply nearby. 'And, by that God of yours, I have made some terrible choices in my time.'

'They say a man's choices will define him,' Dederic mused, tracing the tip of his stake through the dust. 'But what if he makes the wrong choices for the right reasons?'

Apion heard the question, his thoughts snared once again on Mansur's farm and on that last day he had ever laid eyes upon it. His poor choices had led to that day. 'Then he will live to regret it evermore,' Apion replied absently, staring into the dust.

Then his thoughts were curtailed by the echoing clop-clop of hooves. He shot his gaze to the Scorpion Pass. *Approaching horses?* he wondered, firing glances to Igor and Romanus. *No, it is too soon, surely.*

Gregoras was the first to stand, his eyes darting, his tongue poking out to moisten his lips. Then the infantry rose and stretched on their toes like a crop field rippling in a breeze, their faces eager.

Apion looked to Igor. 'Something is wrong,' he whispered, 'gather around the emperor.'

Igor nodded and barked to his varangoi. Immediately, they rushed to surround Romanus. Igor hefted his axe, his head dipped and his scarred eye trained on the opening. Apion stood by their side.

Then a single rider trotted sluggishly from the pass.

'It's Niketas!' one skutatos cried out. 'Where is our water?' A babble of voices broke out, confused and curious.

But Romanus raised a hand to hush them.

Niketas slowed to a canter, then halted, halfway across the pass and some twenty strides from the head of the column.

'Rider – report!' Romanus bawled.

The rider opened his mouth to speak, but no words were forthcoming. The cicada song seemed to grow deafening. Then Niketas' head lolled forward to reveal the circle of scalp that dangled from his crown and the matching disc of blood-smeared skull that it exposed. Niketas' shoulders lurched and he retched. Blood erupted from his nostrils and lips, soaking his mount. Then he toppled to the dust with a thud, revealing the arrow shafts quivering in his back.

A heartbeat of stillness and silence ensued. Then a rumbling of hooves started again. But this time it grew like thunder, and it came not from the Scorpion Pass, but from up above, somewhere atop the valley sides.

The Byzantine column broke into a babble of murmuring and then cries of panic split the air as men looked around in terror. Apion's eyes locked on the southern lip of the valley. All along it, plumes of red-gold dust rose like demons.

'*Basileus*,' he stabbed a finger to the south, 'form up for a flanking strike!'

But at that moment the tip of the southern valleyside came to life. A cluster of ironclad riders burst into view, shimmering in the sunlight, directly across from the emperor and his retinue.

Apion's heart froze. Ghulam riders, the cream of the Seljuk heavy cavalry. There were more than two hundred of them, each encased in armour and clutching lance, bow and blade. Behind them, a crescent of nimble ghazi riders swept into view. Another eight

267

hundred. As one, the Seljuk riders flooded down the scree and onto the valley floor, thundering straight towards the column head like an arrowhead. Apion stumbled to take his place with Dederic between the Varangoi and the Optimates. His mind echoed with a thousand thoughts and orders formed on his tongue, but without his army to command he could only watch on.

'Ready spears!' Romanus cried out. The order was echoed along the lines of the Optimates Tagma who were nearest the approaching horsemen. But, caught by surprise, they were unprepared, many having stowed their arms and armour in the touldon. Those on the front ranks who had spears levelled them, while those in the ranks behind lifted their rhiptaria. The resulting phalanx was blunt and weak in vast stretches, and the raiding horsemen were only strides away.

'Rhiptaria, loose!' Romanus cried.

At that moment, Apion saw three things. He saw the twisted, snarling and mutilated face of Nasir at the head of the Seljuk charge, he saw the devious sparkle in his nemesis' eyes and he saw the knuckles on Nasir's right hand grow white on the reins of his mount.

'No, Shields!' Apion cried. But his shout was drowned out by the hoarse cries of those all around him. Thousands of Byzantine javelins streaked into the air.

Then Nasir yanked on his mount's reins and barked his cavalry into a swift turn, pulling out of the charge and haring right, parallel to the column. The Byzantine javelins punched down harmlessly into the dust in the Seljuk riders' wake. Then the ghulam hurled their spears and the ghazi loosed an arrowstorm into the massed and unprepared Optimates ranks. Apion, without a shield at the edge of the Optimates lines, could only watch the incoming hail. Then, at the last, Dederic snatched up a shield and held it over both of them. The shield battered and buckled as the barrage rained down. The ripping of flesh and crunching of bone rang out all around them. Skutatoi fell in swathes, gouts of blood staining the air and soaking them. The densely packed toxotai further back were also cut down like wheat before they could loose in reply.

Then the barrage slowed as the Seljuk cavalry thundered on past the head of the column, along the valley floor and to the east.

Dederic lowered the shield and he and Apion gawped around them. Many hundreds lay dead or dying. Amidst the screaming of the stricken, the varangoi clustered around Romanus, their shields peppered with arrows. The emperor's eyes were locked on the Seljuk cavalry.

Nasir and his riders stopped a few hundred feet away, before two pillars of rock that pinched the valley. There, they took to cantering in a sweeping circle, those nearest the head of the Byzantine column firing and those furthest away nocking fresh arrows. Once more, Byzantine men all around the emperor fell like harvest wheat and chaos reigned.

Apion heard Philaretos growl from under the ceiling of varangoi shields; 'We outnumber them, urge our riders forward!'

Then Gregoras added to this, snarling; 'Aye, seize the opportunity, *Basileus!* The vanguard are nearly ready to charge.' He stabbed a finger at the cluster of three hundred riders, most now mounted and armed once more.

The emperor seemed swayed by their hubris. Apion grabbed the reins of his Thessalian from the nearby squire, then leapt on the saddle and kicked the beast forward to intervene; 'No!' he cried as he pushed in amidst the cluster of Rus axemen. 'Get shields to the men and wait out the arrow storm! Do not pursue those riders. Our column will lose integrity and the Seljuk mounts are swift and well-watered – even our best riders will do well to catch them.'

Philaretos scoffed at this as arrows rattled down on the shields overhead. 'Enough! This is not a decision for a thematic strategos!'

Apion ignored the jibe as he strapped on his plumed helmet and took up a shield. '*Basileus?*' he gasped.

At that moment, a stray arrow slipped inside the varangoi shields, grazing the flesh on the leg of the emperor's stallion. The beast reared up dramatically and the emperor threw his sword arm up to balance, punching through the roof of shields.

The beleaguered Byzantine front saw this and cried out in anticipation of an advance, and the vanguard took it as so. '*Nobiscum Deus!*' the lead rider of the vanguard roared, then dropped his spathion, pointing it forward like an accusing finger at the swarm of Seljuk cavalry. As one, the riders rumbled forward and burst ahead of the column.

'*Basileus!*' Apion gasped, 'you must stop them.'

Romanus looked to Apion. His gaze was acquiescent. 'It is too late, and I could never have ordered the men to wait here and die.' With that, he kicked his stallion fiercely, and the beast whinnied and bundled clear of the varangoi then charged out to lead the vanguard. 'Forward!' he roared, his purple plume dancing in his slipstream.

At this, the varangoi cried out in dread. Igor was the first to leap onto a saddle. 'Strategos,' he cried to Apion, 'With me!'

Apion nodded and the pair kicked their mounts into a gallop after the emperor. The rest of the column surged forward too; masses of skutatoi, toxotai and pockets of semi-prepared riders. But Apion and Igor broke ahead of them all, lying flat in their saddles to catch up with Romanus.

Apion saw what he expected to see up ahead; the Seljuk horsemen waited until Romanus and his riders were a handful of strides away, then they broke from their swarming circle and burst into a retreat eastwards along the valley.

'They're drawing the emperor away from the rest of the column!' Apion growled over the rush of wind in his ears.

Then the Seljuks slipped between the two pillars of rock that pinched the valley and the emperor's riders were quick to follow. Apion's gut twinged as he and Igor passed through this choke-point. Then his heart froze when he glanced up to the southern valleyside behind it.

A storm of roaring akhi were streaming down the scree. At least two thousand of them. These Seljuk spearmen then streamed across the valley floor and Apion and Igor only just burst past them before they blockaded the narrow choke-point.

Apion shot a glance over his shoulder. The akhi had dug in, nearly twenty ranks deep, spear butts dug into the dust and facing the rest of the onrushing Byzantine column, bodies braced. 'We're on our own,' he hissed.

Igor frowned, then looked back over his shoulder to see the swell of Byzantine infantry surge against this wall of spears. Ribs popped and men were disembowelled as skutatoi were pushed onto the spearwall by their over-eager comrades behind. Blood showered the akhi, screams rang out and Byzantine corpses piled up. The pressure was immense, but the akhi stood firm. 'Aye, then my axe will be busy today,' the big Rus said as he looked forward again.

There, just a few hundred paces ahead, the emperor and his three hundred were now at the mercy of Nasir and his thousand riders. The ghazis were circling, raining arrows, while Nasir led his ghulam lancers in darting charges at the kataphractoi flanks, each time felling clutches of the precious riders. Romanus' purple plume whipped and billowed as he fought like a demon, hacking and slaying when he could get within striking distance of the Seljuk riders. But nearly half of the kataphractoi had been felled. It was only a matter of time.

Apion's heart thundered. It could not end here. Surely this was not the island in the storm the crone had spoken of?

As he burst forward to join the emperor and his riders, he caught sight of Nasir glaring at him then roaring with laughter.

'The emperor will die, and now the *Haga* comes to join him! This is a fine day to take our glory!'

With that, Nasir broke from his pack of ghulam, lifted a javelin from the body of a dead kataphractos and fixed his sights on the emperor. Then he hefted the shaft and launched it.

Apion kicked his mount forward, lunging to the front of his saddle to punch his shield out just as the javelin sped for the emperor's throat. His shoulder jolted and popped as the missile smacked from the shield and sclaffed clear of Romanus.

The emperor looked at him, wide-eyed and blinking as they rode side by side.

'*Basileus,*' Apion cried over the thunder of hooves, 'break your men into two wedges. We must separate the ghulam from the ghazis.' He punched a fist into his palm. 'Snare and lure!'

Romanus nodded briskly then raised a hand and flicked a finger in one direction and then another. 'Split!' Eighty of the kataphractoi read this and wheeled away behind the emperor to charge at the ghazi circle.

Apion led the remaining seventy in a charge towards Nasir and the ghulam wedge. 'With me – stay tight to my path! Every man on the right, ready your bows!' he bellowed, then swept the scimitar down and straight at Nasir.

The dark door crashed open in Apion's mind as the two wedges thundered for one another. The two men at their heads roared, scimitars raised.

Then, only paces apart, Apion wrenched on the reins of his mount, pulling right. He parried Nasir's swipe, then hacked and parried as he galloped along the edge of the Seljuk wedge. The rest of the wedge fell in tight behind him and followed suit, smashing and parrying. The sides of the two wedges scraped together like the hulls of a pair of opposing warships colliding. Splintered spearshafts, crimson spray, the tearing of iron and flesh and a cacophony of curses filled the air.

Then Apion cried out; 'Archers!' The riders in the right half of the wedge stood tall in their stirrups, twisted to their left, stretched their bows and loosed a small but dense volley of arrows down into the flanks of the ghulam. At such close range, the missiles punctured limbs and punched through the gaps between iron plates. The Seljuk wedge wobbled at this barrage, many falling, mounts tumbling over in the dust. Then the two wedges broke apart.

Nasir roared his men into a tight turn. Despite his losses, his riders were fresher than the Byzantines and they wheeled round nimbly, lining up to pierce into the flank of Apion's slower wedge. Apion saw that he could not ride clear of the threat and stay in formation. 'Break, break!' he cried. But it was too late.

Nasir's wedge smashed into the Byzantine kataphractoi, lancing men from their saddles, throwing others under a storm of hooves. Apion kicked at his mount to break clear when he heard a whirring. He glanced up then snapped his head to one side just in time to dodge a flanged mace hurtling for his face. The metal wings on the bludgeon gouged the skin from his cheek before spinning onwards to rip the mail veil and jaw of a kataphractos clean off. The man's eyes

273

bulged as he clawed at his jawless face, tongue dangling, blood soaking his chest before he toppled to the ground. Apion twisted in his saddle to see Nasir cursing the near miss.

Apion heeled his Thessalian round to face his foe, when a wooden spear shaft swept round like a club and knocked him from the saddle. He crashed to the dust, dazed and winded momentarily. Through the forest of horse legs, he saw Romanus' riders, thinned even further, pursuing the ghazis but still unable to snare them. He saw the akhi spearwall holding firm at the choke-point despite the swell of Byzantine riders and infantry pressing against them. Then he saw Nasir's scimitar blade scythe down for his neck.

At once his vision sharpened and he rolled clear of the blow, the blade splitting a jagged rock where he had lay moments before. He scrambled to his feet, turning to face Nasir. He backed away, dodging and ducking between the swiping swords and rearing mounts of the kataphractoi and the ghulam all around him.

Then a ghulam mount reared up and kicked out, a hoof whacking into his shoulder and sending him staggering towards Nasir. Nasir lunged for him, swinging his blade in a flurry of swipes with no thought to defence. Apion parried as best he could, but his limbs were numb, his parched and starved body weak and every blow seemed to be stronger than the last. Then Nasir's blade sliced across Apion's forearm and his scimitar fell from his grip. Before he could grasp out to catch it, his heel stubbed on the split rock and he toppled onto his back, weaponless. Kataphractoi thudded all around him, impaled on ghulam spears and torn by Seljuk blades.

Nasir approached, scimitar extended, chest heaving. 'We once swore an oath to protect one another,' he cried over the tumult, lifting his scimitar tip to Apion's throat. The ruined side of his face was coated in dust, the exposed eye bulging. 'Today, I rescind that oath.'

Apion squared his jaw, waiting. 'Then why do you hesitate, brave bey of the sultanate? My actions led to the death of your betrothed, did they not? If not for my mule-headedness, Maria would still be by your side. I do not deny this. So spill my blood and be on about your business.'

For a heartbeat, Apion saw something behind the rage. Nasir's good eye was shot red with blood and for that moment it was glassy.

Apion searched Nasir's gaze. 'Nasir?'

Nasir offered him a look that broke through the tortured, burnt and bitter features of the man he had become. Then it was washed away with a look of sober finality. He raised his scimitar and readied to swipe. 'Goodbye, old friend.'

The roars all around them died away like a gale dropping.

Apion held Nasir's gaze.

Then a rumble of thunder filled the air and the Seljuk roars of impending victory turned into cries of anguish. Nasir frowned, sword still aloft. Then he snatched a glance at the eastern end of the valley.

Apion looked there too. There, another wall of silver flickered, growing like an onrushing flood. A bobbing sea of Crimson banners emerged from the heat haze.

The cry was jumbled at first, then it grew unmistakable.

'Nobiscum Deus! *Nobiscum Deus!*'

The men of Chaldia were coming to war.

At this, the ghulam and ghazis broke from the melee, kicking their mounts into a frenzied flight up the southern valley side. Then the akhi spearwall hemming in the bulk of the Byzantine column saw this and a panicked wail broke out from them. They disintegrated and scrambled for the valley sides, clawing at the scree to reach the top. The kataphractoi and skutatoi pegged back by their spears now flooded forward like a raging river bursting its dam.

Nasir glanced to the Byzantine tides washing towards him from either end of the valley.

Apion scrambled to his feet and snatched up his scimitar once more. 'Perhaps this means our oath remains?'

Nasir turned to him, then roared in frustration and leapt onto his mount. As he did so, he pointed his blade accusingly at Apion, his gaze trained along its length, his expression darker than night once more.

'Your time is short, *Haga*,' he spat, before heeling his mare round for the southern valley side and taking flight with his army.

Apion watched him go, then fell to his knees, panting. He closed his eyes to see the dark door slam shut. All around him he could hear only the shrill cries of carrion birds descending to begin their feast.

17. Land of Honey

Dusk settled on the plain surrounding Melitene. A baritone chanting of evening prayer started from the centre of the city. It grew in intensity, echoing out over the broad, tall limestone battlements. Then it spilled across the marching camp that hugged the southern walls and gate. Inside the near-deserted camp, Apion sat alone at one of the many benches laid out for the feast that was to come.

He traced his fingertips across the rough oak table – yet to be adorned with fare. The holy chanting reverberated through the timber and caused him to shiver. He shuffled, pulling his crimson cloak tighter.

Three weeks ago the army had limped to this, the last of the Byzantine strongholds in southeast Anatolia. Romanus had proposed that they rest here, waiting until October to march into Seljuk territory.

For, by then, the Syrian sun will have lost its fire and the men will not fall sick under its glare.

Apion knew how eager Romanus was to press on and seize victory, so this was a generous concession from the man. Yet these few weeks had passed like bad meat through a beggar's belly, Apion thought, for the Ides of October was upon them already. Tomorrow the army would set out on the march once more, leaving Byzantine lands behind them. Yet the doubts and questions surrounding the Seljuk ambush in Lykandos still plagued his thoughts like a swarm of gnats.

More than eleven hundred skutatoi, one hundred toxotai and four hundred kataphractoi had been lost in that valley. Their lives had been claimed by Seljuk blades, but they had been condemned to death by whichever dark soul had informed Nasir of the campaign route. The same dark soul, no doubt, that had seen the wells poisoned and the supplies taken.

This unanswered riddle had hung like a grey cloud over the march to Melitene. Rumours had spread amongst the ranks. The men were nervous. These fears seemed to fade somewhat once they reached the safe haven of this city and the men indulged in the local delights – the wine, the renowned honey and the well-wishing local ladies. But the cloud still remained over Apion's thoughts.

He eyed the white-specked peaks of the Antitaurus Mountains to the south. The precipitous passes that led through there would be treacherous, but at least such terrain meant they were unlikely to face another Seljuk warband. Then he thought of what lay beyond the mountains. Syria, the start of the Seljuk heartlands, a desert studded with Seljuk strongholds. Nasir. Alp Arslan. He shivered once more and shook his head.

Then he realised that the chanting had ceased. Slaves had begun swarming around the tables. They brought platters of goose and lamb joints, cheeses, bowls of yoghurt and pots of the renowned Melitene honey. The aroma of the cooked meat wafted across the table and hunger stabbed at his gut. Still they came with fruits, berries and blissfully aromatic freshly-baked breads, then amphora after amphora of wine, soured wine and water. Crackling torches were brought out and staked all around the feasting area as the soldiers and the populace poured from the city to crowd around the tables, taking seats and tucking into the fare. They had made their peace with their god and now they were ready to celebrate. A rumble of kettledrums started and then the plucky melody of a lyre joined in. Laughter and chatter broke out all around. Then a fresh clay cup was slammed down before him. Blastares sat down beside him with two cups of his own.

'Drink up, sir,' the big man insisted.

Apion raised a hand in refusal, swirling his near-finished drink. 'I've had my time seeking answers at the bottom of a cup . . . ' he started. But then Dederic, Procopius and Sha sat opposite him, cups in hand.

' . . . and perhaps tonight you will finally find them,' Sha grinned, pushing the fresh cup towards him.

Apion relented and took a swig of the wine – tart, fruity and unwatered. First it invigorated his flesh, warming his belly and blood. He savoured the sensation for a moment, then tore a piece from a charred, still-warm flatbread offered by Procopius and dipped it in yoghurt. Then he took another deep swig of wine to wash it down. This time he felt it begin to pierce the troubles in his mind. He listened as Procopius and Blastares bickered about a lost cloak.

'I gave it to you, when you were training your men in that rainstorm last week,' Procopius insisted.

'Nonsense,' Blastares waved a hand. 'I borrowed it yes, but I gave it back to you. Not my fault if you've misplaced it.' He gulped at his wine and tapped a finger to his temple, cackling. 'Old age, you see, plays tricks on your mind.'

Procopius gawped at this. 'I can remember every ripping fart, watery belch and grating snore you've subjected me to, so there's no way I would forget . . . '

'Hold on, you're talking about your green woollen cloak?' Sha interrupted, swigging his wine. 'The one I saw that lady wearing this morning in the market square? What's her name,' he snapped his fingers over and over, then he wagged one finger and his eyes sparkled. 'Ah, yes, Tetradia!'

Procopius' jaw dropped. 'Tetradia? The fat Rus whore? You gave my cloak to her?'

At once, Blastares' face fell ashen. 'Aye, all right, I might have left it with her. But she's not just a whore. She's nice.'

'Aye, nice to rut with?' Procopius countered, winking at the others and then rising from his bench slightly to perform a few robust pelvic thrusts.

'No,' Blastares scowled. Then he examined his filthy, cracked fingernails. 'Well, yes. But she's nice to talk with as well. She listens to my problems.'

At this, Sha and Procopius shared and incredulous glance, before erupting in laughter. Dederic nearly choked on his wine at this.

Apion took another swig of wine and grinned. 'Damn, but I've missed your banter in these last months. Dederic will be a fine fit for our group.'

Sha, Blastares and Procopius looked to the Norman and then to Apion.

'He will be the fourth tourmarches for Chaldia.'

The three frowned at Dederic for a moment, and the Norman shuffled where he sat.

Then Blastares leaned forward. 'You're not an artillery bore, are you?' he said, flicking eyebrows at Procopius.

Dederic shrugged. 'I'm a simple man. Give me a horse, a lance and men to lead. I'll lead them to victory or die trying. That's me.'

Blastares' scowl remained for a moment, then he raised a cup and broke into a grin. Apion, Procopius and Sha followed suit and Dederic joined them, clashing the cups together, before gulping at the wine. A cheer erupted from those nearby at this.

Then, when it died, Apion looked them each in the eye. 'The emperor relies on me and the other strategoi and doukes as if we were his limbs. Likewise, I look to each of you as mine. I want you to remember this; what we do out there,' he said, flicking a finger to the south, 'could bring an end to the suffering of these lands. Anatolia has been riven with bloodshed for too long. Syria can be a safe and secure imperial border for the southeast, and if I die and we achieve this, then it will be a good death.'

Their eyes sparkled as they listened.

'I'm ready for it,' Blastares drummed his fingers on his spathion hilt, grinning like a shark. The big man's eyes betrayed a giddiness from the wine.

'I've lost too many dear to me to think of anything else,' Procopius agreed, lifting his cup. The old tourmarches had lost his brother and his son to the war, and he wore a steely look that Apion was all too familiar with.

'Mali is my birthplace,' Sha stabbed a finger into the table, 'but this land is my home, and you are my brothers.'

Then they looked to Dederic. He seemed a little cowed by the bravado of the others. Apion knew the man was here only to earn coin to save his family.

'We fight for different reasons, but know this; I came here to do whatever it takes to see that my family are safe.' Dederic thumped a fist into the table, looking each of them in the eye with solemnity, coming to Apion last. 'Whatever it takes.'

Apion and Dederic shared a lasting gaze.

Then, suddenly, the men all around him put down their cups and slid from their benches, dropping to one knee. The kettledrums and flutes stopped as well and the musicians fell to their knees.

Apion twisted to see Emperor Romanus behind him, flanked by Igor, Philaretos and Gregoras.

'At ease,' Romanus motioned to the soldiers around him to sit once more. 'I too am here to feast and ready myself for what is to come – just as you are.' The men cautiously returned to their benches and the drums and flutes picked up once more. Despite this, the banter was muted. Romanus cast Apion a wry look, then drew his sword and held it aloft by the blade, examining the spectacularly bejewelled hilt. All eyes turned to this spectacle. 'This monstrosity was bestowed upon me, much to my chagrin.' He boomed. 'But know that despite such seemingly necessary ostentation, I am just like every one of you. When we march, I may march at the head. But when we fight,' he clenched a fist, 'I fight by your side.' He lifted a cup of wine, took a gulp and then held it high. 'Nobiscum Deus!'

The surrounding soldiers echoed the sentiment. '*Nobiscum Deus!*'

Romanus sheathed his sword and lifted both arms in the air. 'Now drink and eat until your bellies are fit to burst!' A raucous cheer erupted at this before tapering back into a lively babble.

Apion had heard of many emperors before, some hiding from reality on their thrones while the enemies clawed at the borders, others leading campaigns as if they were gods, being carried above their men or meting out brutal punishment upon the soldiers for any breach of discipline. Romanus was not one of either ilk. He was a man of the armies. It was little wonder the men of the Istros frontier loved him so much. The golden heart pendant around Romanus' neck glinted in the torchlight. Apion looked upon it and welcomed the one word that echoed through his thoughts.

Hope.

Romanus straddled the bench to sit by Apion's side, Igor, Philaretos and Gregoras taking a seat nearby. Sha, Blastares and Procopius bantered amongst themselves, while Dederic shared some ribald tale with Igor. Philaretos and Gregoras were hunched together, chatting quietly.

'We'll meet in the citadel before dawn to review the route one last time,' Romanus said, leaning in towards Apion. 'But it should be unchanged; we take the passes through the Antitaurus Mountains. Then we are there, Apion, and it will all be within our grasp. Syria! The strongholds of Aleppo, Edessa and Antioch can be ours in good time. The Euphrates can be our border once more. With its banks well-manned, we can hold the Seljuks at bay with a minimum of bloodshed. With the south secure, we will only have the borders of eastern Anatolia to contend with.'

Apion thought of the many fortresses, citadels and well-walled towns and cities dotted around Syria. If needed, the Seljuks could muster a vast army. 'There are many strongholds on that baked land, *Basileus*. We must choose our first target carefully.'

'Exactly,' Romanus agreed. 'But I feel we should defer that decision until we lay eyes upon the Syrian sands. Sometimes it is best to descry your enemy before you decide how to tackle him.'

Apion nodded and tore off more bread. 'Aye, and perhaps our destination should remain concealed for now,' he said, shooting furtive glances around at the sea of faces, some sanguine, some narrow-eyed, some scowling, 'for other reasons.'

'As we have spoken of in these last days, your thoughts and mine are one and the same,' Romanus spoke in a hushed tone. 'There is a rogue in our midst. But as ever, this campaign must push on. For, behind us, Psellos awaits like a sharpened dagger. And if it was not Psellos, then it would be another. Such is the fate of an emperor.'

Apion nodded. 'Aye, ever onwards.'

Romanus grinned at this and drummed his fingers on the table. 'Ever onwards with one hand on your sword hilt and a dagger under your pillow.'

Apion smiled at this. The emperor was no fool.

Romanus then lowered his voice to a whisper. 'But this much we can discuss: I plan to leave Doux Ausinalios, his Rus and his Norman riders to garrison these walls. Together with the three banda of skutatoi already posted here, it should prove redoubtable against raids in our absence. This will leave us with just shy of seven thousand fighting men for the march into Syria. Over seven hundred kataphractoi, twelve banda of skutatoi, four banda of toxotai, a handful of my varangoi and scout riders, plus over a thousand horse archers – Pecheneg and Oghuz. A fine ratio of abilities, don't you think? Our patience should pay off too – the men should be able to march through the mountains at a fair pace given that the cool of autumn has settled upon their peaks.'

Apion nodded at this and looked to the south. 'And then on into the inferno,' he smiled wryly.

Romanus slapped him on the shoulder with a chuckle, then stood and left.

Apion then turned to those sitting around the table. He set his doubts to one side and raised his cup. 'Let tomorrow bring what it brings,' those seated around him raised their cups too. He took another generous mouthful and let the tart liquid wash around his tongue. 'And the day after? We will drink to it tomorrow night!'

A raucous cheer erupted around the table.

***

Zenobius supped at his water, cheering along with the fools of his kontoubernion, laughing when they laughed, pretending to enjoy their banter. Then they turned to him.

'So, Zenobius,' Trolius, the pug-nosed *dekarchos* slurred, 'tell us a story. You're from . . . ' he frowned.

'Ancyra,' Zenobius lied, disguising his disdain for this weak man. The leader of his kontoubernion, like the rest of the men, had been cold and guarded around him. Just like everyone else in his life had. It was only now they were drunk that they seemed to warm to him.

'Aye, Ancyra,' Trolius snapped his fingers. 'So, what are the women like in Ancyra?'

Zenobius looked at them, their faces expectant. Then he forced a smile, mimicking their inebriate expressions. 'I'll need another cup of this stuff before I can talk about the women of Ancyra!'

He took his leave as the men roared with laughter at this. He had no intention of returning. Instead, he passed around the feasting area. He glowered at a pair of buxom women who barged past him; the pair shared the warmth of a green woollen cloak as they jabbered about some burly soldier who only seemed to want to talk about his problems – the main one being a bulbous wart on his genitals. The two women shared a look of disgust, then they both shrieked with laughter. Then a staggering drunk fell across his path, slurring an apology, his breath wretched.

Finally, Zenobius reached the table where the emperor sat, whispering with the *Haga*. He offered a faint and cold nod to his accomplice, sat there too. Then he picked a seat nearby – close enough that he could see the emperor's face. He pretended to swill from his empty cup, all the time watching their lips move. He read it all; the emperor's plans for his forces and his ambitions once they reached Syria.

At last he turned away, looking south to the tall and treacherous shadow of the Antitaurus Mountains.

If they reach Syria, he mused.

***

Dekarchos Trolius hiccupped as he swaggered back through the dark streets of Melitene. The air was still spiced with the tang of roasted meat and woodsmoke from the feast. The few torches that still glowed showed that the streets were empty bar the odd inebriate soldier like himself. His thoughts were on the curvy and milky-skinned Rus woman, Tetradia, he had just left behind in the brothel. He could still smell her sweet scent, and could still see her pendulous breasts bobbing in his mind's eye. Guilt and pleasure tugged at his conscience. Then a grin stretched over his face.

'Ah, just wait till I tell the others,' he grinned inanely, thinking of his fellow soldiers who had run out of money earlier that evening. 'They'll be raging!'

He looked up, his eyelids half covering his pupils, and a hiccup escaped from his lips.

'Now which way was it?' he muttered, dragging a finger along the streets before him, looking for the way to the main gate on the southern walls that would take him back to the imperial camp. He chose one shadowy alley behind the granary and set off that way.

The shadows danced around him as he stumbled over the loose and worn flagstones. Then the alley opened up to reveal the main gate, only paces ahead. A grin spread across his features, then settled into a frown. Locating the main gate was the easy part of it. Sneaking through it and then back into the imperial camp and his pavilion tent during the hours of curfew would be somewhat stickier though. He thought again of the others in his kontoubernion – probably sound asleep in their tents by now, obeying the curfew just as he had drilled them to do. Guilt touched his thoughts once more.

He looked up to the walkway above the gate and saw that the two skutatoi on sentry duty up there were talking, doubtless trying to fend off the urge to sleep. The single sentry by the gate hatch inside the city was less fortunate. He rested against the gate, head slumped, chest heaving to the rhythm of his snoring. Satisfied with this, Trolius strode forward and slipped under the shadows of the gatehouse, lifting the iron latch carefully despite his blurring vision. Then he opened the hatch and readied to slip outside. He cast one last glance at the sleeping sentry and shook his head. 'Disgraceful . . . ' he whispered, then clamped a hand over his mouth just in time to stifle a hiccup.

The sentry stirred but only enough to grumble and reposition himself.

Trolius closed the hatch and made haste through the imperial camp. The sky was peppered with scudding clouds, and this caused the moonlight to come and go. Right now, the full moon shone strongly, revealing the imperial banners fluttering in a light breeze in the centre of the camp where the emperor and his varangoi were situated. Surrounding them was the sea of pavilion tents of the themata and tagmata, each cluster marked out by the fluttering, multi-tailed banners of those armies. He tried to pick out the distinctive colours of his banda standard – yellow cloth emblazoned with the Chi-Rho, then three coloured tails: yellow for the thema, blue for the tourma and green for his bandon. Locating it by the outer edge of the camp, he picked his way forward through the tent ropes, avoiding the main thoroughfare for fear of being spotted. He stifled a curse as the moonlight faded under a veil of cloud, causing him to nearly skewer his foot on a tent peg.

Eventually, he reached the tent. A warm sense of relief washed over him. He paused for a moment before entering. He yawned, groaned and stretched then cast a glance out over the palisade camp

287

wall. The darkness to the south betrayed only the dark outline of the Antitaurus Mountains. A sliver of fear snaked through his heart as he remembered what lay ahead tomorrow. A few hours with the busty Rus lady had served only as a distraction. He shrugged and turned to enter the tent.

But then he spun back to the south and froze.

Out there, in the darkness, something had moved.

He rubbed at his eyes, then crept towards the palisade, gripping it, lifting up onto his toes to peer out.

Again, the shadows rippled.

Suddenly, he became very sober.

He glanced up to the nearest watchtower; the sentry there appeared to be sleeping at his post, head lolled forward on his chest.

He squinted back out at the shadows, desperate to be wrong. But then he saw it; a horseman passed under a brief shaft of moonlight, galloping for the mountains. The rider shot a glance over his shoulder and Trolius' heart thundered. A ghazi rider? But there was another figure out there too – someone in a dark cloak, standing where the rider had set off from. Trolius gasped, filling his lungs to raise the alarm. But then a cloud covered the plain in darkness once more.

The breath stuck in his throat, and he rubbed his eyes, peering into the blackness. Then the cloud passed from the moon and the plain was illuminated again in an eerie grey light. It was deserted. No rider, no cloaked figure. The panic faded from his breast. Was it a trick of the light? He scratched at his jaw; if he was to report it, reeking of wine whilst breaking the curfew, the skin would be flogged from his back. But if there was to be some kind of Seljuk attack on the camp tonight . . . his head ached with indecision. Then he recognised the sleeping sentry in the nearest watchtower. It was Sittas, a good man and a friend. Perhaps he could waken Sittas, pass on the warning and then retire to his tent quietly.

Satisfied with this, he jogged over to the timber watchtower, trying to keep the image of what he had seen fresh in his mind. A rider and a dark cloaked figure. The rider was racing to the mountains and the dark cloaked figure was . . .

His brow knitted into a frown as he saw some dark stain on Sittas' chest, then he saw the blood washing from the wound on the man's throat.

Trolius sucked in a breath to cry out in alarm, but the breath never left his lungs.

The cloaked figure from the plain leapt over the palisade to land in the camp only paces ahead of him, then plunged a dagger in his heart. Trolius saw only silver eyes and a ghostly pallor under the figure's hood. *Zenobius?* He mouthed silently.

Then he fell to his knees. A bitter cold gripped his body as the lifeblood pumped from the wound. Behind the albino, he saw some other figure slinging Sittas' body over one shoulder, then bringing it down from the watchtower. As he toppled to the ground to bleed his last, this second figure dropped Sittas' corpse beside him.

Trolius' last thoughts were for his brothers in the camp all around him.

What devilment was to befall them?

18. Mountains of the Bull

The lofty and narrow path that clung to the side of the grey-gold limestone mountain shimmered as the imperial army traversed it like an iron serpent. The kataphractoi vanguard led the way like the tongue and the fangs. Then, some distance back, the head was formed by the emperor, the Cross-bearing priests, the varangoi and the rest of the cavalry. Behind them, the body of infantry writhed like silvery scales for miles, wrapping around this mountainside and the one before it. Then came the supply touldon, the wagons nose to tail in single file, the mules blinkered to the precipitous drop by their sides and the ravine far below. Then the Pecheneg and Oghuz archer cavalry formed the tail.

The sky above was azure and flecked with white cloud. A wake of red-beaked Egyptian vultures circled above the imperial column, eagerly anticipating a meal. Then one bird grew tired of waiting to be fed; it swooped down over the column, gliding over the chain of iron helmets and speartips until it came to the crimson banners of the Chaldian infantry. Here it screeched as it passed over the pair of riders heading them up.

'What the?' Blastares stabbed his spear up in fright then squinted up into the morning sun, scowling as the bird rejoined its shameless comrades. He tilted his helmet back to scratch at his stubbled scalp. 'They're a bit bloody presumptuous are they not?'

'Aye, if I perish up here I hope the feathery bastards break their beaks on this,' Procopius tapped at the chest of his iron klibanion.

Then he looked to his fellow tourmarches and shrugged. 'To be fair, though, they could probably smell you from a few miles away.'

Blastares eyed his friend, then whistled as he nodded to the precipice only inches from Procopius' horse's hooves. 'Big drop, that . . .'

As if to side with the big tourmarches, a section of the rocky path crumbled away, dust and scree toppling silently down towards the foaming waters in the ravine.

Procopius gulped. 'Look I told you, I'm not good with heights. Next time this track broadens, we swap places.'

Blastares grinned at this then looked away and all around him, nostrils flared, shoulders squared. 'Perhaps. Depends on the impudence I get from you before then.'

Procopius frowned and fell silent like a scorned child. His wrinkled features were tinged with a shade of green and his eyes took to darting along the precipice.

Then Blastares thought of the echoing scream that had filled the mountain passes a few days ago, when the column was becoming bold and confident of traversing these tracks. A kataphractoi of the vanguard had trodden and slipped on a patch of slime near a waterfall. The man and his mount had no chance of halting their fall. It was a blessing indeed that the column did not hear the impact of the pair on the rocks far below. Blastares had the misfortune to see the tangle of both bodies being washed downstream like broken kindling. Since then, the column had marched with extreme care. He looked to Procopius; 'Aye, fair enough, we'll swap,' he relented. 'I tell you though, if I was to plot our route through these mountains, this certainly wouldn't be it.'

Procopius nodded. 'Goes without saying that I agree. I understand why the emperor has chosen it though.'

'Next to no chance of a pitched assault along the way? Aye, I can see that,' Blastares looked around again. The place was majestic and barren at once. The towering mountainsides were pierced with a smattering of hardy shrubs and vulture nests, but otherwise they seemed devoid of life. The central mountains towered above all else, their snow-capped peaks ghostly in the haze. For the last eight days, they had marched in daylight and the temperature had been cool and pleasant. In the evenings, they had camped on what patches of broader track they could find, huddling together to stave off the bitter chill that came with the darkness. This ferocious cold had been the only enemy they had encountered – that along with the thin air and the wretched carrion birds. Still, Blastares was sure he preferred this to the heat.

Just then, Sha and Dederic fell back from the cluster of varangoi and the Imperial Tagmata to ride just ahead of them. 'Good news!'

'I'm about to wake up back in Melitene?' Procopius muttered, never looking away from the precipice.

Dederic frowned at this, then shook his head. 'No, the *Haga* and the kursores of the vanguard have ridden well ahead and returned to report that the Syrian plain is within a day's march.'

Blastares and Procopius shared a grin. The skutatoi marching behind Procopius and Blastares heard this and erupted in a cheer, a welcome sound after so long marching in nervous silence.

'The strategos encountered no signs of danger?' Blastares asked.

'No, not yet at least,' Sha replied. 'He and a handful of kursores have remained out front. They're plotting the best path for the rest of the column to take. He will rejoin us by the afternoon.'

'Then on to Syria. Where the ground is flat!' Procopius marvelled. 'Flatter than the piss-brew from the tavern in Kryapege!'

Blastares cocked an eyebrow. 'Aye, and it's hotter than fire and the place is swarming with insects and Seljuks.'

Procopius sighed and shrugged, then motioned with one hand to the inside of the mountain track. 'Look, can we just swap places now?'

* * *

Apion stood by his gelding, stroking its mane as it drank from a babbling waterfall that tumbled down the cliff-face. Here the warm Syrian air mixed with the cool mountain climes and thus the grey-gold rock was dappled with verdant growth. Vines clung to the mountainside and clusters of Syrian Juniper trees sprouted along the edges of the track, lending a tang of pine to the air. A short distance down the track behind him, the three kursores who accompanied him were sitting by their mounts, eating and drinking from their rations. Apion reached up to pluck the berries from the nearest tree and then fed the waxy fruit to his mount. Then he took a dried fig from his rations and chewed upon it as he squinted at the forked path ahead.

One route would take them on a short but high and narrow track to the plateau that marked the end of this mountain range. The other path was long and winding, but wider. The second route was definitely safer but it would mean they would not be clear of the mountains until the following day, probably around noon. Morale had been poor since they had entered the thin air of these passes, so perhaps the safer, longer option was not necessarily the best. He uncorked his water skin and held it up to the waterfall to fill it, then sipped at the meltwater – still ice cold.

The truth was there was little to suggest that any danger lay between them and the Syrian plain on either route – he and the kursores had already ridden to the end of each trail and spotted nothing to be wary of. But something itched at the back of his mind, something that had niggled his thoughts since they had left Melitene. On that last morning before they left, one of the officers of the Thrakesion Thema had been found dead. Murdered. It was the Dekarchos, Trolius. His heart had been cleaved by a blade. They suspected he had been quarrelling with the sentry, Sittas, whose body they found beside him. They thought that perhaps Sittas had deserted his watchtower and, when Trolius had questioned him, the pair had taken up their daggers and torn the life from one another.

During his years in the ranks, Apion had grown well-used to seeing good soldiers die on the battlefield. But that good men should die in their own camp, over what? Some quarrel? And at the end of a comrade's blade . . . his lips grew taut in disgust as dark memories of his past swirled. If only that was the end to it, but it wasn't. That nobody had seen anything, anything at all, provoked doubt in Apion's heart. That the bodies had been found right at the camp perimeter only stoked his misgivings further. His thoughts churned. He plucked a nomisma from his purse. He had found this wedged into the dust near the dead sentry's body. It was no ordinary coin – it was pure-gold and recently minted.

And it was identical to those used by Psellos to buy loyalty.

What if this was the work of the traitor amongst the ranks? And if so, there had to be more than one individual at work here – slaying a sentry and stealing from the camp unnoticed was near impossible for a single man when there was a full watch. He frowned and gazed through the waterfall, his thoughts spinning.

'Sir, it's nearly mid-morning, we should be getting back to the column,' a scout rider interrupted his thoughts.

Apion blinked, turning to the three riders. They were saddled and ready to move out. 'Aye, we should.' He led his Thessalian from the waterfall and slipped one foot in the stirrup, then hoisted himself onto the saddle. He heeled the gelding back along the track towards the column, and the kursores fell in behind him.

They rode until the sun was nearly overhead. At this point, the smattering of white cloud had gathered and had taken on a dark and portentous shade of grey. Indeed, the first spots of rain pattered down around them before long, giving rise to an earthy scent and casting a vibrant rainbow across the mountains. Then a wind picked up. At this the clouds seemed to grow bolder, taking over most of the sky, until the sun was hidden and there was not a patch of blue left. The land was gloomy and grey. Finally, to seal their misery, the gentle rain suddenly turned sheet-like.

When Apion reached for his helmet, a rumble of thunder echoed across the sky and a fork of lightning streaked from the darkest part of the storm clouds. He placed his helmet back on his saddle and cast a contemptuous look towards the heavens. In moments his hair and his cloak were sodden, and the rain lashed from his beard. The kursores barely disguised their distaste for the change in weather, grimacing as their felt caps and jackets grew soaked and heavy. Apion called out to them over the next clap of thunder; 'Let's make haste. This looks like it will last for some time, and I don't relish the prospect of being exposed to a thunderstorm up here any longer than is necessary.' He waited for the three kursores to nod their assent, then dug his heels into his gelding's flanks, moving from a canter to a gallop. 'Ya!'

Now the rain picked up a fresh impetus, driving into their faces as the wind became a gale. The mounts hurled up mud in their wake from the mire underfoot.

'This would have been a blessing back in the valleys of Lykandos!' One of the kursores roared over the howling wind, shivering with his shoulders hunched.

Apion laughed at this, turning his head from the storm, his drenched locks plastered to his face. 'Aye, so enjoy it while you can. For it will be a rarity once more when we reach the deserts of Syria.'

The rider responded with a mirthless laugh through chattering teeth. Then another of them called out. 'Look, sir – the column!'

Apion shielded his eyes from the rain and slowed a little as he looked ahead.

The last stretch of the most treacherous track, clinging to the sheer face of the mountain, dipped and rose like a saddle. Halfway along it, the vanguard had dismounted and now inched along. The rain was driving at them, soaking the cliff face, and their boots slithered and slipped as the path grew slick. He thought back to the kataphractos whose mount had lost its footing on a wet piece of track only days ago. He made out the figure of Romanus, further back. He and his varangoi had also dismounted. The water was rushing past their heels in floods before toppling into the ravine below – its depths now obscured by the spray of the falling rain and the swollen torrents. The priests chanted as they inched along the path. Apion hoped their God would not desert them now. Yet at just that moment, lightning flashed across the sky and illuminated the soaked cliff face and the gilded campaign Cross – and then the storm clouds unleashed an even more ferocious torrent of rain.

First, one skutatoi was washed from his feet. He clawed frantically at the edge of the precipice, only to grasp at loose root and earth before falling into the spray, his scream drowned out by the tumult of the storm. Then, in the distance, a braying rang out as a pack of mules and a supply wagon of the touldon toppled into the foggy abyss, armour and grain sacks spinning free as they fell.

Apion spun to the kursores and spotted the length of rope looped on the nearest's saddle. 'With me – bring your rope and stakes.'

The three dismounted and followed Apion. He took a stake and rope offered by one rider, then looped the rope around the wood. Then he battered the stake into the earth with his heel. The earth was muddy and soft, but at a depth of half a foot it took to the drier ground below. He looked up to see that the three riders had read his plan and were staking the ground further along, connecting each one by a length of rope. He grabbed another rope and stake and edged onto the cliff-path. It was slick with rainwater and every step felt doubtful. He called out to the kataphractoi at the head of the column, only a handful of paces away but pinned where they stood for fear of falling;

'Do as I do – if you can!'

He squatted to tie and stake another rope into the inner edge of the path. The kataphractoi threw him one end of their rope and he tied this to the stake also. In the moments when the storm changed direction and the tumult hushed, he heard the dull thud of stakes being kicked and hammered into the ground likewise, all along the column.

Then the storm grew ferocious once more. He beckoned the nearest of the kataphractoi, then cupped his hands around his mouth and bellowed; 'come forward!'

The nearest rider guided his mount forward with one hand, while clinging onto the rope with the other, white-knuckled hand. Slowly, the column began to shuffle onwards.

Apion helped the first of the riders to safety, onto the wide and flat path. Then he turned to help the next, when another streak of lightning tore across the sky. The flash illuminated the cliff face and

297

the armour of the ironclad amongst the Byzantine ranks. But there was something else. High above, atop the sheer cliff. Something glinted.

'Sir, did you see it as well?' the rider nearest to him gasped.

Apion did not answer as the next fork of lightning revealed the sight once more. A cluster of figures, less than forty of them. They scurried around behind row of eight large rocks – each as tall and broad as a man. The rocks were balanced at the edge of the cliff and directly above the emperor and the varangoi.

Then, with a groaning of timber and snapping of rock, the first of the boulders tumbled. *No!* Apion pleaded, mouth agape. Romanus and his riders could only gawp as they saw it coming for them. Then, only feet away from their heads, one end of the boulder clipped the cliff face, sending the rocky mass spiralling away, towards the ravine. A thunderous deluge of rocks and debris showered the emperor and his men.

Then the next rock wobbled as the figures up above strained at it.

'Come on, come on!' Apion roared at the nearest men of the column. Now they moved at haste, some slipping and sliding, but saved by the one hand they kept on the staked rope. Then the next rock fell, and this time it hit home, some fifty paces behind the emperor now. The gargantuan rock smashed down, crushing packs of skutatoi and toxotai of the Bucellarion Thema like ants. Black blood washed over the edge with the rainwater along with shards of crumpled armour and snapped limbs. Then the track itself let out a titanic groan, and a vast shard of it shuddered and then slid away, taking with it reams of skutatoi of the Anatolikon Thema. Their bodies spun through the air and their screams died in the next clap of thunder. The rest of the rocks fell and another two struck home with equal devastation.

Apion clasped the hand of Romanus and helped him from the cliff path.

The emperor twisted to look up, but the ambushers were gone. 'Seljuks?'

'I think so,' Apion nodded as the floods of survivors stumbled to safety around him, falling to their knees on the wide path.

'They knew we were coming this way,' Romanus' eyes narrowed. 'Just as they knew we were coming through Lykandos.'

Apion squared his jaw and looked up to the clifftop where they had been.

His thoughts churned.

***

Atop the dusty plateau that overlooked the Syrian plain, the weary men of the Byzantine campaign army worked in the last light of sunset to set up their tents and dig the last of the ditch that would mark out their camp for the night.

Apion shivered by the campfire, still cold and sodden despite the temperate climate they had descended into. He lifted a pot from the fire and poured its contents into a clay bowl. The heated mixture of yoghurt, honey and nuts instantly warmed him and he washed it down with warmed sour wine.

He looked out to the south, where the arid flatland of Syria stretched out; a golden infinity that seemed to blend with the deep red of sunset. From memory, even the autumn days there could still be as blistering as Anatolia in mid-July.

He took a small round of bread from his rations, skewered it on his dagger and toasted it over the fire. The men who milled around him sneezed and shivered. Some chatted, some stared to the south while others warmed themselves in silence by their own fires. Six and a half thousand men had set out from Melitene, now six hundred of them lay broken and unburied at the bottom of that ravine. He glanced around the tents of the Chaldian ranks, heartened to see that few of his men had been struck by the falling rocks.

He plucked the toasted bread from his blade and chewed at a piece absently, his gaze darting around the many unfamiliar faces. There was no doubt now that somebody was informing the Seljuks. That they had known the exact route through the mountains was not chance alone. Word had been sent out from the camp at Melitene, he was sure of it now. Sittas the sentry and Trolius the dekarchos had been slain to allow some traitor to steal from the camp.

He caught the gaze of many soldiers. Many faces he recognised, many more he did not. Some looked weary, others wore dark looks. Then, through the sea of milling bodies he saw the emperor's tent a short distance away. The strategoi and doukes were clustered there. Sha, Blastares, Procopius and Dederic talked with Igor. Then, right beside the emperor's tent, Philaretos boomed with laughter, his face illuminated like a demon in the firelight. Gregoras sat by his side, his shifty eyes darting as always.

It could be any of them, he thought as he thumbed at the pure-gold nomisma in his purse. Rotten to the core. Responsible for the deaths of all those men in Lykandos and in the mountains. Such dark-hearted individuals could be the death of the campaign. The death of hope.

He looked to Syria again.

The dimming land offered no answers, and he turned to his tent, tiredness overcoming him.

**

Night descended over the plateau. Zenobius sat alone outside his kontoubernion tent, looking on at the gathering by the imperial tent. As a mere skutatos, he would never be allowed past the ring of varangoi that encircled the gathering. It was as life had always been for him, alone in the cold and dark, looking on at those who lived true lives. But this exclusion mattered little, he mused, his eyes following the movements of his accomplice, near the fire.

The varangoi threw more kindling upon the fire and it roared in gratitude. With wine in their blood and warmth on their skins, they and the others clustered around Romanus became momentarily less vigilant, it seemed. Indeed, the pair of Rus guarding the imperial tent stepped forward to heat their hands.

Zenobius' breath stilled. This was the moment.

His accomplice stole away from the fire, then slipped inside the imperial tent.

Then Zenobius' gaze sharpened as the two varangoi ambled back round to the tent entrance and one reached out to open it.

Do not fail me now, you fool, he thought.

Then, as if hearing his thoughts, the back of the tent ruffled and his accomplice slipped out from underneath just as the varangoi entered. Nobody had noticed.

The gathering slowly dispersed and the fire died.

When it was but a pile of embers, Zenobius heard footsteps approaching.

'Well?' he said without looking up.

'I know where the emperor plans to march; I saw his maps and the markings he had made upon them,' his accomplice whispered.

'Excellent,' Zenobius said flatly. 'Then I will make contact with our Seljuk friends tonight.'

19. Syria

The column snaked down the winding path that descended from the plateau. The riders of the vanguard were the first to spill onto the Syrian plain, shimmering in the fierce morning sun. Apion rode near Philaretos, Gregoras, Igor, Sha and Dederic, with the emperor riding in their midst. To a man they marched in full armour. The lessons of Lykandos had been hard-learned.

'Feel the warmth of the sun on your skin. It feels good, does it not?' Romanus boomed, sitting proudly on his stallion and looking fresher than ever.

'Like a salve,' Apion forced himself to smile as he replied. For although he had slept a deep, dreamless sleep, and woken in the position he had lain down in, he still felt somewhat cobbled together. His bones ached from a light fever caused by the icy rainwater, and now the sun seemed to sear his sweat-soaked skin. Moreover, the neck of his klibanion and his scale aventail were chafing on his collarbone. And then there was the dust. The golden dust seemed to coat his skin and his throat in a matter of moments. He reached for his water skin and then hesitated, shaking his head. *Not yet*, he chided himself.

Then Romanus leaned in closer and dropped his voice to a whisper. 'If it is any comfort, I also feel as if I have slept on a bed of cold rocks at the bottom of a cesspit.' He flashed a grin. 'But I fear the men would rather not hear this from me.'

Apion chuckled at this. Then he noticed the signophoroi lifting their banners, readying to change the column's direction.

'You have decided on our destination, *Basileus?*' Apion asked.

'Indeed,' Romanus nodded, dropping his voice to a whisper. 'We march for Hierapolis, Strategos.'

Hierapolis. Apion shivered, despite the heat. It was as if someone had touched an icy finger to his heart. He glanced back over his shoulder to see that the retinue were just out of earshot.

'Relax, Strategos. You are the first I have spoken to of this,' Romanus said, pointing to the signophoroi. 'Even the banner-wielders know only our general direction. I will only announce it to all in a few days' time, when we are closer to the city.'

Apion saw Romanus' look darken as he said this. 'A wise choice, *Basileus.*'

The pair rode ahead a little so they could talk without being overheard.

Apion thought of Hierapolis. He had skirted past the city once, over a decade ago. 'The city is well-walled, with a strong citadel at its heart. From what I hear, the wells of the settlement never run dry – only a short distance from the broad waters of the Euphrates.'

Romanus nodded. 'Best of all,' he glanced over his shoulder to see who was within earshot, 'the garrison there is thought to be weak. Barely a few hundred line its walls according to reports from last year.'

Apion frowned. 'When I see few Seljuks, I tend to worry more about those who go unseen.'

Romanus drummed his fingers on his saddle. 'The Fatimid rebellion in the south still occupies the sultan's main forces, and it is expected to remain this way until next spring.'

'Then let us hope the Fatimids are dogged in their battles,' Apion said, squinting into the strengthening sun.

They trotted on in silence for some time. In that time, the intense morning heat grew into a midday inferno. A golden heat haze blended the dust with the sky in every direction. The popping of corks and gulping of water was becoming as rhythmic as the crunch of boots on dust. Romanus sent the Oghuz and Pecheneg riders on ahead to locate fodder, water and forage.

Apion twisted in his saddle to see how the men of Chaldia were faring, a hundred feet or so back, behind the kataphractoi. He saw Sha, Blastares, Procopius and Dederic marching at the head of the ranks, their faces bathed in sweat. The sight of them fortified his resolve.

Then, as he drew his gaze round again, it snagged on something.

Just a few paces behind him, Strategos Gregoras rode slumped in his saddle, a foul look on his ruddy and sweating face as he cooked inside his armour. But he balanced something on his knuckles, rippling his fingers to move the object back and forth. The sunlight caught it.

A nomisma.

A pure-gold nomisma.

***

The nights in southern Syria at this time of year were blessedly fresh, and the clear, star-studded sky overhead made it even more so. After nearly two days of ceaseless riding, Nasir inhaled a fresh breath and then slowed his mount as he approached the Seljuk war camp. For miles, the plain was awash with yurts, wandering akhi sentries, and ghazi and ghulam riders leading their mounts to the nearby oasis to drink and eat. The men were beleaguered, their faces smoke-stained and laced with cuts. But the Fatimid rebellions were over, or so he had heard.

'I bring news from the north,' he called out to the sentries, who waved him inside. He dismounted and handed his reins to a stable boy, then walked through the camp, bearing in on the sultan's yurt.

He wondered if this would be the time; the time when finally he could vanquish the past. He touched a hand to the angry welt of burns coating one side of his face, remembering how Maria had winced upon seeing him like that for the first time. Even after all these years, the *Haga's* touch still wreaked havoc with his life. A growl startled him, then he realised it was his own.

Then he slowed, hearing another noise. A weak moaning. Frowning, he scanned the tents and then set eyes upon the inhuman sight in the centre of a circle of yurts. A man lay, legs splayed out on the ground, impaled through the rectum on a thick, splintered post. The man's bloodshot eyes gazed skywards and his mouth lay agape. Every heartbeat saw him shudder and wince.

Nasir squinted, then realised he recognised the man. It was the captain who had been tasked with organising the rockfall in the mountain pass. So the man had failed Alp Arslan and this was his punishment.

He turned from the sight then composed himself as he approached Alp Arslan's yurt. He nodded to the two dismounted ghulam who stood guard there, their flinty expressions semi-concealed behind finely polished conical helms and gilded nose guards.

'Bey Nasir!' they bowed in unison then stepped apart, away from the entrance. One of them fired a furtive glance at Nasir's ruined face and his eyes sparkled with fear.

Nasir grunted, then brushed past them and into the tent.

Inside, the floor was draped with a sheet of silk and the air was thick with incense. The aged Vizier Nizam sat cross-legged near the entrance, poring over papers; city plans, taxation calculations, deeds of ownership, trade agreements and placement of warriors, warhorses, livestock and grain. This man was the operational prodigy behind Alp Arslan's military genius.

Nizam looked up. 'Bey Nasir? The sultan is not expecting you, is he?'

'No, but he will be glad of my visit,' Nasir replied.

Nizam raised his eyebrows in intrigue, then motioned to the far end of the tent where a semi-opaque veil of silk divided the space.

Nasir pushed through it, with Nizam following close behind.

There, in guttering candlelight, Alp Arslan was kneeling, dressed in a light woollen robe, his thick, dark locks loose, dangling to his shoulders like his moustache. He twisted a silver goblet in his hand, near-full with a ruby-red wine. His gaze was intense as he studied the shatranj board set up on a timber stool before him. Nasir's top lip curled at this. The pieces on the board had not been moved since the sultan had started a game with the *Haga* back in Caesarea. *You treat him with too much respect – you could have had him in chains in Caesarea, then peeled the skin from his body and let the dogs feast on his flesh while he breathed his last.*

'Nasir,' Alp Arslan spoke suddenly and without surprise, not looking up from the shatranj board.

Nasir started at this. Then he felt the breath of another on his shoulder. His skin prickled with unease as he realised Alp Arslan's rugged bodyguard, Kilic, had slipped from the shadows behind him. Nasir glanced over his shoulder and down to the big bodyguard's boots; the dagger that had ended so many lives on the sultan's command would doubtless be tucked in there. He had been spared such a death twice already in recent times, he thought, his mind spinning back to his allegiance with Bey Afsin and then his failure to destroy the imperial column in Lykandos. The image of the staked man outside needled at his thoughts. This was surely his last chance.

'Sit,' Kilic grunted, gesturing to the other side of the shatranj board.

Nasir knelt before his sultan and bowed. Nizam and Kilic looked on.

Alp Arslan's gaze remained on his shatranj board. He lifted one pawn piece and held it over a square that would block the opposing war elephant, then shook his head and replaced the piece. At last, he looked up. 'I told you to return home, Nasir, to spend time with your family.' The sultan's brow knitted. 'You have failed me once too often and I fear you need to rest. Yet now you come to me in my war camp?'

'I rode from my home two nights ago and have not stopped since. I have swapped mounts all along our tracks to get here with the utmost haste,' he stopped to nod to Nizam at this – the old vizier was responsible for the network of messenger ponies dotted around the Seljuk dominion. Then he locked his gaze back onto the sultan. He thought of the messenger who had come to him two nights ago. 'I know where they are headed. The Byzantine army march for my home as we speak. Hierapolis is their first target.'

Alp Arslan's brow furrowed, his gaze igniting.

'The emperor and the *Haga*,' Nasir nodded, a rapacious grin forming on his ruined face. 'They are just over two days from Hierapolis' walls.'

Alp Arslan shot his gaze back to the shatranj board before him. 'Then the time is upon us . . .'

'Sultan, your armies are still recovering from the Fatimid Wars and will not be ready to march for weeks yet,' Nizam said.

Alp Arslan flexed his fingers then balled them into fists. 'Aye, you are right.' Then he looked up to Kilic. 'But that does not render us incapable. My bodyguards are still fresh, and we have allies to call upon. Ready a messenger.'

Kilic nodded and left.

Then the sultan looked to the shatranj board. 'We have much to plan. There will be little sleep tonight. The days ahead could well scribe the destiny of our people.' He looked up to Nasir.

'Be ready to ride at haste once more, loyal bey. For you will be part of that destiny.'

***

The sky overhead was dark blue, and the first band of starry blackness stained the eastern horizon. Five horsemen rode at a gentle trot from a rare dip in the land that wound up from the banks of the Euphrates. Then they stopped as they neared the top where the land levelled out onto the plain. Apion, Dederic, Sha, Blastares and Procopius slid from their mounts and then flitted up the rest of the sandy incline in silence. Their faces were smeared with earth and they wore only linen tunics and boots. Apion cast a glance back over his shoulder, downhill to the north. The marching camp was out of sight, well hidden in the sunken crescent of land near the banks of the Euphrates. Even the glow of firelight was masked.

When they reached the top of the slope, Apion stopped and the four stopped with him. They crouched as they looked to the south and the Syrian plain that stretched out before them. It was arid and featureless. Apart from one thing.

Hierapolis.

Apion tucked his hair behind his ears as he studied the place. An odd shiver danced across his skin. He blinked away the feeling and focused only on what he saw before him. Torches dotted the battlements of the broad, squat and sun-bleached outer walls. A handful of akhi were posted along the battlements and atop the towers. The city inside was built on a gentle hill. Immediately inside the main gate he could see a grand mosque, cornered by four vividly tiled minarets. Adjacent to this was what looked like a palm-studded and stall-lined market square, in its last throes of activity for the day. This was surrounded by a patchwork of villas, gardens and palaces. South of the square, towards the heart of the city, was the domed rooftop of an old Roman bathhouse. This, the bulky limestone cistern and the granary opposite had a few akhi posted upon the roofs. These buildings and a maze of alleys and lanes masked what looked like a barrack complex further up the hill – a dilapidated baked red-brick structure nodding to an earlier era when the city was under Byzantine control. The barrack complex backed onto the base of a steep – almost sheer – man-made hill that formed the city's acropolis. The acropolis was topped with a sturdy, tall and round-cornered citadel built from immense limestone blocks and topped with a crenelated roof.

'All looks normal?' Dederic suggested. 'There are few spears on that wall.'

'Aye, as normal as normal can be,' Blastares countered, the whites of his eyes stark against his dirt-smeared features, 'but I've come close to being lanced through the heart by normal. There could be a fair few scimitar-wielding whoresons cooped up in the barracks or in that citadel . . . ' his words trailed off and he nodded to Apion's swordbelt. 'No offence, sir.'

Apion looked to his men. 'I agree with Blastares – apart from the scimitar comment. The emperor feels compelled to push ever

309

onwards. I understand his position – he needs a victorious campaign to validate his reign.' Then he bit his lower lip and shook his head. 'But something feels wrong about this. It feels too easy.' Then he hesitated, doubting his own doubts for a moment. The men had only found out they were headed for Hierapolis just over a day ago. There was no way the rogue in the column could have alerted Seljuk forces in that time. Equally, he had discussed his theory about Gregoras with the emperor. *I cannot denounce one of my strategoi without solid evidence. I need his men,* was all Romanus had said in reply. *Then let me and my men ride between you and him, Basileus,* Apion had replied. The emperor had agreed to this at least. 'Or perhaps I am looking for trouble when there is none? Either way, we cannot charge ahead, blind. We must be certain of what forces lie within those walls.'

Dederic's eyes darted, then locked onto Apion's. 'A spy could infiltrate the city, sir?' he suggested.

Sha nodded at this, slapping a mosquito from his neck. 'That could be the perfect balance. We need to be swift in our taking of this city and sure of the forces we will face.'

'Aye, but it will still take some time to get a man in there and then back out again . . . ' Procopius started.

'Then we leave him inside,' Dederic finished for him.

All looked to the little Norman.

'We send someone in disguised as a trader. They ascertain the true strength of the garrison. If they look susceptible to a sudden, blunt attack, then our man could signal from the walls.' He pointed to the battlements, and the tower on the left side of the main gate – larger than all the others. 'By noon tomorrow we could be here with the whole army, waiting on the signal; three flashes for an advance, five flashes to hold back?'

Apion looked around his men.

Sha was the first to offer his opinion. 'It'd take a brave man to wander in there alone, but it sounds like a plan, sir.'

Apion clicked his tongue and then nodded. 'Then I will suggest this to the emperor.' He looked up to the sky to see that it was almost overcome with blackness. 'Now let us return to the camp – else the men will presume we have taken leave of our senses and tried to storm the place ourselves.'

***

Laskaris always knew he had been destined for greatness. When he joined the Chaldian Thema as a skutatos, he knew he was going to be led by a fine man. Indeed, the *Haga* and he shared certain traits; Laskaris had been brought up by a Seljuk mother and an Armenian father, thus he could speak the Greek tongue and the Seljuk tongue interchangeably just like the strategos. Yet, after four years in the tourma led by the Malian, Sha, it had become clear that perhaps he was not destined to excel as a warrior of the ranks. He was twenty four now, and had fought in many battles. Yet he hadn't even been promoted to the front rank and provided with the iron klibanion and helmet that distinguished the brave warriors who fought in that most perilous position. Despite this, the strategos had regularly taken the time to encourage him, telling him that he was a valued soldier, and that his time would come.

And today, it seemed, was that time. For he was to ride forth to Hierapolis and infiltrate the city dressed as a lone Seljuk trader. He had inherited his mother's swarthy complexion and bore the jet black hair and moustache that was the common style for the Seljuks.

He checked his things once more; a water skin, a bag of orchid root, a parcel of saffron and a purse of coins minted in the eastern

Seljuk heartlands. He glanced around his kontoubernion tent at that which he was to leave behind; his felt jacket, cap, spear, spathion and shield, all piled up next to his bedding. It was ironic that his rise to recognition would come without his skutatoi equipment.

He sucked in a deep breath and pushed back the tent flap. The morning sunlight blinded him for a moment and the contrast in temperature was stark. He walked through the camp. A crowd of soldiers followed him, wishing him well. They all wore anxious but excited grins. All except the ghostly white skutatos from the ranks of the Thrakesion Thema. He realised he was staring at the albino and dropped his gaze. Then he approached the *Haga*, who held the reins of a small, thick-necked fawn steppe pony. He was flanked by Sha and the other three tourmarchai.

Laskaris saluted to each of them. His salute to Dederic was subconsciously diluted just a fraction. Dederic had proved to be a noble warrior in his time with the Chaldian Thema and the man had a pleasant and unassuming way about him. Despite this, Laskaris could not help but feel the tendrils of jealousy coil around his heart. This westerner had shot to prominence with such apparent ease while he had languished in the ranks, undistinguished.

Perhaps that was about to change with his efforts today, he reasoned, his mood brightening.

'Sir,' he looked to the strategos, taking the reins of the pony, 'I am ready.'

The strategos nodded. 'Take great care, Laskaris, for today, the fate of your comrades lies in your hands.' Then he stepped forward and clasped a hand to Laskaris' bicep. 'These are weighty expectations to place upon a man's shoulders, but I know you have it in you. That is why I have chosen you for this task.'

Laskaris felt a few inches taller at this reassurance. He sprung into the saddle and nodded to the gathering crowd of skutatoi. The albino had disappeared, it seemed. But the others called out to him as he trotted through the camp, and more came to offer salutes and pats on the back. Hubris coursed through his veins until he left the south gate of the camp. There, the bustle fell away as he wound his way up the rise in the land. Out here the patches of greenery and the merciful breeze of the riverside fell away sharply. Out here it was scorching hot and silent. Finally the land levelled out and he came onto the vast Syrian plain. Hierapolis beckoned him.

He made his way across the featureless plain towards the city's north gate. The walls flickered in the heat haze ahead, and then he noticed the licks of silver atop the gatehouse; akhi and their sharpened spears. His mouth was suddenly as dry as the dust around him and his bowels took to turning over with a series of groans. The cicada song seemed to grow in intensity at this moment, as if the insects were screaming at him to reconsider.

Then a distant clopping of hooves caught his attention. He shot a glance to the east. There, ambling along the east-west track about a half-mile away was a small caravan of traders. They rode from the banks of the Euphrates to the city's east gate, their wagons pulled by Arabian horses. A contingent of men stumbled along behind them, their wrists in chains. One of the Seljuks lifted and swung something. The sharp cracking of a whip rang out and one of the shackled men stumbled as if broken by the blow. Laskaris gulped at the sight; were they slaves, being taken to market – or perhaps Byzantine captives, being taken for execution? He dropped his gaze to the ground, trying to stay his fears. Then he noticed something odd there on the dust before him.

Hoofprints. Relatively fresh. They led all the way to the north gate as if mapping out a path for him. He frowned and twisted in his saddle to locate their origin; the hoofprints weaved around his own, all the way back to the dip in the land and the sunken crescent that hid the camp. He frowned at this.

Just then, a voice split the air.

'Who goes there?'

Laskaris spun round to the ancient-looking gatehouse. The moustachioed sentry up there was wrapped in a white linen robe and wore a red felt cap. The man leant on his spear and peered at Laskaris, brow furrowed.

Laskaris licked his lips and realised just how much dust had lined his throat in this short ride. He coughed and held up the sacks of orchid root and saffron. 'I bring spices for the market,' he bellowed.

The sentry eyed him, then spoke to some unseen other within the gate tower. Laskaris' heart thundered under the silent scrutiny that ensued. He was sure the sentry could see right through his ruse, and at that moment he was also convinced he had inadvertently kept some piece of giveaway Byzantine equipment on his person.

Then the sentry shrugged. 'Be on about your business then.'

Laskaris' terror turned to relief for a moment, then his blood iced over once more as he passed under the shadow of the gatehouse and into the sun-bleached interior of the ancient city. The noise was in stark contrast to the arid plain outside. The hubbub of bartering and gossip echoed down the broad street that led into the palm-lined market square. Here, the babble of man was mixed with a chorus of animal noises; lowing oxen, groaning camels, the clucking and screeching of distressed chickens and the bleating of goats. Men hauled sacks of grain. Traders pulled carts, yelling to their customers.

Women carried babies and led children through this throng. They seemed to be in a hurry, many packing grain and clothing in carts.

Laskaris guided his mount through the swell, trying desperately to avoid making eye contact with anyone in the sea of sweating faces all around him. It felt as if, at any moment, his veil of disguise could fall away.

He slid from his mount and led the pony along the southern and western edges of the square. He took care to shade his eyes whenever he looked around, to disguise the subject of his gaze. The squat lower city walls were indeed thinly manned with akhi in little or no armour – militia rather than battle-hardened warriors. Still, it would be no simple task for the campaign army to take these walls, he thought, noticing the pair of ballistae mounted on each of the towers and the thick and well bolstered gates. And no doubt there would be a reserve garrison, he affirmed, a number of men who could rush to strengthen the wall guard at the first call of alarm. Ascertaining their number was his next task, he realised, turning his sights uphill towards the acropolis. The old red-bricked Byzantine barrack compound at the foot of the acropolis mount was just visible through the jumble of buildings.

He led his pony along the main street, thick with people cutting across his path, barging ahead of him or coming towards him. One, an aged man with a false eye, seemed to glare at him in the way a wolf would eye a wounded deer. His step grew erratic under this perceived scrutiny. *Compose yourself,* he chided himself.

The broad main street tapered off after a few hundred feet as it rose up the slope towards the acropolis. Then it disintegrated into a dozen or more spidering streets and tight alleys – this was the layout of the original town. He glanced up to see which path would take him closest to the barracks; one narrow, shaded alley lined with stained, whitewashed tenements looked like the best bet. This took him past a few craggy-faced beggars and a three legged, mangy dog – even it seemed to cast him a suspicious glare.

At last, he reached the end of the alley when it joined a less claustrophobic street. The crumbling barrack compound was on the other side of this street. He pretended to fasten his belt as he scanned the few patches of shade nearby. Then his eyes locked onto one spot; an unplanned, triangular gap between the barracks and the Seljuk granary that had been built adjacent to it. The space was thick with gathered dust and tapered off at the far end where the barrack and granary walls touched. There, a pile of tumbled red bricks presented a rough set of stepping stones leading up to the top of the crenelated barrack wall.

Perfect, he thought, leading his pony across the street and into the gap.

Then a hand slapped on his shoulder.

Laskaris spun to face the pair of akhi who glowered at him. All his fears surged into his heart at once, and he barely controlled his instinctive urge to grasp for his spathion – which was back in his tent anyway. He was sure he shook visibly from the thudding of his every heartbeat. The two were dark-eyed, sallow-skinned and moustachioed. One was tall with a razor-nose and the other shorter and flat-faced. Both were finely armoured and equipped, wearing felt caps and horn klibania over pristine white, long-sleeved linen tunics. Their fingers flexed on the freshly-hewn spear shafts they carried. Laskaris' brow knitted momentarily at the condition of their garb.

'What are you doing?' the tallest of the two asked him abruptly, interrupting his flicker of thought.

'Stopping for a little shade,' he heard himself say, wiping his sweating brow.

'Where are you headed?' the shorter one continued, his tone a little less terse.

'To the spice market by the south gate,' Laskaris heard himself say. He held up the two sacks. 'Though when I get there I may keep some of this orchid root for myself,' he forced a grin. 'A mouthful of warm salep on a day like this drains the heat from you.'

The two soldiers looked to one another and a painful silence ensued. Then the tall, razor-nosed soldier nodded. 'You'll do us a deal, yes?' he muttered, rummaging in his purse.

Laskaris' lips opened and closed wordlessly.

Then the big soldier's face cracked into a grin and he produced a silver *dirham*. 'For some orchid root?'

Laskaris suppressed a gulp and nodded, taking the coin. He loosened the orchid root sack and poured a generous measure of the root into the small pouch the shorter akhi held out.

'We will raise a toast to you when we drink, trader!' the taller one grinned once more and then the pair turned and marched away, downhill towards the northern market square.

Laskaris watched them go. Something about them stuck in his mind. Something wasn't quite right, but he couldn't place his finger on exactly what. He shook the doubt from his mind and glanced around to check that nobody else was watching him.

He tethered his pony to an iron ring jutting from the granary wall, before slinking back into the shadows of the dusty, dead-end gap by the barracks. He clutched at the collapsed pile of red bricks. Some crumbled in his grasp, throwing puffs of dust into his eyes and he had to stifle a curse when this happened. But he climbed swiftly and in a few moments he was almost level with the parapet. He waited there for a heartbeat, hearing the snorting of horses inside the compound. Then, he pushed up ever so carefully. The crenelated roof of the citadel

317

stronghold overlooked the barracks. But, on snatching a glance up to the top of its lofty roof, he saw that just one sentry stood there, gazing lazily out to the south, back turned. Reassured by this, he pushed up just a little more, then looked down into the heart of the barrack compound.

His gaze fell upon the drill square and he gawped.

This wasn't right. This wasn't what he had expected.

He thought again of the fine garb of the two akhi who had stopped him. His heart thundered under his ribs. Then he realised what he had to do. He spun away from the sight and looked downhill, to the main tower at the north gate – he had to get there to give the signal.

The Byzantine assault had to be stopped.

He scrambled down the tumbled brickwork, then hobbled towards his pony, fumbling in his purse to check he had the finely polished disc of bronze in there. Instead, he pulled out the dirham he had earned moments ago. His eyes hung on the inscription.

In the name of Allah.

Then something scuffled, just behind him. Before he could spin around, a hand clasped over his mouth and he was yanked to the ground. He saw the face of the tall, razor-nosed akhi glowering down at him, twisted in malice. He kicked and thrashed, but the akhi knelt on his shoulders, pinning his arms to the ground. Then another face appeared over him. Ghostly white, silver-eyed and laced with sweat and dust from his breakneck ride, still panting. Confusion danced through Laskaris' thoughts.

'This is him?' the akhi asked the albino.

'Yes,' Zenobius said flatly, stooping to rummage in Laskaris' purse, pulling free the shard of polished signalling bronze. 'All is in hand. Now tear out his throat.'

318

Laskaris' eyes bulged as he writhed but his roar was stifled by the akhi's palm. Then the akhi ripped something under his chin. He felt a sharp pain in his throat and a warm wetness spread across his chest.

This wasn't right, Laskaris thought as his limbs stilled. His moment of greatness was not supposed to end like this.

20. Siege

'Once, twice . . . three times!' Sha whispered, squinting at the flash from the tower over the north gate. 'It's closing in on noon,' he shot a glance to the sun. There's no doubting it, sir. That's our man signalling us.'

Apion was lying prone in the hot dust alongside his tourmarches, just where the dip in the land levelled out. His heart willed him to give the word, but he hesitated. He looked immediately behind him. The emperor was crouched there, surrounded by Philaretos, Igor and the handful of varangoi who had survived this treacherous campaign so far. Blastares, Procopius and Dederic flanked them along with the doukes and strategoi of the thematic and tagmatic armies. All looked on expectantly, eyes wide. Gregoras looked on like a wily predator.

Behind this cluster of leaders, the slopes of the dip were awash with the Byzantine army. They stood in silence, their faces keen and glistening with sweat, their fingers flexing on shields, swords and reins. A sea of iron, bobbing with a thick flotsam of speartips, fluttering banners and the swishing manes of war horses. To the rear, hidden in the lowest part of the dip, the skeletal frames of siege engines stood silent and ominous.

There could be no more hesitation.

Apion looked to the emperor and nodded.

Romanus' eyes sparkled at this. He stood tall and strode up from the dip in the land, hefting his spathion aloft. 'Nobiscum Deus!' He roared.

At this, the Byzantine army cried out in reply. '*Nobiscum Deus!*' With that, they poured up the slopes, spilling onto the flatland like a tidal wave.

The skutatoi of the Optimates Tagma formed a solid centre, with their thematic counterparts marching on the wings to present a wide crescent of over three thousand spearmen. The first few ranks of the skutatoi all along this arc presented an iron-fronted spearwall, with those to the rear clutching their javelins and every tenth file carrying a siege ladder. Behind them, the thousand-strong toxotai jogged into place, stretching their muscles, readying their bows, checking their quivers one last time. Then the hardy kataphractoi of the themata formed up on the flanks, one hundred and fifty strong on either side, each wing resembling an iron talon. The five hundred Oghuz horse archers milled in loose formation behind the left flank, and the five hundred Pechenegs took up a similar stance on the right. The ironclad riders of the Scholae Tagma – three hundred and fifty in total – formed a central reserve, just behind the infantry line, with Doux Philaretos barking at them to form up in a wedge so they could punch forward at haste if required.

Behind this vast bull horn formation, two siege towers wobbled forward, the skutatoi at their bases straining as they worked the racks and pinions that drove the great devices. The towers split the infantry line evenly as they passed through and settled to a halt just in front of the centre. Then, a cluster of eight catapults rumbled into place, four either side of the towers, and an iron-tipped battering ram waited in reserve behind the stone throwers. Then, as if to add the finishing touch, sixteen siphonarioi in iron full-face masks and conical helmets stepped forward to the right of the Byzantine centre, carrying their deadly fire siphons. Each man carried a flint hook in his belt, ready to ignite their devices and set the world aflame.

At first sight of this iron tide, the sentries on Hierapolis' walls took to scurrying back and forth, sounding horns and ushering men to the battlements. Within moments, around ninety Seljuk archers were clustered atop the gatehouse, nocking arrows to their bows, and some three hundred or more akhi spearmen lined the battlements either side of the gate. At the same time, the mounted ballistae on each of the gate towers came to life, being twisted and raised to point at maximum range, readying to fire when the Byzantine lines came into their reach.

But the Byzantine ranks were not deterred by this. The coloured banners of the skutatoi were pumped in the air again and again and the ranks cried out. Then the priests walked back and forth solemnly, the campaign Cross and the image of the Virgin Mary raised overhead.

'Nobiscum Deus! *Nobiscum Deus!*'

The chant continued unabated, then it rose to an unprecedented level as Romanus took to cantering along the front ranks, hefting the imperial banner in encouragement, his purple cloak lifting behind him in his slipstream. He carried his purple-plumed helmet underarm, allowing his broad jaw, billowing flaxen hair and unrelenting distant stare to inspire his subjects. The men roared as he passed, beating their swords on their shields. Eventually he settled at the Byzantine centre, and Igor and the varangoi hurried to surround him, their pure-white armour and polished axes gleaming in the sun.

Apion, Sha, Blastares, Procopius and Dederic worked their way through to the front. Apion led his mount on foot, carrying his helm. Sha and Blastares were mounted, fully clad in helmet, greaves, veils and klibania and Dederic rode too in his weighty mail hauberk that hung to his knees. Procopius had foregone his mount, having been tasked with leading the artillery crews today.

Apion led them to the emperor.

Romanus turned to him, his eyes sparkling. 'We are on the cusp, Strategos,' he spoke through clenched teeth.

Apion cast his gaze to his left and then his right. Sweeping walls of iron and speartips stretched off in both directions. 'I have rarely witnessed such a show of might from the empire, *Basileus*. At once it both gladdens me and strikes fear into my heart. For I feel that many men are fated to die today.'

Romanus squinted into the azure sky. 'Then let us take a swift and clean victory. Today is a fine day to defy fate,' he grinned.

Apion felt a flare of hope in his heart at this. Then he vaulted into the saddle, placing his black-plumed helm on his head. 'Give the word, *Basileus*, and we shall make the first move.' He motioned towards Procopius. 'Procopius will unlock the city for you.' Then he looked to his tourmarchai. 'And my men will present a dogged left.'

Romanus nodded. 'Then let us begin.'

'Aye, *Basileus*,' Apion replied. Then he heeled his gelding round into a trot along the line. Sha, Blastares and Dederic followed him while Procopius strode forward to the artillery crews. They rode past the spears of the Optimates Tagma and on to the Byzantine left-centre. Here, the crimson banners of the Chaldian Thema were clustered and waiting for him in silence. Adjacent to the Chaldian left was the ranks of the Thrakesion Thema. Gregoras stood at their head, his shifty eyes catching Apion's gaze momentarily.

Apion's brow dipped at this. This man would have to be watched. Lined up here he would be like a dagger hovering near Apion's flank. Gregoras took to rallying his troops at this point.

At this, Apion turned back to Sha, Blastares and Dederic. 'Fight well, and I know we will drink to victory tonight.'

'Sir!' They each saluted. Then the three tourmarchai trotted off to the head up their tourmae.

323

He squeezed the Thessalian's flanks, bringing it into a gentle trot along the Chaldian front, casting his gaze along each of his men. Then he drew his scimitar and held it aloft. 'The sultan has left a sparse garrison to man the walls we see before us. But walls are not taken easily, as well you know from the countless years of struggle we have faced to hold our own. So stay together, defend your brother's flank and he will defend yours. Let every swipe of your spathion be the one that will turn the battle. Seize victory today, seize this chance to let our empire breathe once more, for your wives, for your children, for the men who have fallen for the cause!' Their steely silence erupted at this. Sword hilts thundered on shields, the din spreading along the line like a coming storm;

'*Ha-ga! Ha-ga! Ha-ga!*'

Then he turned to the city, sliding on his splinted arm greaves and then his studded leather gloves on top of them. As he did so, he saw the first fleeting glimpses of the dark door. The flames were ferocious, licking out from around its edges. Finally, he buckled the triple mail veil across his face. Only his emerald eyes remained visible to remind those he was about to meet in battle that he was human.

Then it began.

The signophoroi clustered around the emperor, strode forward a few paces. Then they hefted their purple and gold banners, before dropping them, pointing directly to the catapults. A chorus of notes rang out from the buccinators by their sides.

At this, Procopius was spurred into action. The aged tourmarches spat into his palms, then rubbed them dry, his wrinkled features scanning the walls. Silence fell across the plain and all eyes were upon him. At last, he nodded, then spun to bark orders to his crew.

'Catapults, forwaaaaard!' he screamed.

The stone throwers rumbled some fifty paces ahead of the front line and then halted. Then the crews rushed to stretch the ropes and load the devices with rocks. But before they could even prepare, the first of the Seljuk ballistae – one of the two on the tallest tower – let loose. With a twang and a whoosh, a five foot, iron-tipped bolt shot forth and smashed into the rightmost catapult, shattering the device and pinning the leader of the crew to the ground where he stood, his head slumping forward and a wash of blood erupting from his mouth. Then another bolt sailed over the next-nearest catapult and skated along the surface of the ground, ploughing into the front ranks of the Opsikon Thema, breaking legs and sending up a wail of terror.

'Smash those bolt-throwers!' Procopius yelled as the first of the catapults groaned and then bucked violently in riposte. The first rock sailed over the tower and into the city. The next one to fire hit the face of the tower, which shook but was otherwise unharmed. Then the third volley sent a rock sweetly into the crenelated tower-top. The limestone blocks shattered under the impact. Tendrils of dust and rubble shot into the air, accompanied by two screams and a thick crack of timber. One of the ballistae crew toppled soundlessly from the tower before crunching into the ground outside the walls. Then the dust cleared. The ballista hung limp, its bow was shattered and the other crewman was draped lifelessly over the gouged, bloodstained battlement like a discarded robe.

A cheer rang out from the Byzantine lines at this.

Apion watched in sombre silence. In the next heartbeat, another Seljuk ballista bolt crashed through the offending Byzantine catapult, throwing one crewman into the air and snapping the neck of another.

Then, as the catapults and ballistae exchanged fire at will, Procopius twisted to the emperor. Romanus nodded. Then the old tourmarches bawled, lifting both arms and dropping them to point forward. 'Towers – forwaaaaard!'

At this, the skutatoi clustered in the base of the two tall and ungainly timber-wheeled towers took the strain, grappling the handles jutting from the pinion and pushing until the cog engaged with the rack. Like wakening giants, the towers rumbled towards the walls, one either side of the gate. The towers were not the tallest Apion had seen, but Procopius had designed them to perfectly match the height of the squat outer city walls of Hierapolis. He had also ensured they would have a decent rate of movement and a broad enough base and weight distribution to provide stability while they moved. The front and sides of the towers were clad in timber and scrap iron, like a cobbled together foulkon. Only the rear was uncovered, revealing the two floors and connecting timber stairs inside. A clutch of toxotai was positioned on the bottom floor. This extra weight stabilised the towers while the archers fired their bows through narrow slats in the frontage at the defenders on the walls.

The Seljuk archers were quick to react to this new threat. At once, an orange glow bobbed above the gatehouse, and then they raised their bows, each nocked with a blazing arrow. With a gentle whoosh, the fiery missiles arced skyward and then fell upon the siege towers, their flames licking up the sides of the timber.

'Aye, it would be as easy as that,' Apion muttered under his breath as he watched, 'had you faced a less astute artillery master.'

The surfaces of the towers glistened in the raging heat of the arrows, but neither tower caught light. A stench of vinegar permeated the smoky air that wafted over the watching Byzantine line. Procopius had insisted on soaking the towers in vinegar that morning. The liquid would neither ignite nor evaporate too quickly in the dry heat, rendering the towers impervious to fire. The archers seemed to lose heart as volley after volley of fire arrows were ineffective. But they quickly re-nocked their bows with unlit arrows, turning their weapons instead on the Byzantine skutatoi pushing the devices. A handful fell, screaming, clutching thighs and clawing at throats, but most were shielded by the hulking towers. Then the akhi captain on the walls barked out a command. At this, the three remaining Seljuk ballista twisted, taking aim at the siege tower nearest the walls, on the Byzantine right.

The first ballista bolt smashed through the frontage of the siege tower. Shattered splinters of timber flew from the frame and the bolt punched one toxotes out of the back of the tower like a piece of slingshot. A fine cloud of his blood settled like mist on the skutatoi below.

Then another ballista bolt whooshed from the walls and destroyed the broad beam that supported the first and second floors of the tower. A crack rang out that caused all in the Byzantine ranks to gasp. The tower halted, then there was an eerie hiatus before the wooden frame groaned, buckled, then pitched forward, its structure compromised. The screams of the toxotai rang out as they scrambled to the back of the tower, but the floor turned vertical under their feet as the tower crashed into the ground like a slain giant. The toxotai were dashed on the ground, some killed by the impact, others prone, limbs snapped. They could only lie where they had fallen and watch as the Seljuk archers took aim to finish them off. The skutatoi who drove the device were likewise exposed and in range of the archers. They dropped into a foulkon formation, pulling their shields around them instinctively as the Seljuk arrows rained in upon them. But, heartbeats later, another ballista bolt smashed into their midst. Blood erupted from the strike, and the men inside the foulkon fell away, injured, bloodied or dead.

A groan of despair sounded across the Byzantine ranks.

But then, the tower on the Byzantine left clunked into place against the battlements. The skutatos leading the crew who pushed this device turned and waved his banner frantically. At this, the cries of despair turned into a defiant chorus of cheering.

'Now,' Apion whispered, firing glances to the centre of the line, 'send the ladders forward now!' He willed the emperor to think as he did once more.

Blessedly, the buccinators lifted their horns to their lips and the instruments wailed across the plain. Then the signophoroi around the emperor strode forth again. They waved their banners in a chopping, forward motion, and this was echoed up and down the line by the bandophoroi of the ranks, where every komes bawled;

'Ladders! Forward!'

At last, the caged fury of the Byzantine line was unleashed, and the wide crescent of iron washed forward. The earth shook and the cries of men echoed across the land.

Apion rode in the midst of the Chaldian ranks, urging them onwards. The plain jostled before him. Dust stung in his eyes and the stench of blood, vinegar and fear thickened the air. Arrows smacked down around him. 'To the walls!' he roared over the thunder of boots.

He twisted to his right and saw the fate of the brave Optimates Tagma. They were being torn asunder by the ballistae, doomed to lose many of their number just to force home the taking of the walls. Their shields and armour were pierced like paper with every strike. Men were ripped apart at the waist, others were pinned to comrades. Blood and dirt streaked the air like a gory blizzard.

He glanced up to the nearest of the gate towers; the ballista crewman there was taking aim for another strike at the Optimates. Apion lifted the javelin strapped to his back, tensed his shoulder, hefted and hurled it. The missile stayed true, arcing up and directly for the man. But at the last, the man ducked under the javelin. Then he rose again, grinning like a shark as he turned the ballista on Apion and the Chaldian ranks.

Apion's heart froze. Until another javelin burst through the man's chest. Apion glanced over his shoulder to see Gregoras punching the air at this, celebrating his feat of marksmanship. Apion frowned, then fell back.

'You saved my life?' he cried over the tumult.

'Aye, what of it?' Gregoras growled, 'every man in the ranks is my brother.'

Just then, a Seljuk arrow hissed down and smacked into Gregoras' thigh, finding a gap between the iron plates of his klibanion. Black blood pumped from the wound in gouts. Gregoras' smile dissolved, and he solemnly slid from his mount and slumped to sit, cross-legged, panting as his lifeblood soaked the dust.

Apion leapt down from his mount, crouched and grappled the dying strategos' hand, lifting his shield to protect them from the Seljuk arrow hail. 'If you have any light in your heart then tell me before you die, who are you working with?'

Gregoras could barely manage a frown, his face greying. 'What?'

'The Seljuks have known our route all along this campaign. I know you had something to do with it. I found your coin near the body of the murdered sentry at Melitene.' He plucked out the pure-gold nomisma and held it before Gregoras.

The dying man laughed a weak laugh. 'Ah, Psellos has given out many of those in the last year. We have all taken coin at times, Strategos. I took mine for delaying the works at the armamenta. Yes, I took Psellos' bribe, but only because I feared what might befall me had I refused. But I have had nothing to do with the ill-fortune on this campaign. Aye, there is a dark bastard at work, but it is not me.'

Apion saw nothing but truth in the man's eyes.

Then Gregoras' pupils dilated and his head slumped forward.

Apion frowned, backing away.

Then the clatter of ladders rang out all along the walls.

Apion spun to the sound. The matter of the traitor would have to wait.

He smacked his gelding on the rump to send it galloping back from the fray, then he turned to the walls, looking for a ladder to climb. Arrows smacked down all around him and he could only snatch glances over his shield rim as he ran to the nearest ladder. But it was already thick with skutatoi, unable to force their way onto the battlements. The sight was the same all along the walls. Despite the sheer weight of Byzantine numbers, the akhi on the battlements were holding steady. Apion knew that just a few hundred men could fend off many thousands if marshalled well, and these akhi were ruthless. And they weren't just akhi, he realised, squinting. Some of the men on the battlements held two-pronged spears. Daylamid spearmen, he realised. Rugged and burly mountain warriors and tenacious whoresons who would fight to the death. This was unexpected. Doubt swirled in his thoughts as he wondered what other surprises awaited them.

He saw skutatoi topple back from the ladders, their faces cleaved by spear thrusts. One fell away when the top of his head was sliced off like a piece of fruit, brains and blood showering his comrades below. Then one ladder was pushed back from the walls, toppling to the ground, snapping the limbs of the screaming men who clung to it and scattering those in its path, making them easy targets for the Seljuk archers.

Next, a pair of Seljuks appeared at the battlements, carrying a wide urn of something. They moved to the top of one packed ladder and tilted the urn, unloading a heap of glowing sand on the climbers. A terrible screaming rang out as the scorching sand penetrated every gap in the skutatoi armour, fusing with their skin. One skutatos fell from the top of the ladder, clawing at his face. He roared, thrashing to pull off his helmet and klibanion, heedless of his horribly shattered leg. His skin was ruby red and blistered and one eye had burst in the intense heat. The stench of his melting flesh pierced the air before the stricken man was peppered with Seljuk arrows.

The sight was the same all along the walls. There was no bridgehead, no foothold to allow them to press onto the battlements. Apion looked to the siege tower; it was yet to spill soldiers onto the battlements. 'The tower is the key – fill the tower!' he cried.

'It is full already!' one skutatos roared, staggering, clutching at an arrow shaft in his thigh. 'They won't lower the drawbridge.'

Apion frowned, then pushed through to the rear of the tower, arrows thudding into his shield as he did so. Indeed both floors of the tower were packed with skutatoi. But many were the young, feeble boys who had been rounded up to bolster the numbers of the Bucellarion Thema. He pushed through and flitted up the stairs to the second floor. The air was stifling in the cramped space.

The pair who held the drawbridge rope wore the expressions of terrified lambs.

'What are you waiting for – another ballista strike to cripple your tower? Our men are falling like harvest wheat out there!' Apion roared. 'Lower the drawbridge!'

The first man gulped and nodded. The second – a man of his own age with a thick dark beard – was white with fear, his hands trembling.

'I . . . I can't,' the man stammered.

Apion pushed him away, grappling the rope in his place. Then he fixed the first man with a glare. 'Are you ready?'

The man gulped and nodded again.

Apion cast a glance around the fearful faces surrounding him. 'How many years have you spent, fearful of Seljuk raids? How many of you have lost those you love to this war?' He stabbed a finger at the drawbridge. 'Out there you can change this; stand together and you can bring it to an end. Know this and you will know victory.'

They nodded, some shouting in agreement.

'Now, are you ready?' Apion roared.

'Yes, sir,' some called. 'Yes, *Haga*,' cried others.

Now he ripped his scimitar from his scabbard and held it aloft. This time he cried; 'I said . . . *are you ready?*'

'Yes, Haga!' came the reply. Even the uncertain bearded man he had pushed away had taken up his spear and held it in shaking hands, his jaw clenched.

'Onwards!' Apion cried out, then scythed the scimitar down on the ropes. The drawbridge toppled onto the battlements and the white heat of the day flooded the insides of the tower. Snarling daylami and the din of battle awaited them.

Apion leapt through the dark door and into the fray.

***

The fighting on the battlements was ferocious. The stonework was slick with blood and littered with skutatoi corpses. Still the Seljuk akhi and daylami were holding good around the gatehouse, but Apion and his men had established a foothold on the walls and now more and more reinforcements were piling up there through the siege tower. On the ground outside, the Byzantine battering ram had reached the gates and now smashed at the timbers like a giant demanding entry.

Apion pulled his blade across the swipe of an akhi scimitar, then kicked out at the man's gut, sending him over the edge of the battlements and plummeting down into the city streets.

Then a daylami spear came forking down at him like lightning and he toppled backwards to dodge the blow. He sprung to his feet and swiped at his challenger. The scar-faced man wore only an iron conical helmet and a light horn klibanion, and he was fast and nimble for it, evading Apion's strike. The man then feinted to jab his spear at Apion's gut, and followed up with what he thought would be a death blow to the throat. Instead, Apion ducked right, pulled his war hammer from his belt and swung it round in a wide arc to bring the pointed head crashing into the daylami warrior's left temple. The man's helmet flew from his head as his skull crumpled under the blow. Blood gushed from his ears and nostrils, then his eyes rolled in his head and he crumpled to a heap.

Apion leapt over the body to thrust his scimitar between the twin prongs of the next warrior's spear. But the man was strong. He freed one hand to smash a fist into Apion's nose. Apion's head was filled with white light and the crunching of breaking bone and cartilage. He fell to his knees, shaking his vision clear just as the twin-headed spear edged towards his heart. Apion's limbs trembled as he pushed back with his scimitar, but the daylami would not relent. The man pushed until the prongs ground against Apion's klibanion. The speartips parted the iron plates to pierce the skin of his chest, then ground into his breastbone. Apion saw the past flit before him.

Then the pressure fell away and the spear clattered to the ground. His foe staggered back, gawping, clutching at the spurting stump where his arm had been. His eyes were fixed on the severed limb by his feet, still gripping the spear shaft.

The thick-bearded skutatos who moments ago had been paralysed with fear inside the tower leapt forward to finish the daylami. Then he twisted back to Apion; '*Haga!*' he barked in acknowledgement before plunging forward into the fray. Another wash of fresh skutatoi spilled from the towers and onto the walls and then more joined them, finally winning the battle of the ladders. Then Igor and his comrades leapt into the walls just ahead. Their once pristine, white armour was now spattered with blood and their faces streaked in gore too. The big Rus swung his axe overhead and unleashed a cry that seemed to shake the walls and his blade cut through man after man, cleaving bones, lopping off limbs and splitting skulls.

At this fervent onslaught, the remaining few daylami seemed to lose their infamous nerve, and scrambled back to take shelter in the gatehouse towers. At the same time, the walls shuddered as the battering ram smashed the gates apart.

Apion panted as the men of Chaldia flooded past him. He glanced around the battlements and the ground either side of them. Skutatoi lay dead or dying, hundreds upon hundreds of them. Nearly a third of the toxotai had been slain too, having bravely exchanged fire with their Seljuk counterparts above the gatehouse. A clutch of kataphractoi lay broken near the gates, where they had fallen foul of a ballista barrage.

Yet cries of victory rang out when one bull-like soldier scrambled up to the top of the tallest gate tower, grasping a crimson banner of the Chaldian Thema. It was Stypiotes, the big komes. He hefted the banner high and waved it. At this, the remaining Byzantine soldiers outside the walls broke into a raucous cheer.

The outer walls had fallen, Apion realised as he unclipped his mail veil. Then he drew his gaze across the maze-like streets that clung to the inner city slope, and up to the citadel perched high on the acropolis. Handfuls of akhi fled through those streets, headed for the stronghold. They carried their spears and shields – clearly determined to fight on there.

Just then, the Byzantine infantry spilled through the shattered gates and poured into the market square. The emperor rode into the city in their midst, punching the smoke-streaked and crimson-spattered imperial banner towards the acropolis. 'Onwards!'

The battle for Hierapolis had only just begun.

**

Seljuk arrows and deadly iron bolts rained down like a storm from the rooftops onto the tapering, sloping street that led up to the citadel gate. The flagstones were littered with slain skutatoi, and the gutters ran red.

Apion inched forward to poke his head out from one alleyway and look uphill once more. The street rose sharply, past the granary and the crumbling barracks, then it narrowed and rose from the land around it like a ramp as it came to the arched citadel gate. The smooth limestone walls of the round-cornered bulwark shimmered in the afternoon sun, lifted from the city around it by a steep, rubble-strewn slope. The stronghold was five storeys tall, and looked as though it had been set there by giants. The crenellations ringing its flat roof seemed impossibly high from this angle, with iron glinting in the sun betraying the akhi, archers and ballistae up there. The gate was the only way in and it looked as sturdy as the walls, made of thick timber and barred and studded with iron. Already, several brave charges had faltered; the ramp before the gate was carpeted with broken skutatoi corpses and the battering ram they had tried in vain to bring to the gate. *There has to be a way,* Apion affirmed.

Then, as if willed by this frustration, one brave komes burst from the next alley and onto the rising, tapering street. He held his shield overhead, his arm juddering with every arrow strike, his step faltering as he picked his way through the dead. Then, with a hoarse cry, he beckoned his ninety remaining skutatoi with him. They roared in reply, holding their shields overhead to brave the worst of the hail. They reached the ramp and came within paces of the unmanned battering ram.

Yes! Apion clenched a fist, readying to wave his own men out to support them.

'Take the strain!' the komes roared, swiping his spathion forward to usher his men around the device. Then the two ballistae mounted atop the citadel dipped like the beaks of watching birds of prey. The komes' eyes widened under the rim of his helmet and he staggered back. The ballistae loosed. One bolt hammered into the spine of the ram and a sharp crack of timber rang out; the device was ruined. The other ploughed into the skutatoi, blowing their tight formation apart. At once, the arrow storm from the rooftops turned on the scattered men. Their cries were short lived and the street was piled higher with corpses.

Apion stared at the sight. He ducked back only when another arrow smacked against the whitewashed wall, inches from his eye, sending a shower of dust and grit across his face.

'Back!' he hissed, waving his eighty dirt, smoke and bloodstained men flat against the wall. This alley, like all the others they had stolen through to get here, was deserted. Doors lay ajar, belongings lay discarded. The populace had been evacuated. The Seljuks had anticipated the fall of the lower city walls. Planned it, even. Doubt was taking shape in Apion's gut as he thought of the hidden traitors in their midst.

In the alley directly across from Apion, Sha and his contingent were pinned down too. All up and down the broad street that ran steeply up the hill towards the citadel gate, the scene was the same. The army had been fragmented and immobile like this for over an hour, pinned down in the labyrinth of alleys. Apion looked to the rooftops all around the citadel. The granary, the bathhouse and the tenements were packed with Seljuk archers, pointing to targets, nocking their bows and loosing with ease. The buildings themselves were bristling with akhi, who had so far fended off Byzantine attempts to storm them.

Just then, Komes Peleus returned. He darted across the street, diving into the alley beside Apion, a storm of arrows smacking down in his wake. 'Many hundreds of them, sir. I lost count after that,' the little Komes panted, jabbing a finger up to the rooftops. 'I don't understand it. Laskaris signalled . . . ' Peleus started.

'Laskaris is long dead,' Apion cut him off. 'We have been lured into this, Komes. There are far more men garrisoning this city than we were led to believe. And they're no militia – they are the sultan's best men.' He stabbed a finger at the pure white tunics and the horn vests worn by the archers. 'And they're keeping us pinned down here.'

'What for?' Peleus' eyes widened.

'I fear the answer to that more than any of the missiles that might tear my throat out.'

Then a defiant cry rang out from above. Apion looked up, shielding his eyes from the sun. Three storeys above, a pair of skutatoi had somehow fought their way onto the bathhouse rooftop and were struggling with the Seljuk archers at the roof's edge. Then a bundle of akhi appeared behind them. With the flash of a scimitar, one skutatos crumpled out of sight. The other toppled from the roof, screaming, limbs flailing. Then he crunched onto the ground, blood, entrails and grey matter exploding from the shattered corpse. Apion turned away, sickened.

'We have to take the citadel, we need the high ground,' he spat, flexing and unflexing his fists. Far down the hill, he could see Procopius and his crew waiting in frustration beside the two remaining catapults – the only thing capable of breaking through that citadel gate. Yet the aged tourmarches and his men could not hope to move upon the citadel while the two ballistae on the stronghold roof were trained on anything that approached. Nothing could break through. Not while the ballistae remained. He closed his eyes and breathed. His heart slowed and he imagined himself as an eagle, soaring over the sun-baked city. Then he thought of the men of the campaign army as shatranj pieces and the walls of the citadel as enemy pawns in a tight square. Every piece he tried to move had to best the enemy pawns in order to break into their midst. But the knight . . . the knight could move up, over and inside their lines.

He blinked, his eyes sharp and focused, then looked to Peleus. 'You are a climber, Komes?'

Peleus frowned.

'I have seen you climbing the cliffs outside Trebizond.'

Peleus nodded, bemused. 'Aye, keeps me limber, sir, and falcon eggs fetch a good price at market. What of it?'

'Can the citadel walls be scaled?'

'Sir?'

Apion pinned him with his gaze. 'Can they be scaled, Komes?'

Peleus' face was etched with doubt. He risked a glance around the corner. 'They look sheer and smooth, but there will be gaps in the mortar. In theory, yes. But the archers on the rooftops will pick . . . '

'Do not fear the archers,' he flicked his head up, to where the Seljuk marksmen were still scouring the streets below for easy targets, 'they are clustered on the roofs and streets here, around the northern side. They're not paying attention to the other side, and they won't expect climbers,' he cocked an eyebrow with a ghost of a grin, 'as that would be a foolish plan.'

Peleus looked up, the fear and doubt on his face dissolving as he squared his jaw and nodded briskly. 'Then yes, we can do it.'

Apion clasped his shoulder, then looked to two toxotai near the back of his group. 'Steal back downhill. Take word to Tourmarches Procopius. Tell him that the ballistae will soon fall silent. Tell him that when they do, he must unleash a storm of rock upon the gates.'

Then he turned to the bandophoros and pointed to the filthy crimson Chi-Rho banner on the staff he carried. 'I'll be needing that.'

Finally, he beckoned Peleus and seven others equally lithe and light. 'Now, come with me.'

***

Apion pressed his back against the southern wall of the citadel and filled his lungs with a few good, deep breaths. He looked to the eight with him. Like him, they were dressed only in boots, tunics and swordbelts. A few were still stretching their limbs so they were supple enough for the climb. It was a blessing that they had made it this far.

They had picked their way through the alleys unseen to come round to the south of the acropolis mount. A brief glance around had confirmed that only a few Seljuk archers had part-sight of this area and

339

in any case, they seemed to be focused on the scurrying Byzantines below the gates on the north side. So, Apion and his men had picked their way up the scree of the acropolis mount unseen. That had been tense enough, but the most perilous part of the plan had still to come.

He turned to the walls, running his palms across the surface. The blocks were vast indeed, but they were also old, and in places the mortar between had crumbled.

'Good hand and footholds, sir,' Peleus confirmed. 'Whereas these,' he pressed his fingers into the shallowest of depressions where the limestone had been weather worn, 'are enough to hold you to the wall, but do not use them to climb with.' The seven skutatoi with them nodded. Their chests were rising and falling rapidly, some darting looks to the Seljuk archers – only a glance away from spotting them.

'You will not be sighted if you stay close to the wall,' Apion reassured them. 'And if you stray from the wall then an arrow will be the least of your worries,' he added with a half-grin. They laughed at this, some of the nerves dissipating as they did so. Then he fixed each of them with an earnest look. 'I'll be following Peleus' every move, so you follow me. We will get to the top.'

'Sir!' they replied in unison.

All eyes fell on Peleus. The limber komes nodded and turned to the wall. He crouched to pat his hands in the dust, then clapped them together.

'Good for grip,' he nodded, motioning for the others to do the same.

Next, he slid one foot into the first gap and then stretched out an arm to reach the next one. He groaned then swung his leg up and kicked it into the next gap in the mortar. The little komes picked his way up the citadel wall like a spider. Apion memorised his every hold, then followed suit.

As he rose, the din of battle became distant. He heard only the thudding of his own heart and every scrape of his fingers and boots in the limestone. The sun seemed intent on blinding him. His spathion seemed to pull at his belt like an anvil, and the higher they climbed, the more precarious and tenuous each hand and foothold became. Worse, his arms took to trembling with fatigue. His legs were strong from running and his arms were lean and muscular from battle but this climb seemed to pull on tendons and muscles he had not used in years. His vision became hazy and his mouth dry. It was then that a breeze served to remind him of how high he was. He glanced down to see the other skutatoi below gawping up at him, their hair flapping in the breeze, their eyes wide. He realised he could not afford to show any sign of weakness or those below him would let fear creep back into their hearts.

He reached out for the next handhold and then hesitated – it was barely a dent in the wall. *Did Peleus climb with this? He said we should avoid these but I am sure he used it.* Then he realised he had lost track of the little komes' path above him. *No time to delay,* he affirmed, then worked his fingers into the depression and hoisted himself up.

In that instant, his grip was gone. His body jolted in alarm as he dropped, his fingertips gouging at the surface. Fingernails were ripped clear as he fell and he braced himself for death. Then his body jolted as his scimitar guard wedged into one foothold below. All was still. He panted, staring at the ivory hilt. This was not the first time old Mansur's sword had saved him. *Don't let it be the last,* he mouthed, seeing the old man's solemn features in his memories, *you owe me that much.* Then he glanced down to see the skutatoi below had halted in horror at his fall.

'Bad handhold,' he said flatly, before continuing on the climb as if nothing had happened.

When Apion neared the top of the wall, he found Peleus waiting, clinging like a limpet. The others soon joined them.

'Take a few moments to breathe and reinvigorate your limbs,' Apion whispered over the gentle breeze. Their chests rose and fell and they looked all around them. On the shimmering Syrian plain, outside the western wall, the riders of the Scholae Tagma had set up tents and laid down their armour and weapons. Packs of them were now setting out to locate fodder, forage and water as Romanus had ordered them too, for it had swiftly become apparent that the city had been stripped of all food and the cisterns had been drained too. The Antitaurus Mountains stood defiant in the north. The waters of the Euphrates sparkled in the east. Then his gaze snagged on something, far to the south. A train of wagons and a disorderly mob. The populace of Hierapolis, fleeing from their homes.

Guilt stabbed at his heart at this. Relief washed around his veins too – that they would not be slain. But there was something else. A shiver passed over his skin again; there was something about this city, something about those fleeing people. He frowned, unable to turn away from the sight.

***

Maria swept her robe over her mouth to block out the worst of the dust. Then she felt Taylan wrench clear of her grip, spinning round to look north once more.

'I should be there, to fight them off, to save our city, to save our home!' he spat, staring back at the besieged city. His fingers flexed on his spear, knuckles white. The fleeing families and wagons broke around him like a river around a rock. Women, children and elderly flinched at his snarling expression as they passed.

Maria placed a hand on his shoulder as she looked to Hierapolis with him. She knew what was to happen there today. She could not bring herself to tell Taylan. She pulled him round from the sight, grappling him by the shoulders. 'Your duty is to see your people safely to Damascus.'

He dropped his gaze. 'But I should be there, by his side . . . '

Maria placed her forehead against his, cupping his face, silencing him. 'Turn and walk with me, Taylan. I need you to be strong.'

At last he nodded, and they set off together once more.

Maria afforded one last look back at the city. Her gaze lingered on the top of the citadel. An odd chill passed over her skin.

***

'Sir?' Peleus hissed.

Apion snapped out of his thoughts, turning from the distant exodus.

He eyed each of his men. They all wore flinty looks. They were ready.

Then he sucked in a breath. 'Now!'

They scrambled up and over the crenellations, thudding down onto the rooftop. There were twelve archers lining the northern edge of the roof, and then the ballistae were each manned by crews of three akhi.

One Seljuk archer spun to the noise and loosed an arrow instinctively. It took the skutatos nearest Apion square in the throat, and he toppled back over the wall.

Apion lurched for the archer, then swept his scimitar round, knocking the bow from the man's grip before ramming the blade into his gut. He twisted to hammer his elbow into the face of the next nearest, then wrapped an arm around the man's neck to use him as a shield against the arrows loosed by the man's comrades. Then he pushed the man forward, bundling him and another from the roof. Peleus and two skutatoi had already cut down six of the others, while the other four Byzantines despatched those manning the ballistae, one of the skutatoi taking a fatal cut to his belly in the process. The remaining three Seljuk archers fled, descending into the citadel. Apion ran to the leftmost ballista, chopping down on its bow with his scimitar then kicking out to snap the device. 'Peleus, shatter the other ballista,' he yelled. 'The rest of you, guard the staircase!'

As Peleus crippled the second ballista with a series of furious swipes of his spathion, Apion hastily pulled the rolled up crimson Chi-Rho cloth from his sword belt and stood tall, unfurling it and waving it overhead. The maze of alleyways below looked like a map from up here, and it was no wonder the Seljuks had been content to fall back to this citadel. He searched down the hill until he saw it; Procopius and his catapult crew driving forward, pushing the two catapults up the hill and into range with a guttural roar. The Seljuk archers on the rooftops of the granary and the baths realised what was happening, and took to firing upon this new threat. Crewmen toppled, peppered with shafts, and the catapult slowed. But then a cry burst from the alleys.

'The ballistae have fallen . . . forward!' Apion recognised the booming voice of the emperor.

At once, the men pinned back in the alleys burst forth, no longer fearful of the bolt throwers. Hundreds upon hundreds of them rushed to collect around the catapults, helping to push them ever closer, holding their shields over the heads of the crew.

Apion spun from the scene. 'Our men are coming for the gates! Soon the citadel will be . . . ' he halted at what he saw. Three of his five skutatoi staggered back from the top of the stairs, arrow shafts quivering in their unarmoured chests. The other two backed away, faces pale.

From the shadows of staircase, baleful grey eyes and a broad, glittering scale vest sparkled as a figure ascended the rooftop. Then the sun shed its light on the face, melted and ruined on one side, the dark hair scooped back in a ponytail. He wore a dark cloak on his shoulders and his expression was fixed in a scowl.

'Nasir,' Apion uttered.

'*Haga,*' Nasir replied, then snapped his fingers. Four akhi rose behind him, clad in the pure-white robes, horn armour and studded conical helmets of the sultan's personal guard. Without hesitation, they punched their spears into the hearts of the last two skutatoi, then kicked the dying men clear of the spearpoints, sending them toppling from the roof.

Peleus rushed forward, spathion raised.

'No!' Apion pulled him back.

'Save your breath, *Haga*. For he will die today, as will you.'

'Then you had best be swift about it,' Apion replied. 'For in moments, the doors of this stronghold will be blown from their hinges in a blizzard of rocks and my men will flood this rooftop.'

As if old Procopius was joining the conversation, a whoosh sounded from the street below, followed by an almighty crash and a groaning of timber. The rooftop shook under them.

Nasir did not flinch. 'That matters little,' he said, his eyes pinning Apion. 'My sultan asked for volunteers to come here. Men who wished to give their lives for the Seljuk cause. To snare the emperor and his armies.'

Apion frowned, noticing something over Nasir's shoulder. To the west, something stained the horizon, a few miles distant. *A dust storm?*

But Nasir's face had bent into a rapacious grin. 'Now you see it, don't you?' he swept a hand to the west.

Apion's vision sharpened like a blade. His heart iced over as he saw glinting iron amongst the dust clouds. This was no dust storm. Speartips, scimitars, iron masked mounts, spike-bossed shields. A Seljuk war machine. Only now, the unprepared riders of the Scholae Tagma outside the walls saw what was coming for them. Now, men ran between tents in a panic, unarmoured riders hared back from their foraging, cries erupted and horses bolted in fright.

'The Emir of Aleppo commands a fine army. Some ten thousand fresh and well-equipped riders and infantry. This is why I allowed your forces to tire, dashing your heads against Hierapolis' walls. You are snared within this broken city and now the emir will slay your forces to a man. Alp Arslan rides a short way behind with his retinue. The sultan looks forward to having your emperor bow before him.' Then Nasir beckoned another akhi from the stairs. The man brought a hemp sack, stained brown at the bottom. 'And know this,' Nasir continued, opening the sack and tossing the grey, staring head of Laskaris across the rooftop towards him. 'Every step of your journey here has been planned, planned so that you would arrive at this shabby end. Planned not by my sultan, not by me, but by your very own kin in the place you call God's city. Those who oppose your new emperor sponsor his downfall.'

One name rang in Apion's thoughts.

Psellos.

'I have known this for some time,' Apion growled. 'Yet still the emperor and his armies stand. This emir will have a gruelling fight on his hands, and the dark heart in our ranks who brought this upon us has not won.'

Crash! Another catapult strike pummelled the citadel gate.

Nasir's brow dipped like that of an angered bull. 'Do not trouble yourself with the emir or the traitors festering in your ranks and at the heart of your empire. For soon you will lie rotting, your eyes staring at the sky, watching as the carrion birds swoop to feast upon them!' he snarled, shrugging off his dark cloak, sliding his scimitar from its sheath. He raised the curved blade, levelling it at Apion, glaring along its length. 'It is time to bury our oath, *Haga!*'

Crash! The stronghold shuddered violently.

Nasir stalked around behind him. Apion did not move.

'Are you too timid to bring this to a finish? It would give me little satisfaction to strike you down so easily . . . '

Apion heard the whoosh of honed iron coming for him. He spun round, lifting the flat of his blade to parry in one motion. Nasir's blade smashed down upon it, sending a shower of sparks into the breeze.

Apion backed away and the pair circled. 'All those years ago, you hated me at first, Nasir. But you learned to accept me. You knew happiness in that time, as did I.'

'I knew happiness when she was mine. *Maria was mine!*' he roared, thumping a fist against his chest. His eyes were shot red with blood. 'Then you took her from me!' He cried, lunging forward with a flurry of swipes.

His anger carried him forward with speed and strength, and Apion could only parry each of the blows.

Finally, Nasir fell back, panting.

'I did not take her from you, Nasir,' Apion gasped. 'She was taken from us both by creatures who did not deserve to walk this earth.'

Crash! A splintering of timber rang out as the gates collapsed and Byzantine cheering filled the citadel from below. At this, three of the four well-armoured akhi left Nasir, rushing down the stairs to join the fray. Peleus took to circling with the last of them, the pair exchanging blows.

Nasir looked to the stairwell. Then his face fell and his eyes grew distant. 'Then perhaps the truth will die today along with our oath.'

Apion frowned. 'Truth? What truth?'

Nasir simply glared at him, lifting his blade once more.

'Nasir, tell me!' Apion cried. But Nasir rushed for him, a roar tumbling from his lungs.

Apion instinctively leapt to the defensive. He hefted his scimitar and rested his weight on his left foot. Then, just as Mansur had taught him all those years ago, he bent his right knee, just a fraction.

Nasir saw the bent knee and lunged to his left to dodge the blow and strike out at Apion's right flank.

Apion pulled out of the feint, dipping to his left, sweeping his scimitar round, swiping the blade from Nasir's hand. A popping of bone rang out as the blade spun into the air together with four fingertips. Nasir roared, dropping to his knees, clutching his hand, his ruined face contorted further.

'It's over,' Apion stated stoically. From a few floors below, the clatter of swords rang out as the Byzantine forces swept up through the citadel.

Nasir looked up at him, his grey eyes fierce under his v-shaped brow, his shoulders heaving with each breath. 'It is not over until one of us is dead.' Then he tore a dagger from his belt and stood.

There was something in Nasir's eyes. A finality. It reminded Apion of the lion's gaze on the plains of Thracia.

'Nasir,' Apion panted. 'Do you really think that the death of one of us will bring the victor peace?'

Nasir's rage faded at this. He shook his head and a single tear quivered in the corner of one eye. 'No. Peace will come only for the one who falls.'

Apion's heart stilled and he searched his old friend's eyes. *Don't do it.*

But Nasir rushed for him again, emitting a booming roar, dagger held overhand, his chest completely exposed.

Apion glanced to either side. He was near the edge of the rooftop and had no space to dodge the blow. He closed his eyes and twisted, swiping his scimitar across Nasir's path. The all-too familiar crackle of splitting flesh and bone rang out, and Apion felt blood shower him. He sunk to his knees with Nasir.

'*Haga* . . . ' Nasir rasped.

Only now Apion opened his eyes. Nasir's gaze was distant, his pupils dilating, mouth agape, lips trembling as he tried to speak.

Apion placed his free hand on Nasir's shoulder. 'You have your peace now, old friend. Do not fight it.' He thought of Nasir's long dead father and brother. Perhaps Nasir's faith would provide a final comfort to him. 'Kutalmish and Giyath wait for you.' Then he felt a stinging sorrow behind his eyes as he thought of the past. 'But you must know this. Not a day has passed since Maria died that I have not wished it was me. Were it not for me, then you and she may have lived these last years together in happiness, far from this war.'

349

Nasir's eyes glinted at this and he stared at Apion. It was a stare that worked its way into his soul and witnessed some truth deep inside. At the last, Nasir clutched at Apion's shoulder with his bloodied, fingerless hand. 'Apion, she . . . '

Apion stared through Nasir as the life left him with that breath. A breeze skirled around them like his last, unfinished words. He lowered the body to the ground, whispering a farewell, and then stood.

'Sir?' Peleus stepped forward tentatively, having sent the last akhi running for the stairs.

Below, the victory cries were only just turning into shouts of alarm as word of the emir's approach reached them. Down by the western walls, the approaching tide of iron rushed for the unprepared riders of the Scholae Tagma. The Byzantine riders could only turn and flee. Then they, their mounts and their tents seemed to disappear under Seljuk hooves and boots. Ghulam riders cried out as they skewered the dismounted riders, set light to the banners and fodder and spared none in their path.

'Steel yourself, Komes,' Apion spoke flatly, staring at the tide of iron. 'For the day is yet young.'

***

The charioteers arced around the southern bend of the Hippodrome track and the crowd on the eastern terrace rose as one, punching the air, waving and crying out in fervour. Then the lead charioteer saw the mounts of his nearest opponent slip onto the inside and pick up a good pace. He thrashed his sweating stallions with a whip and snarled, simultaneously pulling their reins to block off the overtaking manoeuvre. But then one overtaking mount foundered, stumbling under the wheels of the lead chariot. A sharp crack of timber rang out.

In an instant, mounts, chariots and men were bundled together, tumbling over and over before spinning into the air and then smashing down again. When the dust cleared, the sandy track was strewn with splintered wood, bent bronze and mutilated flesh. The screams of the riders and whinnying of the horses rang out above the roar of the crowd. One rider lay, halved at the waist, clutching at his spilled bowels and gazing in disbelief at his legs, twitching only paces away.

The roar of the crowd died with a chorus of gasps and pained yelps. Silence prevailed for a heartbeat. Then, in the midst of the long eastern terrace, one sweat-basted bookmaker turned from the disaster and drew his bulging eyes around the crowd, wagging one finger in the air.

'Next race – wager just a single follis on the swift and nimble Xerus and his Phrygian chargers and I'll give you twelve in return!'

As if the poor wretches writhing on the track were little more than an inconvenience, the spectators burst into an excited babble once more, clamouring around the bookmaker, waving fistfuls of coin in the air.

Psellos' nose wrinkled as he looked down on the populace from the *kathisma*, shaded by a purple silk awning. The imperial box was perched high enough over the terracing to catch the southerly breeze and prevent their foul odour from offending him. Then his chest prickled in agitation at the figure shuffling and sighing in the emperor's chair next to him.

John Doukas glowered at the gold and silver coins being passed around on the terrace below, scratching his dark beard in irritation. Then he took to shuffling and wriggling his shoulders despite the cushioned, silk-lined comfort of the chair.

'It is money well spent,' Psellos whispered in reassurance. 'The people must remain our pawns.'

351

But John merely grumbled at this. 'It is not the spending of my family's money that concerns me. Paphlagonia will always produce rich and flavoursome wines and furnish us with riches. No, it is the continued occupation of the imperial throne that boils my blood.' He twisted to look behind him, to the spiral stairway that led up here. Only the pair of numeroi that had escorted them here were present. 'Yet all day I have been tormented with the possibility that my troubles could be over?'

'Be patient, Master,' Psellos urged him, twisting to look over his shoulder. Through the latticed arches to the rear of the imperial box, the tower on the far side of the Bosphorus was just visible in the midday haze. 'The signal from Chalcedon was only a short while ago. The messenger will be escorted here without delay once his ferry docks in the Neorion Harbour.' Then his gaze snagged on the rooftop portico at the heart of the palace. There stood a silhouette, gazing eastwards. Eudokia. Flanking her as ever were the stocky shapes of her precious varangoi. *If Romanus has fallen, then no number of axes will protect you from my forces, my lady.*

A panting broke through his thoughts. He turned round to see a dusty, red-faced young man ascend to the top of the spiral staircase. He held a simple scroll. *Yet he has no comprehension as to its weight*, Psellos mused. He and John shared a rapacious grin. Then he beckoned the messenger, snatched the scroll and unfurled it. His eyes darted across the text.

Master, our designs have been thwarted so far. Romanus and his armies have reached Syria, and I write this as we march onto that arid plain . . .

'It is done?' John Doukas asked, hands grasping the arms of the emperor's seat like claws. 'The signal can be given today, the Numeroi can move on the palace.'

Psellos' chest tightened as he crumpled the scroll. 'Romanus lives.'

John's face reddened and his hands trembled. 'He *lives?* I chose you to be my adviser, and I could just as easily have you exiled!' John roared, grappling Psellos by the collar. 'Or worse!'

Spectators below looked up, squinting in the sunshine, frowning.

I could let the ignorant fool boil himself into a seizure, Psellos mused as he eyed the man who would be his puppet.

'Be at ease, Master,' Psellos calmed him. 'Our men within the campaign ranks have prepared for this eventuality.'

John frowned in confusion, his nostrils flared. But he set Psellos down nonetheless.

Psellos held his gaze. 'Now that Romanus and his loyal retinue are in Seljuk lands, subtlety is no longer a necessity.'

John's eyes darted. 'The campaign army will doubtless meet vast Seljuk armies and be battered by them, yes. But how can we be sure that Romanus falls in any such onslaught?'

Psellos' grin stretched and his eyes sparkled. 'Whether Romanus falls to a Seljuk blade or a Byzantine one matters little. Should the sultan's men fail, then our men will make sure that it happens. Indeed, in the days it has taken for this messenger to arrive, it may already have happened.'

John's face split with a baleful grin at this. He released Psellos and threw back his head, roaring with laughter. Then he stood and spread his arms wide.

As one, the crowd rose with him, roaring in applause.

21. Light in the Darkness

The Seljuk war horns wailed across the sweltering Syrian plain as the Byzantine army rushed to man the western walls of Hierapolis.

'Ten thousand men, Strategos?' Romanus gasped to Apion as they galloped downhill from the citadel towards the western gate. The emperor was wide-eyed, his face and hair streaked with grime and gore, his armour laced with battle scars.

'At least.' Apion fumbled to fasten his klibanion buckle as he galloped, then slid on his helmet. From the slope he could see the slaughter outside the walls. The emir's army dominated the plain, part-silhouetted in the late afternoon sun. A thick pack of ghulam were ripping the Scholae camp asunder, swooping and darting through the screaming and unprepared kataphractoi, cutting off limbs, sending heads spinning clear of bodies. A broad wall of akhi stood back from this, flanked by two packs of ghazis, bows nocked, mounts shuffling in anticipation. To the rear of this assembly, a pair of green banners fluttered in the dust storm kicked up from the fight. The emir was between them, clad in gilt armour and saddled on a grey mare. Then, emerging from the western horizon, a fleet of a dozen war towers, a dozen more tall trebuchets and some forty catapults were being hauled forward, eager to smash the city walls from their path and capture the emperor as a prize for their sultan.

'We have barely three thousand men!' Romanus growled through gritted teeth, pointing to the western wall. The battered remnant of the Optimates Tagma had reached the battlements there first, and now filtered into a thin line. The ragged remnants of the themata spilled up there to join them; banda of spearmen missing helms and shields, carrying blunted blades and limping on bloodied limbs, many of their comrades lost. Pockets of archers scrambled onto the gatehouse with their quivers depleted, their numbers thin. To a man, they glanced to the storm on the plain and then over their shoulders, seeking out their emperor, seeking out hope. 'The outer walls will not hold their artillery back. And the citadel is breached – so we cannot fall back to its walls. Defending this place is nigh on impossible.'

'The emir knows this. Yet he is bargaining on us clinging to the battlements like fearful limpets, defending to the last. That is what Byzantium has become in the eyes of men like the emir,' Apion shouted back, 'and that is why we must abandon the walls.'

Romanus' face curled into an incredulous frown. 'Retreat, *Haga?*'

Apion's brow dipped and he stabbed a finger out to the plain. 'No, *Basileus*. We must ride out to meet them in the field.'

'I have stolen some unlikely victories in my time, Strategos. But the emir's men are fresh and numerous . . . ' Romanus frowned.

'They expect an easy victory, *Basileus.*' Apion pointed to the ragged few of the Scholae who fought their last out on the plain. 'They think they have slain all of our riders, no doubt.

Romanus looked to him. 'They all but have!'

'Do not discount the riders of the themata, *Basileus,*' Apion pointed to the packs of ironclad kataphractoi just ahead, milling inside the western gate. 'Three hundred, three hundred and twenty, perhaps. Let the emir feel the wrath of their steel. If we engage the Seljuks in the field, then their artillery will count for little. What use is a war tower against a swarm of skutatoi? Will they fire their trebuchets or catapults into a mass of fighting men?'

Romanus looked to him wordlessly as they slowed under the shade of the western gatehouse.

All around them, men cried out, appealing for their emperor's words.

Apion, Romanus and Doux Philaretos gathered together to discuss their next move.

Then, at last, Romanus nodded. 'Doux, you have the infantry. Lead them out onto the plain to face down the emir,' he said to Philaretos, nodding to the western gate. With that, the emperor kicked his stallion round. 'Sally forth!' he roared to the amassed ranks. 'It is time to end this long and bloody day. With God by our side, victory will be ours! Nobiscum Deus!' he boomed, emptying his lungs.

'*Nobiscum Deus!*' the men of the ranks roared in reply, the panic shaken from their hearts by the emperor's hubris.

Doux Philaretos dismounted and strode forward to head up the exodus. 'Onto the plain!'

The signophoroi waved and their banners and the western gates were thrown open. Men streamed onto the plain to the song of the buccinas.

Then Romanus turned to Apion. 'Take half of the riders to the southern gate, Strategos. I will lead the other half to the north.' He heeled his mount round, a dry grin spreading across his face as he clutched a hand across his heart, the golden pendant dangling there. 'And I will see you out there in the fray.'

Then the emperor waved Igor, the varangoi, half of the thematic kataphractoi and the Pecheneg riders with him, northwards along the inside of the western wall.

Apion waved the kataphractoi of Chaldia plus a handful of those from the Bucellarion Thema – some one hundred and thirty riders combined – over to him. Then he waved the cluster of Oghuz riders over too. Just over five hundred men in total.

He kicked his Thessalian along the inside of the western wall to the south and in contraflow to the flood of infantry. He slowed momentarily as he came to the torn crimson banners of Chaldia as they made for the western gate. Sha, Blastares, Procopius and Dederic led them. They were matted in the filth of battle like the few hundred spearmen and archers that remained of the Chaldian army.

'*Haga!*' Sha barked. 'You will lead us out?'

Apion slowed his mount and shook his head. 'No, but I will be joining you soon.' He looked each of them in the eye. 'Have the men proceed in a line. Present the emir's men with an irresistible target. Then . . . ' he pressed his hands together, making a diamond shape. 'Doux Philaretos knows this already,' he paused, shooting a furtive glance at the scowling doux. A traitor was still amongst their ranks. Apion longed for it not to be the man who would lead the infantry into the fray. 'Just be sure your ranks are ready for the move. And stay strong. Today can still be ours!''

'Aye, sir,' Sha nodded firmly.

'Aye, sir!' Blastares and Procopius barked in reply.

Dederic offered him a solemn gaze. 'Whatever it takes, sir.'

Turning from his trusted four, he waved his riders with him. 'To the southern gate!' he cried.

***

The earth trembled beneath Sha's feet as the Byzantine spearmen marched forward in a phalanx. It was only two men deep and an atypical formation for the banda, and even then it barely stretched to match the breadth of the emir's horde. All along the line, faces were

357

stained with blood, wrinkled in defiance, jaws jutting, tears streaming from eyes. Banners were held proudly, spears and shields grappled in white-knuckles. Doux Philaretos led the centre on foot, heading the few hundred remaining spearmen of the Optimates Tagma. The Chaldian army marched left centre, with Sha, Blastares, Procopius and Dederic on foot at the head of their depleted tourmae. Behind them, the toxotai rumbled forward in a pack of six hundred, arrows nocked to bows, wide-brimmed hats cocked forward to shield their eyes from the dropping sun. With them marched eight siphonarioi, their fire siphons grasped tightly, their iron masks betraying nothing of the fear they doubtless felt. Then, to the rear, the priests held the campaign Cross high and chanted, eyes closed.

'Halt!' Doux Philaretos cried when they were some two hundred paces from the smoking remnant of the Scholae camp. The buccinas sang and the bandophoroi waved their banners to reinforce this. As one, the phalanx slowed to a standstill.

Ahead of them, the Seljuk centre was obscured by the devastation of the Scholae camp. Tents lay ablaze, smoke smudging the air. A smattering of the broken tagma fled, some on their mounts, some on foot, precious few unwounded and carrying arms. Those who did escape – thirty seven, Sha counted – thundered in behind the phalanx where they formed together once more.

The flames ahead died, the smoke grew thinner, and through the sweltering heat haze, the full might of the emir's forces were revealed. The two wings of ghulam reformed on the Seljuk wings, cleaning their bloodied lances. Ghazi archer cavalry milled close behind, and a broad and deep wall of some eight thousand akhi spearmen formed the centre.

He glanced to his side. Blastares and Procopius returned his solemn look.

If today is to be my last, then it has been a pleasure fighting alongside you, he thought. Then he saw Dederic. The Norman was muttering some prayer, his gaze sombre. *Aye,* he thought, his mouth drying and his bladder swelling, *let us pray our riders come soon.*

Then his thoughts dissolved as the emir raised both hands. The babble died to silence for but a heartbeat. Then he dropped his hands forward like blades. The Seljuk war horns wailed and the battle cry rose up, then the emir's army washed towards the phalanx like a tidal wave.

'*Allahu Akbar!*'

Sha's eyes flicked from the advance to the scowling Philaretos. The lives of the infantry lay with this man. If his order was just a fraction too early or too late, thousands would die and the Byzantine campaign would be crushed.

'Hold!' Philaretos cried.

'Hold!' Sha barked along with every other tourmarches along the lines.

Still the Seljuk horde thundered forward. Sha could see the whites of the ghulam mounts' eyes, their grinding teeth, the glint on the scimitar blades of their riders.

'Hold!' Sha repeated.

The akhi now loosed javelins towards the phalanx like a hailstorm. The missiles rained down all along the front of the ranks, most falling just paces short. But one missile punched into the skutatos by Philaretos' side. The doux gawped at the gap where the man had stood.

Then he looked back up at the advancing horde. 'Fall back! Form square!' he cried at the vital moment.

At once, the buccinas sang and the banners waved, but the ranks were moving even before these signals. The centre of the phalanx bunched closer, the two ranks becoming sixteen deep. The men with the longest spears and iron vests formed the front ranks, and those with shorter spears fell in behind. The left and the right of the phalanx folded round to form the other three sides of the square, enclosing the toxotai and the few surviving Scholae riders. Then the siphonarioi bustled forward to present their fire siphons alongside the wall of spears, two men posted at each corner. In just moments, the broad, thin Byzantine line had transformed into a compact square, bristling with a palisade of spears, the centre packed with readied archers.

The emir's horde did not falter at this, curving their broad and deep line around the square like a flooding river around a feeble rock. The ghulam riders swung round at the end of this line to charge at the left and right of the square, while the wall of akhi charged towards the front.

The toxotai focused their aim on the approaching akhi wall, sending a thick cloud of arrows skywards, then nocking their bows once more while this volley rained down on the spearmen. The shafts punched into shoulders, burst through eyes and shattered the skulls of those without helms. The stricken suddenly dropped from the approaching horde as if the ground had opened up beneath them. Then the ghazi riders replied in kind, circling on their mounts a few hundred paces away. The square scrambled to pull their shields overhead. A rattle of arrowheads on shields rang out, with a chorus of screams and wet punch of iron in flesh from those too slow to react.

Then, when the akhi were some thirty paces away from the Byzantine front, Sha raised his hand like every other tourmarches.

'Rhiptaria . . . *loose!*'

Like a bristling porcupine, the rear ranks of the skutatoi hefted and loosed their javelins. This thick cloud of iron-tipped timber crashed down on the akhi advance, punching akhi from their feet, dashing the lives from their bodies. Many hundreds fell. But many hundreds more rushed to the fore to replace them, spears trained on Byzantine throats, only paces away.

'Stay together!' Sha roared with all the breath in his lungs, but the din of the Seljuk cry rendered it useless. He felt his comrades' shoulders press against his, their bodies shaking with hubris and terror.

Then the Seljuk charge met the Byzantine square with a tumultuous rattle of shields, screeching iron and screaming men. A thick spray of blood burst into the air. Many skutatoi crumpled, many akhi ran onto spears, some surging up and over the Byzantine wall such was their momentum. At the same time, the ghulam riders plunged into the square's flanks, hacking off Byzantine speartips and heads as if they were one and the same. Mounts reared up, hooves dashing out skutatoi brains or shattering ribs, the ironclad Seljuk riders leading a dance of death through the Byzantine spearmen. In moments, the front of the square was battered out of shape and the flanks fared little better.

Sha's spear arm jolted as he thrust his spear through an akhi warrior's breastbone, the tip erupting through the man's back. The akhi's face fell expressionless, and a wash of black blood and broken cartilage vented from his lips and nostrils, the spray coating Sha's eyes. He blinked to clear the mess. The corpse fell under the continuing akhi push and pulled Sha's spear down with it. He clutched for his spathion hilt and lifted his shield to brace against the push, but the pressure was immense, and he felt his feet slip on the red-white mire of blood, flesh and bone underfoot. He pressed shield to shield with another screaming akhi before him and both found their arms pinned to their sides, unable to wield their weapons. He could do little but scream back in defiance at his foe. The square was wobbling, the

361

front face bending inwards. The toxotai behind cried out in alarm at this.

'Give them fire!' Sha cried to the corners of the square.

At this, the siphonarioi were hoisted onto the shoulders of the men around them. They hurriedly struck their flint hooks to ignite their siphons. Then, with a thundering growl, they sent forth far-reaching jets of orange flame. At once, the akhi and the ghulam were ablaze, the fire clinging to them like clay. The ghulam riders cooked inside their own armour, their panicked mounts carrying them, screaming and ablaze, back from the fray. Their pained roars were short as corpses toppled, acrid smoke billowing from their burnt out faces and throats.

At once, the deathly crush was relieved. But only briefly.

The emir rode behind the akhi, marshalling them into line once more. Sha watched as the gilt-armoured leader and his retinue took to chopping their blades down on the heads and necks of those of the men who did not obey the commands. Then the emir ordered his ghazi to fire upon the siphonarioi. A cloud of arrows hammered down on the fire throwers and, without shields, all but one of them fell under this hail. At this, the akhi and ghulam halted their retreat, and came crashing back towards the Byzantine square.

'Reform the square!' Sha barked. Blastares, Procopius, Dederic and Philaretos echoed the command all around him and the front and sides of the square bent back out to present flat walls of spears. But this time the square was smaller – much smaller. Nearly one in three of their meagre ranks had fallen in the first Seljuk assault, Sha realised. Another such charge and they would surely break.

He plucked a spear from an akhi corpse, then pushed up against the spearmen either side of him. The akhi came at him in their thousands, spears levelled, eyes bulging, screaming. Sha's limbs trembled, his heart thundered, and he cried out in defiance.

***

Dederic's ears pounded with every heartbeat and he heard little of the screaming all around him. His arm juddered as he brought his longsword across the throat of man after man. His lips were caked in blood and the vile metallic tang permeated every breath he managed to snatch. This was survival and little more.

Then an akhi speartip punched through the top of his shield, sending splinters into his eyes and scoring across the hood of his hauberk, tearing it and splitting his ear, knocking his helm to the dust. Dederic dropped his shield, clutching at his ear, momentarily deafened. In the silence, he saw the speartip lancing towards his heart, the akhi wielding it roaring in fervour.

Two emotions pierced his heart as he saw the certainty of death. Guilt that he would now never free his family from serfdom and tyranny, and relief that he would now no longer have to carry out the deed he had been paid to do. He looked the akhi in the eye, searched for an image of Emelin and the children, then prepared for death.

But it did not come.

The akhi's snarling face widened in shock as a spathion hammered down into the side of his skull, cleaving it through to the nose. Blood spurted from the fissure and then the body crumpled under the press.

Gawping, Dederic felt his shield being pressed back into his hands. At this, his deafness passed and the din of battle returned. He parried at the flurry of spear thrusts that rained in on him and glanced to his side to see who had saved him.

Zenobius was a sickly, vivid red, his pallid features caked in gore and the brains of the slain akhi.

363

'Your job is not over yet, accomplice,' the albino said. 'With me,' he demanded and then stepped back from the front and melted into the heart of the Byzantine square.

Dederic felt his legs move and he followed the man. Now his heart was awash with guilt alone.

***

Apion clipped the mail veil across his face as he galloped along the base of the southern wall. Then he and his wedge burst round the corner tower and onto the western plain.

Before him he saw the vast swarm of akhi and ghulam feeding on a pocket of Byzantine resistance in the centre. Before him he saw skutatoi falling in swathes as if being swallowed by an underground predator. Before him he saw the fiery tendrils engulfing the dark door. He felt his hands trace its scorching timbers, and welcomed the goading, sibilant voice that lay behind it. *I'm coming for you*, he mouthed behind the veil. He saw the door smashed back upon its hinges. The flames gouged at his flesh, and he lunged into the fury of battle.

'First, the ghazis!' he cried, waving his wedge towards the thick pack of Seljuk archer cavalry. These riders were focused on the attack on the Byzantine square. They loosed an almost constant storm of arrows upon the trapped skutatoi there and were oblivious to Apion's charge. He saw some of them cheer when their missiles hit home. Others punched the air in delight as they watched the akhi and ghulam cut further into the beleaguered square.

Only when Apion and his riders were around forty paces away did the rearmost ghazis turn, faces etched with confusion. Then their eyes bulged, their lips flapped wordlessly. Now they slapped the shoulders of their fellow riders in alarm. But it was too late.

The kataphractoi lanced into them, ploughing through their pack like an axe through kindling. Few ghazis had time to draw their blades before man and mount were thrown to the ground. Their cries were short lived. Apion hacked the bow from one ghazi's grip and then chopped at the man's shoulder, shearing the bone and relieving him of his arm.

Then the Oghuz riders, riding close behind Apion's wedge, loosed their arrows rapidly, picking off the ghazis who tried to break from this kataphractoi strike. Many of the archer cavalry did manage to break away though. They raced to the north, readying to adopt their deadly tactic of firing and circling, remaining clear of the Byzantine lancers.

Not today, Apion mouthed behind the veil, looking to the north.

The ghazis stumbled and slowed when they set eyes on another iron wedge coming from that direction.

Emperor Romanus charged at the head of this second pincer, holding the purple imperial banner aloft. His cry sounded across the plain. Igor and the varangoi echoed his cry as did the kataphractoi who fanned out in their wake. Even the Pecheneg cavalry racing alongside them joined in.

At this, the ghazis' nerve broke. They wheeled round, ready to break to the west from where they had come. But the two Byzantine wedges crashed through their flanks to see them off. Mounts were turned over and over and riders were thrown clear of their saddles under the impact.

At once, Apion turned from the fleeing riders and looked to the swarm of Seljuk akhi and ghulam, a few hundred feet away. In their midst, the few men of the Byzantine square were fighting their last. Across the fray, Apion locked eyes with the emir.

The emir gawped back at these silhouetted riders who had appeared on the plain unexpected, as if the ghosts of the Scholae Tagma had come back for him. Then his face curled into a hateful grimace and he yelled at his ghulam riders.

Apion panted as he sidled up to the emperor. 'It is time to finish this, *Basileus,*' he said with a solemn finality.

Romanus' gaze was flinty. 'To the last, *Haga.*' He clutched one hand over his heart and raised the other to wave the riders forward. 'To the last!'

The men of the two Byzantine wedges kicked their mounts into a gallop. At the same time, the ghulam riders peeled from the attack on the Byzantine square and hared headlong for this charge. They were evenly matched in terms of numbers. Some three hundred ghulam to the same number of kataphractoi. The ghulam rode as one pack while the Byzantine riders rode as two.

The ghulam leader was brave and brash, urging his men on with a guttural roar. Apion squeezed his gelding's flanks and burst ahead of the wedge, training his lance on this man. The lead ghulam tensed his arm, bracing as he guided his spear tip towards Apion's throat. At the last, Apion saw that the ghulam lance was nearly a foot longer than his and knew he would die on the end of it if they clashed. So he fixed his gaze on the man's bulging white eyes, then hefted his own spear and hurled it forward like a javelin. The shaft was heavy, but at only paces away, the tip smashed through the rider's veil, shattered his face and punched his lifeless body from the saddle. Apion burst past the riderless mare, and the two wedges collided with a cacophony of screaming and clashing blades. Then, moments later, Romanus' riders piled into the fray too.

The ghulam and kataphractoi fought like centaurs, at once dealing out and evading death. The arrow storm from the nearby Oghuz and Pechenegs was thin but carefully placed, the shafts falling only on the enemy, panicking the mounts or debilitating the riders. Apion twisted in his saddle to swipe his scimitar at the ghulam who charged for him. The curved blade scythed into the rider's neck, breaking through the chain mail and tearing out the man's larynx. Then he felt the presence of another attacker on his flank, and spun instinctively, swinging his mace down to crumple the plated iron vest of his foe and burst the man's heart. Through the dust and crimson fog all around, he saw Romanus wheeling and hacking, never ceasing to cry out in encouragement. Before him, Igor and the varangoi swung their battle axes overhead, cutting a path for their emperor. Riders on both sides fell in swathes, but the two Byzantine wedges tore at the brave ghulam with a ferocity that the Seljuk riders could not match. The storm of hacking and stabbing ended only when Apion came face to face with Romanus. Both panted, glancing all around, expecting another foe. But there were none. The mighty Seljuk ghulam riders had been broken. Less than seventy kataphractoi remained, the rest lying tangled amongst the fallen.

Apion turned his sights on the mass of leaping, hacking, roaring akhi, and the near-invisible Byzantine square holding out to the last at the centre of this horde.

Now the emir was berating his infantry, waving his arms. 'The threat lies behind you, you fools!' his voice echoed across the plain. His mount reared up in the centre of the crush, the hooves breaking the neck of one helmetless akhi. At this, the rearmost of the akhi ranks began to turn away from the assault on the tattered Byzantine square, their faces etched with panic at the small but bloodied pack of riders forming up behind them. First a few, then hundreds of spears were turned round to protect the rear.

'*Basileus!*' Apion gasped. 'We must act!'

Romanus' eyes bulged. 'Onwards!' he bellowed.

The plain juddered before them once more. Apion saw the emir force his way into the swarm of akhi that had turned to face the rear, keen to find protection behind their myriad spears. The finely armoured leader even chopped his blade down at men in his way and kicked out at them from his saddle. At that moment, Apion realised that the Seljuk warriors would fight for this man only as long as they feared his reprisal. Thousands of lives would be lost today, but thousands more could be spared if this man was slain.

Apion plucked a ghulam lance from the body of a comrade and readied himself in the saddle. 'With me!' he roared, waving his wedge into a charge at the akhi who clustered around their leader. He lay low in his saddle and levelled his lance. Crucially, it was longer than those held by the Seljuk infantrymen. He waited until he could see the panicked eyes of the nearest of them, then he braced. His shoulder jarred and jolted as his spear plunged through the man and then again through the next two men behind. Likewise the rest of his riders carved into the akhi cluster like a blade and Romanus' wedge ploughed into them too. The dull crunch of crumpling armour, the sickly ripping of flesh and serrated screams of torn men sounded all around. Apion did not blink throughout it all as he barged through the enemy lines. His gaze and his spear tip were fixed on the emir.

The gilt-armoured emir snarled at the few akhi left immediately before him. But, at the last, all bar a few ducked out of the way.

The emir fell silent, his eyes wide, his lips trembling. Only four akhi remained to defend their leader.

Apion hurled his spear into the nearest of the defenders, then pulled his scimitar from his scabbard and ripped the blade up and over the next man's chest. The third threw his spear, and Apion tumbled from the saddle to avoid the lance. He rolled where he landed and saw the akhi rush for him, sword in hand. The akhi sliced the blade down, and Apion spun from the blow, then dealt a counter swipe, scoring across the man's throat and bringing forth torrents of lifeblood. He kicked the man backwards, then turned to the last defender – a giant of a man with a smashed nose who bore a huge spike shield and a silver-tipped spear. Apion drew his war hammer and hurled it at the giant's skull. But the giant hoisted his shield and punched the hammer from the air, then lunged at Apion, bringing his spike shield crashing down. Apion threw up his shield arm. The small shield strapped to his bicep caught the brunt of the blow, but the rusting, serrated spikes of the giant's shield were long and found a way through the gaps in Apion's klibanion. White-hot pain streaked through his ribs and blood washed from under his armour.

He had only an instant to get his bearings. He scrambled back from the giant's next scimitar strike, which splashed into the gore underfoot. Then the giant came at him again. Apion leapt as if to meet the man, then dropped into a crouch, swiping his blade round to cut across the giant's left hamstring. The giant fell with a guttural roar. On his knees and unable to stand, the big man swiped out as if wanting to finish the fight. Apion kicked the man over into the gore. 'Your fight is over,' he panted.

Ignoring the giant's roars of derision, Apion turned to the emir. The kataphractoi had driven the rear-facing akhi back like an axe hewing into soft timber, and now the emir was alone. Apion stalked towards the man. But his tunic and legs were now soaked in his own blood and his stride was sluggish. His vision blurred as he approached the emir. He shook his head, but it did not help.

The emir backed away from Apion, his face twisted into a bitter scowl. The jewels studding the rim of his ornate helmet sparkled, illuminating the hatred in his eyes as he looked down from his black mare.

'Byzantine dog!' he roared, levelling his scimitar.

The words sounded distant and echoing to Apion. Then, seemingly lightning-fast, the emir swept the blade down as if to split his skull. Apion was slow to react, his limbs heavy. He only just held up the flat of his blade, two-handed, to parry the strike. Sparks showered as the blades collided.

The emir strained and grunted, pushing down with an unexpected strength. Apion felt his own strength sapping quickly, his limbs growing numb and cold. Then, behind him, he heard an animal grunting. He twisted to see the giant bodyguard whose hamstring he had torn, propped on a spear shaft, hobbling towards his back. The giant held a scimitar in his other hand, and a foul grin stretched across his face as he lifted the blade and readied to swipe it at Apion's neck. Apion shot glances to the giant and to the emir. All the other riders were locked in battle with the akhi. He was alone and his vision was spotting over. He could slay either one of these men, but only one. And then he would die on the blade of the other.

The emir leaned closer, sensing Apion's weakness. 'Your head will be rotting on a spike by dusk,' he spat. 'My sultan will dine in the shade as he watches the vultures feast on your cold, staring eyes.'

For Apion, the decision was made. 'Your sultan is my enemy, but at least he carries honour in his heart.' With that, he dropped back from the emir's blade, twisted round and rammed the tip of his scimitar up, under the emir's armour and deep into his chest. The emir's eyes widened in shock, and black blood poured from his lips in gouts.

As the light left the emir's eyes and the corpse toppled, Apion heard the whoosh of iron swiping round for his neck. He turned to see the giant's blade sweeping round to behead him. He locked his gaze upon his killer and waited upon the death blow.

I will march on in your nightmares, whoreson!

Then a whinnying split the din of battle, and he saw the faint outline of a white stallion behind his killer, bursting from the nearby melee. Something glowed on the rider's breast. Something golden.

A crunch of iron chopping through flesh and bone ended it. Hot blood washed down Apion's body. But there was no pain. Blinking, he looked at the headless body of the giant. Blood pumped from the raw stump of a neck, the arm was still outstretched, quivering, holding the scimitar only inches from Apion's jugular.

Then the corpse toppled away. Romanus stood behind it, his face twisted in a grimace, his chest heaving, his bejewelled spathion dripping with blood.

As news of the emir's slaying spread, many akhi broke from the battle. Spears were thrown to the ground and they spilled past the kataphractoi like a flooding river, fleeing to the west. The Byzantine square broke apart like an exploding mirror, striking out to hasten their flight. Joyous and hoarse victory cries rang out as the tide turned.

Apion frowned as he looked around him, swaying on his feet, the last of the akhi barging past him in their hundreds. The dark door slammed shut and tendrils of smoke spiralled from the edges. He saw only the carpet of corpses all around. He glanced down to see the blood washing freely from under his klibanion. He felt cold, so cold.

Then he saw something else. A Byzantine spearman, on horseback, galloping through the fleeing akhi. It was Zenobius the albino from the Thrakesion ranks.

Apion frowned. Those of the ranks who gave chase to their enemy wore twisted scowls and pained, tear-streaked grimaces. But this rider wore an empty look on his face. Empty and cold. And he was riding against the tide. Something chilled Apion to his heart at that moment. Then he saw the albino lift a bow from his back and load the wooden channel fixed to it with a solenarion bolt. At that moment he realised where the rider was headed.

'*Basileus!*' he cried weakly.

But it was too late, Zenobius loosed the bolt at Romanus' back. The emperor spun, eyes widening. The varangoi cried out, pitching forward. But none were fast enough.

Except one small rider in a mail hauberk.

Dederic's mount flashed in front of the emperor at the last, and the bolt took the Norman high in the chest. His lifeblood burst over Romanus. Then he slid from the saddle and into the gore.

Zenobius' expressionless face cracked into a sneer of confusion and disgust. He had time to snatch up his spathion before a pair of varangoi axes swung down upon him, one cutting his chest open, the other slicing his sword arm off. Then Apion's scimitar spun through the air and swiped his head from his shoulders.

The varangoi and the men of the ranks cried out in confusion, swarming past Apion to surround the emperor. Apion felt his thoughts merge with blackness as he staggered to where Dederic lay.

The Norman clutched at the solenarion shaft, sputtering blood from his lips, his eyes searching the sky above.

Apion dropped to his knees, panting weakly. 'How did you know?' he croaked. 'Even the varangoi were caught unawares.' His vision was slipping away, and all he could see now were the Norman's eyes, fixed on him.

'Whatever it takes . . . ' Dederic whispered. 'They promised me gold, Apion – enough to free my family. I betrayed our every move.'

Apion shook his head. 'No!' he whispered.

'I made my choice.' He clasped Apion's forearm, his eyes bulging as another mouthful of blood burst from his lips. 'But I pray that my choice at the last will define me. I pray that God will not let my family suffer.'

With that, Dederic of Rouen shuddered in a death rattle and he was still.

Apion's heart turned as cold as the rest of his body. He gazed at Dederic's dead eyes.

All around him, the skutatoi chanted for the emperor. '*Ba-si-le-us! Ba-si-le-us!*' and this chant became intermingled with that from the tattered remains of the Chaldian Thema; '*Ha-ga! Ha-ga! Ha-ga!*'

At this, Apion's head lolled round weakly and he glanced to the setting sun in confusion. Dusk was coming on faster than normal, he thought as his vision dimmed.

'Strategos!' he heard Romanus cry as if from a distant place. He felt hands grapple at him, men calling out in alarm. He heard the voices of Sha, Blastares and Procopius, pushing to the fore. But they were slipping away. And he was falling.

As Apion toppled into the gore beside Dederic, the distant chanting changed to a solemn tone as the priests heralded the victory and bemoaned the lost, accompanied by a chorus of screeching carrion birds.

***

Alp Arslan halted his retinue of seventy ghulam with a raised hand. Not a man spoke.

Upon their approach, he had watched in disbelief as the small pockets of Byzantine cavalry had carved the emir's army apart. Now his gaze hung upon the sight before him. Thousands of the emir's men washing past, leaderless, weaponless, their eyes wide. The fleet of trebuchets, towers and catapults had been abandoned in the middle of the plain, their crews having fled. 'Fleeing what?' he said, eyeing the bloodied rabble that stood outside the western walls of Hierapolis. 'I see only a tattered band of men.'

'Including the two that matter,' Nizam whispered, by his side.

Despite the distance, Alp Arslan recognised the white and crimson form in the Byzantine heart as that of Romanus. Beside the emperor knelt a bloodied rider with a black eagle plumage, shoulders draped in a crimson cloak. It was the one who had slain the emir.

'The *Haga* has shown honour today. He slew the emir, knowing it would end the battle swiftly,' Nizam mused.

'Honour or the ruthless nous of a man soaked in battle-blood?' the sultan countered.

'It matters little,' Kilic cut in, grinning. The big bodyguard pointed to the crimson-cloaked form. 'Look, he has fought his last.'

Alp Arslan squinted, seeing the *Haga* collapse to the ground.

He found no joy in the sight.

'What now, Sultan?' Kilic asked.

Alp Arslan's eyes never left the *Haga's* body as he heeled his mount round to the south. 'We are beaten today and so we return to our homes.' His eyes glazed just a little as he added. 'Tomorrow, and every day after, we will pursue victory. Fate is with us. Byzantium must fall.'

22. The Grey Land

The cawing of the birds faded and was replaced with the skirl of an angry wind. It roared and roared until he could bear it no more, and so he opened his eyes. At once, the roaring wind stopped and there was utter silence.

He was in no pain. All around was a grey and lifeless world. Mountains tapered up to jagged peaks that pierced a curious sky. It was as dim as twilight, but the sun was present, yet shrouded by a dark veil that seemed to withhold its brilliance. And it was cold. So very cold.

He looked down to see that his faded red tunic seemed to be draining of colour, turning as grey as the dust. At the same time, he felt his thoughts fall away like dead leaves from a bloom in the first frost of autumn.

'I feared I would meet you here, Apion,' a distant voice spoke.

He turned to see the crone. She shuffled across the still land towards him with the aid of a cane, her off-white robes betraying bony knees as she moved. Behind her and stretching off as far as he could see was her trail of footprints in the grey dust, as if she had journeyed far to be here. Her puckered features were etched with sadness. Then, as she came closer, she lifted the cane and held it out to him.

Apion eyed the walking aid. At once, his heart seemed to spark with fondness as he recognised old Cydones' palm prints, worn into the top. For a moment, the fading memories and greying of his thoughts slowed.

'Where am I?' he asked.

'A place that every man visits eventually. A place that I have long grown weary of,' the crone replied, looking up to the veiled sun, her sightless eyes slitted as if she could see and the sun was blinding.

'I cannot remember how I came to be here. All I feel is a terrible pang in my heart – as painful as any wound I have suffered. Is it . . . betrayal?'

The crone avoided his question. 'This place soothes a man's soul and takes away many things . . . including some things best forgotten.'

Apion's eyes darted as fleeting images of the battle pierced the numbness. 'Am I dead? I must be, for the battle is over and I find myself on this lifeless plain.' He thought of the frantic last moments of the fray, Romanus' sword swinging alongside his own, seizing victory from the flames. Then the crone's words danced across his thoughts.

At dusk you will stand with him in the final battle . . .

' . . . like an island in the storm,' he finished. Then he looked up at her. 'This last part of your vision has come to pass?'

She shook her head. 'Today was but a grim portent. The final battle and the island in the storm have still to come.'

'But I surely will not be there to stand by his side?' Apion said, looking to the skin on his forearms – the white band where the prayer rope had once been tied was gone. Then the *Haga* stigma started to fade until it too was gone. Now the network of scarring on the skin was disappearing before his eyes, leaving grey, smooth flesh in its place. 'This place seems eager to draw the life from me, to drain me of those things that make me what I am.'

She reached forward, clutching at his wrist with her talon-like fingers. 'Then fight it, before it gnaws into your heart – the one place that truly defines you.' She raised a bony finger and pointed to the pair of grey, fang-like mountains, dappled with shadows. 'Look, what do you see?'

'I see a wasteland. What of it?' he said, then turned his gaze once more upon his disappearing scars.

She stared at him, her eyes weary. Then she reached over, placing Mansur's bloodied shatranj piece in his left palm, and Cydones' cane in the other, before closing his greying fingers over these two items. She placed a hand on his breastbone and pointed to the jagged mountains again. 'Let the iron melt from your heart, Apion, then look again.'

Apion frowned, shaking his head. 'Then I must be dead inside and out, for I see only . . . ' he started. But he felt the hand holding the cane growing warmer. The draining of his thoughts slowed and then stopped. He thought of Cydones and the many days he had spent with his mentor, supping wine, playing shatranj, and with both men recalling the happy times in their lives. Like Apion, Cydones would speak little of the many years that spliced these precious and happy times. The old man had no family, and his life was entwined with the war. In Cydones, Apion had found a reflection of himself. These memories were rich and vivid. Their colour did not fade.

Before him, the shadows seemed to fade from the grey mountains and they turned a warm russet-gold. Then the veil fell from the sun, bathing the land in warmth and light. When he frowned at this, the crone pressed his fingers over the shatranj piece in his other palm.

At once, his thoughts were filled with old Mansur's laughter. Memories of the years they had spent together danced in his mind's eye. Orphaned, Apion had found a Seljuk father in the old man. Then his lips grew taut as he remembered the bitter truth that had followed. But the anger faded as a tear danced across his cheeks. Without Mansur's mistakes, would the old man have grown to become the fatherly figure he was in his latter years? Without Mansur, would he ever have had those precious few years with Maria?

As his thoughts swirled, the mountains before him altered likewise. The jagged peaks relaxed into the rounded, gentle sloping hills of a valley. Beeches grew from seedling to sapling to verdant thickets in heartbeats. Then a babbling of running water filled the air and a gentle river spilled through the valley, in between the two hills. The ground below him rose up, lifting him to the top of another modest hill. Cicadas sang, goats bleated and the heat was like elixir on his skin.

'I know this place,' Apion spoke as he twisted to look around him.

'And you must never forget it,' the crone spoke.

Then he heard the lowing of oxen in the distance behind him. He spun round and looked down into the valley, and the sight wrenched at his heart. The weary farmhouse with the bowed roof. The goats. The ageing grey mare tucked into a patch of shade, munching on hay. Then, in the heart of the valley, a short stroll from the farmhouse, he saw a portly figure driving a pair of oxen along a square of flat ground, ploughing the soil. *Mansur?* His heart hammered under his ribs. Then it seemed to stop dead. Beside the farmer, a young woman stood in a frayed, red robe. Her hair was dark and sleek. 'Maria?'

He glanced to the crone. 'What is this?'

'From darkness, you can find strength,' she replied. 'Many mourn what they have lost. The strongest use it to drive them onwards. That is what makes you what you are, Apion. That is why I came here. You *must* not give up.'

'But this is not real.'

'No, most of the things you see here live on only within your heart.' The crone stared at him, then reached out to offer him something else. A lock of sleek, dark hair, bound together by a fine golden thread. 'But not all.'

He took it, then lifted it to his nose and inhaled Maria's sweet scent. He looked up to the crone, his eyes widening.

A smile had spread across the crone's face. 'Your old friend, Nasir, left it with me when he passed through here only a short while ago. At the last, he wanted you to know the truth.'

Apion gawped at the lock of hair and then at the figure down in the valley. 'She is . . . no, I saw her blood. She was . . . ' he looked back to the crone. She was gone. In her place a swirl of grey dust rose and then dissipated.

He set off at a sprint downhill as an eagle screeched out above him. The wind rushed past his ears and he slid down the scree at the foot of the valley, tumbling over, kicking up dust as he scrambled towards them. Maria turned to him. She was frowning. She looked older than he remembered. He held out a hand to her, stretching his fingers out as he ran to her. But then she started to slip away. He tried to cry out to her but found his voice was simply not there.

Then all around him the verdant valley crumbled like a fading dream.

Blackness overcame him.

23. The Few

Winter had gripped the lands of the Sebastae Thema like a predator's claws. A winding track snaked across the land, still, empty and frozen hard with sparkling frost. A dark-red sun dipped towards the western horizon, retreating from the blanket of chill darkness encroaching from the east.

Then a steady crunching of boots and clopping of hooves stirred the icy stillness. From the horizon on the south-east, a weary column of men bearing tattered banners and a smoke-stained campaign Cross marched into view, their breath clouding above them as if to compensate for the lack of a dust plume. The priests carrying the Cross chanted as they marched, lamenting the fallen.

Some way back from the head of the column, Tourmarches Sha rode solemnly, flanked by Blastares and Procopius. He stared dead ahead when the thud of another man falling to the ground sounded from not far behind him. Of the sixteen hundred wretches that had survived the Syrian campaign, nearly a third had died on this march home, succumbing to their injuries and the cold. As such, the path behind them was littered with dead men and mules. Hierapolis had been secured and with it, the beginnings of a new, more defensible borderland in the southeast. But at what cost, he mused, thinking of the six thousand men who would never return home.

Then his eyes fell upon the crimson cloak, tied up to form a parcel and balanced on the front of his saddle. It contained an ivory-hilted scimitar, a battered helmet plumed with black eagle feathers and a folded iron klibanion scarred with a russet, blood-encrusted tear near the midriff.

'Many widows we make of waiting wives, with so little thought we squander men's lives,' Sha spoke gently, his breath clouding before him.

'Aye,' Procopius nodded, his aged features creasing as he squinted into the sunset. 'For an old bastard like me to ride home unscathed while so many boys and young men lie buried back in that dusty plain is strange indeed.' He pointed upwards furtively. 'Makes you wonder, doesn't it?'

Blastares frowned. 'Eh?'

Procopius glanced this way and that, eyes wide. 'If God has chosen those who live and those who die, then on a day like today, you have to question his judgement.'

'You shouldn't question him,' Blastares replied flatly, clutching the Chi-Rho amulet dangling around his neck. A troubled frown wrinkled the big tourmarches' features.

'The strategos gave up on God a long time ago,' Sha said, looking to the parcel of armour he carried. 'What that tells us, I don't know.' He looked up to the sky with the other two as if searching the coming gloom for an answer.

A chill wind whistled around them.

'Tourmarchai of Chaldia,' a hoarse voice called out from behind.

They turned to the voice. The gaunt and pale, amber-bearded rider was saddled on a scarred chestnut Thessalian, shivering under a pair of thick woollen blankets. He held one hand to his ribs and his face was wrinkled in pain.

'Strategos!' Sha gasped, dropping back to ride level with Apion.

'Ah, so you have my armour, I've been all along the touldon looking for that,' Apion said as if Sha hadn't spoken. He reached out to lift the crimson bundle from the Malian, poorly disguising another wince of pain as he did so.

'Sir?' Sha searched Apion's battered features. His eyes were open for the first time in weeks. Only that morning, the strategos had been strapped to a stretcher, wrapped in blankets. He was muttering and feverish. 'The skribones insisted you would be confined to the stretcher for the rest of the journey,' Sha frowned. 'Even then, they were sure you were . . . '

'Aye, well, they were wrong,' Apion replied, his eyes avoiding Sha's, a bead of cold sweat dancing down his forehead.

Sha's brow furrowed. 'Sir, for the last two weeks, you have been near-lifeless, face tinged with blue.'

'True, I feel well rested,' he started to chuckle and then stopped, flinching and clutching his ribs. 'The skribones have done their job. My wound is already healing well.'

'Then perhaps that old hag should join the skribones?' Procopius added with a dry snort.

Apion's gaze snapped round on the white-haired officer. 'Tourmarches?'

Procopius jabbed a thumb over his shoulder. 'About a week ago, after we came back through the mountains, she started walking with the column. She was bare-footed and withered like a dried berry. The men grew tired of heckling her after a few days and then she started walking alongside you. The skribones saw no harm in this, until they caught her smoothing some foul-smelling paste into your wound.'

'I was there,' Blastares cut in. 'The open flesh had absorbed most of it by the time they hauled her away and cast her out of the column. We feared she had poisoned you, but that evening, the colour returned to your face and you started to show signs of life once more. But still it was not pleasant; you were feverish, moaning, crying out in pain. You really should be at rest, sir.'

'I'll journey as I see fit,' Apion grunted, scowling, then failing to disguise another shudder of agony. 'Besides, the skribones fed me a pot of warm stew and bread – I am in fine fettle.' Sha, Blastares and Procopius stared at him, their brows knitted in frowns.

'What's wrong – do I command no respect without my armour?' Apion barked, patting the parcel then pinning each of them with a flinty glare. The three gawped back at him until at last his features melted into a weak smile; 'Or does the mighty *Haga* look more like a wounded sparrow in his current state?'

The three could not stop laughter tumbling from their lungs at this, rousing the attention of those nearby.

Apion nodded back down the column. 'Now fall back and ready the men. For we will soon depart for Chaldia. We're going home.'

'Aye, sir,' Sha grinned in reply.

***

As his tourmarchai fell back, Apion rode for the head of the column. Every stride of the Thessalian's canter sent fiery waves of agony through his torso. Every wave washed at the memory of that curious grey place, pushing it back into the depths of his mind like a fading dream. Not for the first time since he had crawled from the stretcher, he looked to the palm of his hand. Empty. The lock of hair was absent. He looked to the sky in search of an answer. It offered nothing.

When we speak again, I have much to ask you, old woman.

He slowed as he approached the front of the column. Romanus rode there, back straight and jaw squared, his cobalt eyes narrowed as he looked to the deep-red sunset. He carried his purple-plumed helmet underarm. His moulded breastplate was battered and scarred. The golden pendant hung on his breast, glinting in the sunset. Igor and the four surviving varangoi flanked him, their braided locks caked in dust and their armour in tatters.

The Golden Heart lived on. This was the spoil of victory. But then sadness and a dying ember of anger touched his heart as he thought of Dederic, lying in the gore by Zenobius' side. He had shed blood with the Norman. He had allowed himself to trust the rider. But the man had betrayed him. Yet Dederic had died a hero, Apion having concealed the rider's shame. Then he thought of Nasir, their days together in adolescence, the war that had torn them apart and the festering scar that had remained between them in the years since. Then that last moment, that unspoken truth. *Damn, but I miss you both like brothers, despite it all,* he thought, tears pushing into his eyes.

He rubbed his eyes clear and looked ahead. Romanus was the talisman of hope. Romanus was the future.

Psellos' minions had been slain, but the adviser himself still loomed like a venomous asp. Indeed, Apion wondered what troubled the emperor more; the vast Seljuk armies that would doubtless fall upon Byzantium's eastern flank in retaliation for the taking of Hierapolis, or the snakepit in the west he was to return to. Romanus' hard stare at the western horizon suggested the latter.

A cry pierced the air as the Strategos of Sebastae ordered his handful of men to fall out from the column, readying to lead them back to the farms and forts of their homeland.

Romanus turned to the noise, then gawped as he saw Apion. 'Strategos? Are you sure you are fit to ride?' Philaretos, Igor and the varangoi frowned in concern likewise.

Apion pulled his woollen blanket tighter and cocked a half-smile at the question he had become so familiar with since prising himself from the stretcher. 'I'll ride until I drop.'

Romanus frowned at this. 'Aye, that's what I'm afraid of.'

'I will recover my strength soon, *Basileus*. For I must,' Apion looked to the north. 'It will soon be time for my men and me to depart for Chaldia. The people of my thema have been without the protection of their army for too long.'

Romanus nodded earnestly. 'Return to Chaldia and aid your people, Strategos. Then turn your thoughts to readying your army for what is to come. Syria will serve as our south-eastern border now, and a fine one at that; Hierapolis will be garrisoned by the Doux of Mesopotamia and his army, and the city's walls will be rebuilt taller and stronger. The passes through the Antitaurus Mountains will be maintained and the city will never be starved of reinforcements or supplies. But Eastern Anatolia is still porous, as you well know. Before long we must march into that rugged land. The forts and passes there must be secured if we are to have any hope of holding the sultan's armies at bay.' He balled one fist and punched it twice against his palm. 'Manzikert, Chliat. These strongholds must be secured. With them under imperial control, Lake Van and the surrounding lands will be stable once more.'

A shiver passed over Apion's skin. *I see a battlefield by an azure lake flanked by two mighty pillars. Walking that battlefield is Alp Arslan. The mighty Mountain Lion is dressed in a shroud.* Then he looked to Romanus as the rest of her words echoed in his mind. *At dusk you and the Golden Heart will stand together in the final battle, like an island in the storm . . .*

Then Romanus rode a little closer, his voice dropping. 'For Alp Arslan's Fatimid troubles appear to be over. He will never again turn away from battle as he did in Syria.'

'He will never relent, *Basileus,*' Apion said, thinking of the sultan's steely resolve. 'Likewise I will always be there to stand against his armies.'

'Then we will always have hope, *Haga,*' Romanus' eyes sparkled and he held out his forearm.

Apion clasped his forearm to the emperor's. He thought of a thousand words that demanded to be spoken. To plead that Romanus stay clear of Psellos and his minions. To stay close to the axes of Igor and his men at all times. To protect Eudokia and her boys. But behind Romanus' assured gaze, Apion saw a sharpness, and awareness of all the ills he would return to. The words did not need to be said.

'Until we meet again, *Basileus.*'

They shared a lasting and earnest gaze and then they parted.

As the imperial banners marched on towards the setting sun, Apion dropped back to the ranks of the Chaldian army. Blastares was leading them in the chorus of a song extolling the benefits of a plump woman's figure. On seeing Apion approach, the men abandoned the song and threw up their hands in salute.

'*Haga!*'

He eyed each of them. One hundred and sixty three men. Each bore scars, bruises, bloodied bandages and some walked on crutches. 'We have fought long and hard. Now another long march lies ahead of us. But it is the march home.'

At this, a raucous cheer erupted and the crimson banners were pumped in the air.

He smiled at this and heeled his mount round to lead them north, away from the column.

'Sir,' a voice called as they peeled away from the column.

Apion frowned, looking down on the lean, gaunt man. It was one of the skribones who had carried him on the stretcher. He offered something in his hand.

'This fell from your grip, when you were feverish,' the man said, dropping the object and then jogging back down the Chaldian ranks.

Apion stared at the dark lock of hair and the golden thread that bound it.

The pain inside him was swept away and tears welled in his emerald eyes.

24. As You Sow

A chill winter wind swept around Trebizond's market square and searched under Apion's crimson cloak and thick woollen tunic. His wounds were bandaged and healing well, and the pain had dulled. He weighed the purse in his palm. It had been stripped from the body of Zenobius. The gold coins clunked together, lifeless and cold.

'Sir, I must leave before sunset,' the rider said nervously.

Apion looked up. The scrawny lad was mounted and the mules of the fast post were burdened with two wagon-loads of papers and small parcels. Two impatient kursores flanked him, wearing thick woollen cloaks and felt caps and holding spears, their muscular mounts snorting and their breath clouding in the winter dusk.

'Aye, the empire never sleeps,' he said with a wry grin, tossing the purse into the lad's hand.

The rider looked at the purse. 'Where is this to be taken?'

Apion's thoughts drifted back to those first days when Dederic had ridden with him. The Norman had won his trust swiftly, proving himself a good-hearted soul. Yet he had blackened his blood by taking Psellos' gold. Then the Norman had shone once more, at the last, giving his life by way of atonement. So was Dederic a good man poisoned by evil, or an evil man struggling to be good? Darkness or light?

'To be a man is to be both,' he muttered absently, a thousand dark memories flashing through his mind, 'and the struggle is endless.'

'Sir,' the rider frowned, 'the purse?'

Apion looked up, his thoughts falling away. 'The purse is to go west. Far to the west. Outside the city of Rouen in Normandy, there is a smallholding by a clear brook, ringed by gnarled and aged oaks. A widow by the name of Emelin lives there with her children. See to it that this reaches her uncorrupted.'

The lad nodded earnestly. 'Yes, Strategos. On my life I will see that it reaches this place.'

Apion stood back from the rider's path and the mule train clopped into motion, rumbling to the southern city gate.

He watched the train leave and head to the west. From the barrack compound nearby – glowing orange in firelight – he could hear Blastares and Procopius recounting some ribald tale with their comrades. Every passage was punctuated with a roar of wine-fuelled laughter from those they entertained.

Then a biting wind howled over the chatter, and Apion realised the last of the market-goers had retreated indoors to their warm homes. He was utterly alone in the deserted streets of the city and now the sky was near-black. The stars over the eastern horizon sparkled brightest. So much lay out there. The sultan's vast armies. The empire's hopes of salvation. But what else?

He reached into his purse and stroked at the dark lock of hair as he gazed eastwards.

Can it be true?

***

Taylan finished the last of his meal of flatbread and cheese, then rose from the table. He pulled on a woollen cloak and opened the door to the bitter, clear night that cloaked the streets of Damascus. A chill draught filled the hearth room of the small house and caused the dying fire to gutter.

'Come straight back as soon as you have the firewood, you hear?' Maria called after him. The streets of this vast city were foreign to her and she knew Taylan was but a spark away from trouble. Indeed, he had been foul-mooded since the refugees had arrived here.

'Aye, Mother,' Taylan called back.

The door swung shut and at once the room was still and quiet apart from the crackling of the embers in the hearth. Maria washed down her meal with a mouthful of warm salep, before lifting the two plates from the tiled table. Then her smile faded as it fell upon the third plate - clean and unused.

She traced a finger along its edge, her thoughts flitting with images of Hierapolis, of Nasir's insistence that he should stay. Indeed, he had tricked young Taylan into leaving the city, swearing that he would be following them shortly.

She took the plates to the water barrel, humming a tune from her childhood in an attempt to stave off the unwelcome thoughts. Then she heard footsteps approaching the door. She twisted around, smiling, expecting Taylan to enter. But the footsteps died right outside but the door did not open. Then knuckles rapped on the timbers.

She frowned, then moved to the door, drying her hands on her robe. Something caused her blood to ice as she reached for the handle and opened it. Outside stood a grim-faced and weary akhi. One of Nasir's men. The man's eyes told her everything before he uttered a word.

She felt little other than numbness in her heart.

'I bring dire news,' he started. 'Bey Nasir finally confronted the *Haga*.' She heard nothing else, seeing only his lips repeating something, his brow wrinkling in concern. He reached out a hand to her, but she stared through him.

Then she realised he had gone. The man had placed one of Nasir's cloaks, neatly folded, into her arms.

She felt no sadness in her heart, only a raking guilt at its absence.

Suddenly, the room grew warmer, and the dying fire rose into full flame once more.

'Grief can take many forms, Maria,' a croaky voice said behind her.

She spun to the corner of the room. In the shadows, a withered crone sat in the wooden chair there. It was the old lady who had nursed her back from near-death, all those years ago after the murder of her father. The crone's milky-white eyes sparkled in the firelight and she wore a benevolent half-smile. Maria's heart warmed at her presence.

'Most grieve for dead loved ones, and that grief comes in floods, thick and fast. But some must watch as those they love die inside, and that grief is long and wearing. You have grieved long enough, Maria.'

The crone leaned forward and reached out to place a hand on her shoulder. Maria felt the weight lift from her heart at this. The crone's sightless gaze searched hers, and then she felt something being summoned from the recesses of her mind. A rich and treasured memory. For a moment she was there – on the hillside by Father's farm. The nutty scent of barley hung in the air, cicadas chattered incessantly and oxen lowed in the fields. She heard chattering voices behind her and spun round. Young Nasir was there, climbing up the hill towards her. His cinnamon skin was unblemished with the scars of war, his grey eyes bright and youthful, his charcoal locks swept back into a pony tail and he toyed with a stalk of wheat as if it was his only

391

care in the world. Beside him was another; a smiling, amber-haired boy, resting his weight on a crutch, emerald eyes sparkling as he climbed. *Apion!*

The image faded. The tears had fallen, staining Maria's cheeks.

'I loved both of them once.'

'They both loved you, Maria. Nasir may have neglected to show you just how much he cared for you, but believe me, he did. As for Apion . . . he carries your memory in his heart to this day. And it is Apion you love still, is it not?'

Maria's gaze fell to the floor at this.

'Do not trouble yourself with guilt, Maria.'

'I promised Nasir I would never so much as speak of him.' She looked up, her eyes glassy. 'Apion has lived out all these years believing me to be dead, and that it was his doing. I tried to get word to him, but Nasir begged me not to. I granted him this.'

'A sad day. For that was the start of the long, slow death of Nasir's soul,' the crone concluded. 'But do not loathe your husband for his choices. He made them only to protect you.'

Maria looked to the crackling flames in the hearth. 'Perhaps those choices were for the best, for I hear that Apion's life has mirrored Nasir's.' She shook her head, a tear dancing down her cheek. 'Why are men drawn to bloodshed so?'

The crone's face fell. 'Just as the sun marches west every day, it is man's very nature to seek out war.'

Maria's heart grew heavy at this. 'Then Taylan will doubtless follow in his father's path,' she said, her gaze falling to the floor as she thought of her son.

At that moment, the door opened behind her and the winter chill swept around the room once more. The fire died to a dull glow and the room darkened.

'Who are you talking to, Mother?' Taylan's voice broke the silence.

Maria twisted to his silhouetted figure, then back to the chair in the corner. The crone was gone and in her place was a dancing shadow. In the howling gust outside, the faint screeching of a lone eagle sounded. 'Nobody, I . . . '

'Father's cloak!' Taylan cut her off, dropping the firewood he carried. For an instant, his face lifted as he searched the room and the bedroom doorways for sight of Nasir. 'The Byzantines were repelled? The city stands?' Then his face fell, mouth agape, eyes wide as he saw his mother's expression. 'No . . . '

Maria shot to standing and embraced her boy. As Taylan sobbed on her shoulder, he shuddered with grief. In between sobs, she heard muffled growling. 'The Byzantines will pay for this. I will slay his killer, Mother. I swear it to you. I swear it to Allah!'

At this, her heart froze. The truth that she and Nasir had withheld from the boy could remain tacit no longer. The truth that had riven their marriage from the start and sent Nasir spiralling into bitterness.

'Taylan, there is something you must know,' she started.

He pulled back from her, his face contorted in grief and confusion.

As she sought out the words, she searched over his features. His charcoal dark hair, his fine, fawn skin.

His sparkling emerald eyes.

* * *

I stretch my wings and the zephyrs lift me high above the frozen Anatolian plateau. I look down upon the white-capped mountains like a god. But if any man could take my place they would understand the bitter truth of my existence. Yet I must go to where I am drawn, and on this dark and chill night, I am drawn west, to a place I loathe, for it is infested with the darkest of hearts.

I swoop across a frost-coated forest and then the heavens open, unleashing a driving snow-storm across my path, as if willing me to turn back. But I cannot. I battle through the whiteness until I come to the narrow strait that takes me from Anatolia to Europa. Greeting me on the far shore are the tall and broad walls of the place they call God's city. Here, I must seek out one man and find out what lies within his soul . . .

***

A blizzard howled around the Boukoleon Palace. On one balcony looking out over the sea walls, Psellos stood with John Doukas.

'It cannot be!' John spat over the howling wind, thumping a balled fist onto the edge of the balcony, sending settled snow toppling down into the gardens.

Psellos remained silent, gazing stonily through the storm. Just for a moment, the blizzard slowed to change direction, revealing the sea walls. The torches there pierced the night, illuminating patches of the choppy grey surface of the Bosphorus.

'Our assassins failed? Despite months of planning – he lives?' John raked his fingers through his hair.

Psellos' nose wrinkled at John's panic. The man was just like every other Doukid puppet he had operated in the last twelve years; a blunt and witless character that would do well to stay on his good side. *After all, the portatioi act on my word alone.* But he swallowed his annoyance and replied calmly; 'Unfortunately, yes. Romanus will return to Constantinople in the next few weeks, and he will herald the re-taking of Hierapolis.'

'He will be the people's new hero,' John laughed mirthlessly.

'All we need is another chance – and there will be plenty,' Psellos offered. He clasped a hand to John's shoulder. 'The people will love him for now, but he cannot live off of this victory for long. When winter lifts from the land, he will have to campaign once more. Every stride he takes will be watched by one of our own. Watching, waiting . . .' he clenched his other fist as if throttling an imaginary foe.

John Doukas' scowl faded at this, and then his face bent into a determined grimace. 'Aye,' he nodded, 'and the sooner his blood is spilled, the sooner the throne will belong to its rightful owners once more . . .'

Psellos smiled, satisfied that he had his puppet under control once more.

'We will speak again tomorrow,' John nodded, then turned and strode from the balcony and back into the palace.

Psellos allowed himself a moment of reflection. So many wretches had died – and died horribly – on this initiative, yet he had not even a bruise on his skin nor a dent on his grip on power to complain about. *God's city, where the emperor reigns as God's chosen one,* he thought with a sense of satisfaction. 'Then he who chooses the emperor must be . . .' he started, grinning like a shark.

' . . . a dark soul indeed,' a voice spoke, inches from his ear.

Psellos stumbled back, startled. Where John had stood moments ago, a cloaked and hooded figure loomed. The storm picked up with a ferocious howl. He panicked, backing up against the balcony edge. An assassin? No, this figure was knotted and withered. The numeros spearman posted on the adjacent balcony looked out to the Bosphorus, seemingly oblivious to the presence of the stranger. His lungs filled to call the spearman, yet his tongue was tied and his voice was but a whisper.

'Yes, you have something to say?' the figure asked.

Psellos clutched at his throat. 'Don't kill me,' he hissed.

'I may or I may not.' The figure laughed gently and reached up with knotted, aged hands to lower the hood. The puckered, sightless features of a silver-haired hag stared through him. The gale dropped at that moment, the snow falling silently around them. 'It depends on your answers to my questions.'

Psellos looked around. 'Then ask me,' he said in a hoarse whisper.

'You have grand plans, visions of greatness.'

'Don't all men?' Psellos shrugged, his face expressionless.

'Your machinations have already brought about the deaths of many, many souls.'

Psellos' gaze darted nervously across the crone's face.

She continued; 'And fate shows me what will come to pass if your scheming continues. On a battlefield far to the east, by an azure lake flanked by two mighty pillars, blood will be let like a tide,' she extended a bony finger and pointed it at him, 'and it will be your doing. Does this please you?'

'My doing?' Psellos squared his shoulders and tilted his pointed features haughtily at the crone. He was surprised to find that his voice had returned and thought of shouting to the nearby spearman. Then he touched his fingers to the hilt of the dagger tucked up his sleeve. 'Bloodshed cannot always be avoided,' he said, then wrapped his fingers around the dagger hilt, tensing his arm, 'sometimes it simply begs to be spilled.' He swung the blade out and round for the sightless crone's throat. But her gnarled hand shot up to grapple his, shaking the blade from his grip. Then she clasped her other hand around his throat like a viper's jaws and lifted him up and towards the edge of the balcony. He gasped and spat soundlessly, his legs kicking, his free hand thrashing.

The crone threw her head back, unleashing a shrill cackle into the night sky. 'So you do not know the meaning of remorse. You are Fate's pawn indeed!' At that moment the storm picked up into a ferocious roar once more, hurling the stinging snow horizontally across the balcony, sweeping her hair back from her withered features. Her eyes bulged and her yellowed teeth were revealed in a baleful grin. 'I have found out all I need to know about you, Psellos of Byzantium. And now . . . ' she started, edging him ever closer to the lip of the balcony.

Panic shook every part of Psellos' being as he saw the three storey drop onto the flagstones below. For the first time in his life, he was utterly powerless. Then the storm quelled once more, and she set him down carefully. Psellos panted, cupping his throat, trembling in disbelief.

'Now I will leave you with one musing; as you sow . . . ' she lifted one fingertip to his chest ' . . . you shall *reap!*' She jabbed the fingertip into his breastbone as if thrusting a dagger. It burned like fire and he cried out once more, falling to the balcony floor.

As he threw up his hands to shield himself, cold hands pulled at his wrists and he struggled to beat them away, crying out for mercy.

'Sir?' a voice pierced the shrieking gale. 'Sir!'

Trembling, Psellos blinked open his eyes. The numeros had him by the wrists and wore an anxious frown. The crone was gone.

'What's wrong?' the spearman asked as the thick snow whipped around them.

Psellos scrambled up to standing. 'Get your hands off me,' he spat, pushing the soldier away. He staggered back towards the doorway, snatching glances up and around at the barbarous storm.

Over the howling, he could hear the faint shrieking of an eagle. As his panic subsided, he frowned, feeling a dull stinging on his chest where she had touched him. He pulled at his robe to see that there was nothing but a coin-sized, blood-red blemish on his breastbone. It itched, but that was all. His terror waned; if this was the worst the crone could do then he had little to fear of her.

His eyes darted across the storm as her words rang in his ears; *On a battlefield far to the east, by an azure lake flanked by two mighty pillars, blood will be let like a tide . . . and it will be your doing.*

'So be it,' he said, a winter-cold grin spreading across his features.

Author's Note

Dear Reader,

I'd like to thank you warmly for trying my work and I truly hope that the tale of 'Rise of the Golden Heart' has allowed you to escape to Byzantium for a precious few hours.

After I left Apion at the end of 'Strategos: Born in the Borderlands' I often found my thoughts returning to him. In these moments I did not ask myself where I would take him next, but wondered instead where I would find him. So it has been a cathartic experience to enter his world once more, and I know that world has already moved on again without me since I wrote the final words of this volume.

Now, as always, a work of historical fiction weaves a tale around events of the past. The core aspects are based on solid historical fact, others are skewed slightly to aid a dramatic narrative and some are entirely fictional. I'll try to summarise the main elements of the plot which I feel are noteworthy in these areas.

In 1067, Alp Arslan was at war with the Fatimids to the south of his dominion, offering a brief period of respite to the Byzantine borderlands. But only until Bey Afsin slew a member of the sultan's court, then fled west with an army. His subsequent raids into Anatolia ripped through the heart of the poorly defended Byzantine Themata. The rogue bey led his men in the sacking of Caesarea, which saw the tomb of St Basil pillaged and the sarcophagus broken. My portrayal of Alp Arslan halting Bey Afsin at this juncture is fictional, but when Alp

Arslan finally did bring Afsin's raids to an end in 1068, he magnanimously pardoned his bey and welcomed him back into his ranks.

My depiction of Emperor Romanus Diogenes comes chiefly from the chronicler, Michael Attaleiates. Attaleiates' History is considered slightly anti-Diogenes, but with a grudging respect for his bullish determination to right the wrongs of the previous imperial dynasties and to stop the decay of the armies. Attaleiates' writings also provide priceless eyewitness accounts of Diogenes' imperial campaigns. He tells how the emperor's Syrian campaign in 1068 took them through Anatolia where he tried to muster the themata, but found them in a grievous condition:

For the most part they had been neglected, because no emperor had marched east for many years and they had not received their due pay having been subdued and turned to flight little by little by their opponents due to their wretchedness and ill preparedness for attack, and thus fallen into cowardice and impotency, of no good use. To put it plainly, their standards were dirty as if from smoke with easily countable, wretched attendants beneath them. They were greatly discouraged when reckoning how they would return to the old days of their former martial honor and get it back after so much time, since the men who remained in the legions were few and lacking in arms and mounts, a band of inexperienced youths with the most warlike and war-experienced opponents arraigned against them.

The campaign continued to the south east and culminated in the siege and taking of Hierapolis. Attaleiates records that the lower city was taken swiftly, but that the citadel was tall, well-defended and hardy, and that it took a 'snowstorm of artillery' to breach its walls. He goes on to describe how, while the citadel was being taken, the Emir of Aleppo marched from the west and fell upon the unprepared

Byzantine units posted outside of the walls, routing the Scholae Tagma and capturing their standards. Romanus Diogenes only learned of the emir's arrival whilst still battling to take the citadel. The emperor took to rallying his fearful army and then led a brave sally, eventually turning the emir's forces to flight.

One place I have knowingly strayed from Attaleiates' text is in my depiction of Romanus Diogenes residing on the Istrian frontier prior to his accession to the imperial throne. Attaleiates states that he was in fact exiled in his native Cappadocia at the time.

As for Michael Psellos; he has been hailed by some as a great thinker, by others as an imperial sycophant, and by some as a power-hungry and shrewd individual. Among modern commentators, Psellos' penchant for long autobiographical digressions in his works has earned him accusations of vanity and ambition. He rose to prominence in the eleventh century, spearheading the initiative to establish the University of Constantinople and serving at various times as a provincial judge and in the imperial court. It was in the reign of Constantine IX Monomachus (1042-1055) that he became an influential political adviser. He then played a decisive role in the transition of power from Michael VI to Isaac I Komnenos in 1057; then from Isaac Komnenos to Constantine X Doukas in 1059. Then, in 1067, the strident Eudokia Makrembolitissa decided to renege on the oath she had made to her husband and manoeuvred to raise Romanus Diogenes rose to the imperial throne. Psellos and the Doukids were bitterly opposed to his accession and then to his reign, and actively sought to confound him at every turn.

So, while much of my portrayal of Psellos' behaviour and deeds is entirely speculative, he was clearly a shrewd operator. You have to question how one man can remain at the side of the imperial throne for so long while emperors (God's chosen ones) come and go.

It was Psellos' role as kingmaker and his hand in the events that followed the Syrian campaign (which I will cover in the next volume of the series) that proved fuel enough for me to draw the darkest possible conclusions.

Regarding the themata; Apion's home – the Byzantine Thema of Chaldia – was a bastion of the imperial borderlands for many centuries. However, by the mid-eleventh century, many themata were in the process of becoming, and some had already become, 'ducates'. In other words, they would have been ruled primarily by a doux rather than a strategos, and the border tagma commanded by the doux would have diminished the importance of the strategos' thematic armies. I have portrayed Doux Fulco as Apion's ostensible superior in this respect. However, I do confess to exaggerating Apion's position and the doggedness of his thematic ranks.

One question that has been raised about 'Strategos: Born in the Borderlands', that is likely to be raised again from this volume, is my depiction of Byzantine soldiers using Latin war cries. After all, in the eleventh century, Latin had been a dead language for several hundreds of years and the people of the Byzantine Empire undoubtedly spoke Greek.

The cry of 'Nobiscum Deus' was attested to in Maurice's 'Strategikon' (written in the 6th century AD) and then referred to in John Haldon's 'Warfare, state and society in the Byzantine world, 565-1204' where it is grouped as one of many practices that 'remained constant throughout the existence of the empire.' The paucity of compelling evidence of any one particular Byzantine cry – possibly Greek – usurping this, and the likelihood that the original, simple, Latin phrase would have gathered an air of mystique after centuries of use, led me to stick with the Latin. Certain phrases can and do transcend the death of their parent language while maintaining their semantic origins. Indeed, a friend pointed out to me that the Irish Rangers' (a British Army regiment) cry is in Gaelic, which most of their men can't speak. Added to this, many other Latin phrases persisted right up to the end of the Byzantine Empire, albeit partially graecofied (e.g. skutum = scutum, kontoubernion = contubernium). I don't think we'll ever have concrete proof either way, but I think there is a certain romance in the notion of a war cry from antiquity echoing through the centuries.

Regarding heraldry, historians believe that, by 1068 AD, both the Seljuks and Byzantines had come to use the double-headed eagle as their symbol of power. This image is thought to have represented their declaration of power over the east and west. Interestingly, on the Byzantine side, Emperor Isaac I Komnenos (1057-1059 AD) adopted the symbol, having been inspired by legends of the *Haga* (the actual Hittite myth – not the fictional Apion!). However, I have deliberately neglected to depict this symbol on Byzantine and Seljuk banners, as I felt it would cause some confusion in the narrative, being identical to Apion's *Haga* stigma.

There are hours of discussion to be had on many more aspects of the history. As ever, I'd be delighted to hear from you on these or any other aspects, and I can be contacted at my website (below).

In the meantime, rest assured that Apion's journey is not over yet. The *Haga* will return, and I hope you will too.

Yours faithfully,
Gordon Doherty
www.gordondoherty.co.uk

Glossary

Akhi: Seljuk infantry armed with long anti-cavalry spears, scimitars, shields and sometimes armoured in lamellar.

Armamenta: State funded imperial warehouses tasked with producing arms, clothing and armour for the armies. They were usually situated in major cities and strongholds.

Bey: Seljuk military commander, subordinate to an *emir*.

Ballista: Primarily anti-personnel missile artillery capable of throwing bolts vast distances. Utilised from fortified positions and on the battlefield.

Bandophorus: The standard-bearer for a Byzantine *bandon*.

Bandon: The basic battlefield unit of infantry in the Byzantine army. Literally meaning 'banner', a *bandon* typically consisted of between two hundred and four hundred men, usually *skutatoi*, who would line up in a square formation, presenting spears to their enemy from their front ranks and hurling *rhiptaria* from the ranks behind. *Banda* would form together on the battlefield to present something akin to the ancient phalanx.

Basileus: The Byzantine emperor (feminine: *Basileia*).

Bey: The leader of a Seljuk warband.

Buccina: The ancestor of the trumpet and the trombone, this instrument was used for the announcement of night watches and various other purposes in the Byzantine forts and marching camps as well as to communicate battlefield manoeuvres.

Buccinator: A soldier who uses the *buccina* to perform acoustical signalling on the battlefield and in forts, camps and settlements.

Chi-Rho: The Chi-Rho is one of the earliest forms of Christogram, and was used in the early Christian Roman Empire through to the Byzantine high period as a symbol of piety and empire. It is formed by superimposing the first two letters in the Greek spelling of the word Christ, chi = ch and rho = r, in such a way to produce the following monogram:

Daylamid warriors: Fierce and rugged warriors from the mountains of northern Iran. It is thought that they may have fought with twin-pronged spears (though many argue that this is a mistranslation and that they actually fought with double-edged blades).

Dekarchos: A minor officer in charge of a *kontoubernion* of ten *skutatoi* who would be expected to fight in the front rank of his *bandon*. He would wear a red* sash to denote his rank.

Doux: One of the titles for the leader of a Byzantine *tagma*.

Dromon: Byzantine war galley with twin triangular sails. Capable of holding up to three hundred men.

Droungarios: A Byzantine officer in charge of two *banda,* who would wear a silver* sash to denote his rank.

Emir: Seljuk military leader, roughly equivalent to the Byzantine *strategos.*

Er-ati: A Seljuk warrior name.

Fatimid Caliphate: Arab Islamic caliphate that dominated the area comprising modern-day Tunisia and Egypt in the Middle Ages.

Follis: A large bronze coin of small value.

Foulkon: The Byzantine heir to the famous Roman *testudo* or 'tortoise' formation.

Ghulam: The Seljuk heavy cavalry, equivalent to the Byzantine *kataphractos.* Armoured well in scale vest or lamellar, with a distinctive pointed helmet with nose guard, carrying a bow, scimitar and spear.

Ghazi: The Seljuk light cavalry, a blend of steppe horse archers and light skirmishers whose primary purpose was to raid enemy lands and disrupt defensive systems and supply chains.

Haga: A ferocious two-headed eagle from ancient Hittite mythology. Also the basis for what would become the emblem of both the Byzantine Empire and the Seljuk Sultanate.

Kampidoktores: The drill master in charge of training Byzantine soldiers.

Kataphractos: Byzantine heavy cavalry and the main offensive force in the *thema* and *tagma* armies. The riders and horses would wear iron lamellar and mail armour, leaving little vulnerability to attack. The riders would use their *kontarion* for lancing, *spathion* for skirmishing or their bow for harrying.

Kathisma: The imperial box at the Hippodrome in Constantinople. This was connected directly to the Imperial Palace via the Cochlia Gate and a spiral staircase.

Kentarches: A Byzantine officer in charge of one hundred Byzantine soldiers or the crew of a *dromon*. A descendant of the Roman centurion.

Kentarchia: A notional unit of one hundred Byzantine soldiers, commanded by a *Kentarches.*

Khagan: The title of the Seljuk chieftain prior to the era of the sultanate.

Klibanion: The characteristic Byzantine lamellar cuirass made of leather, horn or iron squares, usually sleeveless, though sometimes with leather strips hanging from the waist and shoulders.

Komes: An officer in charge of a *bandon* who would wear a white* sash to denote his rank.

Kontarion: A spear between two and three metres long, the *kontarion* was designed for Byzantine infantry to hold off enemy cavalry.

Kontoubernion: A grouping of ten Byzantine infantry who would eat together, patrol together, share sleeping quarters or a pavilion tent while on campaign. They would be rewarded or punished as a single unit.

Kursoris: Byzantine scout rider, lightly armed with little or no armour.

Milareum Aureum: The gilded bronze mile pillar situated just north of the Hippodrome in Constantinople.

Nomisma: A gold coin that could be debased by various degrees to set its value.

Numeroi: A Byzantine imperial *tagma*, stationed in Constantinople. They guarded the prisons, the walls, the site of the Baths of Zeuxippus and parts of the Imperial Palace.

Paramerion: A one-edged, slightly curved blade carried by the *kataphractoi*.

Pamphylos: A small, round-hulled Byzantine cargo ship, used typically to transport horses and artillery.

Portatioi: A shadowy subset of the *Numeroi*. It is thought that they were employed as torturers.

Rhiptarion: A short throwing spear. *Skutatoi* carried two or three of these each.

Salep: A hot drink made with orchid root, cinnamon and milk.

Shatranj: A precursor to modern-day chess.

Signophorioi: Byzantine standard bearers for the *tagmata*. They would carry sacred purple and gold banners on campaign.

Siphonarioi: Operators of Greek-fire throwing siphons. They operated large siphons mounted on towers or walls, and it is thought that they also carried smaller, hand-held siphons into field battles.

Skribones: Byzantine medical personnel who would carry the dead and wounded from the battlefield.

Skutatos: The Byzantine infantryman, based on the ancient hoplite. He was armed with a *spathion*, a *skutum*, a *kontarion*, two or more *rhiptaria* and possibly a dagger and an axe. He would wear a conical iron helmet and a lamellar *klibanion* if positioned to the front of his *bandon*, or a padded jacket or felt vest if he was closer to the rear. *Tagma skutatoi* may well all have been afforded iron lamellar armour.

Skutum: The Byzantine infantry shield that gives the *skutatoi* their name. Usually kite or teardrop-shaped and painted identically within a *bandon*.

Solenarion: A wooden channel that can be fitted to a standard bow to create a rudimentary crossbow. This allows quick aiming and firing of short, weighty darts.

Spathion: The Byzantine infantry sword, derived from the Roman *spatha*. Up to a metre long, this straight blade was primarily for stabbing, but allowed slashing and hacking as well.

Strategos: Literally 'army leader'. The *themata* armies of Byzantium were organised and led by such a man. The *strategos* was also responsible for governance of his *thema*.

Tagma: The *tagmata* were the professional standing armies of the Byzantine Empire. They were traditionally clustered around Constantinople. These armies were formed to provide a central reserve, to meet enemy encroachment that could not be dealt with by the *themata,* and also to cow the potentially revolutionary power of those *themata.* They were well armoured, armed, paid and fed. Each *tagma* held around five thousand men and was composed exclusively of cavalry or infantry. In the 11th century AD, some of these *tagmata* were moved closer to the borders to deal with emerging threats. In addition, a raft of smaller, 'mercenary' *tagmata* were formed in these regions, comprising largely of Rus, Normans and Franks.

Thema: In the 7th century AD, as a result of the crisis caused by the Muslim conquests, the Byzantine military and administrative system was reformed: the old late Roman division between military and civil administration was abandoned, and the remains of the Eastern Roman Empire's field armies were settled in great districts, the *themata*, that were named after those armies. The men of the *themata* would work their state-leased military lands in times of peace and then don their armour and weapons when summoned by the *strategos* to defend their *thema* or to set out on campaign alone or with the *tagmata*. The manpower of each thema varied vastly, with some able to field only a few thousand men while others could muster as many as ten or fifteen thousand men. The diagram at the front of the book depicts the structure these forces would be organised into. In the 11th century, the thematic system was in steep decline, with the *tagmata* gradually taking over as defenders of the borderlands.

Tourmarches: A Byzantine officer in charge of the military forces and administration of a *tourma*.

Toxotes: The Byzantine archer, lightly armoured with a felt jacket and armed with a composite bow and a dagger.

Tourma: A subdivision of a Byzantine *thema*, commanded by a *tourmarches*. Each *tourma* was comprised of some two thousand soldiers of the *thema* army and encompassed a geographical subset of the *thema* lands.

Varangoi: An elite infantry unit of the Byzantine army, employed as a personal bodyguard to the emperor. These axemen were primarily Rus or Germanic, and were thought to be both loyal and fierce in battle.

Vasilikoploimon: Byzantine imperial fleet stationed in the Bosphorus. This fleet was responsible for patrolling the Propontus Sea and for transporting campaign armies.

Yalma: A close-fitting, long-sleeved and knee-length silk shirt worn by Turkic peoples.

*The use of a sash to denote rank is backed up by historical texts, but the sash colours stated are speculative.

If you enjoyed Strategos: Rise of the Golden Heart, why not also try:

The Thief's Tale by S.J.A Turney

It is 58 BC and the mighty Tenth Legion, camped in Northern Italy, prepare for the arrival of the most notorious general in Roman history: Julius Caesar.

Marcus Falerius Fronto, commander of the Tenth is a career soldier and long-time companion of Caesar's. Despite his desire for the simplicity of the military life, he cannot help but be drawn into intrigue and politics as Caesar engineers a motive to invade the lands of Gaul.

Fronto is about to discover that politics can be as dangerous as battle, that old enemies can be trusted more than new friends, and that standing close to such a shining figure as Caesar, even the most ethical of men risk being burned.

Galdir: A Slave's Tale by Fredrik Nath

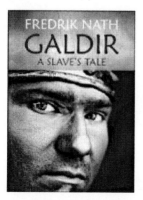

A Roman slave with a serpent tattoo uncovers his true barbarian identity... A battle for power among Frankish warlords leads to a mass exodus across the Rhine... All the while, Marcus Aurelius' Roman army pushes further north, changing everything. These three events meet in a cataclysm that changes the course of history. In the background, the ageing witch Chlotsuintha predicts it all. Or is she the one pulling the strings to shape her people's future?

When Sextus escapes Rome with a pocketful of gold and a knife, how could he even have dreamt of what the fates might have in store for him?

Pursued by Roman soldiers for the murder of his master, Sextus enlists the help of a retired gladiator, and falls in love with the gladiator's niece. An invading German army drives them further north, where Sextus discovers his true birthright, and his real name - Galdir. He becomes caught up in a bitter feud as one of the heirs of a dead Frankish warlord; but the blood feud must be put aside when the Romans invade and besiege the Frankish capital.

'Galdir' is enthralling Roman fiction - a tale of love, brutal battles and conflict, in which a mystical prophecy winds its way through an epic saga of struggle against Rome, and the consequences of resistance by the Frankish people, its Warlord and its witches.

Lightning Source UK Ltd.
Milton Keynes UK
UKOW02f1456120415

249489UK00017B/76/P